AF560278

Fundamentals of Textiles and Their Care

Fifth Edition

SUSHEELA DANTYAGI

Orient BlackSwan

FUNDAMENTALS OF TEXTILES AND THEIR CARE

ORIENT BLACKSWAN PRIVATE LIMITED

Registered Office
3-6-752, Himayatnagar, Hyderabad 500 029, Telangana, India
e-mail: centraloffice@orientblackswan.com

Other Offices
Bengaluru, Chennai, Guwahati, Hyderabad, Kolkata,
Mumbai, New Delhi, Noida, Patna

First published 1959 by the Indian Women Writers Cooperative Publishing Society, New Delhi
Second edition published by Orient Blackswan Pvt. Ltd. 1964, reprinted 1968
Third edition published 1974, repinted 1977
Fourth edition published 1983, reprinted 1984, 1987, 1989, 1991, 1994
Fifth edition 1996
Reprinted 1998, 2002, 2004, 2006, 2007
First Orient Blackswan impression 2008
Reprinted 2009, 2015, 2017, 2024

Cover and book design
Orient Blackswan Pvt. Ltd., 2008

ISBN: 978-81-250-1027-2

Typeset by
Scribe Consultants
New Delhi

Printed in India at
B B Press, Tronica City, Ghaziabad, U.P. 201103

Published by
Orient Blackswan Private Limited
3-6-752, Himayatnagar, Hyderabad 500 029, Telangana, India
e-mail: info@orientblackswan.com

To

the late Rajkumari Amrit Kaur

Acknowledgements

The author gratefully thanks the following organisations for their kind and generous permission to use and reproduce the various photographs and diagrams.

The Lady Irwin College, New Delhi
The Delhi Cloth and General Mills Limited, Delhi
The Millowners' Association, Bombay
Modella Woollens Limited, Bombay
Modella Knitwear, Ludhiana, Punjab
Calico Mills, Ahmedabad
Bombay Dyeing and Manufacturing Co., Bombay
Hindustan Lever Limited, Bombay
Handloom Board, New Delhi
Silk and Artsilk Research Association, Bombay
Calico Museum Ahmedabad
Apex Societies of Handlooms, Union Ministry of Textiles, New Delhi

Contents

Preface to the Fifth Edition

There have been many new and interesting developments in the field of textiles since the publication of the fourth edition of my book *Fundamentals of Textiles and Their Care*.

- The production of man-made fibres has overtaken that of natural fibres.
- New fibre blends and fabric trends have arrived in response to fashion changes and market demand.
- The programming of computerised knitting machines permits the translation of patterns from paper to fabric in minutes, in an infinite variety of colours, in response to fast-moving fashions and markets.
- The development of our handloom and knitting industry has gained momentum, and both have expanded their markets at home and abroad.
- The garment industry has grown enormously, making significant contributions to India's exports.
- New laws have been passed to protect consumers of textiles, by requiring, for instance, clear and informative labels.

This edition has been revised taking these changes into account. The general organisation of the original text has, however, been largely retained because the study of textiles from raw material to finished product follows an orderly and logical progression.

Fundamentals of Textiles and Their Care was written with the primary objective of imparting information on textiles to students of an introductory college course so that they develop an interest in textiles that motivates further study, and to recognise the values that enter into the selection and care of textiles. While the information has been updated, the basic objectives remains the same.

My grateful thanks to my colleagues at various home science colleges. Acknowledgements must also be made of the kindness of authors and publishers who have given permission for the use of their material; their names are given in the bibliography.

New Delhi
1st January, 1992.
SUSHEELA DANTYAGI

Preface to the Fourth Edition

Due to popular demand, both from students and consumers, the fourth edition of the book has been suitably revised and expanded.

In response to a demand from students, particular topics as: scope of textiles, high tenacity viscose rayon, permanent press in fabrics, 'Home-dyeing—the Batik way' have been added.

Admittedly, our textile industry is scaling new heights and entering new horizons. Our manmade fibres/fabrics are not used to satisfy apparel needs of the country alone. They have industrial household and defence uses also. While it is not only necessary to buy these textiles wisely it is equally necessary to care for them suitably. The right choice and use of cleaning supplies and detergents is a must. Realising a need, a chapter on synthetic or soapless detergents has been added. The topics include: The place of detergents today; the advantages offered by soapless detergents; the manufacture of soapless detergents, soapless detergent powders, liquid soapless detergents and their use.

The author is greatly indebted to the Research Department of the Hindustan Lever Limited; Dr O P Singh, Professor and Head, Department of Textiles, Punjab Agricultural University, Ludhiana, Punjab; and to Miss B Daftary, Head of Department of Textile and Clothing Construction, S.N.D.T. University, Bombay, for their kind association and revision of the book.

S.D.

Preface to the Third Edition

The importance of textile Education is increasing day by day specially among women and girls. Today more than ever before, we have entered into the market for manufacture of nylons and other synthetics.

The scope of this book has been considerably extended in the present edition. A special chapter has been added on synthetics and their use in the home.

The author is greatly indebted to Dr. Maria Friesen of Ohio State University, USA and Dr O P Singh, Textile Specialist of the College of Home Science, Punjab Agricultural University, Ludhiana, for their kind assistance and advice in the revision of the book.

S.D.

Preface to the Second Edition

The need for printing the second impression of the *Fundamentals of Textiles and Their Care* had been felt in less than three years, but due to several reasons it was not possible to get this edition published. It was gratifying to note that the response to the first edition of this publication was very encouraging. This book was well received by various agencies and areas. I appreciate the interest of persons in the material presented in this book.

In this second edition serious attention has been given to improve the material by making the necessary alternations and changes. Some of the common problems which are very pressing have been taken up in this edition such as consumers' problems, art of selecting wearing apparel, detergents, and use of indigenous dyes, etc. A special attempt to make the description simple and understandable without going into technical details and terms of Chemistry has been made. During the period after the first edition there have been many developments of textiles. We have more and more of synthetic fibres, mixtures and blended fabrics, which need to be explained to consumers. For students especially, there is a definite need to indentify and recognise the performance and to have a basic knowledge of the interrelations of these textiles, I hope and trust that the efforts made to include these changes and additions will be of relevance to persons interested in this field.

It would not have been possible to bring out this edition without the help of friends and experts. My thanks are due to the Lady Irwin college, where I have worked for several years. I am also grateful to the experts in this subject who have always been so kind and helpful. The commercial companies and the government agencies have been kind enough to give me the necessary information and illustrations for this book. I would like to once again thank all the friends who have given me a helping hand in this endeavour.

S.D.

Preface to the First Edition

The material presented in this volume is the result of years of work developing a practical course for Textiles and Laundry Work in Lady Irwin College for Home Science.

In 1948, the book was made available in cyclostyled form to my students. With more experience the book was revised and enlarged and is now printed in response to pressing requests from several friends, and colleges and schools.

In India, the one serious mistake which every Indian housewife makes is the amount of soiling that she allows to accumulate on linen before sending it to the dhobi. Perhaps the idea is to squeeze a little more value out of the cost of laundering. But in doing that the housewife is only cheating herself; for though she may gain a little through a slight extension of each wearing period she is indirectly shortening the life of the fabric. The dhobi's crude method of laundering is the distress of all housewives. His bhatti not only ruins precious fabrics but is also a carrier of many a disease.

The aim of this volume is to create an interest in, and impart some knowledge of, the fundamentals of textiles, dyeing and laundering processes. As the country is planning for more and more electricity at cheaper cost, a chapter has been added to deal with electrical equipment for laundry work.

The book is intended mainly for the use of students taking training in Home Science, but it is hoped it will also prove helpful to the vigilant housewife who is anxious to be thrifty and know something of the why and how of the textiles now in the market and of their appropriate treatment in the home without drudgery.

I wish to acknowledge my grateful thanks to (Late) Mrs Hannah Sen, the first Director of the Lady Irwin College.

My indebtedness is also due to Mrs B Tara Bai, B.A., L.T., B.Sc., London, the Ex-Director of Lady Irwin College and to my friends Dr (Mrs) M B Kagal and Dr M Baliga for their valuable suggestions and kind help in the preparation of the book in its various stages.

Last but not least my sincere thanks go to my husband for his never-failing guidance and encouragement.

Acknowledgement is also made to the authors and publishers who have so kindly given permission for the use of their materials.

S.D.

1

Plant Fibres

The word 'textile,' is derived from the Latin term *textiles* for woven fabrics. Thus by textiles we understand those objects which have been prepared by weaving. Laces, nets, knitwear, felt, etc., though not woven, are included in the textile category as also cords, ropes and similar materials.

From ancient days India has been famous for its beautiful fabrics. The art of India's gold brocades and filmy muslins 'comely as the curtains of Solomon' is older than the Puranas. The Puranas tell us that spinning and weaving were important handicrafts and that Vedic Indians were fond of *Suvasas* or beautiful garments. The Vedic hymns sang of Ushas, the daughter of Heaven, 'clothed with radiance ... day and night spreading light and darkness over the earth like two female weavers weaving a garment'. From the Arthashastra we learn that the materials then employed for spinning were wool (*urna*), cotton (*karpasa*), hemp (*tula*) and flax (*kshauma*). The work of weaving in those days was done by women only, and their wages depended on the fineness of the yarn they spun.

Textile fabrics originally took their names from the place where they first acquired excellence and retained these names long after the local manufacture had been transferred elsewhere. Thus we have damask from Damascus, satin from Zaytun (modern Tsingking) in China, sindon or sandalin from Sindh, calico from Calicut, worsted from Worsted in England, and muslin from Mosul (in Iraq). Chintz is derived from chint or *chete*, which in Hindi means 'spotted,' whence chitta and cramoisy from the insect *kermes* from which a scarlet dye was made.

Almost every region in India has its own exclusive textiles. For example, Kashmir is noted for its exquisitely embroidered fabrics, and its carpets are famous all over the world for their elegance, designs, workmanship, colour schemes and fine texture. Yet another of Kashmir's unsurpassed handmade textile treasures are pashmina shawls. Charles Dickens said of them 'If an article of dress could be immutable it would be the Kashmir shawl, designed for Eternity in the unchanging East, copied from patterns which are heirlooms of the Orient'. From other parts of India, Banaras has for long been the home of brocades and other select fabrics, and there are the exquisite *patolas* from Patan, silky muslin saris from Chanderi, delicate fabrics from Bengal, phulkaris from Punjab and so on.

Textiles in Our Lives

Our primary needs are food, clothing, shelter and energy. Textiles serve the clothing requirements of the individual, the home and the country. They add to our comfort, appearance and to our happiness in several ways by their exceptional versatility. We use them to help enhance the beauty of our homes. In the larger sphere, they help serve our country in the army, navy, air force and in manifold industries. In recent years, there has been a growing demand for our textiles and clothing, both at home and abroad.

In order to gain a better understanding of the place of textiles in our lives, we need to view the field in relation to India's total planning process and the objectives envisaged for the socio-economic development of our country. Each of our five-year plans presents a picture of continuous evolution in our basic economic and social policies. These plans seek fresh ways to strengthen institutions, establish methods and machinery and broaden the manpower base. To this end the plans have assisted in establishing specialised institutions to train technical and professional personnel, including textile technologists.

Over the past few decades, a new textile world has emerged. New fibres, new fabrics and new finishes make new demands for understanding and evaluation. The development of rayons, the advent of new synthetic fibres and finishes speak volumes. Today lightweight, soil-resistant, permanent-pressed fabrics, durable-pressed garments are becoming increasingly popular. Modern production methods overcome some of the old difficulties in making fibres into fabrics.

We can now make some fibres usable which formerly were not, and there are a whole range of fabrics which are crease-resistant, lustrous, matte or any other quality. They do not 'pill,' accumulate dust or dirt or static electricity. Our manufacturing plants make fabrics in weaves, knits, felts, etc. Lightweight, 'drip dry' garments have become household words. We have fabrics for furnishing, for industry and the military.

The Handloom Export Promotion Council, set up by the Government of India, takes steps to promote the export of India's handloom fabrics. In order to achieve this, the Council organises trade missions and overseas market studies. This should open a communication channel that will continually feed back information about international market trends, consumer preferences and distribution facilities. Among its many responsibilities are the collaboration and publication of literature concerning the handloom industry for dissemination in foreign countries, and the staging of exhibitions abroad to inform the foreign public of the beauty and splendour of our handloom fabrics and the varieties of uses to which they could be put. The Council looks after quality standards and takes prompt action to settle complaints. It helps the producer get quality raw material and also helps exporters effectively in such matters as shipping opportunities, freight rates, credit problems, foreign exchange, sales-tax, etc.

This growth of the textiles industry is largely the work of our professional personnel. These ingenious technologists have invented and refined new methods of serving our clothing needs. The consumer too is more willing and able to pay for the improved services and goods.

On the other hand, there needs to be informative labelling, quality marking, indication of brands and standardisation to help the consumer get his money's worth. A pioneering effort in this direction is being made by the Indian Standards Institution and its ISI certification mark.

The year 1987 was memorable for India, when the government passed the Consumer Protection Act. This Act, has been rightly termed "a policy of mutual help and collective self-reliance."

With the implementation of this Act, the country could look forward to a great expansion in the field of textiles.

The Consumer Protection Act emphasizes the following basic rights.

- the right to be informed
- the right to choose
- the right to safety
- the right to be heard and
- the right to be protected

To advise the consumer 'free legal cells' have been constituted so that he or she can seek compensation for damages suffered on account of restrictive and unfair trade practices.

With reference to textiles, the Act has led to more informative labelling, quality marks and certification, and the suggested retail prices. Laundering and care instructions (ironing, bleaching, drying) should also be attached.

The common textiles fibres may be classified as follows:

	Natural
Cellulose	Cotton (Seed Hair) Flax (Stems) Ramie (Stems) Jute (Stems) Hemp (Stems) Sunn (Stems) Sesal Coir
	Manufactured
Cellulose (Regenerated)	Rayon (pure cellulose) Viscose Cuprammonium High-tenacity rayons

Protein	*Natural* Wool (sheep) Mohair (Angora goat) Cashmere and other speciality wools Silk (silkworms) *Manufactured* Ardil (peanut fibre) Vicara (zein of corn) Casein (milk protein)
Thermoplastics	Acetate (cellulose ester) Nylon (polymide) Dacron (polyester) Orlon (acrylic) Vinyon
Mineral	*Natural* Asbestos *Manufactured* Fibreglass Metallics *Other common fibres* Rubber Alginates Paper

CELLULOSIC OR VEGETABLE FIBRES

Cotton

Cotton is the most widely produced textile fabric today. It is believed that India was the first country to manufacture cotton. Among the finds at Mohenjodaro are a few scraps of cotton sticking to the side of a silver vase. This at least shows that cotton must have been used in India as far back as the 2nd millennium B.C. Historically painted and printed clothes are known to have been sold in Egypt and some parts of Europe long before the time of Alexander. (300 B.C.)

Fig. 1.1 A wood cut of the 'wool plant'

It is not known when Indians first started to trade with Europe, but the use of the oriental word 'carbasina' (Sanskrit *karpasa*) for cotton suggests that it must have been in use before 200 B.C. To the Greeks who came to India with Alexander the Great in 326 B.C. India was a land of mystery. They were so surprised to see cotton that they called it 'wool nuts.' They wrote: 'The wild trees of that country (India) bear fleeces as their fruit, surpassing those of sheep in beauty and excellence, and the Indians use cloth made from this tree wool'. We also learn from them that the Indians of those days, in contrast to their simple life-styles, loved finery. Many of their garments were worked in gold and ornamented in precious stones, or they were made of the finest 'flowered muslin'.

Even earlier, during the time of the Buddha, Banaras and Dacca were noted for the finest cotton fabrics—'so soft and smooth was their texture and the bleaching so perfect'. It is said that the mortal remains of the Buddha were covered with cloth from Banaras. Dacca has long been famous for its muslins, a word derived from the city of Mosul in Iraq where the fabric was first made. Marco Polo, during his travels in the East in the thirteenth century, says, "All the clothes of gold and silver that are called *mosolines* are made in this country." This shows that mosoline or muslin had a very different meaning from what it has now. Although chiefly devoted to the techniques employed in the weaving of the famed Indian muslins, the process shown in Fig. 1.2 can be taken as suggestive of the weaving of delicate fabrics, such as silken brocades and 'kinkhabs'

Early records tell us of a rare muslin produced in Dacca which,

PROCESS OF TEXTILE WEAVING IN INDIA

steaming clothes during the process of bleaching

arranging displaced threads in cloth

Fig. 1.2 These reproductions from a nineteenth century print depict the different steps involved in the process of textile weaving in India

when laid on wet grass, became "invisible", and because it was indistinguishable from the evening dew it was named *shabnam.* Another kind was called *abrawan* or running water,' because it became invisible in water. Yet another variety was named after *Arikamedu* near Pondicherry, showing that large-scale bleaching, starching and dyeing operations were undertaken in the immediate vicinity. It is related that the Emperor Aurangzeb one day reproached his daughter Zebunnisa for lack of modesty for her dress revealed her body through their weave. Whereupon the princess humbly replied, 'Father, I have already entwined myself eightfold with the *shabnam.*'

These muslins were of various qualities and had different designations. The finest of all Dacca muslins was called *mulmul khas* or the 'king's muslin'. It was generally made in half-pieces 10 yards by 36 inches. It weighed about 30 oz and the yarns had a count of about 250 to 300.

Abrawan muslin was considered of second quality. This usually measured 20 yards by 1 yard and weighed only 7 ½ oz. A story goes that in the time of Nawab Aliwardhikhan, a weaver was chastised and turned out of the city of Dacca for his neglect in not preventing his cow from eating up a piece of *abrawan* which he had spread out on the grass. Besides Dacca, fine muslins were produced at Banaras, Chanderi, Kotah and Arni too.

Another variety was *jamdani* or 'figured muslin'. These have been spoken of as the *chef d'oeuvre* of the Indian weaver. They are seen in artistic designs displaying superb skill in the manipulation of loom embroidery. Chikkan (needle work) embroidery muslins and printed muslins are other varieties of much beauty. A popular method of testing fineness was to ascertain that a piece of cloth could be passed through a lady's finger ring.

The bright cotton fabrics of ancient India were unmatched for hundreds of years. The Indus Valley sent out its popular cotton cloth known as 'sindhu' or 'sindon' to Baluchistan and Babylon. Over land and sea routes, a brisk trade in printed cotton fabrics was carried on with Egypt, Arabia, Turkestan, China, Thailand and Java. The trade was of such magnitude that new villages sprang up engaged solely in supplying the demands of foreign markets.

Much later, when Arab merchants plied the Arabian Sea carrying goods to Europe, they took with them shiploads of Indian printed cottons. According to Jacquemont, a French writer, these Arab

Fig. 1.3 A sea-going ship of the sixth century carrying textiles and cargo (From Cave II at Ajanta)

traders got the 'chipas' or printers of the Coromandel coast to print fabrics for them on the spot for a pittance. They then sold the fabrics at fabulous prices in the southern countries of Europe, where many an ignorant buyer was told they were from Arabia. The bright cotton fabrics of Hindustan remained a source of wealth and prosperity to the Arab countries for several centuries and were the envy of the rising nations in Europe.

Cotton manufacture did not establish itself on a large scale in Europe until the last century. The first three hundred years of the Christian era saw an all-round expansion of Indian culture, beyond the Gangetic region and into central Asia. There is evidence of profitable commerce between India and the Roman Empire, Egypt and Arabia. Among the most profitable of the items traded were the

Fig. 1.4 In England cotton fibre was first used to make candlewicks and not for clothing

fine Indian muslins known as *ventis textiles* or *nebula*, painted and embroidered cloths form Masulipatam, the Coromandel coast, Surat and Burhanpura, Painted chintzes with delicate shadings of floral patterns were also produced through a masterly use of mordant and dye. The main textile centres for export to European and Arab traders were Gujarat, Sindh and Rajputana in the west, the famed Coromandel coast from the Krishna delta to Point Calinere in the south, and Bengal, Orissa and the Ganges valley including Benares in the east. Before this the art was carried from India to Assyria and Egypt. Thence it passed over to the Italian states in the thirteenth century, reaching England only in the nineteenth.

With the help of the Industrial Revolution, the English tried ways and means to produce cotton textiles, and soon made such rapid progress that they surpassed the East in their manufacture. The introduction of machinery for spinning helped this progress.

Sources

The fibre comes from the fruit of the cotton plant, which grows in the tropical regions of the world. It is the downy 'boll' that surrounds the seeds of the plant. Cotton fibre is also called 'seed hair' because it is the fluffy, fibrous material which envelopes the seeds of the plant, as distinguished from stem or bast fibres such as flax or hemp.

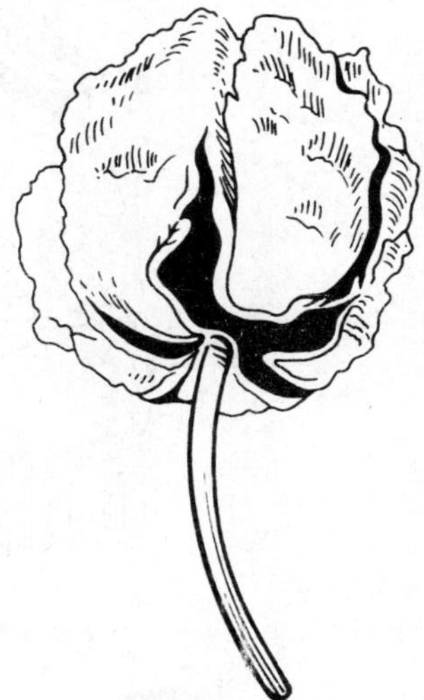

Fig. 1.5 The cotton 'boll'

The principal cotton producing regions are Egypt, the Southern United States, India, Brazil, the western and southern coasts of Africa and East Indies. The U.S.A produces more than 40 per cent of the world's cotton, while India ranks second to the United States as a producer and exporter of cotton.

Manufacture of handmade cotton in India

The tools and appliances used by cotton weavers consist of a spinning wheel *(charka)* and a spindle *(takli)*. The cotton is first separated and "carded." A bow-shaped beater known as a *dhun* is used for the purpose. The string of the bow is placed on the cotton and is made to vibrate by means of a wooden hammer. These vibrations disentangle the fibres and cleanse them of all foreign matter such as

Fig. 1.6 Takli

Fig. 1.8 Handloom

Fig. 1.7 Spinning wheel (*Charka*)

seeds and leaves, leaving soft, fine cotton behind. This fine cotton is next rolled on a stick to form a cylinder, about half a cubit (six inches) long and half an inch in diameter. This is fastened to a spindle or *takli*. The *charka* wheel is turned and the thread is gently drawn out, until it is about three hundred yards long. It is then taken off the wheel and rolled on the *chakra*. After a sufficient quantity of thread has been spun and collected, it is wound on to a bamboo reel.

Between 1000 and 2400 threads—according to the material required—are worked on a mill. The length of the warps is generally 50-1000 yards. The yarn is now ready for weaving on a handloom.

After weaving, the cloth is "calendered" with a blunt beater to give it a gloss and to soften it. It is finally passed to the hand-folders to give it a final fold. The cloth is then stamped, ticketed, and made ready for sale.

In recent years there has been a rapid development in the handloom sector to meet the demand for technically and aesthetically improved textiles.

The handweaving sector has socio-economic importance in our country, and some of the improvements introduced include

1. modernisation of looms;
2. training weavers in improved techniques;
3. development of cooperatives for production and marketing;
4. diversifying production and increasing the use of multifibres;
5. Promoting consumer awareness for handloom products, through fairs and exhibitions. Steps are also taken to introduce new spindles to meet the full demands of the handloom sector for yarn, both for the home and export markets.

Manufacture of cotton by machinery

Preparation The fibres are first removed from the seeds, which are them used for the production of seed oil, hydrogenated fats, soaps and cosmetics. The fibre mass is compressed into bales and shipped to the spinning mills.

Every bit of the fibre is used. The short ends (linters) left on the seed after the longer 'fabric' fibres have been removed, go to make rayon, plastics, dynamite and many other by-products.

In the spinning mills the cotton is fed into machines which remove the dirt and form the mass of fibre into a soft roll or lap. Several laps may be combined into one.

Carding The next process is known as carding, in which the fibres are smoothed and drawn together to form a loose rope or sliver.
Drawing The sliver is then combed, smoothened and stretched. The sliver may be drawn three times, reduced further in size and given a slight twist by a process called roving, in which the sliver is passed through rollers and wound onto bobbins set in spindles. This is done in a speed frame.

Fig. 1.9 Draw frame

Combing This process is really a continuation and refinement of the carding process. Cotton yarns for fabrics are carded but not all are combed. Yarns that are only carded are not so clean; whereas combed yarns are finer, even and free from all woody stalk of the plant. They are used for finer quality fabrics such as voile and organdie.
Weaving and Dyeing The yarn is then knitted or woven in any one of a variety of weaves and structures. Warp yarns are usually more strongly twisted than filling yarns, since they must withstand

Fig. 1.10 Speed frame

Fig. 1.11 Weaving (automatic loom)

Fig. 1.12 A 'Buser' automatic screen-printing machine, which prints up to 12 colours on a continuous piece of cloth

greater strain in weaving and finishing. Dyestuffs may be applied to raw cotton, yarn, or piece-goods.

Finishing The cotton cloth is now ready for finishing, which includes starching, calendering, sanforizing, schreinerizing, mercerising or other finishes as is necessary for the particular use for which the cloth is intended. These finishes may be applied to the yarns, but are usually applied to the fabric. The fabrics may be given these special finishes before or after dyeing. Some of these finishes are durable, others semi-durable. Scientists are improving on them every day.

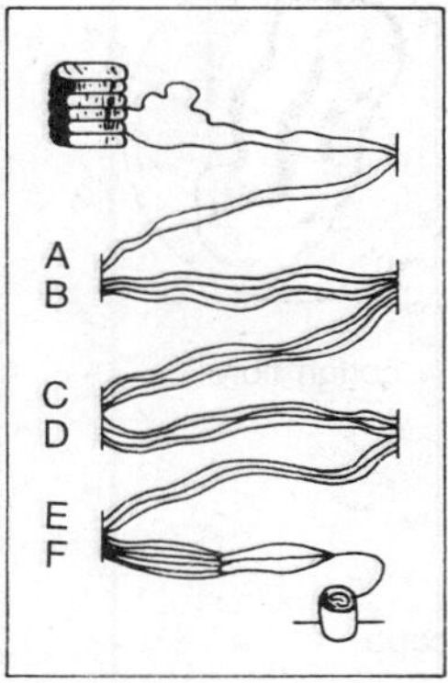

Fig. 1.13 Diagram of processes from cotton bales to spool of thread

Structure and composition of the fibre

The cotton fibre is short (1/2 inches to 2 inches) and cylindrical or tubular as it grows. After ripening, the sap inside the fibre dries up so that the fibre flattens and twists. This natural twist is of great importance, as it helps to keep the yarn firm and strong and makes it easier to spin it into long threads. These twists are called convolutions. Fibres vary in the number of convolutions, mature cotton fibres having as many as 300 per inch, while immature fibres have none. Long length and many convolutions help in the spinning of the fibres. When untwisted the fibre of the yarn appears straight and inelastic.

Cotton fibre is essentially cellulose, that is carbon, hydrogen and oxygen in the proportion $C_6H_{10}O_5$. Bleached cotton is almost pure cellulose. Raw cotton contains about 5 per cent of impurities, consisting principally of cotton seed oil, pectic acid, colouring matter, albumen and wax. The wax acts as a protective coating to the fibre, making it water-repellant.

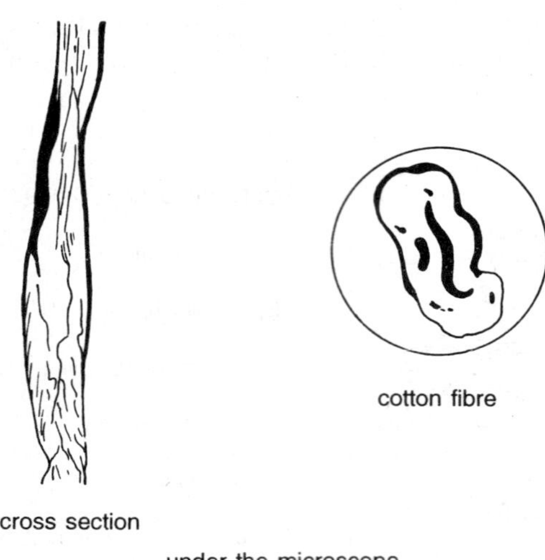

Fig. 1.14

Examined under the microscope, the fibre is a narrow, flattened structure with a spiral twist and thick irregular edges.

Mercerized cotton appears smooth and cylindrical, and shows a slight suggestion of twist, because usually all of the twist is not removed in the mercerizing process.

Quality

The quality of cotton is measured partly by the length and brightness of the fibre. This depends on the species, the quality of the seed and soil, the mode of cultivation, and climatic conditions. Sea Island (West Indies) cotton has the longest and finest fibres, with the highest lusture. Then come Egyptian American and Indian cotton, which has coarser, shorter fibres, but is very strong.

The best qualities are those capable of being spun into the finest yarns, and these are found to possess the greatest hair-length, with a corresponding decrease in diameter and a greater number of convolutions per unit length than in the lower qualities. The following table indicates these relations.

Type of cotton	Length in mm	Diameter in mm	Convolutions per mm
Sea Island	45	0.014	14
Egyptian	40	0.014	12
American	38	0.019	8
Indian (High)	25	0.020	6

Types of cotton

Kapok This is the fibre from the seeds of a large tree of India and the East Indies, called silk floss. It is unsuitable for spinning as it has no natural twist but is useful for lifebuoys, belts and mattresses. Kapok is resistant to vermin and moisture, drying quickly when wet and so is used for articles that are constantly exposed to moisture. Kapok is used for sound proofing on airplanes and as insulating material. Under the microscope, kapok is easily distinguished from cotton as it appears as a hollow circular tube with very thin walls and no twists.

Flannelette and Flannel A soft napped cotton fabric, its warmth in wear is due to the fact that the nap traps a layer of air between the body and the cold outside. In composition it is the same as ordinary cotton, but treatment in weaving makes it very inflammable. For this reason attempts have been made to make it fireproof by saturating the fibre with metallic salt, but in general the fireproofing does not withstand washing. Flannelette is napped on one side only, while flannel is napped on both sides.

Organdie A thin light fabric in plain weave with a very stiff finish. It is made from good quality combed yarn. The yarn is made from long staple cotton and is spun with many twists. This, along with the finishing process, produces its characteristic transparent crispness. The aim is to give a permanent finish. The fabric is used for summer and evening wear.

Muslin This is a cool, very light, plain weave cloth also used for summer wear. The name derives from the city of Mosul where the fabric was first made. Muslins were not always plain, silk and even gold stripes woven in when made in Mosul, but as cotton was grown more plentifully, and the women could spin yarns of great fineness, cotton yarns gradually superseded silk. During the first century A.D., Indian muslins and jamdanis became famous in Rome under such names as *nebula*, *gangetika* and *venti* textiles (woven winds).

Chemical reactions

Mild alkaline substances such as ammonia, borax and silicate of soda are not harmful to cotton fibres but they may affect the colour of dyed cotton. However, prolonged boiling, in the presence of air is likely to tender it.

Dilute caustic alkali can be used safely in the absence of air, but concentrated caustic solutions change the nature of the fibre.

Dilute acids, such as sulphuric and hydrochloric acids, have little or no effect on cotton, but if they are allowed to remain in the fabrics for long, the acid will become concentrated during drying and the fabric will be weakened. Concentrated mineral acids destroy the fibre.

All bleaches can be used with safety, but the use of oxidizing agents demands great care, since they tend to weaken the fibre. Hence thorough rinsing is necessary to ensure the removal of all traces of acid from the fabric.

Other reactions

Long exposure to water or moisture has no harmful effect on cotton fabrics. In fact, the tensile strength of cotton is greater wet than dry, increasing by about 25 per cent when wet. This is important in washing and ironing. Fabrics which are stronger when wet can be handled with less care. Hardness of water has no action on the fibre but dislocation may result from insoluble soap deposits produced by the action of soap on the hardening substances in the water.

Friction can be applied and the fabric stretched without any harmful effect, but the fineness of the fabric and looseness of its weave have to be taken into consideration, otherwise, shrinkage and undue wear may result.

Heat is not harmful unless scorching takes place. The fibres can be safely exposed to moist heat at boiling point but scorch readily when heat is applied by an over-heated iron. Prolonged steaming at 99°C to 100°C has a tendering effect.

Exposure to light tends to weaken the fabric.

Cotton absorbs moisture as well as wool or silk. Thus if worn next to the skin, it absorbs perspiration readily and feels cool.

Affinity for dyes

Cotton does not dye as readily as wool or silk, but its affinity for colours is considerably increased when the fibre is mercerised.

Direct cotton dyes have great affinity for cotton and can be applied from their aqueous solutions without the help of a mordant. Similarly, azoic dyes, sulpur and vat dyes have affinity for cotton. Cotton has no affinity for the acid dyes used for wool and silk.

Cotton is resistant to moths but is attacked by mildew and silverfish. Mildew and mould occur under most warm conditions. Micro-organisms need heat, moisture and food to grow. Hence it is advisable to store cotton fabrics unstarched in a dry place and care taken to see that soiled clothes are dry before being put into the laundry basket.

Conclusion

Despite the increasingly rapid inroads being made into its market by synthetics, cotton continues to be the world's major textile fibre. It is one of the oldest and most versatile of all fibres and is able to contribute all of its good properties when blended with other fabrics. Some of the main reasons for the use of cotton are its good weaving qualities, low cost, high absorption, excellent abrasion and pilling-resistance and stability to repeated blending. It is excellent if preshrunk, and can be safely ironed even at temperatures of 425°F, is colour fast, has excellent wash and wear and wrinkle resistance, and is also good if resin treated.

Linen

The art of making linen from flax goes back to the ancient Egyptians. According to Egyptian mythology, flax was the first thing created for themselves by the gods before appearing on earth. A series of graphic pictures depicting the entire process of flax culture were discovered in 1881 in one of the tombs of the Pharaohs, dating to about 2500 B.C. Even if Egypt was not the birthplace of linen, it was at least its cradle, reaching a perfection seldom equalled and never surpassed elsewhere in either the ancient or the modern world. Warden writes, "The very finest cambric or linen of the present days looks coarse besides these specimens of Egyptian looms in the days of Pharaohs."

There is also evidence that Swiss lake-dwellers of the Stone Age used the fibres of a wild flax for fish lines and nets.

Linen is mentioned often in the Bible, sometimes as an emblem of peace. The Biblical description of a Jewish tabernacle, tells us that the curtains were of fine linen, and that when the high priest entered he put on a holy linen coat and girdle, and upon his head a linen mitre.

From Egypt, linen manufacture spread to other countries. Phoenician merchants opened up new channels of commerce, introducing flax cultivation and linen manufacture throughout the Mediterranean, perhaps even to Ireland. However, it was not until the twelfth century that flax production was organised into an industry in Europe. By 1685, Ireland had become the centre for the manufacture of linen. The flax industry in the U.S.A dates from the early 1800s when many Irish linen weavers emigrated to that country.

In India, linen was commonly used during the time of Manu. The *Arthasastra* mentions materials made of flax or *kshauma*. Linen was also a popular fabric during the days of Lord Buddha. It was particularly selected and used for the robes of Buddhist monks or *bhikshus*.

Sources

Linen fibre is obtained from the stem of the flax plant, which grows throughout the temperate climate wherever there is sufficient moisture. The Baltic states, Germany, France, Holland, Ireland, Central Asia and some parts of America are the regions where flax is grown extensively.

The botanical name for the common flax plant is *Linum usitatissimum*. There are two types of flax grown; fibre flax and seed flax. The former is grown mainly for its fibre, with the seed crop secondary; the other is grown for its seed, the fibre qualities being secondary.

Flax is an annual plant growing to a maximum height of about

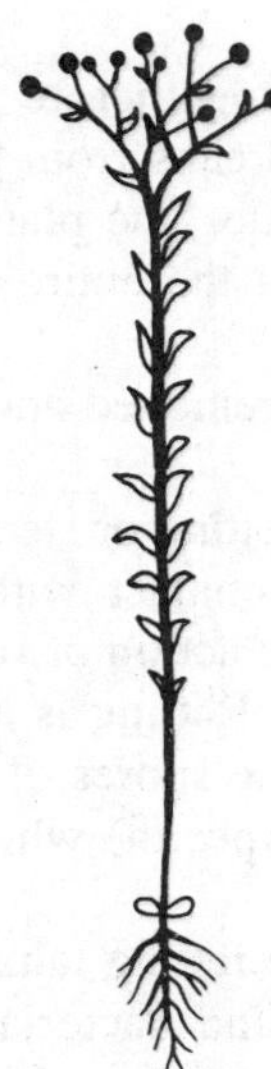

Fig. 1.15 Flax stalk showing the seed head, the long straight stem with small leaves, and the roots

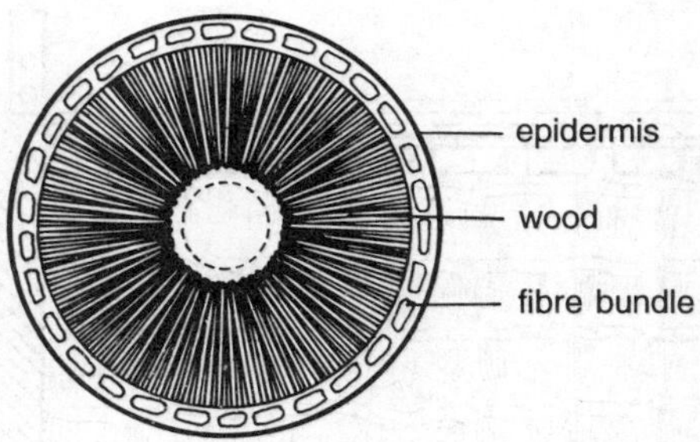

Fig. 1.16 Diagrammatic cross section of flax stalk showing the distribution of the linen fibres in a bundle

40 inches. The stem is slender and straight; and the flowers are pale blue.

The fibres for linen yarns grow in the bast oı woody part of the stem of the flax plant. Thus they are called 'bast fibres'.

Manufacture

Flax plants are grown close together to prevent the stems from branching, for once a branch breaks from the parent stem the fibre above that point is of little value. The plants are pulled by hand or machine, and care is taken that the entire fibre from top to root is intact.

After pulling, the seeds are removed and used for the production of linseed oil.

Retting This is followed by retting or steeping, in which the fleshy part of the stem is rotted by contact with water. This process is carried out by exposing it to the action of running or stagnant water, or to the action of dew or sun. Retting is a fermentation process in which (pectin eater) bacteria, the spores of which exist in the plant, come to life and eat the gum (pectin) which binds the fibre to the stem.

Retting is now done in large retting tanks where the composition and temperature of the water and bacterial count can be carefully controlled (Fig. 1.17). Retting requires about a week and is an important step in flax preparation, since it determines the looseness. The stem is finally removed by pressing the stems between fleeted rollers and beating them with revolving blades. The bundles are then dried in the fields.

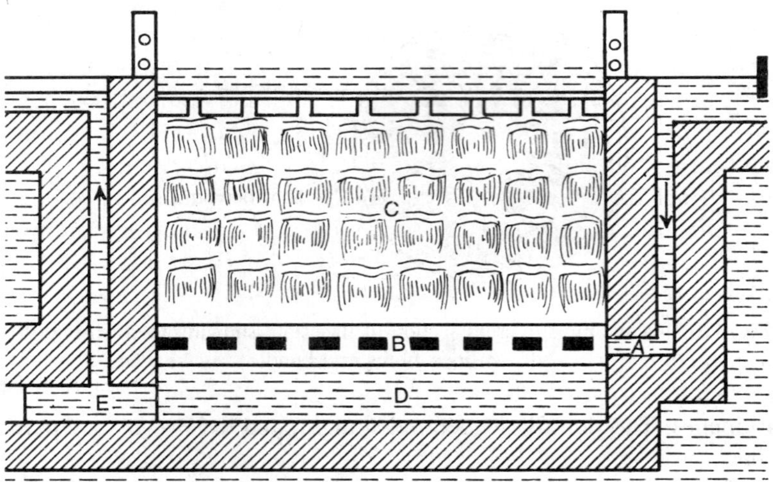

Fig. 1.17 Retting tank

Scrutching By this process the softened woody outer portions are broken up and removed. An early method of scrutching was to place a bunch of fibres in the cleft of a "scrutching post" and striking it with a flat beater. Scrutching machines are now used, operating on the same general principle.

Hackling or Combing The inner part that is left forms the linen fibres. These vary in length from ten inches to several feet. They are separated into short and long linen fibres. The long fibres, called 'line,' are passed through a series of combs until they emerge smooth, fine and glossy, ready for spinning. The shorter fibres, known as 'tow,' are used in the manufacture of inferior linen materials. The fibres are now ready for spinning into yarn.

Spinning The long glossy yarn is either spun wet to give very fine yarns or dry to form coarser yarns. After the fabric has been woven it may be bleached. Dressing is also added to the cheaper varieties of fabric, but the effect is lost after washing.

The natural colour of linen varies from dark to yellowish grey Linen is sold in different degrees of bleach, full, half bleach and

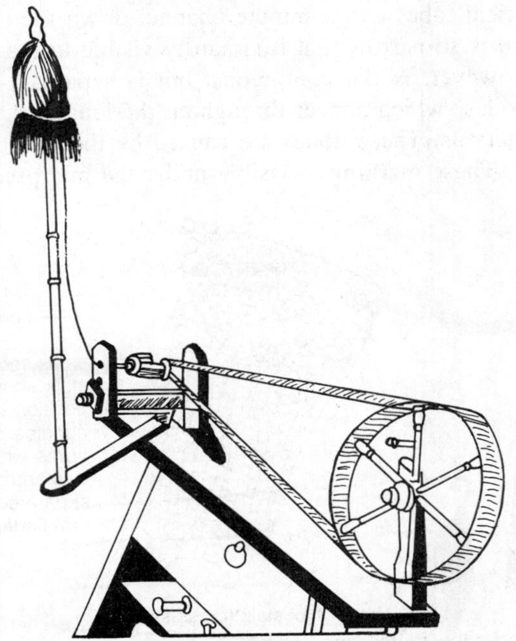

Fig. 1.18 An ancient spinning wheel for flax used in the home

natural. This bleaching is done chemically by spreading the cloth out on grass in the sun. The more the cloth is bleached the more it is weakened so that a piece of full-bleached linen is weaker than one only half-bleached. Long line fibres are used for better quality linen fabrics. They give the lusture and body so typical of linen. Short tow fibres are used for less expensive linen.

Linen fibres are naturally stiff, and fabrics made from them usually have more body than those made from softer fibres. Because of the natural stiffness of the fabric, linens wrinkle readily and have to be pressed with each wearing. This objection is overcome to some extent by special finishes given to linen.

Structure and composition of the fibre

Linen or flax, classed as a bast fibre, is long, round, smooth and semi-transparent. Untwisted from the yarn it has the same appearance as cotton fibre. Linen or bast fibre is composed of a large number of tiny cells compacted together to form a single fibre. The fibre ranges from 12 to 36 inches in length and has the appearance of a cylindrical tube with a minute channel down the centre. This central canal is so narrow that it is hardly visible to the naked eye. The tube however, is not continuous, but is separated by distinct joints or 'nodes' which appear throughout the length of the fibre at irregular intervals. These nodes are caused by the irregular growth of the stem. These markings—visible under the microscope—serve

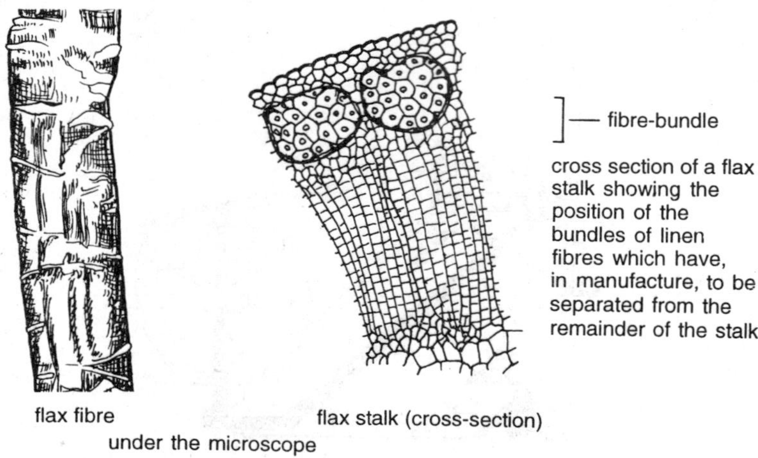

Fig. 1.19

as a positive means of identifying the flax fibre. Each flax fibre is further sub-divided into minute fibrils invisible to the naked eye.

The composition is the same as that of cotton, almost pure cellulose.

Seen under the microscope, the fibre is cylindrical, straight, firm, smooth, round and transparent, with notches or nodes at intervals which give it the appearance of bamboo. Like bamboo, its structure makes it capable of being split both length-wise and across.

If ignited the fibre flares up and burns like cotton.

Properties and Uses

Linen fabrics are smooth, cool and crisp to the touch and have a natural gloss or sheen. They are resistant to tearing, take great strains without breaking or stretching and do not lose their shape or go limp. Linen material is hard-wearing, washes very well (in fact it is 20% stronger when wet). It never fluffs, does not soil readily and holds dye very well. It is also normally moth-proof.

The material can crease easily if the fibre is not mixed with other fibres to prevent this or if the material is not treated to resist creases. It can also be subject to mildew. It discolours if stored in a cupboard with hot water pipes running through it or in wood-lined drawers or chests. The material regains its whiteness easily, however. To remove discoloration it is washed in the normal way and dried in the sun to bleach.

The material is used for table and bed linen, drying cloths in the kitchen and bathroom, inner lining and clothing, including protective clothing against radioactivity, handkerchiefs, mail bags, hosepipe covers, insulation in telephones and telephone switchboards, parachute harnesses, lightweight suitcases and fishing lines.

The thread is used to stitch aircraft and railway carriage upholstery, carpets, suitcases, life-belts, tarpaulins, footballs and cricket balls.

The fibre is also made up into many types of material such as duck, canvas, double and single damask and slubbed dress linen. There are textured suitweights where different effects are given in the weaving to simulate tweed, hopsack or herring-bone, and there are also twill weaves and houndstooth checks.

Linen drinks in moisture more readily than any other fabric. Wet the cloth and if smears and streaks of water are left on the surface it is not made of linen. Linen cloth has an irregular thickening of single threads (slubs) which is characteristic of its fibre.

Laundering and storage

Give stains prompt attention, soaking the material for a short time, then wash and iron in the usual way. Separate white from coloured linens, and to maintain the freshness of colours wash in a good soap in hand-hot soft water. White linen may be washed with soap or detergent by hand or machine and the water can be of any temperature up to the boiling point. Rubbing is rarely necessary. Rinse thoroughly and stretch the damp article to its natural size and shape. Iron while still quite damp with a hot iron (on the wrong side only for coloured dress linens).

For extra special clothes such as damask table-cloths, fold once and roll around a cardboard cylinder of stiff paper. Other linen should be put on slatted shelves to allow air to circulate.

Common tests for linen and cotton in cloth

The marked difference in the cost of linen and cotton has led to urgent requests for physical tests that will make the identification of linen possible.

1. Tearing is the most commonly accepted test, though not reliable. Linen, when torn, shows glossy ends pointed and unequal in length with fibres parallel to each other, contrasting with the almost even, brush-like, curling, lustreless fibres of cotton. Linen is much stronger than cotton and tears with a duller sound.

2. Boil a portion in a strong solution of sulphuric acid for 2 or 3 minutes; linen is not destroyed but cotton is.

3. Boil in a strong solution of common salt and water, dry and then burn. If flax, a grey ash is left; if cotton, a black ash.

4. The most positive test for cotton in a linen fabric is to use a microscope. The smooth, straight linen fibre can be easily distinguished from the twisted cotton fibre under an ordinary microscope. However, should the cotton be mercerised, a number of fibres will have to be examined in order to find some that have escaped mercerising. When cotton is mercerised, the fibres untwist but there will always be found a proportion that have remained unaffected.

Jute

Jute is the second most widely used vegetable fibre after cotton. The name of this plant is derived from the Bengali word *jhuto* which means 'to be entangled', probably referring to the irregular fibres which readily mesh together.

The fibre has been used in India as handicraft material since very ancient times. Early Sanskrit writings speak of *pat* or jute as a useful household plant, serviceable both as a pot herb and as a fibre.

Jute is often called 'Calcutta hemp,' but it only receives the name from the fact that most of this fibre enters into commerce through that port. Jute is obtained from the plant *Corchorus capsularis*.

Practically all the jute fibre produced in India, and 85 per cent of the total world production, is from Bengal and Bangladesh. Some jute is also cultivated in other parts of India. Brazil is also making a successful attempt to grow jute.

Jute is an annual plant growing from 5 to 10 feet high. It has a cylindrical stalk as thick as a man's finger. There are no branches except near the top. The plants are grown not only for the fibre, but also for the leaves which, as stated before, are used as a pot herb.

The crop is ready for cutting when the flowers begin to fade. If gathered earlier, the fibre is weak; if left until the seed is ripe, the fibre, although stronger, is coarse and lacks the characteristic lustre. The best fibre is secured by hand-stripping, when each stalk is peeled separately.

Structure and composition of the fibre

The fibre consists of bundles of cells with sharply defined polygonal outlines. The individual bast cells of the jute are very fine and much shorter than flax fibres. The best quality of jute fibre is a clear yellowish colour with a fine silky lustre. It is soft and smooth to the touch.

The jute fibre is decidedly less strong than flax or hemp. It is highly hygroscopic. In a dry atmosphere it may have no more than 6 per cent of moisture, but in damp conditions the moisture may be as high as 23 per cent.

Manufacture

The plants grow to a height of up to ten feet, and are gathered just as the flowers fade.

Retting The cheapest method of removing the fibres from the jute plant is to steep the stems in streams or pools until bacterial action destroys the tissues in which the fibres are embedded. Great care has to be taken. If over-retted, the fibres are injured; if insufficiently retted, the fibres cannot be handled by the spinner.

Softening Jute is naturally very harsh owing to a low wax content and also its lignified nature. For this reason it must be softened to permit the division of the fibre, and also lubricated. Water and oil are added to the fibres, and they are passed through a series of rollers until the desired change is obtained.

Preparing the Yarn The fibres are sent to the carding machine and made into long round slivers. These slivers are drawn out by combining a number of fibres into one. These then go to the roving frame, where they are drawn out to about eight times their length, given a slight twist and wound on bobbins. The yarn now is ready for weaving.

Properties and uses

The finished material is lustrous and can be bleached to a cream shade or dyed. Jute is used mostly for making hessian, sacking, *durries* and cheap pile fabrics. Bleached jute is also used as filling weft to cotton warp in "linen" towelling. Lately, a variety of novelty fabrics for dress goods have also been made from jute used in conjunction with woollen or cotton yarns. Jute is also used in the manufacture of twine, rope and carpets.

Jute is susceptible to microbiological decay, especially under conditions of high temperature and high relative humidity. It is especially weak in salt water. Rot-proofing is accomplished by the use of insoluble antiseptics which are fixed on or within the fabric. Mineral salts, organic metallic compounds and phenolic derivates are among the substances used. Modern jute is both water resistant and fireproof. It is also converted into a wool-like fibre by treatment with caustic soda. (See chapter on Yarn Construction)

Jute can be distinguished from linen or cotton if the fibres are stained with iodine, and then concentrated sulphuric acid and glycerine are applied. Jute fibres remain yellow, but cotton and linen turn blue.

Hemp

Hemp was much used by the peoples of Asia from before the Christian era. It was used for carpets, tapestry, ropes, soles of shoes and even to tie together letters carved on slats of wood. Some of these antiquities were brought to India by Sir Auriel Stein from his expeditions to the heart of Asia and are now exhibited at the Archaeological Museum in Delhi.

Hemp is grown chiefly in the Philippine islands, China, Mexico, Russia, the West Indies and India. The Manila variety is white.

In India, Deccan hemp is grown both as a crop and as a hedge plant. It is cultivated largely in Maharashtra, Karnataka and Tamil Nadu. It grows best in the alluvial soils of north Gujarat and in medium black soils.

Structure and composition of the fibre

The fibre is lustrous and has the microscopic nodes and joints of linen, but the central canal is wider. The cells are blunt ended.

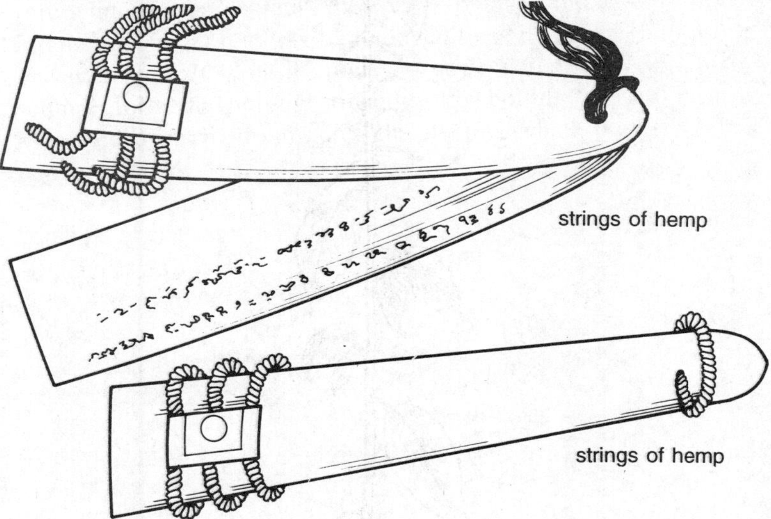

Fig. 1.20 Double-wedge tablets like these were generally used for official correspondence in central Asia (where Sir Auriel Stein found this example) and in northern India in the first to the third centuries. The tablets are about 15 inches long and fastened together with strings of hemp

Manufacture

The manufacture of hemp follows the same processess as flax.

Uses

Being stronger than linen or jute, it is ideal for twine, ropes, cables, carpets, canvas, ship cordage and sailcloth, as it is not weakened or rotted by water. Today, even fine fabrics are made from hemp.

Ramie

Ramie is a vegetable fibre from nettles, grown chiefly in India, China and in other neighbouring countries. The Chinese variety is often known as China grass or rhea.

The finished fibre is fine, silky and strong. This makes it suitable

Fig. 1.21 The Ramie plant

for weaving into fine table-linen, like tray cloths, table cloths, napkins, etc. Ramie has many properties similiar to those of linen. A slight amount of gum in the fabric, makes starching unnecessary as the material will stiffen sufficiently if ironed damp.

Another quality of ramie that makes it unique among fibres is its behaviour when in contact with water. Ramie is more absorbent than cotton, holding water to the extent of 28 per cent of its dry weight, whereas cotton holds only 26 per cent. More over, instead of losing strength when wet, as do many fibres, ramie is 30 to 60 per cent stronger wet than dry. It also dries more rapidly than flax or cotton. That has the additional advantages of making it unshrinkable and highly resistant to mildew as well as to the attack of micro organisms that cause rot.

Structure and composition of the fibre

Ramie, like linen, is a bast fibre. The fibre is made up of cells about one inch long, and the whole fibre has longitudinal markings. It is fine and silky in appearance, and makes strong, lustrous fabric. Ramie is well adapted for use in light-weight summer suits. It is also blended with rayon, cotton and wool to make attractive new fibres.

Under the microscope the ramie fibre resembles flax with definite nodes. The diameter varies like flax, but its average is wider than that of flax.

Manufacture

It is manufactured in the same way as linen.

Sunn

The Sunn (or san) plant is a native of southern Asia, chiefly India. There are two varieties, Bhadoi san and Rabi san. The former is planted in May and June and harvested in October and November, and the latter, which is the better variety, is planted in October and November and harvested in February and March.

In order to secure the best grade of fibres, the plants are cut when they flower. They are exposed for 36 hours, then retted in water for three to four days and the fibres immediately stripped off owing to their tendency to rot. They are then dried and sorted.

Sunn is better in quality than jute, being lighter in colour and with greater tensile strength. It contains 80 per cent cellulose as against 64 per cent in jute.

Sunn is used for fishnets, twines, rug yarns, sacking fabrics and in paper making.

Abaca or Manila

This plant is a native of the Philippine islands, where it is cultivated on a large scale. It is also grown in Sumatra and Borneo. It is planted clear of other trees and ten feet apart each way. It is a perennial and grows to a height of 9 to 10 feet. A single plant yields about 1 lb of fibre. The fibre is white and lustrous, light and hard, and easily separable. It has good tensile strength and great durability. The cellulose content is 64 to 65 per cent. It is used in the manufacture of rope and heavy cordage.

Sisal

Sisal is grown on large plantations in East and West Africa, the East Indies, Java and Mexico. The plant is a triennial. The leaves grow from the base of the plant, and each leaf is cut by hand close to the ground. The leaves are beaten by hand and the fibres removed. The fibres are washed simultaneously with scraping. They contain 72 per cent cellulose and 14 to 15 per cent lignin. The fibre rots readily in salt water. Its principal use is in the manufacture of commercial tying twines, ropes and cords. It can be admixed with cotton to alter the quality and price of the rope.

Coir

Coir is obtained from the shell of the coconut. The fibres are about 10 inches long. Kerala and Sri Lanka are the home and centres of coir fibres. The coconut husks are softened by steeping them in sea-water and the wood is separated from the fibres by pounding with a stone, hackled with a steel comb and then dried. The fibres are changed into yarns from which cordage and coarse cloths are prepared. Bristles for brushes are made directly from the fibres.

Coir fibre has a natural affinity towards dyestuffs. Coir being a vegetable fibre, shows greater sensitivity towards the primary colours, and good, brilliant colours are obtained when the fibre is dyed with such dyestuffs. Although basic colours are not stable to sunlight, they are used on coir fibre because dyed coir mats are usually placed indoors.

Rayon

One cannot imagine the modern world without synthetic textiles. 'Man-made' or synthetic fibres, as they are more loosely known, were invented only this century. The commercial production of rayon goes back no further than about forty-eight years. It blends well with all other fibres. Rayons are regenerated cellulose fibres. Yet within this short time, rayon—or artificial silk as it was originally known—has become an intrinsic part of everyday life. It has brought to many a standard of luxury once enjoyed only by a few.

The main object in manufacturing rayon was to provide a cheap substitute for silk. Softness, coolness, lightness in weight and attractive appearance, all count for the popularity of rayon. So clever is the imitation that many cannot distinguish silk from rayon without prior knowledge.

For the first time in the world, bamboo and eucalyptus have been successfully used for the manufacture of rayon grade wood pulp. India's first rayon factory was started in 1946 in Kerala, followed since then by several more.

Manufacture

All varieties of rayon are of vegetable origin and are derived from a cellulose base. There are four main procedures by which cellulose is transformed in to rayon:

a) the nitro-cellulose method;
b) the cuprammonium method;
c) the viscose method; and
d) the cellulose acetate method

The general principles of rayon yarn production involve making a treacly liquid and then forcing it through the fine holes of a jet.

There are, however, variations on this procedure, and they give each type of yarn distinct properties.

All processes for producing rayons are common in that they copy the technique of the silkworm of forcing a sticky fluid through a small hole and then hardening the thread to obtain filaments. Some of the important differences in rayons are due to the method of treating the cellulose raw material. The viscose method converts the cellulose by the addition of carbon bisulphate, whereas it is copper sulphate and ammonia that are the chemical agents used in the cuprammonium method. In the acetate method the purified cellulose is treated with a mixture of acetic acid and acetic anhydride.

The Nitrocellulose Method was the first to be used for the production of rayon fabrics. It was invented by Count Hilaire Chardonnet of France in 1884. The fibre is produced from cotton linters (short stapled cotton) which, treated with a mixture of sulphuric and nitric acids, produce nitro-cellulose. The inflammable material thereby produced is dissolved in spirits, and the solution is denitrated to make it non-inflamable. But the method is expensive and little used today.

The Cupramonium Process was first used in Germany in 1897. Cotton linters or wood pulp are treated with caustic soda solution and steeped in cold saturated copper sulphate solution. It is then squeezed and dissolved in strong aqueous ammonia to give cuprammonium solution, which is forced through fine jets into dilute acid to give threads that may be stretched into fine fibres. This rayon closely resembles silk. The American Bemberg Corporation is a specialist in the production of these rayons.

Manufacture of Bemberg Yarn The accompanying drawing (Fig. 1.22) depicts the most important steps in the manufacture of cuprammonium cellulose yarns by the Bemberg stretch-spinning process.

1. The raw material may be cotton linters or wood pulp. Cotton linters formerly supplied the chief source of cellulose in the production of cuprammonium cellulose yarns by the Bemberg stretch-spinning process. Cotton linters are the fine, soft fibres adhering to the cotton seed after the long fibres have been removed during ginning. These fibres are separated from the cotton seed, cleaned and bleached before use for conversion into rayon yarns. Now highly refined wood pulps serve also as a raw material in this process.

2. The cellulose is bleached to a pure white in a washing machine. This is the only bleaching required for this type of rayon yarn.

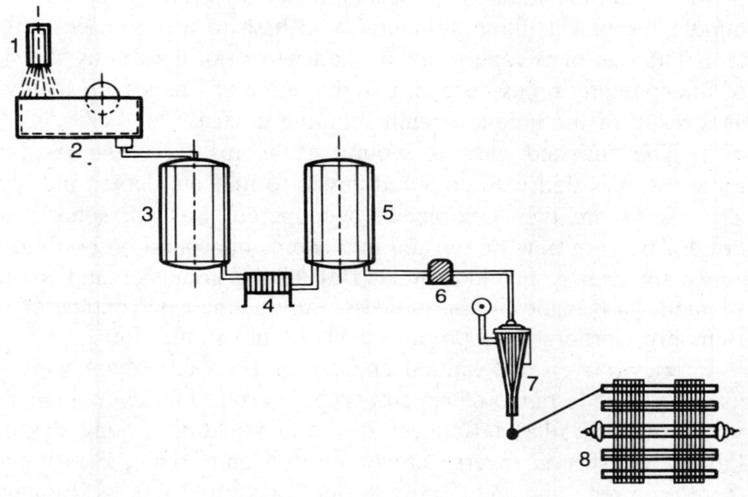

Fig. 1.22 Manufacture of bemberg yarn
(Courtesy: American Bemberg Corporation, USA)

3. Next, cuprammonium cellulose spinning solution is prepared in a solution mixer by dissolving the cellulose at low temperature in aqueous ammonia containing basic copper sulphate.

4. The impurities are then filtered out in a solution filter. The pure, clean spinning solution is dark blue and has the consistency of honey.

5. The spinning solution is allowed to mature or age in a storage tank.

6. The solution then passes through a spinning bath supply of purified, slightly alkaline water which causes coagulation of the filaments as they leave the spinneret.

7. The diagram depicts the stretch-spinning apparatus where the spinning solution is forced through the comparatively large holes of the spinneret, which is fitted into the top of a glass cylinder containing a long, tapering glass funnel. The water from the spinning bath supply is admitted at the bottom of the cylinder, flows up and descends through the funnel. The action of the water coagulates the spinning solution coming through the spinneret and at the same time stretches the filaments thus formed. Final coagulation and stretching

of the combined filament is accomplished by passing the filament bundle through a dilute sulphuric acid bath to a driven collecting reel. The size of Bemberg rayon filaments is not limited by the size of the spinneret holes instead, a high degree of fineness is achieved as a result of the unique stretch-spinning device.

8. The finished yarn is wound as skeins on reels. As it is removed, it is tied with coloured thread to indicate denier and type. The skeins are then completely decoppered, washed, soaped and dried. The yarn may be twisted into skeins or wound on bobbins or cones for use by manufacturers. Due to the great demand for the filament yarn made by this process, only a small percentage of the Bemberg Corporation's product is made into staple fibre.

Fabrics woven and knitted entirely of Bemberg rayon yarn are used for a wide range of apparel types. Formal fabrics include velvet, satin, brocades, taffeta, chiffon and voilette. Among daytime fabrics are sheers, reverse crêpe, shirting and jersey. For lingerie there are crêpe and satin and a variety of knitted fabrics. Bemberg is also used extensively for gloves, scarves and undergarments.

In the interior decoration field, ninon, drapery satin and taffeta, brocades, jacquards and table damask are woven of All-Bemberg rayon yarns.

Combination fabrics The unusual texture, rich appearance or durability of certain fabrics is the result of combining yarns of different fibres. This may be done by blending different kinds of rayon staple fibres together or with natural fibres, by twisting rayon filament or spun yarns together or with natural fibre yarns, and by combining yarns of different fibres in the weaving. (See mixed fabrics.)

In upholstery fabrics Bemberg rayon yarn is mainly used on the surface to add richness to cotton, wool or other types of rayon fabrics, and to increase resistance to sunlight and light deterioration.

Apparel fabrics such as bengaline, poplin crêpes, many sportswear fabrics and novelties receive their characteristic textures through the combination of Bemberg with natural or other man made yarns.

The Viscose Method Viscose was first manufactured in England in 1892 by the chemists Bevan, Cross and Beadle. The largest proportion of rayons today is manufactured by this process, as the cost of production is comparatively low and excellent fibres are produced. In India the raw materials used for viscose rayon are bamboo, eucalyptus and other woods (see Fig. 1.23).

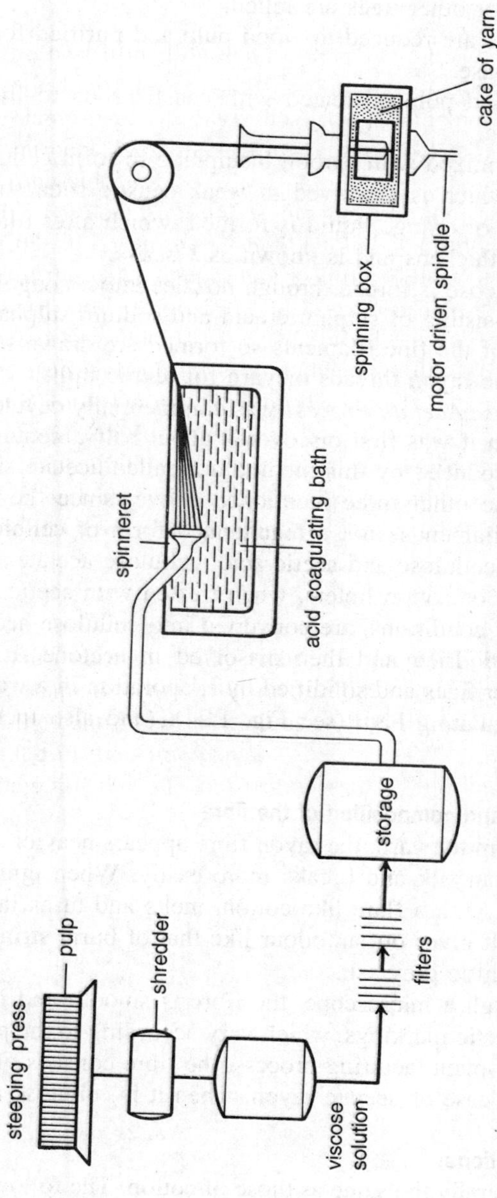
steeping press
pulp
shredder
viscose solution
filters
storage
spinneret
acid coagulating bath
spinning box
motor driven spindle
cake of yarn

1. Spruce or other trees are felled.
2. The logs are reduced to wood pulp and purified for the cellulose base.
3. The wood pulp is treated with caustic soda to form alkali cellulose.
4. This is mixed with carbon bisulphide to form cellulose zanthate, which is dissolved in weak caustic soda solution. A reddish or orange liquid is formed, which after filtering and ageing thickens and is known as *Viscose*.
5. The viscose is forced through nozzles into a coagulating liquid consisting of sulphuric acid and sodium sulphate.
6. Many of the fine filaments so formed are drawn together to form the rayon threads or yarn for textile mills.

The Cellulose Acetate Process was commercially developed after 1918, although it was first discovered about half a century earlier. The fabrics produced by this method are called acetate silks. They differ from the other three mentioned above, since the substance forming the filament is not a regenerated form of cellulose, but a compound of cellulose and acetic acid, cellulose acetate.

Wood pulp or cotton linters, when treated with acetic anhydride under suitable conditions, are converted into cellulose acetate. This is washed and dried and then dissolved in acetone. It is forced through fine orifices and solidified by evaporation in a warm chamber or a coagulating bath (see Fig. 1.24), (and also thermoplastic fibres).

The structure and composition of the fibre

Untwisted from the yarn, the rayon fibre appears heavier, stiffer and less elastic than silk and breaks more easily. When ignited, rayon burns quickly with a flare like cotton, melts and turns into a black thorny bead. It gives out an odour like that of burnt string or paper and leaves a little grey ash.

Seen through a microscope, the fibre is smooth and rounded. It has characteristic markings, which vary according to the process. As shown by the manufacturing process, the fibre consists of cellulose, except in the case of acetate rayon, when it is cellulose acetate.

Chemical reactions

They are generally the same as those of cotton. The following points must, however, be remembered.

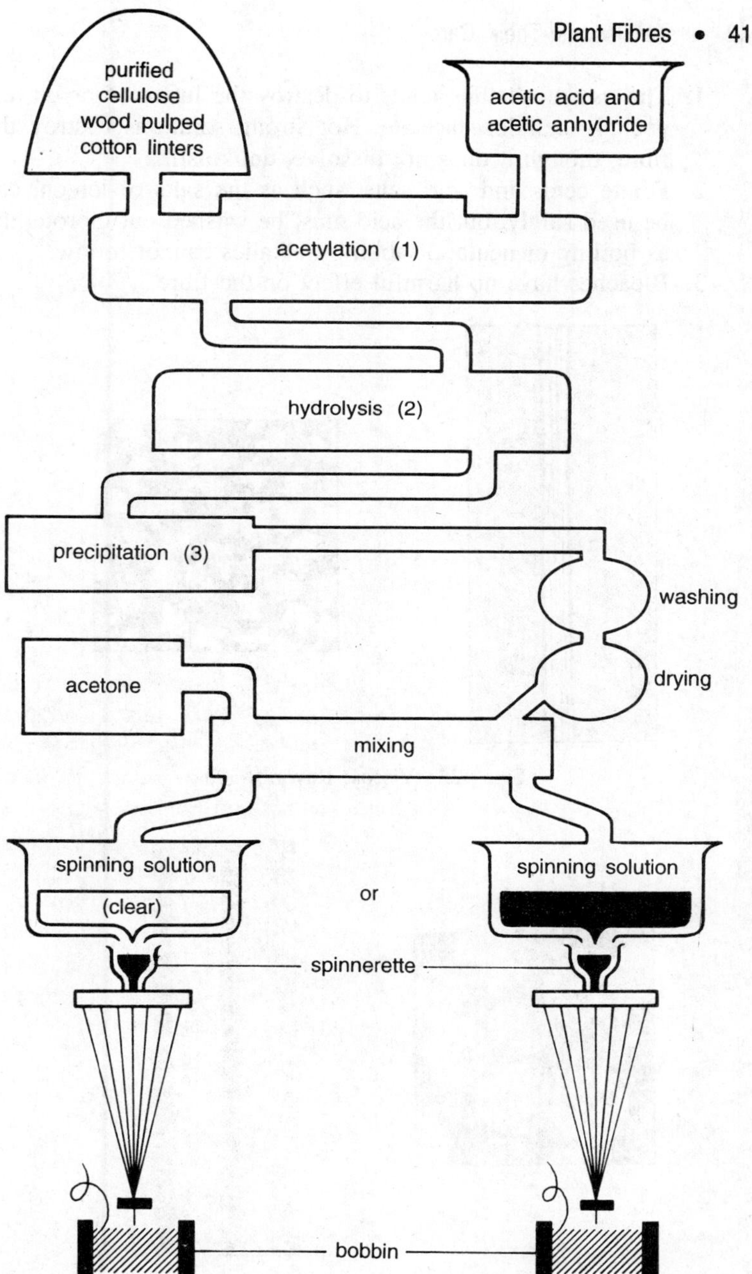

Fig. 1.24 The cellulose acetate process of manufacturing rayon

1. The use of alkalies tends to destroy the lustre of rayon, especially cellulose acetate. Hot strong solutions destroy the fibre, though it does not dissolve, unlike silk.
2. Dilute acids and acid salts, such as the salts of lemon, can be used safely, but the acid must be washed out thoroughly, as boiling or neutaralisation by alkalies cannot follow.
3. Bleaches have no harmful effect on the fibre.

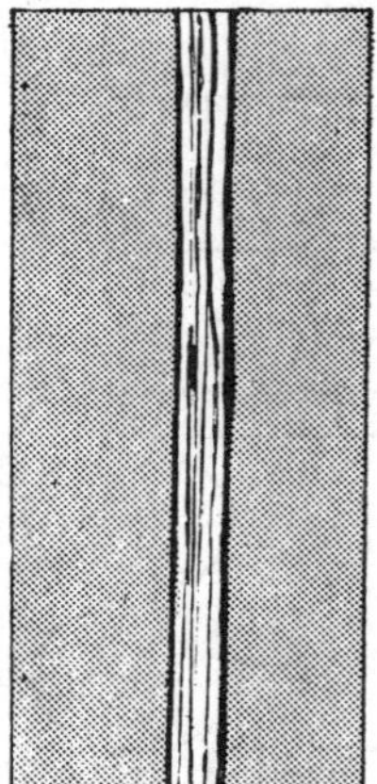

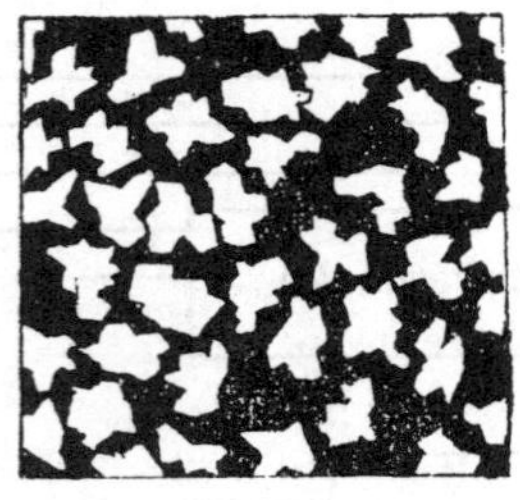

Fig. 1.25 Viscose Rayon × 300

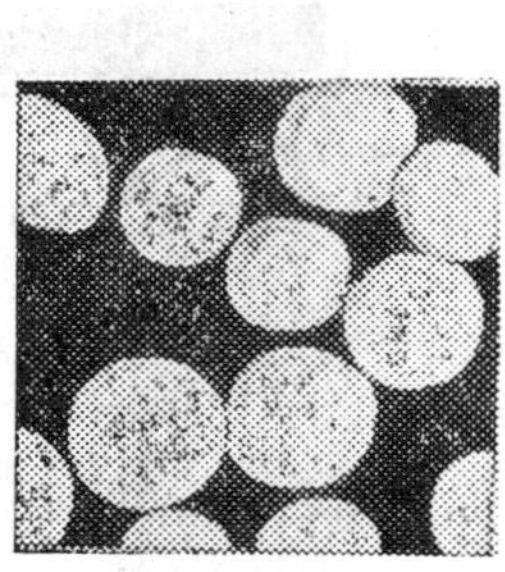

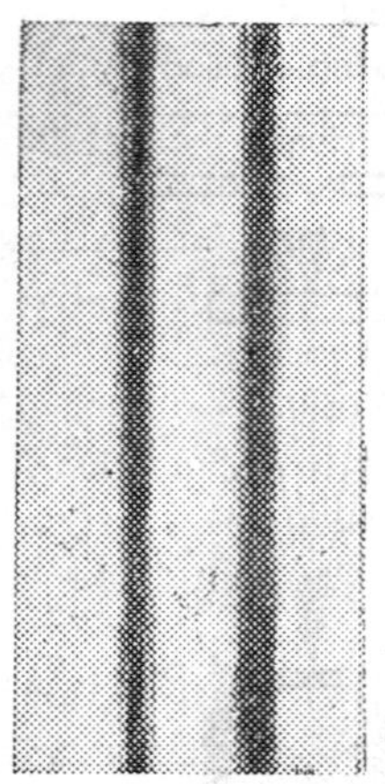

Fig. 1.26 Cuprammonium Rayon (× 400)

Other reactions

Water weakens rayon to such an extent that great care is necessary to prevent tearing or stretching during washing. When rayon is dry again, however, it completely regains its strength. Viscose is easily stretched when wet and swollen.

Friction therefore should be avoided when washing rayon, as it is likely to cause holes or stretch the fabric in such a way as to permanently spoil its shape.

Severe pressure may weaken or split the fibre.

Rayon may be glazed or the fibre damaged by excess heat. The application of a hot iron will at once cause the rayon to perish, changing it from a dry lustrous fabric into a treacly substance which hardens immediately upon cooling.

Exposure to light tends to weaken rayon, and so articles like curtains hanging in a window may perish if they remain in continual sunshine.

Grease solvents like acetone must never be used on cellulose acetate as it will dissolve.

Affinity for dyes

Cellulose rayons are easily dyed in a wide range of cotton dyestuffs, but acetate rayons dye only with their own special dyestuffs.

Test to distinguish the fibre

Many fabrics are composed of a mixture of textile fibres. Often it is difficult to distinguish between the various types of rayons. In order to discover the composition, the quickest method is to burn a piece of it, or some threads, if a mixture. This will help to show whether the fibres present are animal or cellulose.

High performance viscose rayons

High performance rayons have been made by successive improvements on the raw materials and production technology of regular viscose rayons. The most important improvement is an increase in the tensile strength of the rayon.

Polynosic Fibres Polynosic fibre is an improved type of viscose rayon produced by maintaining a higher DP betweem 500 and 700, obtaining a microfibrillar structure that makes the fibres more like cotton. Compared with regular rayon process, higher viscosity viscose is spun into a coagulating bath of lower hydrogen ion activity.

Slower coagulation and regeneration allows stretching by 200% and highly oriented fibre with low lateral order. The polynosic fibre possesses the advantages of viscose staple regarding uniformity of size, length, lustre and low cost, as also excellent dimensional stability, improved wet strength, and a crisper, loftier handle resembling that of cotton fibres.

The physical properties of polynosics closly resemble those of cotton. The fibres have values of wet strength near those of cotton after alkali treatment. They do not have the defects of viscose rayon and do not become rough even after repeated washing and, unlike cotton, they do not turn yellow after prolonged use. Polynosic fibres have a round cross section and silky lustre.

Polynosic fibres are extensively used for blending with cotton, wool, silk and with all other man-made fibres. The blends of these fibres make them luxurious to handle and easy to process. Because of these advantages they are being increasingly used in apparel, home furnishing fabrics and in knitted fabrics as well. High tenacity rayon yarn is used for the production of tyre cord, conveyor belts, fan belts, hoses, fishing lines, sewing threads and rope cordage. They are also used for coated fabrics for rainwear, inflatable rafts, tarpaulins and flexible reservoirs. The Indian sea-fishing industry now uses nets of high tenacity rayon and synthetic fibres which are much stronger than the traditional type. There are defence uses also, as in parachute fabrics and antiballistic cloth for body armour.

Developments in Indian rayon exports have become significant. Rayon velvets, embroidered and other speciality velvets, rayon pile and chenille fabrics are finding good markets abroad.

Among the rayon fabrics exported from India are

Filament rayon: brocade, crêpe, georgette, satin, shirt and suit material, sarees, taffeta, tapestry, twill velvet.

Spun rayon: shirt and suit material, sheets, serge.

Mixed rayon fabrics: spun rayon cotton mixed fabrics, rayon/nylon suit fabrics, mixed shirt fabrics and saree materials.

The basic features common to all regenerated cellulose fibres are tabulated below.

	Properties	From the user's point of view
1.	Good conductor of heat	Cool for summer wear fabrics
2.	Low resiliency	Fabrics wrinkle badly unless finished for recovery
3.	Absorbent	Absorbs moisture, though less than cotton; suitable for summer wear
4.	Not attacked by moths	Simplifies problems of storage
5.	Can withstand fairly high temperature	Must be ironed with a moderately hot iron (375°C)
6.	Not greatly harmed by alkali	Fabrics can be bleached, washed with strong soaps; not greatly damaged by perspiration
7.	Harmed by acid	Fruit stains must be removed immediately to prevent setting
8.	Attacked by mildew	Avoid putting away soiled damp garments
9.	Inflammable	Filmy or loosely-constructed garments should not be worn near an open flame
10.	Pack well into compact yarns	Yarn can be crêped
11.	Identification	Cellulose fibres ignite quickly, burn freely, have an afterglow and grey feathery ash.

2

Animal Fibres

Wool

In cold countries wool was probably the first material to be made into clothing. It was first worn in the form of a skin or pelt. Later the fabrics were matted or felted.

An interesting story is sometimes told of a shepherd boy who twisted together a strand of wool fibres to bind his bundle of faggots. This might well be the beginning of the formation of short fibres into yarns from which cloth could be woven.

Mesopotamia was perhaps the birthplace of wool. The Romans encouraged sheep farming in England and in 80 A.D. introduced wool weaving there. Soon British woollen cloths gained a fine reputation. The cloth sent to the Roman emperors was said to be "so fine that it was comparable to a spider's web".

Woollen Kashmir shawls seem to be as old as the Indian epics. Tradition has it that when Krishna went to the Kurus as a delegate from the Pandavas, Dhritarashtra's presents included ten thousand shawls of Kashmir. The historian Montgomery Martin describes the fabrics of ancient India thus: "The gossamer muslin of Dacca and beautiful shawls of Kashmir … adorned the proudest beauties at the courts of Caesar".

In ancient India, cotton was not known to the Vedic people, but wool was an important material. Fine wool was obtained from the ewes of Ghandhara and the region around the river Ravi, (a tributary of the Indus). From this, wool blankets *(kambala), dhussa (or dursa)*, a variety of woollen cloth, and *sundhyavah* bleached woollen stuff were manufactured. The Mahabharata notes that the Kambojas, the people of Dakshan and Pamir, presented Yudhisthira at the time of Raja Bhoj with woollen cloth embroidered with gold and that the Abhiras brought woollen cloth of various designs manufactured from the soft wool of the sheep and the shaggy hair of the goat and deer. These were manufactured in Cina and Valhika, the province between the Indus and Sutlej rivers.

The people of the Indus Valley used wool for their warmer textiles and cotton for their lighter ones. No textiles of this age have been preserved for us, because of the saline nature of the soil of the valley. However, the statues of that period indicate that hand-spun and hand-woven shawls were in fashion then. For example, a statue from Mohenjodaro shows a man draped with a light shawl decorated all over with a design of trefoils in reliefs, interspersed occasionally

Fig. 2.1 Limestone statuette found at Mohenjodaro (c. 1500 B.C.) depicts a man draped with a trefoil patterned shawl over his shoulders

with small circles, the interiors of which were filled with red pigment.

The Moghul kings, renowned as lovers and patrons of art, encouraged the woollen industry of Kashmir and gave it much stimulus. During Akbar's time, shawls were being sent as valuable gifts to other kings. By the end of the eighteenth century, Kashmir shawls had a vast market in India, Persia, Afghanistan, Russia and Europe. So popular was the shawl in Europe that England sought to shift its manufacture from Kashmir to Paisley. This was a severe blow, and by the end of the nineteenth century, Kashmir shawls became a memory in Europe.

Today, the woollen industry in Kashmir is slowly coming into its own. Among the popular woollen goods are pashmina shawls, both embroidered and woven (*pashm* being the under fleece of the cashmere goat), *shahtust*, *gabha* (a kind of embroidered carpet rug), woollen *chadder* and *lohis*, and *namdhas* (embroidered felt throw rugs). Thousands of *namdhas* from Kashmir and druggets from Mysore are exported to the U.S.A., earning valuable foreign exchange.

At present the chief wool manufacturing countries are Australia, New Zealand, the British Isles, South America and South Africa. Not only wool but also the hair of the camel, goat and rabbit are used to make woollen fabrics. Some breeds of sheep provide wool that is short and curly, while others give long-staple wool that has a smooth, silky appearance. Sheep reared in tropical countries yield wool that is less scaly less curly and more rigid than that from cooler climates. It is not too different from the hair of goats.

Varieties of wool

All wools are graded under the four general classes fine, medium, long and carpet wools.

Fine Wools The wool of the merino sheep is the outstanding example of this type. Fine wool fibres may vary in length from 1½ to 5 inches. 'Botany' or Bolany wool is another name for Merino wool, named after Botany Bay in Australia. Australia is the largest producer of Merino wool, although the first merino sheep are believed to have been shipped to Australia from the state of Bikaner in India. Merino sheep originated in Spain.

Medium Wools These are furnished by the Oxford Shropshire, Hampshire, Suffolk, Dorest and other breeds of sheep. These sheep

Fig. 2.2 Merino ram

are valued for their meat as well as for their heavy fleece. The fibres are of medium fineness and are from 2½ to 6 inches long. Shetland wool, from sheep raised in the Shetland Islands, has a special use in imported and domestic sweaters.

Long Wools Large sheep like Lincoln, Cotswolds, Leicester and Romney Marsh produce long, strong, lustrous wool. The fibre length varies from 5 or 6 inches for a Romney Marsh to 10 or even 15 inches for Cotswolds.

Carpet wools This type varies in length from as short as 1 inch to as long as 15 inches. Strength and resilience are its qualities. To get uniformity of properties, several grades are usually blended in carpet manufacture. These wools are got from various cross-breeds.

Hair-bearing animals

The world's rarest, finest and most expensive fibres, commercially known as speciality fibres, are obtained from animals that grow long,lustrous hair. These animals are the vicuna, cashmere goat, camel, llama, alpaca, angora goat and angora rabbit. They are noted here in the order ot their rarity and cost.

The Vicuna The vicuna is the smallest species of the South

American branch of camels. It yields what is thought to be rarest and finest fabric fibre known to man. The vicuna inhabits the highest plateaux of the Andes, mostly in Peru. Since this small animal is very wild, it has to be hunted to death in order to obtain its fibre. The species almost died out through over-hunting till the Peruvian government took measures for its protection. Now, only a small fixed number of these animals can be killed yearly. Hence a vicuna coat, which may require forty fleeces, is fabulously expensive. The fibres are extremely fine, of velvety softness, and vary in colour from cream to fawn and brown.

Fig. 2.3 Vicuna of the llama family

The Cashmere Goat This animal lives in the Tibetan region of the Himalayas. It derives its name from the fine Kashmir shawls made of the fine down of the goat. Several attempts have been made to transplant the cashmere goat to other parts of the world, but without success.

The outer or beard hair of the goat is straight, long and coarse, while the under fleece is soft and downy and rivals vicuna hair in fineness. It has a distinct silky gloss and is smoother and warmer than wool. Its length is from 1½ to 3½ inches. Cashmere's wearing qualities are unexcelled. The wool blends well with other fibres.

Fig. 2.4 Cashmere goat

Kashmir is the only place in the world which produces the famous 'ring shawls', shawls that can literally pass through a ring. The term 'cashmere,' however, is often used in a broader sense today although technically, only a fabric containing wool from the cashmere goat can correctly be so called. Kashmir woollen goods are of two main varieties. The fleece of the domestic goat is called *pashm* and that of the wild goat, wild sheep, etc., is called *asli* or *shahtush*.

The Camel The Bactrian or two-humped camel is found in Asia, from the cold north of Siberia to the hot deserts of Arabia. The camel's hair protects it not only from severe cold but also from extreme heat. This remarkable fibre is soft, rich in lustre and colour, possessing warmth-giving as well as cooling properties. Unlike sheep, which have to be shorn periodically, camels drop their hair continually in clumps and these are picked up by the camel herders.

Fig. 2.5 Bactrian (two-humped) camel

The coarse, wiry, outer hair is used for ropes, rugs and blankets by desert tribes. Underneath is a mixture of long hair, and the finer fleece is closer to the skin. This fine, soft fleece is the true camel hair used for quality fabrics.

The Llama is another member of the camel family native to South America, where it is used as a beast of burden as well as for its meat and fleece, which is heavy. The colours of the fibre range from almost white to a deep opaque brown. The outer coat is thick and heavy, while the hair underneath is soft and silky.

The Alpaca a domesticated animal from Peru, resembles the llama but is smaller than it. Its fleece, full and soft, grows to the remarkable length of 12 or more inches. Its chief use is for pile fabric coatings.

Fig. 2.6 The South American llama

Fig. 2.7 Alpaca

Angora Goat The hair of the Angora goat is known as mohair. This goat was originally reared in Ankara, Turkey, but is now bred chiefly in Texas and California. It gives the long lustrous, and clean fibres which are so valuable in pile fabrics for blending. Mohair is

Fig. 2.8 Angora goat

somewhat slippery because the fibre has no deep serrations. It also lacks the two qualities of wool, namely a natural crimp and the ability to felt. Mohair dyes readily and retains colours well.

Angora Rabbit This breed of domesticated rabbit also originally from Turkey, has soft, silky hair, which is extensively mixed with wool to give novelty effects, or with yarns used for sweaters, baby clothes, etc.

Manufacture of wool by hand

The great bulk of India's woollen yarn is hand-spun. In the villages it is done by farmers during the dry season, when they are unable to work on the land. The demand for wool cloth is seasonal in India. It is used all the year round in the extreme north, and for most of the year in the hilly country of Assam and Bengal. Further south and in central India, wool is used mainly as a covering at night.

About 75 per cent of the woollen handloom industry is concentrated in Uttar Pradesh, Punjab, Kashmir and Rajasthan. In the plains of the west, south and east, the local wool is used to make blankets, *kumblies*, druggets and coarse carpets. The blankets are frequently sold straight off the loom. As they contain a certain amount of grease, they are used as water-proof capes in the rainy season. In Madras and the slopes of the Western Ghats, where the wool is coarse and hairy, the finished cloth resembles hessian, but in Uttar

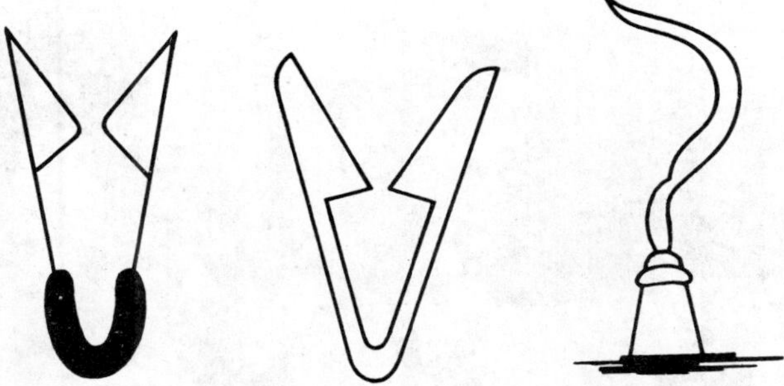

Fig. 2.9 Hand tools used in the woollen cottage industry in India

Pradesh, Punjab and Kashmir, where the wool is good, the finished fabrics come close to those imported from England.

Grading and Sorting To begin with, the wool is graded and sorted. Sorting is the process of breaking up the fleece into distinct qualities. This very important work is done by machines in advanced countries, but in the Indian cottage industry, the fleeces are opened out on sorting tables by hand and separated in accordance with the purpose for which they are to be used—carpets, blankets or good woollen cloth.

Blending and Carding The wool is next blended and carded. Carding is done with the string of a bow made of bamboo or cane. A professional class of carders are the Pinjaris.

Drawing The *takli* and *charkha* are used to draw and twist the loose-wool sliver.

Spinning and Weaving To prepare the warp yarn, a board with a series of upright pegs arranged in a U-shape is frequently used. The yarn is wound on to selected pegs, according to the length required, and this is repeated until the desired number of warp ends is obtained. For blankets (*kumblies*), there are usually 10 to 12 per inch. When the yarn is removed form the peg, the threads are arranged to give the required width and placed on a trestle. After they have been stretched tight, they are brushed with a size A (a stiffening substance) made from crushed tamarind seed boiled in water.

Once it is dry, the yarn is ready for the handloom. This is frequently a throw-shuttle, a type of pit loom, which has the advantage of being simple and cheap. The weaver uses a hollow cane or

Fig. 2.10 Stage 1: Shearing

Fig. 2.11 Stage 2: Carding and spinning of woollen yarn with an ordinary charka

Fig. 2.12 Stage 3: Warping

Fig. 2.13 Stage 4: Carpet (*kumblie*) weaving

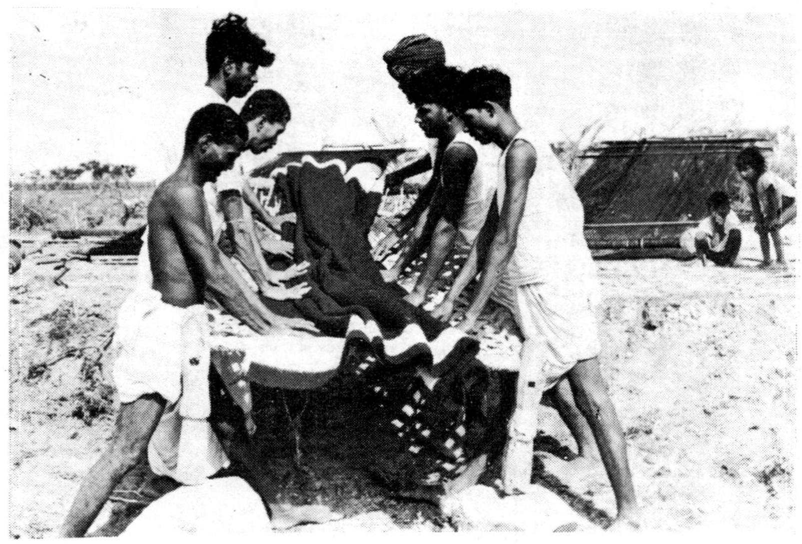

Fig. 2.14 Stage 5: Felling of blankets
(Courtesy: Modella Woollens, Bombay)

bamboo in which is placed the filling yarn, the shuttle is thrown backwards and forwards, the shed being opened as required.

Manufacture of wool by machine

The sheep are washed in early summer and sheared a few weeks later. The wool is packed in bales and sent to the factory.

Sorting and Cleaning This wool is first sorted according to quality, and the dirt removed by a machine called duster.

Washing and Scouring The wool is then washed in a series of four connecting tanks, each containing warm soapy water and weak alkali. This removes grease and perspiration. The fibres are washed in the first tank and rinsed in the others. As it emerges from the last tank, the wool is soft and white. If it is to be fibre-dyed it is sent to the drying machine. If not, it is dried by forcing hot air through the fibres. Usually about 16 per cent of the moisture is left in the wool.

Valuable by-products are obtained from the spent liquors in the scouring of wool. The most important of these is lanolin, which is used in the manufacture of cosmetics, adhesive plasters, disinfectants, ointments and a host of other preparations.

Carbonising Although scouring removes all grease and dirt, some vegetable matter, such as seeds and burrs, may still remain in the wool. These impurities must be removed, and the process used for this is carbonising. The wool is immersed in dilute sulphuric acid, the excess acid is squeezed out and the wool dried under conditions of carefully controlled temperature. The burr cellulose is converted into a brittle state and is crushed to dust by rollers and shaken out.

Drying and Oiling The wool is next rinsed in clear warm water and spread out on racks until it is as dry as the air around it. It is kept soft and elastic by oiling it. This also minimises the chances of fibres breaking in the more violent process of carding, which follows.

Carding The clean wool is by no means in a fit state for spinning. Its fibres will be lying in all directions. It is therefore blended, opened out and converted into a soft, thin, gauze-like band. This is carding. The carding process introduces the classifications of woollen and worsted yarns. Accordingly manufacturing processes from this point differ, depending on whether the wool fibre is to be made into a woollen or a worsted product.

In the manufacture of woollen yarns, the essential purpose of carding is to disentangle the fibres by passing the fibres between rollers covered with thousands of fine wire teeth. This action also removes any remaining dirt and foreign matter. As the fibres are brushed and disentangled by these wires, they start to lie parallel, which would make the yarn too smooth. Since woollen yarns should be a bit rough or fuzzy, it is not desirable to have the fibres entirely parallel. By the use of an oscillating device, one thin film or sliver of wool is placed diagonally and overlapping another. This entangles the fibres while leaving them mostly parallel, giving a fuzzy surface to the yarn. After this the woollen slivers go directly to the spinning operation.

In the manufacture of worsted yarns, carding again disentangles the fibres by passing between rollers covered with fine wire teeth. Since worsted yarns *should* be smooth, the fibres are made to lie as parallel as this process will permit. The worsted wool now undergoes gilling and combing.

Gilling and Combing The processes remove the shorter fibres of 1 to 4 inches in length, called combing noils, places the longer fibres called tops, as parallel as possible, and further cleans the fibres by removing any remaining, loose impurities.

Depending on the original source of the wool, the short-staple containing noils may be of adequate quality, and may be used as fillers for other types of wool fabrics. However, such fibres must be classified as reprocessed wool.

The long-staple tops which are over 4 inches in length excel in colour, feel, and strength. They are used in the production of such worsted fabrics as serge, whipcord, gabardine, and covert.

Spinning and Weaving In the next stage the wool fibres are drawn out and twisted into yarn. Loosely twisted fluffy yarn is made into soft woollen material. The smoother, tight and evenly twisted yarn is used to weave worsted.

Dyeing and Bleaching may now follow. These process can take place at any stage after scouring. In some cases, the yarn is dyed, as for plaids. Bleaching is usually necessary for undyed woollens owing to the yellow colour produced by the scouring process. Acid colours are extensively used in wool dyeing. They are direct dyes for wool and require no mordant.

Finishing The beauty of woollen goods depends largely on the finish of the cloth, and of worsted goods, in the weave. Worsted fabrics taken from the loom, look much as they will in the finished state, but woollen fabrics are still far from attractive, being coarse and rough and needing many more processes. The wool fabric is dried and stretched during drying to retain even width. The surface is brushed to raise the hairs, which are then cut into even lengths. The material is then pressed and folded, ready for sale.

Drawing is an advanced combing operation which doubles and redoubles slivers of wool fibres. The process draws, drafts, twists and winds the stock, making the slivers more compact and thinning them into slubbers. Drawing is done only to worsted yarns.

Roving This is the final state before spinning. Roving is actually a light twisting operation to hold the thin slubbers intact.

Spinning In the spinning operation, the wool roving is drawn out and twisted into yarn. Woollen yarns are chiefly spun on a mule spinning machine. Worsted yarns are spun on any kind of spinning machine—mule, ring, cap or flyer following two different systems of spinning.

Differences in the manufacture of woollen and worsted yarns

Woollens are fabrics woven from shorter fibres that do not lie parallel in the yarn. They are soft and fuzzy in appearance, and are used in heavier items of clothing like tweeds and fabrics of casual weave designs. Woollens have qualities of texture, warmth, suppleness and colours. Knitting may be used instead of weaving, to make sweaters, underwear and hosiery.

Worsted fabrics are woven from yarn whose fibres are long and parallel. They are more tightly woven than woollens, and have a crisp, tailored look. Worsteds are used for men's and women's suits, serges, gabardines and very light-weight tropical suits and dresses. Worsteds drape very well and, are the most wrinkle and dirt resistant of all fabrics.

Typical woollens are made from short-staple fibres, and have a fluffy appearance. Examples: suede, tweed, flannel broadcloth and wool crêpe.

Worsteds are made from long fibres laid almost parallel before being highly twisted. They have a distinctly visible weave, wiry feel, and are somewhat harsh. They are finely woven, free from nap and are smooth in appearance. Worsteds give very good service. Examples: men's suit, gabardine, crêpes and Bedford cord.

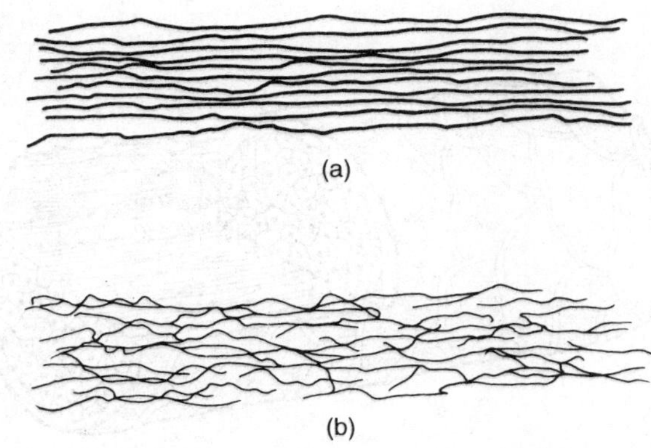

Fig. 2.15 (a) Parallel arrangement of fibres in worsted yarns; (b) Random arrangement of fibres in woollen yarns

Special Finishes Modern research has enabled manufacturers to make wool proof against shrinkage, water and moths.

Unshrinkable Wool Processes to make wool unshrinkable generally aim at removing or modifying the scales on the fibre and so preventing the tendency to creep. For this purpose chlorine is often used to attack the surface of the fibre. In another process the surface of the wool is partly digested by an enzyme called papain extracted from the paw-paw tree, which grows in India, Sri Lanka and Africa. The action of papain renders the scaly surface of the wool fibre soluble, smoothening it and making it shrink-proof and glossy.

Structure and composition the fibre

Untwisted from the yarn it has a kinky appearance. Its length varies between 1½ inches and 18 inches, the long fibres being generally coarser than the short ones. The fibres used for worsteds are usually 3 to 8 inches in length, whereas those used for woollens vary from 1 to 2 inches.

When ignited, the fibre burns or smoulders with a smell like burning hair or feathers, leaving behind a black bead.

The fundamental substance of wool is protein, keratin. Keratin is the fibre material of wool, just as cellulose is of cotton. The following figures are a typical analysis: carbon 50 per cent, oxygen 22-25 per cent, nitrogen 16-17 per cent, hydrogen 7 per cent and sulphur 3-4 per cent.

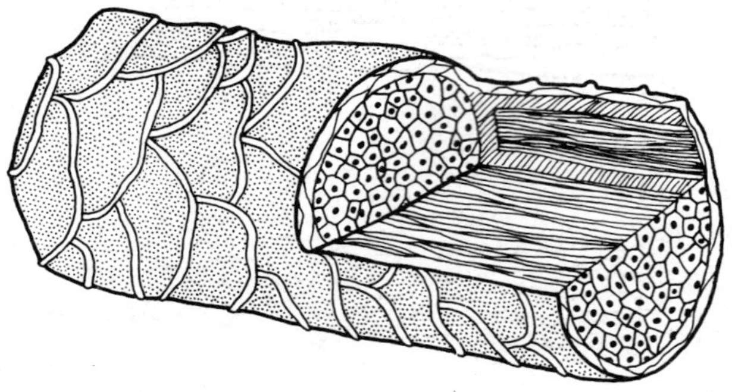

Fig. 2.16 Diagram illustrating the structure of a wool fibre magnified about 5,000 times. Notice the overlapping outer scales (the cuticle) and the elongated cells inside (the cortex). The coarser fibres also have a core of hollow cells (the medulla) (Courtesy: International Wool Secretariat, London)

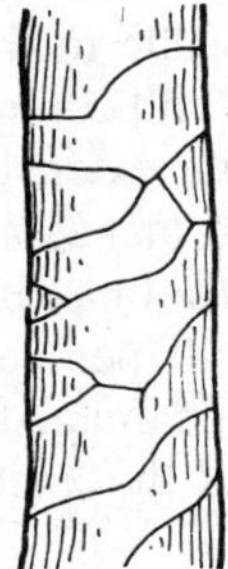

Fig. 2.17
(× 400) Merino wool

Fig. 2.18 Photomicrograph of wool cross-section (× 600)

As seen under a microscope, a wool fibre has an outer surface of scaly cells called serrations or cuticles. Beneath the surface is the 'cortex' of the fibre, made up of overlapping layers of cells that adhere tightly to each other. (See Figs. 2.16, 2.17 and 2.18)

The qualities of wool

Crimp The wool fibre grows in a more or less wavy form with a certain amount of twist. The waviness is called crimp. The finer the wool the more crimps there are. In fine merino wool there may be as many as 30 crimps per inch, but in coarse wools, as few as one or two. Crimp is a most important quality, since it is responsible for some of the elasticity which is so characteristic of wool garments. It also enhances felting power and spinning qualities. Moisture alters the crimp of wool, and it is possible to remove it completely in hot water. After drying however, the crimp usually reappears.

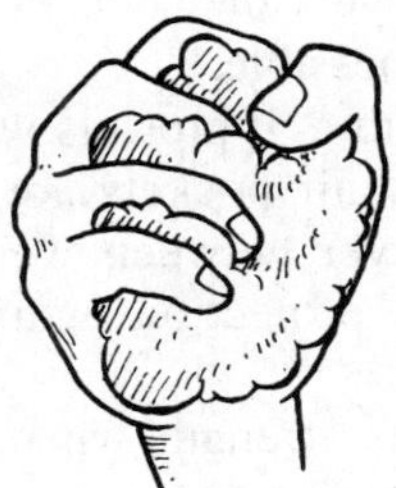

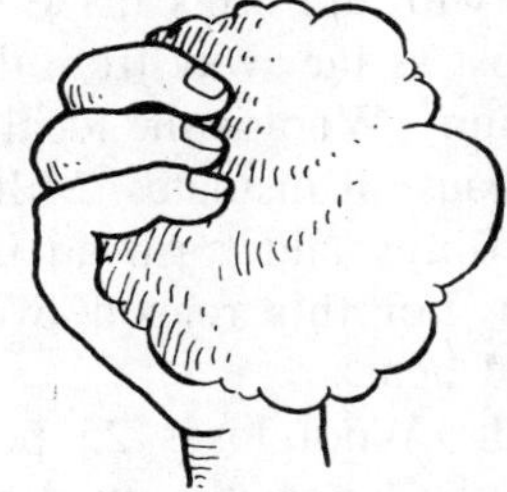

Fig. 2.19 Illustration of resiliency (Courtesy: Sears, Roebuck & Co)

Resiliency Wool is resilient being able to spring back to its original form like a rubber band after being wrinkled or creased. This is a virtue which most other fibres lack and is due to the structure of its fibre, the cells of whose cortex can stretch and contract without breaking. If wool is slowly elongated, a definite extension will result, but when the tension is released, the fibre makes a partial recovery, and slowly loses its temporary 'set'. Wool can be stretched up to 30 per cent and, if the fabric is wet, 40 per cent without breaking, and returned to its original length undamaged. This is a very useful property for materials, used, say, at the knee or elbow of a suit.

Resiliency accounts for the excellent wrinkle and crush resistance that woollen fabrics retain through their long wearing lives. It also explains why woollen sweaters or carpets do not lose their fleecy looks and become thin with wear, unlike materials made of cotton or rayon.

Warmth Wool keeps one warm. This is because the serrations or scale-like projections of the fibre entangle air, a bad conductor of heat, around and in between the fibres. The more loosely a fabric is woven or knitted, the greater is the air entangled. Hosiery fibres have about 80 per cent air to 20 per cent fibres. Even tightly made worsted suits retain about 70 per cent air to 30 percent fibre.

Affinity for Moisture Wool is the most hygroscopic of all fibres. It can absorb moisture up to 50 per cent of its weight from the surrounding air and can carry up to one-fifth its weight in moisture without feeling damp. It dries slowly, thus preventing chilling of the body through too rapid evaporation. Wool absorbs perspiration after strenuous exercise, acting as a thermostat which guards the body against quick changes in temperature. Experience has taught the Indian Army to equip its men on duty along the northern mountain borders with uniforms made of several layers of wool, in order to keep frost as far away from the body as possible.

Insulation Wool is the ideal protective fibre. It protects with comfort, because it insulates. Millions of tiny air pockets are trapped by the fibres and form an insulating layer between wearer and weather. For this reason, wool is good protection against both cold and heat.

Strength Wool loses 25 per cent of its strength when wet. In general, the longer the wool fibre the greater the yarn strength.

Felting Wool fibres interlock and contract when exposed to heat,

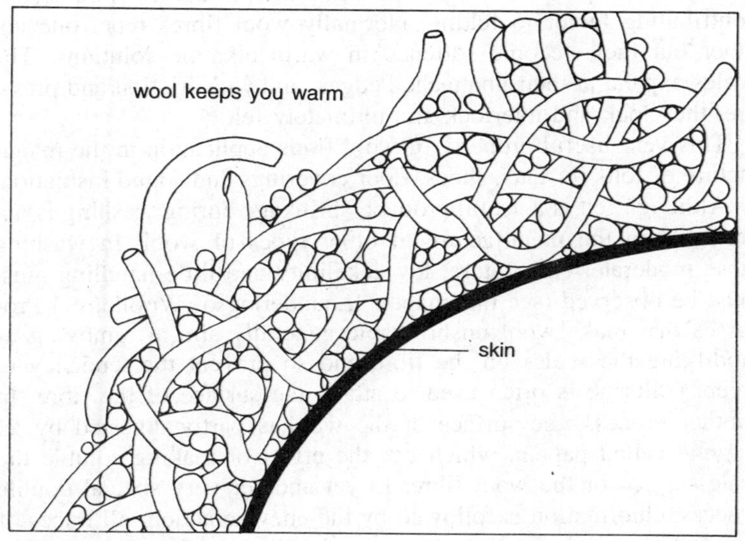

Fig. 2.20 How the fibres of a wool garment worn next to the skin entangle air, forming an insulating layer (From International Wool Secretariat filmstrip "Wool in the Home")

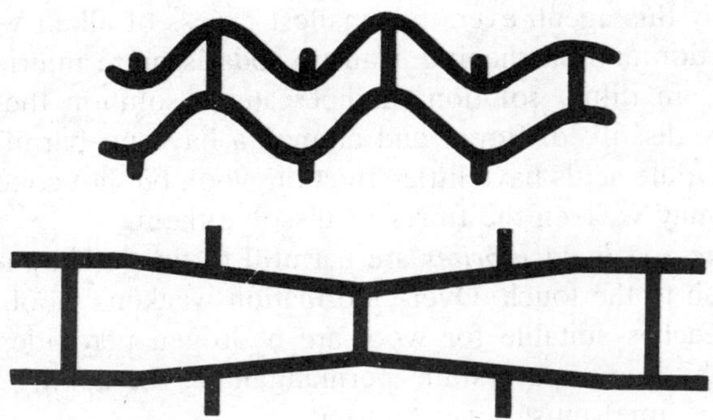

Fig. 2.21 Model showing the molecular structure of wool. Stretching the wool fibre causes the molecular chains to unfold (Courtesy: International Wool Secretariat, London)

moisture and pressure. The scale-like exterior of the fibre is one contributing factor to felting. Normally wool fibres repel one another but they become softened in warm alkaline solutions. The scales expand at their unattached edges, and with friction and pressure, they lock and interlock and ultimately felt.

This very useful property of wool finds application in the manufacture of felts for hats, shoes, floor coverings and sound insulation.

Although felt is a useful product, shrinkage during washing is not desirable in the manufacture of other types of wool. In washing these moderate temperature, low alkalinity and little handling must must be observed (see the chapter 'Laundering of Woollens'.) Processes that make wool unshrinkable generally aim at removing or modifying the scales on the fibre and so prevent the tendency to creep. Chlorine is often used to attack the surface of the fibre. In another process, the surface of the wool is partly digested by an enzyme called papain, which has the effect of making soluble the scale-surface of the wool fibre. In yet another very special double process, chlorination is followed by the enzyme action; all traces of the scales are removed and a smooth fibre results. This 'glossy wool' is completely shrink-resistant.

Chemical reactions

Alkalies tend to make wool yellow, hard and felted instead of soft and elastic. Strong solutions of sodium carbonate, or dilute ones when heated, have a destructive action upon the fibre. If water is softened by this agent, even the smallest excess of alkali will cause discolouration and harshening. Caustic soda is more injurious even when it is in dilute solution. In hot caustic solution the fibre is completely dissolved. Borax and ammonia have no harmful effect on wool. Dilute acids have little effect on wool, but hot concentrated solutions may weaken the fibres or dissolve them.

Chlorine and *hypochlorites* are harmful to wool. They make the fabric harsh to the touch. Over-chlorination weakens wool.

The bleaches suitable for wool are hydrogen peroxide, sodium hydrosulphite and potassium permanganate. Bleaching powder (chloride of lime) must never be used

Other reactions

Water and friction affect the fibres, for when they are wet or damp, the scales on the surface are raised up and roughened and tend to interlock or 'felt' as they are brought together by friction. Felting causes an article to become thick and to shrink. Hence scrubbing, which is normal in washing cotton fabrics, causes serious injury to wool.

Long exposure to moisture is likely to cause shrinkage. So laundering processes should be carried out as quickly as possible and long steeping must be avoided.

Hard water causes no harm during washing if care is taken to preserve a good lather by the addition of more soap when necessary, but if it is used for rinsing, insoluble soaps are likely to be deposited on the fabric. So it is important to use soft or softened water for the washing and rinsing process. Thorough rinsing is essential; for soap left in woollen fabrics causes an unpleasant smell, and is responsible for the yellowing of white wool after several washes.

Sudden changes of temperature may affect the serrations on the fibre and add to the danger of felting. Extremely hot and cold water should be avoided.

Affinity for dyes

Wool absorbs and holds most dyes better than other fabrics. Unfortunately, it also retains odours, as bacteria can breed in greater numbers on woollen garments. If controlled laundering is not feasible, woollen garments should be dry cleaned, as this kills about 98 per cent of the odour-causing bacteria.

Other hair fibres

All hair fibres have a high lustre and react the same way chemically as wool. They are usually combined with other fibres to make them easier to handle, go further and produce interesting effects.

Reclaimed wool

Woollen materials are often recycled by manufactures as an economy measure and to produce utility fabrics. If the starting material is woollen or felted fabric that has never been worn, the term used is *reprocessing*. It includes the mill ends and clippings that accumulate during manufacture. Most reclaimed wool, however, is *reused*. Old clothes and blankets are collected and sorted and sold to the mills, which break them back down to the fibres to blend with new wool. Used wool that is not too damaged makes better blends than synthetic fibres. The term "Virgin" is used to designate wool that has never been processed in any way before being manufactured into a fabric or yarn. In India, the government's Wool Products Labelling Act of 1990 specifies among other things that all woollen garments must be clearly tagged to indicate the percentage of pure wool used.

Identifying wool

Fabrics and garments labelled 'pure', 'virgin' or 'new' wool are made from wool that has never been used before; those marked '100% wool' and 'all' wool may be made partly from reprocessed wool. The term 'wool' is also too often used to describe the hair of the alpaca, camel, llama, vicuna, goat or rabbit. The International wool Secretariat awards its woolmark (see diagram) to manufactures whose products are made of pure, new wool of high quality.

Uses

Merino is used for high-quality worsted, hosiery and hand-knitting wools, blankets and speciality fabrics. Crossbred wools go to make worsteds, felts, hosiery and thicker hand-knit wools. Certain types of tweeds are made from carpet wools, which are also used for carpets and as mattress fillings. The 'heavy duty' wool used for uniforms and coat lengths are serge, gabadine, whip-cord, cavalry twill, beaver cloth and barathea.

Silk

Silk is considered the queen of fabrics even today. Its strength, lustre, softness and the graceful line in which it hangs makes it the most attractive of textiles. This fibre is known to have been used in ancient China. According to legend, a beautiful Chinese princess, while in her garden one day, dropped a cocoon into a cup of tea. On taking it out she discovered that she could unwind the strong continuous fibre from the softened exterior.

Whether or not this is true, it is recorded that about 2640 B.C. Si-Ling-Chi, the young wife of the third Emperor of China, discovered how to reel silk from cocoons, which she later wove into a robe for the Emperor. This was the beginning of a great oriental industry, one that has furnished a livelihood for millions of workers.

For nearly 2,000 years the Chinese jealously guarded the secret of silk manufacture. Throughout these centuries, this fabric of exotic beauty went round the world on camel caravans. Imperial Rome received them in great quantities. Cleopatra took pride in possessing a silk robe woven in China, dyed in Asia Minor, and embroidered in Egypt.

In the meantime many attempts were made in other countries to learn the art of making silk. Slowly the knowledge of sericulture began to trickle out of China starting around 300 A.D. About 550 A.D. two Nestorian monks who had long resided in China learning the art of silk-worm culture, were fortunate in being able to smuggle a few silk worms out of China to Constantinople by carrying them concealed inside hollow canes. These few worms were probably the beginning of the varieties that supplied the Western world for more than 1,200 years. Byzantine silks became famous; the Saracens mastered the industry; and Venice, Florence, and Milan became known as silk centres.

Fig. 2.22

Ancient India knew about silk and the silk worm, perhaps from China via Burma. Silk is referred to in the Indian epics. In his Ramayana, Valmiki says that Sita was clad in silk when she accompanied Ram to the forest. The old name for it was *ketaja*. Country-made silks were called *patta*, *kauseya*, *dhina-shuka* or *chinapatta*.

Around the time of King Harsha, 606-648 A.D., every young bride in Gujarat longed to have a *patolu*, a rich, colourful silk sari. This lovely fabric resembles printed cloth, but unlike it, has no reverse side, being woven in such a way that it has similar designs on both sides. Its warp and weft are both dyed in a rich range of shades along the length of each thread by the technique of tie-dyeing or bandana work. This cottage craft appears to have thrived in Gujarat for many years, well appreciated at home and patronised abroad for its colour scheme and rich configuration. But on account of the long time taken in weaving, its high price, and the substitution of cheaper woven fabrics, the *patolu* very nearly disappeared from the markets. Fortunately, the ancient craft was revived recently, and the *patolu* technique has also been extended to other fabrics, such as curtains, table covers, blouse-pieces, cushion covers and other household textiles. They are chiefly woven in Benaras, Gujarat, Hyderabad, Sambalpur (Orissa) and some parts of Tamil Nadu.

Pitamber was a pure silk *dhoti* of old. It was generally pink, yellow or sun flower coloured and worn on festival days or at meals by orthodox Hindus.

Tussore (*tassar, koshavastra, kaushikvastra*) is a coarse silk cloth known for long throughout India. Ceremonial tussore *pattavastras* of subdued lustre, rich colours and gold embellishments are still used, as are tussore saries woven with lotus, elephant, swan, *rudraksha*, deer and other designs.

Sericulture has had its ups and downs in Indian history. Muhammad Tughlak, 1325-1350 A.D., was a great patron of the industry. Abul Abbas Ahmad, a Damascus traveller who came to India from Egypt during this time, records as follows:

> The Sultan has a manufactory, in which 400 silk weavers are employed, and where they make silken stuffs of all kinds for robes of honour. Every year the Sultan distributes 200,000 complete dresses, 100,000 in spring and 100,000 in autumn. The spring dresses are made of goods imported from Alexandria whilst those of autumn are made of silk manufactured in Delhi. The Sultan keeps in his service 500 manufactures of golden tissues, who weave gold brocades worn by the wives of the Sultan or for presents to be given to the Amirs and their wives.

Sources

Today, most silk is produced in China, India, Japan, France and Thailand. India is the fourth-largest producer of raw silk in the world. The main silk-producing states are Karnataka and Jammu Kashmir. Besides producing mulberry silk, India also produces three types of non-mulbery silk (tussore, *muga*, *eri*) in substantial quantities, a feature not associated with sericulture elsewhere. Assam is the only place in the world where the rare golden-yellow, *muga* silk, an excellent material for embroidery is produced. The state also makes a bulk of (*eri* or *endi*) silk, a creamish-white, soft, cotton-like fabric.

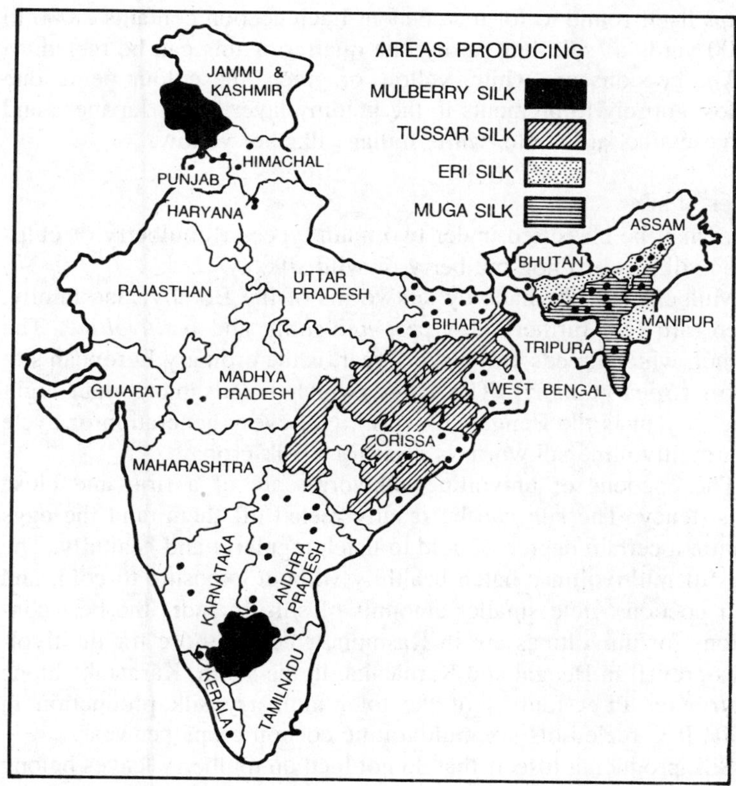

Fig. 2.23 Silk industry in India (Courtesy: Silk Board of India)

The silk worm

Silk is the secretion of the silkworm and is the fibre used by the larva to make the pupal case. The eggs of the silkworm are placed in well-lighted and ventilated chambers to hatch which they do after about twelve days. The larvas are fed on mulberry leaves. When the caterpillar is about eight weeks old, it secrets a viscous fluid from two glands in its head. This substance, called fibroin is forced through two minute channels into a single exit near the mouth. At the same time, two other glands secrete a gummy kind of liquid called sericin, which passes through the same exit. As it emerges from the head of the silkworm, the fibroin sets or coagulates, forming a filament coated with sericin. With this thread the caterpillar wraps itself round to form a cocoon. Each cocoon contains 2,000 to 4,000 yards of silk, but hardly one quarter of this can be reeled.

The cocoons are white, yellow or green, the colour being due almost entirely to pigments in the gummy layer. Most Japanese and Chinese silks are white, while Italian silks are yellow.

Types of silk

Silks may be classified under two main types: a) mulberry or cultivated silk, and b) non-mulberry or wild silk.

Mulberry silk is made by silkworms of the Bombycidae family. There are two further sub-types: *univoltine* and *multivoltine*. The former, which breeds only once a year, is the ordinary European silk worm (*Bombyx mori*). The latter, which breeds more than eight times a year is the Bengal silkworm. Not every generation or cycle of a multivoltine silkworm is used for a silk crop.

The cocoons of univoltine silkworms are of a firm and close consistency. The silk can be readily reeled off them, and the eggs require a certain degree of cold to hatch regularly and healthily. The eggs of multivoltines hatch healthily without exposure to cold, and their cocoons yield smaller amounts of silk. In India the best conditions for univoltines are in Kashmir, whereas those for multivoltines prevail in Bengal and Karnataka. In the south, Karnataka alone contributes three-fourths of the total mulberry silk production in India. It is reeled off six multivoltine cocoon crops per year.

Silk-producing insects that do not feed on mulberry leaves belong to the family *Saturniidae*. The most important of their silks are listed below.

Tasser silk (also written tussore) is obtained from an oak-feeding

Fig. 2.24 Fatwah silk women: mother, daughter, and grand-child. The mother is reeling tasser cocoons

moth, native to India and China. Unlike mulberry cocoons, the tasser cocoons have a 'pedicle' attached to their mouths which support them on the twigs of forest trees like Sai and Asan (see Fig. 2.35). Indian tasser is sought after in Europe and U.S.A for men's suits and other dress materials and for use as tapestry and upholstery material.

Muga silk The muga moth is a native of Assam, where it is domesticated. Although not as widely cultivated in India as the tusser moth, Muga silk is superior to tasser in gloss and other qualities. It is commonly employed for the manufacture of mixed fabrics and for some kinds of embroidery. Assam is the only place in the world producing the rare golden yellow muga silk, an excellent material for embroidery.

Eri or Endi silk. The eri or arrindi moth of Bengal and Assam is fairly widely distributed in eastern India. The eri worm, feeding on castor leaf is reared indoors in Assam, Bihar and West Bengal. The cocoons are a soft white or yellow, and filament so exceedingly delicate that it is impracticable to wind off the silk; instead it is spun like cotton. The earliest European record of this silk is in the year 1676, when the agent of Fort St. George wrote that large quantities were produced in Goraghat.

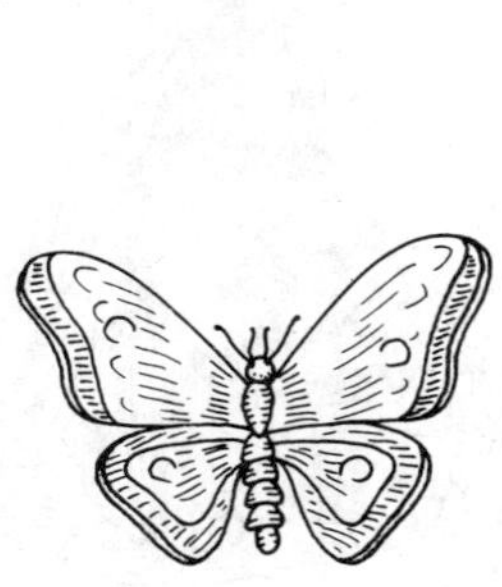

Fig. 2.25 Chinese tusser moth

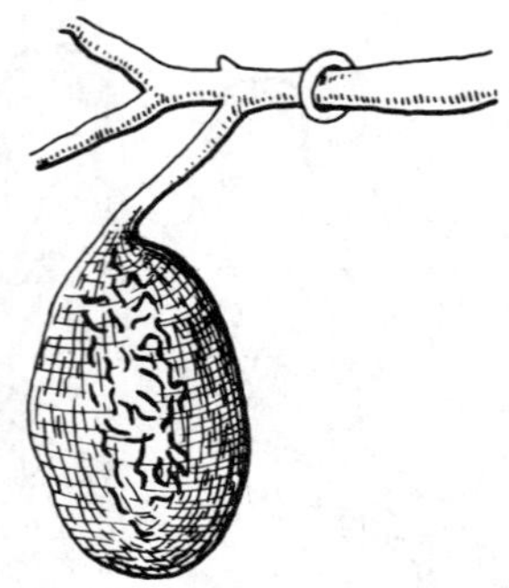

Fig. 2.26 Tasser cocoons with their pedicles with which they attach themselves to branches

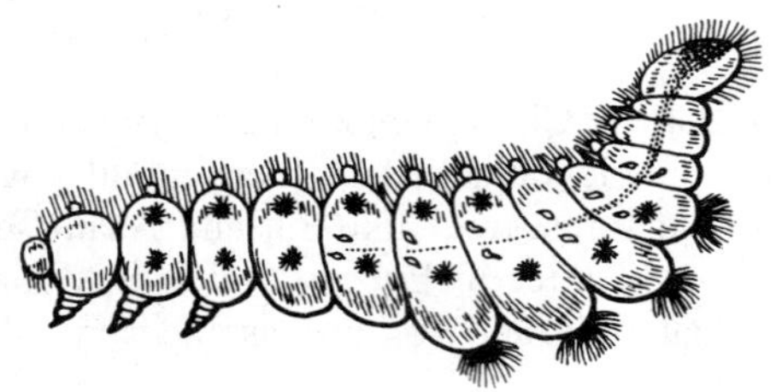

Fig. 2.27 Larva of the tassar silkworm

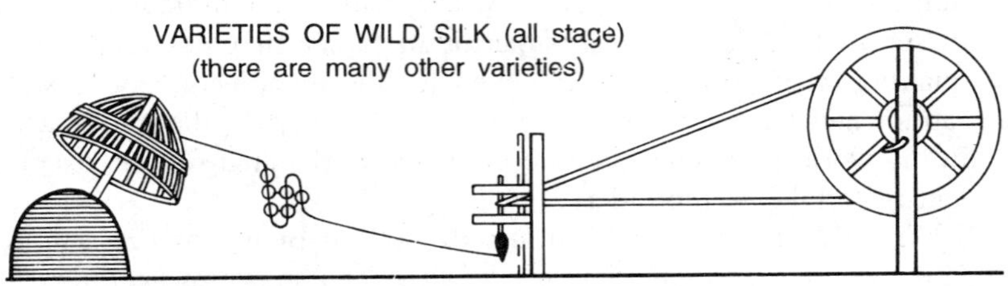

1. vertical bar on hump of clay
2. yarn on cone
3. cone
4. brass rings
5. spokes of charkha
6. handle
7. spindle
8. wheel tier
9. spindle support
10. yarn on spindle

Fig. 2.28 The process of twisting silk in Bengal on the *Paraita* and *Charka*

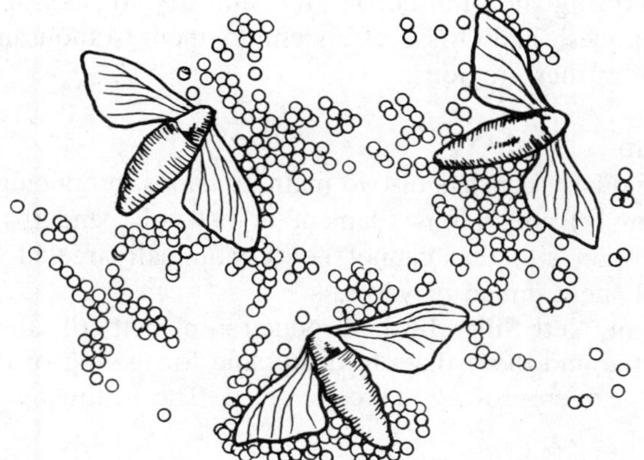

Fig. 2.29 Silk moth and eggs

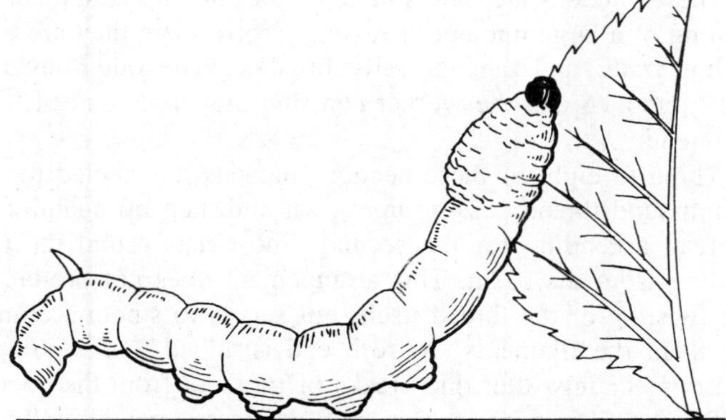

Fig. 2.30 Larva of Italian *Bombyx mori* silkworm moth

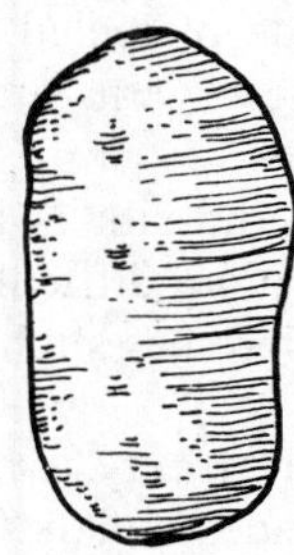

Fig. 2.31
Cocoon of Bombyx mori

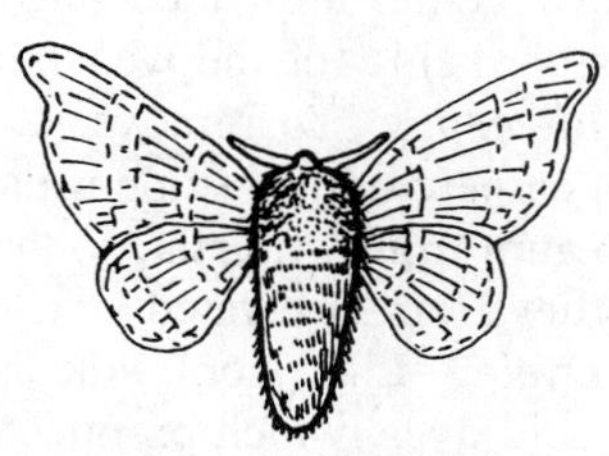

Fig. 2.32 Male Bombyx mori or
mulberry-feeding silkworm moth

The thriving non-mulberry silk industry of Assam, Bihar, Madhya Pradesh and Orissa offers employment to thousands of tribal people in these regions.

Manufacture

The silk industry consists of two main divisions, producing material made from (a) continuous filament or nett silk, and (b) residual, waste or spun silk that cannot be economically reeled into continuous filament thread or yarns.

Filament or Nett Silk In the production of nett silk, the cocoons are collected and those that are unsuitable for reeling or those kept aside for next crop of eggs are removed. The following processes then take place.

1. The cocoons are stifled by steam or hot air in order to kill the chrysalises within them.

2. These cocoons are then sorted for the filatures, establishments consisting of a large number of reeling basins. Here they are treated with hot water and mechanically brushed. The outer layers are thereby removed and the worker can find the single end of the cocoon thread.

3. Three to eight of these cocoon filaments are reeled together, the compound thread passing up, down and then up again, so that the thread ascending for the second time twists round the thread ascending from the basin. This arrangement does not produce any actual twisting of the thread itself, but serves to smooth, compress and cement the filaments. A fresh end is added to the composite thread immediately after one breaks or runs out from the cocoon.

4. The thread now passes to a swift where it is wound in the form of a hank. During its passage to the swift, the thread is dried either naturally or by artificial means. Yarns made of reeled silk threads twisted together are called thrown silk. These yarns are wound on spools or skeins for the weavers.

5. *Bleaching*. To remove residual gum, the silk is treated with hydrogen peroxide or sulphur dioxide. It is more difficult to remove all the gum from wild silk, so the finished fibre has slightly different properties from cultivated silk.

6. *Dyeing*. Like wool, silk has excellent affinity for dyes, especially acid dyes, which produce brilliant shades on silk. As a group, these dyes have a good fastness to washing and light.

7. *Printing*. Silk fabrics may be left plain or they may be printed

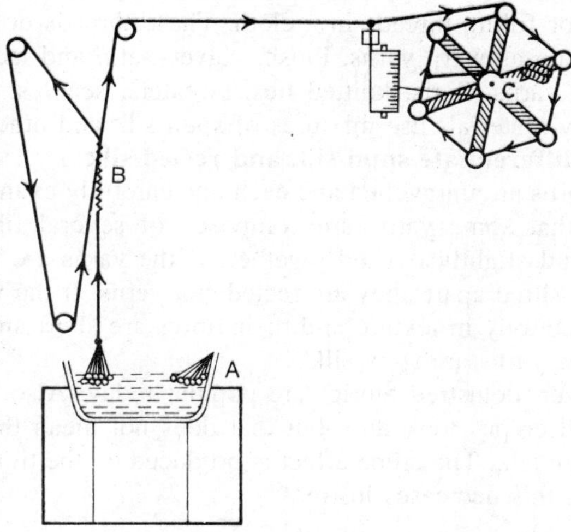

Fig. 2.33 Cocoon reeling basin A. Basin containing cocoons. B. Filament twisted round itself. C. Reel

by any method—roller, screen or block. Silks are usually dyed and then printed.

8. *Finishing*. With its natural lustre and soft drape, most silk fabrics require very little finishing touches.

Spun Silk This silk is commonly called 'waste' silk. It consists of silk that cannot be unwound from the cocoons and reeled into skeins, or it may be got from damaged or unreelable cocoons such as those from which the moth has emerged.

Spun silk yarn requires more twist than reeled silk, to hold in all the short fibres. Twisting decreases lustre, so spun silk doesn't shine as much as reeled silk. It also has less tensile strength, less elasticity, and a rather cottony feeling.

In its manufacture, the silk is scoured, the gum is boiled off and the fibres are dried. They are then combed so as to separate and straighten them, and make them parallel. The filament ends of the fibres are then drawn out several times between rollers. A slight twist called roving is put in; a spinning frame, which winds and rewinds the yarn on spindles, puts in the twists. Spun silk requires a tighter twist than thrown silk.

Spun silk is less expensive than reeled silk, and is often used for the weft or filling threads in a cloth. These threads do not have to be as strong as warp yarns. Plush, velvet, satin and lace may have spun silk yarns. Saris, knitted ties, sweaters, scarves, hosiery and upholstery materials use mixtures of spun silk and other fibres.

How to differentiate spun silk and reeled silk

The yarns are unravelled and each one carefully examined. It will be seen that some yarns are composed of several fibres that lie parallel and slightly twisted together. If the yarns are lustrous and the fibres shred apart, they are reeled silk yarns. If the yarns appear dull and cottony in texture and their fibres are short and of uneven length, the yarns are spun silk.

However, delustred fabrics are popular today. Also, many georgettes and crêpes look dull, but that does not mean that the yarns are of spun silk. The crêpe effect is produced by the tightness of the twist, and this decreases lustre.

Weighing of silk

This is a common practice. When the yarn is prepared for weaving, it is boiled in soap solution to remove the natural gum or sericin. The silk may thus lose from 20 per cent to 30 per cent original weight. Silk has a great affinity for metallic salts, such as those of tin and iron, and the loss of weight is sometimes compensated through the absorption of these metals. In this way, a heavier fabric can be made at a lower price than that of pure silk. Weighted silk does not wear as long as pure unweighted silk, because sunlight and perspiration weaken the fibres. Heavy weighing causes the silk to crack, a process often seen in taffetta and other flat crêpes.

The Fibre

The silk fibre is in every respect one of the most perfect natural substances known for yarn-making. It is smooth and semi-transparent, and is the longest of all natural fibres, ranging from 800 to 1200 yards.

Structure and composition of the fibre

Wild silk fibre is very irregular and resembles flattened, wavy ribbons with longitudinal markings.

Degummed silk is smooth, cylindrical and generally uniformly thick, like glass rods.

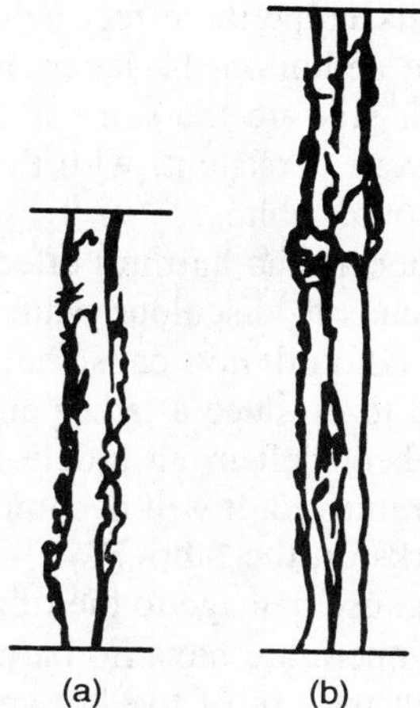

Fig. 2.34 Much enlarged depictions of (a) cultivated silk fibre (b) raw silk fibre

Ignited silk burns slowly like wool, running together to form a black bead, and emitting the smell of burning protein. The ash of weighted silk retains the shape of the silk burnt.

Like wool, silk is chiefly protein, but contains no sulphur. It consists of carbon, hydrogen, oxygen and nitrogen according to the formula $C_{15}H_{23}N_5O_6$

Chemical reactions

Alkali. Alkaline substances are less harmful to silk than to wool, but more harmful than they are to cotton. Hot caustic solutions completely dissolve the fibre, and dilute solutions tend to discolour it and cause it to tender. Weak household ammonia can be safely used. Wild silk is less affected by alkali than cultivated silk.

Acid. Dilute acids are absorbed and retained with tenacity as for wool, and dilute organic acids can be used without risk of injury. But concentrated mineral acids rapidly dissolve the fibre. Wild silk is less affected by the action of acids and more slowly than is the case with cultivated silk.

Increased brilliance and scroop (crisp feel) are imparted to silk by treatment in a dilute solution of sulphuric, acetic and other acids, which are dried in the fabric. A mixture of silk and wild silk treated in this way produces silk crêpe the effect being due to the fact that the bath has little or no action on the latter fibre.

Bleaches suitable for silk are the same as for wool. The yellow colour in wild silk is very persistent, with the result that it is very difficult to bleach it a pure white.

Other reactions. Water has no harmful effect on silk, though long exposure to moisture tends to discolour white fabrics.

Hardness of water should not cause any injury, though the amount of soap needed to produce a lather makes rinsing more difficult. If any acid has been left in an article after the last rinse, or any soap has not been removed, it will decompose, leaving a deposit of apparent grease marks on the fabric.

Excessive heat will cause damage to the fibre, but otherwise, mild heat and changes of temperature have no harmful effect. White silk fabrics turn yellow with the use of too hot an iron.

Affinity for dyes

Like wool, silk takes up colouring matter very rapidly, but it holds it more tenaciously. Wild silk is much less reactive to dyes.

Casein Fibre

Among the modern fabrics is one that is produced from milk protein. The first fibre of this type was developed in Italy by the chemist Ferretti in 1935. Casein fibres are variously named according to the country of manufacture: Lanital (Italy), Tiolan (Germany), Polan (Poland), Lactofil (Holland) and Courtauld's casein fibre (England). Casein is precipitated from milk treated with dilute sulphuric acid. The precipitate is dissolved in a solution of caustic soda, and the liquid forced through jets into a coagulating bath of sulphuric acid and hardened. The filaments are cut into short lengths like wool and spun into threads.

Casein fibre is soft and feels somewhat like wool. Under the microscope, however, it presents a smooth surface like rayons unlike the scaly surface of wool.

The fibre is used as a substitute for wool, as it has similar handle and heat insulating properties. Its great advantage over wool is that it has no felting properties. It readily absorbs alkali from warm soap solutions and becomes plastic. It takes dyes more rapidly and at a lower temperature than wool but fades easily. It is non-shrinkable and is not attacked by insects. However, casein fibre is not as elastic or strong as wool, and stretches much less, especially when wet. It is used primarily as a blending fibre to capitalise on its soft texture.

Soyabean Protein Fibre

Soyabean fibre was first developed by the Ford Motor Corporation about 1939, but the work was dropped around the end of World War II.

The soyabeans are first crushed to extract the oil. The protein is then extracted by means of a weak alkaline solvent. This is treated with various chemicals to produce a solution and forced through jets into a coagulating bath. The finished fibre has a warm, soft feel like wool and has good resiliency. It blends easily with other fibres. It can be woven or spun unblended.

Soyabean fibre has been experimentally made into blankets, carpets, upholstery, hats, suits and other products.

Peanut Fibre

Just prior to World War II the ICI company of the U.K. introduced a new fibre called Ardil, manufactured. from peanut proteins in a manner similar to that used for the production of other protein fibres (see diagram). Ardil is a cream-coloured fibre with moderate lustre and closely resembles wool. Although it can be used alone, it is more usually mixed with cotton, wool or rayon. It is strong, moth and mildew-proof and does not shrink. The fibre has a high resistance to attack by acids but, like wool, is sensitive to alkalies. It is soft and silky to the touch, more expensive than cotton, but cheaper than wool. Ardil can be dyed with direct cotton dyes.

Corn Fibre

Fibres made from zein, corn proteins, were first manufactured by the Virginia-Carolina company of the U.S.A., which gave them the trade name Vicara. It blends well with all fibres, but is weaker than

ARDIL MANUFACTURE

Peanuts Undecorticated → Peanuts Decorticated → Peanut Meal Oil-free → (Protectein) Ardein → Ardil Spinning Solution

Peanuts Decorticated → Peanut Oil

Peanut Meal Oil-free → Residual Meal (Cattlefood Nitrogen 2%)

Ardil Spinning Solution → Ardil Fibre Staple

Ardil Fibre Staple → Ardil Sliver → Ardil Yarn → Ardil Yarn Bleached

(*Courtesy:* United States Testing Company Inc.)

other natural protein fibres. It is creamy white and has the smoothness and softness of cashmere. Vicara does not pill, but lacks the strength of nylon.

Vicara was manufactured in small quantities and found ready acceptance, but production was halted in 1958 and later the plant was dismantled. Zein is now mostly used as an ingredient of varnishes and inks.

For the manufacture of Vicara, the protein zein is removed from corn meal by alcohol and treated with caustic soda. This process is called denaturing, the purpose of which is to straighten out the coiled protein molecules. The spinning solution so obtained is forced through a spinnerette into an acid precipitating bath. The treated fibres are blended with formaldehyde and stretched to orient the molecules for strength. The tow is washed, dried, crimped and cut into staple lengths.

Vicara is resilient, very flexible and has adequate tensile strength. Like all protein fibres it does not support combustion. Unlike wool, it is not harmed by alkalies. It resists shrinking, stretching and wrinkling and gives softness and elasticity to cotton and rayons. Most of the Vicara produced was used in blends with other fibres.

Basic features common to all protein fibres

	Property	From the user's viewpoint
1.	Resilient	Fabrics tend to hold their shape.
2.	Weaker when wet	Wool loses about 40% of its strength when wet, silk about 15%. Handle carefully during washing.
3.	Harmed by oxidising agents	Chlorine bleaches damage fibre. Sunlight causes white fabrics to turn yellow.
4.	Poor conductors of electricity	Good insulation.
5.	High absorbency	Comfortable in cool, damp climates; absorbs odours.
6.	Weakened by alkalies	Use neutral or mild soap or detergent; perspiration weakens the fabric.

7.	Harmed by dry heat	Wool becomes harsh and brittle and scorches easily with dry heat. Silk yellows with heat.
8.	Do not support combustion	Protein fibres tend to stop burning when the flame is removed. Burned protein fibres have the odour of burning chicken feathers. This test can be used to distinguish wool from fibres that resemble wool.

3

Thermoplastic Fibres

The 1920s saw the first of a group of synthetic fibres which have served us in so many ways that they have been called 'magic fibres' and 'easy-living fibres'. The time required for washing, and drying has been reduced to a minimum, and ironing is often not necessary. Their superior strength, elasticity and other versatile qualities have revolutionized the clothing industry.

These fibres are called thermoplastic because they soften and become pliable or plastic with heat. Their softening points vary from quite low to very high. They will also melt if they come in contact with too hot an iron, or if they come in contact with flames or heat from blasts or other sources which have temperatures above their melting points, such as hot cigarette ashes. The hot, melted material can cause severe burns. Like other man-made fibres, thermoplastic fibres must be stretched to orient the molecules in order to increase fibre strength, tenacity and sometimes their dimensional stability. During the processing, spinning and drawing operations, the orientation of the molecules has already occurred. At the same time the linear molecules are under considerable strain which, if released during washing and steaming, may result in considerable shrinkage and puckering of the fabric. Hence heat treatments have been devised to relax such strains in thermoplastic fibres. Heat setting is also the treatment used to achieve dimensional stability of some though not all thermoplastics.

Regenerated cellulose fibres, including all rayon fibres, although man-made, are usually distinguished from the synthetic thermoplastic fibres, whose starting point is a polymerized chemical. Included in the synthetic fibres are acetate, nylon, dacron, orlon, vinyon, acrylic and polyester.

Acetate (The Cellulose Base Fibre)

The acetates are one of the oldest and expensive of all man-made fibres. Acetate was the second of the man-made fibres produced by the Du Pont company, the first being nylon. Like rayon, it is dependent on cellulose for its basic material, and was originally classified with the rayons. Later, however, the Federal Trade Commission of the U.S.A. classed acetate with the thermoplastic fibres, as it has properties that are quite unlike the rayons and because it is a chemically different material.

Manufacture of acetate

Acetate is an ester of cellulose produced by treating purified cellulose with acetic acid. The cellulose is changed both physically and chemically.

Purified cellulose in the form of cotton linters or wood pulp is mixed with glacial acetic acid, acetic acid and sulphuric acid, for a period of 5 to 8 hours until a clear solution of the desired viscosity is formed. The cellulose has now changed to cellulose triacetate. The solution is aged for 10 to 24 hours during which time it hydrolyses to a secondary acetate that is soluble in acetone. Water is added and the cellulose acetate precipitated in the form of flakes. These are dried and several batches of flakes are blended together.

The flakes are dissolved in acetone and spun out into a column of warm air. Delustring agents or colour may be added to the spinning solution before spinning. The filaments are collected and wound onto bobbins ready for shipping to the mills for weaving or knitting. Staple fibres are cut, crimped, lubricated, dried and baled for shipment.

Physical and chemical properties

The acetate fibre, as seen under the microscope, has length-wise striations, but they are fewer in number than those in viscose. Cross-sections resemble a three or five-petalled flower.

Acetate is a cellulose ester composed of carbon, hydrogen and oxygen. It contains chemically reactive hydroxyl (OH) groups and many acetyl groups. Oxidising agents seldom need to be used on acetate. If bleaching is necessary, a mild hydrogen peroxide or a weak chlorine bleach should be used. Acetate is resistant to moth, mildew and soil. Acetate will dissolve in acetone and other organic solvents such as nail polish remover and perfumes, so care must be taken when acetate fabrics are washed.

Acetate fibres and fabrics burn as easily as cotton and viscose, leaving black, syrupy, melted material at the edges. In napped or pile fabrics, however, acetate does not burn with quite the same speed. When acetate is burned, it has a characterisite, vinegar-like odour.

Acetate loses strength when wet, but less than viscose rayon, and regains it completely on drying. Acetate rayon dries more rapidly than viscose, because it absorbs considerably less moisture.

Acetate has little affinity for cotton or viscose dyes, so special direct acetate dyes have been developed. A complete range of shades with good fastness has been available for many years, and new dyestuffs, generally of improved fastness, are now available. Acetate dyes very uniformly, dyeing is unexcelled and it can be cross-dyed with rayon or cotton to achieve an unlimited range of multi-coloured styling effects. In recent years a method of applying vat colours without impairing the material has been developed. These vat colours are fast to light and washing. Certain fluorescent dyestuffs are also applied to acetate yarns and fabrics with full retention of brilliance. This was found useful during World War II for signal flags and identification panels.

Uses

Acetate produces fabrics with excellent drapability and luxurious hand or feel, making it excellent for satins and taffetas. It dries very quickly, which is important in swimwear and lingerie. Acetate helps fabrics keep their shape and resist wrinkles and shrinkage and retain their freshness after drying. It can be woven for warmth and coolness. Acetate fabrics are used for underwear garments, women's apparel, men's wear, children's garments, baby-blankets, curtains, upholstery and for industrial purposes.

Care of acetate fabrics

The care of acetate fabrics is not the same as those of rayon or cotton. They can be either washed or dry cleaned, depending on the particular fabric. For instance, one does not normally wash an acetate taffeta evening dress. Often too, acetate is combined with other yarns, which determine whether or not the fabric is washable. Always check the tag for this information. If washable, acetate fabrics should be dipped lightly in mild, lukewarm suds, rinsed, and allowed to drip dry or blotted to remove excess moisture. When evenly damp, iron gently on the wrong side (never press hard), using the lowest temperature setting. After smoothing out the wrinkles, finish on the right side with a press cloth if necessary, hang on a hanger, and let the fabric air dry.

Nylon (The Polyamide Fibre)

In 1929, the Du Pont company of the U.S.A. began research into the chemistry of substances called polymers, which are long molecules made up of chains of smaller molecules. In particular, they studied the synthesis, properties and uses of the long-chain chemicals called polymides and polysters. Since the company made many kinds of chemical products, the research was not specifically aimed at producing a new synthetic fibre. But by 1938, several long-chain polymides with fibre-forming characteristics had been made. Of these, fibre 66 (6 molecules of adipic acid and 6 molecules of hexamethyline diamine) was selected as having the best all-round properties for fibres. Named 'nylon,' it was first marketed as tooth brush bristles. By 1940, the first nylon textile fibre was put on the market as nylon hosiery.

Nylon 66 was followed by the closely related polymide nylon 6. The major production of polyamide fibre in the world is of nylon 6 and nylon 66. However, because of the lower cost of ingredients and easier processing of fibre, the world production of nylon 6 continues to grow more rapidly. Other related polymides like nylon 4, 79, 11 and 12 have also been developed, but in India only nylon 6 is currently being produced.

"Nylon" is now a generic name although it began as a trade name. It is the name of a family of compounds that vary as to properties, form or use. Some nylon compounds melt at quite low temperatures and others melt at temperatures above 600°F. The type of fibre used for textiles melts at about 480°F. The form into which nylon compounds may be made varies from rigid plastics to fibres to finishes.

Of the fibres, high-tenacity nylon has an average strength of 7.5 grams per denier, and regular nylon fibre average 4.5 grams per denier. Nylon fibres are produced in three forms: monofilament, multifilament and staple.

Manufacture

Nylon salt is heated in an autoclave, a piece of equipment like a giant pressure cooker (see Fig. 3.1). Heat causes the molecules to join together to form linear polymers. The molten nylon is pumped out through tiny holes in a spinerette, a metal disc about 2 inches across.

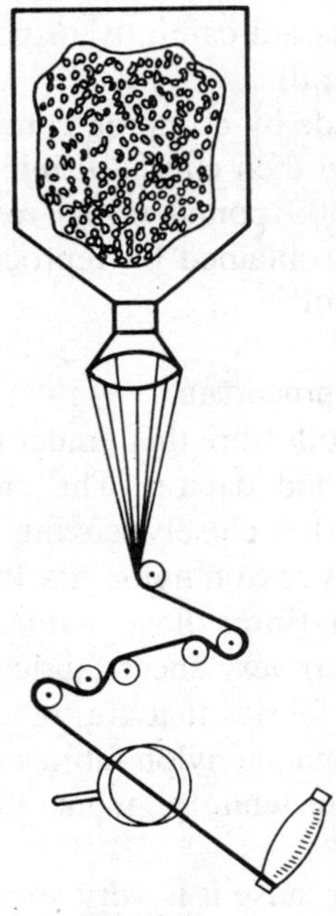

Fig. 3.1

As the nylon fibres emerge from the spinnerette and hit the air, they solidify and are then gathered together into a yarn. Next the yarn is stretched or 'cold drawn' between a system of rollers. The stretching causes changes to the fibre, as illustrated in Fig. 3.2, where the molecules of the fibre are represented by short lines. In the undrawn fibre, the long-chain molecules are arranged randomly

Fig. 3.2

like straws in a haystack. But drawing aligns the molecules into an orderly array, parallel to one another and closer together. Fibre diameter is also reduced. The nylon becomes very strong, tough and elastic, and the yarn develops translucency and luster. After drawing, the filament yarns are carefully inspected and packed for shipping to the weaving mill.

Nylon staple is made by crimping continuous nylon filament tow (untwisted fibres), and then cutting it into short, uniform lengths. It is shipped in large 500 pound packs resembling bales of cotton. Some nylon staple is obtained by reprocessing nylon by a system similar to that for wool.

Physical and chemical properties

Nylon is a round smooth fibre that, under the microscope, resembles cupramonium rayon and dacron. The cross section is round and small so it packs together closely leaving little dead air space in the yarn or fabric. For this reason nylon has less bulking power than the acrylic fibres. Nylon fibres have natural translucency. Filament nylon can be made into very sheer fabrics. But this property makes it difficult to produce fabrics that are light in weight and yet not too sheer. The first thin, opaque nylon fabrics are made by printing them with a resin containing white pigment. Recently opaque nylon has also been developed.

Nylon is durable because it is very strong, elastic and resistant to abrasion. Its strength varies from 4 to 7 grams per denier, and it is possible to have very sheer fabrics with good wearing properties. Garments of nylon are seldom discarded because of worn spots in the fabric, but rather because of seam failure, loss of colour or a gray appearance. Nylon fibre's are so strong and durable that they sometimes 'shear off' or cut through other kinds of fibre during wear. Scissors and clippers need frequent resharpening if used on nylon. The snagging of filament yarn fabrics result from nylon's

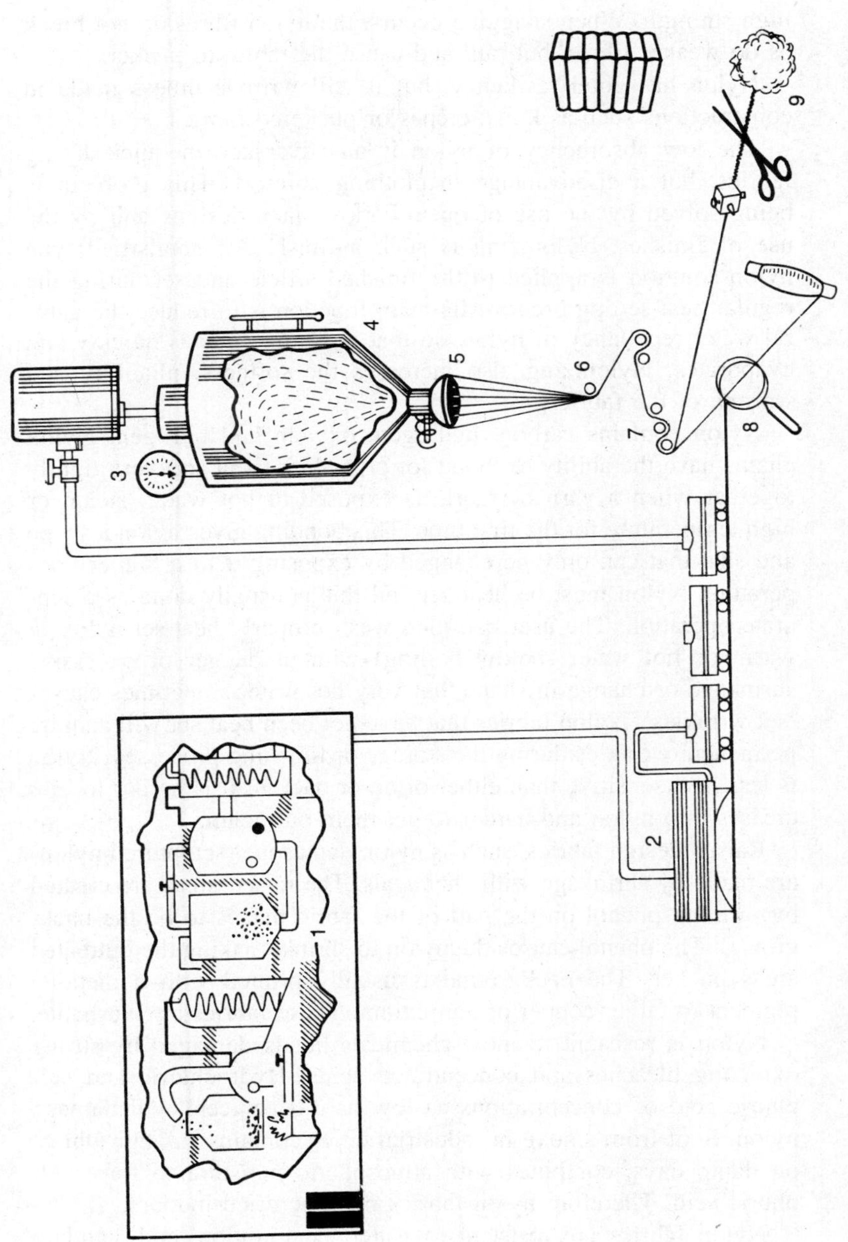
1
2
3
4
5
6
7
8
9

high strength. When snagging occurs, the nylon fibres do not break as do weaker fibres, but pull and cause the fabric to pucker.

Nylon has good resiliency, but it will wrinkle unless made in constructions such as knits, crêpes or puckered fabrics.

The low absorbency of nylon is an advantage in quick-drying fabrics, but a disadvantage in clothing comfort. This problem is being solved by the use of open-work or lacy designs and by the use of finishes. Nylonizing is such a finish. An emulsified type nylon solution is applied to the finished article and set during the regular heat-setting process. Its main function is to reduce the natural water repellancy of nylon, so that moisture spreads quickly and evaporates. Nylonizing also increases the softness, pliability and warmth of the fabric.

Nylon contains carbon, hydrogen, oxygen and nitrogen. Nylon chains have the ability to 'bond' or cross-link (heat set) very tightly together when a yarn or fabric is exposed to hot water, steam or high temperature for the first time. This bonding gives nylon a shape and size that can only be changed by exposing it to a higher temperature. Nylon must be heat set and this is usually done as a separate operation. The user can then wash properly heat-set nylon in warm or hot water (below boiling) without danger of excessive shrinkage or change in shape, but very hot water sometimes causes 'set wrinkles'. Nylon fabrics that have not been heat set will acquire permanent wrinkles during the storage or finishing processes. Nylon is less heat sensitive than either orlon or dacron. It is harder to iron creases into nylon and harder to get them out again.

Raised design fabrics, such as nylon damasque (sculptured nylon) are made by shrinkage with chemicals. The raised areas are created by printing phenol on the part of the fabric that is to be the background. The phenol causes the nylon to shrink, making the untreated areas pucker. The background is usually printed with a metallic pigment of either copper or aluminium. These fabrics are washable.

Nylon is resistant to most chemicals but is damaged by strong oxidizing bleaches and concentrated acids. Hydrochloric and sulphuric acid of concentrations as low as 3.0 per cent will damage nylon. Soot from smoke in industrial cities contains sulphur which, on damp days, combines with atmospheric moisture to form sulphuric acid. Therefore nylon fabrics must be dried indoors.

Nylon fabrics are resistant to water, perspiration, and standard drycleaning agents. The colour, however, may be affected. Nylon also resist damage by moths and mildew.

Care of nylon

Nylon is classed as an 'easy-care' fabric, as it is easy to launder and needs no pressing. Nylon melts with a hot iron and forms a hard black bead. Strong bleaches should not be used. One disadvantage of nylon-cotton blends for garments like overalls, has been the fact that nylon is not resistant to the chlorine bleach needed to keep the garments clean. When it is necessary to bleach nylon, use a mild bleach.

When sewing with nylon, use nylon thread, because it will last as long as the garment. It may be necessary to change the needle often as nylon dulls needles and scissors very readily.

Types of nylon textile fibres

Multifilament yarn is made up of a number of tiny, almost endless strands twisted together into one yarn. The size and number of strands can be varied as well as the number of twists. Most nylon fabrics are made from this versatile type of yarn. In lingerie, blouses, bathing suits and upholstery, multifilament yarns give pleasant surface texture, softness and luxurious drape.

Monofilament yarn is a single, solid strand of continuous length. Very sheer hoisery is a glamorous example of its use. Monofilaments are also used to make sheer blouses, veils and gowns.

Staple consists of many short, wavy strands of nylon cut-lengths varying from 1½ to 5 inches. The wave or crimp in these strands adds springiness to yarn spun from it, giving light, soft fabrics that are pleasant to the touch. Its convenient washability and durability has made this form of nylon fibre especially popular for sweaters and socks.

Recent improvements have brought new textures, effects, styling and uses to nylon. One new yarn has the ability to stretch and fit almost any shape. This makes it ideal for gloves and socks that fit all sizes. Another new yarn is less shiny and see-through than normal nylon. It is used in knit or woven fabrics for lingerie, nurses' uniforms, men's shirts and underwear.

From fibre to fabric

Knitters and weavers use nylon in their fabrics in three basic ways:

100% nylon fabrics, blends and combinations of nylon with other fibres, and as reinforcing material.

Fabrics made of 100% nylon give the wearer the full benefit of all of nylons' many properties, strength with lightness, resistance to wear and tear, shape retention and easy care. Blouses, slips and socks that wash quickly and need little or no pressing are examples of this use.

As a reinforcement. Here nylon is added in small amounts to an article of clothing, giving it longer life. Nylon yarn knitted into only the toe and led of socks made of another material increases the sock's wear life.

Blends and combinations Some materials are made partly of nylon and partly of some other fibre such as orlon, dacron, polyester, cotton, wool, rayon, acetate or silk. Such fabrics can be classified as blends or combinations.

In combinations fabrics a yarn made entirely of nylon and one made entirely of another fibre are woven or knitted together. Many rayon-nylon slip fabrics are of this type. Such a fabric can have the drape and feel of rayon with the added strength, wear and tear resistance, and shape retention of nylon. However, an improper combination of nylon and rayon may result in the nylon fibres cutting the rayon fibres.

In blends, the various short staple fibres are mixed together before the yarn is made. These yarns are then made into fabrics. Blends of nylon and wool can be lighter and stronger then wool alone. If enough nylon is used in the blend, the fabric may need no special care to prevent noticeable shrinking or loss of shape after washing. Nylon and cotton blends can have greatly increased wear and tear resistance without the loss of cotton's characteristic softness. Some of the more common blends are described below:

Nylon and cotton When properly combined with cotton, nylon adds strength, allowing finer textures than is possible using cotton alone. Nylon provides smoothness, silkiness and dirt rejection. It also reduces the weight of the fabric and increases its wrinkle resistance. The cotton contributes softness and moisture absorption. This combination permits the weaving of fabrics that are soft, supple and extremely serviceable. If the combination is not properly balanced, however, the cotton may shrink, causing the fabric to pucker. Also, the nylon fibres may cut into the cotton fibres. A blend of at least

17 per cent high tenacity nylon staple with cotton will produce an extremely durable fabric.

Nylon and wool The proper combination of nylon and wool will produce a lighter weight fabric with greater durability. Such a fabric will retain the hand, drape and warmth of wool as well as the elasticity, resilience, and shape retention of nylon. The relative proportions of wool and nylon determines the properties of the blended fabric. A blend of 10 to 15 per cent nylon and the remainder wool is considered satisfactory.

Nylon and silk In this combination, the silk improves the hand and provides moisture absorption. The nylon improves the stability or shape retention, as well as the elasticity and strength.

Nylon and rayon Here the nylon gives wrinkle resistance and strength, while the rayon gives suppleness, drape and moisture absorption. Such a combination makes for a fine quality fabric of extremely light weight. As with cotton, if the combination is not properly balanced, the rayon may shrink, causing the fabric to pucker. Also, an improper blend may result in the nylon fibres cutting the rayon fibres. Like cotton, rayon staple blended with high-tenacity Du Pont 420 nylon staple can produce fabrics with 70 percent longer wear than all-rayon fabrics if the nylon is blended in a proportion of at least 17 percent. This proportion is used for garments classed as wash-and-wear.

Nylon Acetate The acetate in such a blend provides a luxurious hand, and the nylon gives light weight and strength. As with cotton or rayon, improper blending may result in the nylon cutting the acetate fibre and in some fabrics, puckering may occur. Also, neither nylon nor acetate absorbs much moisture. Such fabrics feel clammy and uncomfortable in warm, humid weather.

Dacron or Terylene (Polyester Fibre)

After polymide, the second big class of synthetic fibres is polyester. The major portion of the post-1945 polymer work at Du Pont was on polymides, resulting, in the development of nylon. This work was extended by the British to the polysters. Starting from ethylene glycol and dimethyl terephthalate, in 1946 they produced a fibre they named 'terylene' derived (by inversion) from polyethylene terephthalate. Du Pont bought the patent rights and developed their own version, called 'dacron'. Terylene and dacron are trade names for polyster, but they have become so common that they are used in the generic sense.

Dacron is not chemically related to any other fibre. It is meltspun like nylon and is much like it in physical appearance and in many of its properties. Dacron fabrics too, are very similar in appearance to nylon.

Dacron is manufactured in the form of filament yarn (used in knit fabrics for men's shirts and women's dresses), and staple fibre (used in upholstery fabrics and filling for pillows). These are the same chemically, but they possess somewhat different physical properties. These differences have been produced intentionally, so as to make dacron suitable for widely different purposes. Filament yarn is processed very much like silk or nylon and the finished fabric resembles these. Staple fibre has a wool-like appearance and character and can be processed on the worstedsystem.

Chemically, dacron and cellulose acetate are both esters and for this reason have similar dyeing properties. Dacron is polymerised at high temperature in a vacuum and is then mill spun. Under the microscope dacron is so much like nylon that identification is difficult.

Physical and chemical properties

It is warm to the touch. It has a low stretch when the filament yarn is used. It is crease-resistant and will keep its shape wet or dry. Since dacron fabrics have low absorbency, stains lie on the surface, so it is easily washed and dries quickly. Dacron has excellent press or crease retention; creases remain sharp even after washing. It is a very strong fabric and has a high resistance to rubbing. Dacron is mothproof, mildewproof and immune from attack by other insects and bacteria. It is resistant to weather and sunlight, especially behind glass. It is not easily affected by perspiration. Its 'wicking' property makes terylene or dacron comfortable to wear in hot weather, even though it is not absorbent. Wicking is the ability of a fibre to pick up moisture and allow it to travel along the fibre without actually being absorbed by it. Thus the moisture is carried from the skin of a wearer outward, where it evaporates.

Dacron has excellent resistance to such oxidising agents as sodium hypochlorite and hydrogen peroxide even with severe treatment. It has a high resistance to hydrochloric, sulphuric, nitric, acetic, formic and oxalic acids, even concentrated, being able to endure long exposures of up to 72 hours, and temperatures up to 176°F.

One disadvantage with dacron is that it builds up static electricity. This however can be controlled by the use of an antistatic agent. Dacron also pills very readily and, because of high electrostatic properties, picks up lint-forming 'lint-pills' which spoil the appearance of the fabric. Unlike the other thermoplastic fibres, dacron has no water repellancy. Instead it has wicking properties; rain drops get through to the skin, causing discomfort.

Dacron has a fairly good affinity for dyes, and can be dyed in a complete range of colours.

Tests for identification

Dacron melts like nylon and forms a hard bead at a temperature below ignition point. The bead may continue to burn, leaving a hard, irregular black mass.

Under the microscope, dacron or terylene filaments are smooth and cylindrical, while their cross-sections are circular. It is very much like nylon.

Dacron retains its fibre form for one minute on treatment with boiling 90 per cent phosphoric acid. This distinguishes it from other synthetic polymer fibres which either dissolve, shrink or lose their fibre form.

Dacron fibre blends

Pure dacron is used to make curtains, upholstery fabrics, women's dresses, underwear and night clothes, men's socks, children's clothes, and knitted garments. But dacron polyester fibre is more successfully used when blended with other fibres. Various effects and combinations of properties are derived from these blends, depending on the fibres used and the percentages in the blends. One of the most important characteristics that dacron provides is its high degree of shape retention for garments that require little or no ironing after they are washed. The more important blends are described below.

Dacron and Cotton For satisfactory wash-and-wear and permenent-press rainwear, tailored clothing, dress shirts and sports shirts should have a blend of at least 65 per cent dacron with the cotton. Dacron provides and retains strength, wrinkle resistance and shape retention while the cotton contributes absorbency and consequent comfort. However, unless properly constructed and properly cared, a dacron-cotton fabric may pucker and lose shape if the cotton should shrink or if cotton thread is used in sewing.

Dacron and Wool In combination with wool, dacron provides outstanding wrinkle resistance and crease retention, so that wet or dry, the shape retention is improved according to the proportions used. The greater abrasion resistance of dacron also provides longer wear. The wool component provides good draping quality and elasticity, and also reduces the hazard of burning cigarette holes. A blend of 60 per cent dacron and 40 per cent wool provides a cloth warm enough for year-round suits.

Dacron and Rayon Blended with viscose rayon, dacron gives greater resiliency, shape retention and durability. The viscose rayon provides absorbency and variety of colour and texture. For satisfactory wash-and-wear service, a blend of at least 55 percent dacron with the rayon is desirable. A blend of 65 percent dacron and 35 percent high wet-modulus rayon provides a strong, durable and serviceable fabric that has a good hand and drapes well. The rayon again provides the absorbency that dacron lacks.

Dacron and Nylon Nylon contributes strength and abrasion resistance, while from dacron we get outstanding wrinkle resistance. Such a combination offers stability, easy laundering, quick drying, and resistance to damage from mildew and insects. The fabric will be clammy to the skin, however, in warm, humid weather. Since both the fibres are thermoplastic and neither is very absorbent, any combination in the blend will provide good wash-and-wear characteristics. Care should be taken to avoid pilling of fabrics with this type of blend.

Care of dacron fabrics

Wash, knead and squeeze. Drip dry. The weight of the water will press it as it dries. Be careful to turn all garments wrong-side out. This will reduce any surface pilling that might occur on the right side. Dacron garments can be dry cleaned satisfactorily.

Vinyon

This manufactured fibre is one in which the fibre-forming substance is any long-chain synthetic polymer composed of at least 85 per cent weight of vinyl chloride units.

Production

Some of the raw materials required for the manufacture of vinyon are petroleum, chlorine, acetic acid and acetone, from which ingredients, a fluffy resin powder is made. This powder is dispersed in a solvent, de-aerated and spun by extrusion. The fibres so formed are heated under tension to 90° to 100° and stretched to develop strength, elasticity and resilience. The fibre may have a crimp induced by controlled heat-setting or by a suitable bath.

Vinyon may be delustred by the usual procedure of incorporating pigment into the solution before it is spun, or by a less destructive new process using water. Thus like rayon, it can be made into dull or bright yarn and can be dyed in various colours.

Physical and chemical properties

Vinyon is warm to the touch and feels like silk. It is water resistant and non-inflammable. It is not attacked by bacteria, moulds or fungi, and is satisfactorily resistant to sunlight. Vinyon is a non-conductor of electricity, and as water does not affect it, an excellent insulator. Unlike most man-made fibres, vinyon has the same tensile strength in both dry and wet states. It is a thermoplastic and exceptionally resistant to mineral acids and alkalis.

Uses

The short fibres of vinyon can be blended, like rayon with natural fibres such as cotton and wool. They are also mixed with wool and used for felts. They make excellent fabrics for pleated garments the vinyon serves as a binder, and the garments do not shrink whilst the pleats are held well.

Because of its water and fire-resistant properties, vinyon is used for umbrellas, waterproof garments, bathing suits, tents, draperies, fish nets, awnings, industrial filter-cloth, etc. It is also used as a binding fibre in certain kinds of paper. Vinyon is sometimes woven with other fibres in carpets to make embossed designs. When woven or tufted carpet is treated with heat, the vinyon shrinks, producing the design.

Orlon (Acrylic Fibres)

Orlon is another of the synthetic polymer fibres developed by the Du Pont company. It was first produced in 1948. The name 'orlon' is a proprietary trade mark of du Pont. Modern practice prefers the generic term acrylic, which is defined as any long-chain synthetic polymer composed of at least 85% by weight of acrylonitrile units.

Manufacture

Orlon is made from a chemical compound called acrylonitrile, which is formed by the reaction of ethylene oxide and hydrocyanic acid. These two chemicals are derived from elements found in coal, air, water, petroleum and limestone.

Acrylonitrile contains carbon, hydrogen and nitrogen. A close relative of acrylonitrile is the acrylic resin used to make lucite, found in items such as brushes, handles and combs. Lutice too is a du Pont trade mark.

To make the fibre, single molecules of acrylonitrile are processed in a reactor containing water and a catalyst until the molecules connect into long chains of acrylonitrile polymer. Then the water is removed and the polymer is pressed through perforated plates and cut into bits.

The hard bits are dissolved with a solvent to make a concentrated solution. After being filtered, the solution is forced (extruded) through a spinnerette, a small, round metal plate with tiny, barely visible holes in it. The polymer is extruded in the form of long threads, (filaments), which are dried in hot gases and drawn (i.e. stretched) while hot. The drawing process orients the long-chain molecules parallel along the length of the filament. Drawing controls the stretch of the fibre and improves its strength.

Orlon in filament form resembles long silk strands. This form is used in smooth, sometimes shiny, fabrics such as satins. As for other synthetic fibres, orlon is also made in staple form, which resembles raw wool or cotton. Staple is made by putting a crimp (permanent wave) into the filaments, and then cutting them into lengths ranging from 1½ to 4½ inches.

A variety of acrylic with the trade name acrilon is manufactured similarly to orlon. Natural gas and air are combined to form ammonia, then the ammonia is combined with natural gas to produce

Acrylonitrite
polymerization reactor
mixer
dimethyl formamide
filter
spinneret
dryer
to stretcher, robbin or cutter, crimper, opener and baler

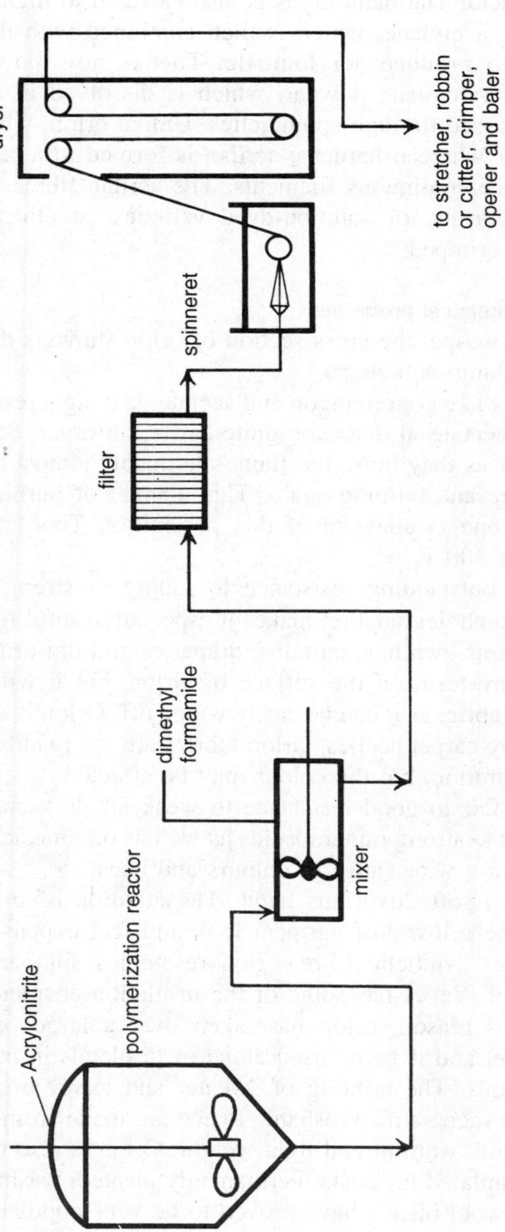

hydrocyanic acid. The natural gas is also elevated to high temperatures to make acetylene, which is then combined with the hydrocyanic acid to produce acrylonitrile. This is now polymerized, making polyacrylonitrile powder, which is dissolved in a suitable solvent and passed through spinnerettes. Unlike orlon, which is extruded into air where it hardens, acrilan is formed in a coagulating bath to produce continuous filaments. The acrilan fibres, produced in semi-dull, bright, or solution-dyed varieties, are then washed, stretched and crimped.

Physical and chemical properties

Under a microscope, the cross-section of orlon shows a distinctive, dog-bone or dumb-bell shape.

Orlon burns like cotton, rayon and acetate, leaving a residue similar to that of acetate. It does not ignite easily, however. Some orlon fabrics sputter as they burn, the flame alternately almost dying out, then flaring up and burning again. This manner of burning can be dangerous if one is unaware of this possibility. The safe ironing temperature is 300°F.

Orlon has outstanding resistance to fading in strong light. Its resistance to such degradation makes it especially useful for outdoor purposes such as awnings, curtains, draperies and uniforms.

Mildew may form on the surface of Orlon, but it will have no effect on the fabric, as it can be easily wiped off. Orlon is unaffected by moths or by carpet beetles. Orlon fabrics are not readily deteriorated by perspiration, but the colour may be affected.

Orlon has fair to good resistance to weak alkalies, and exceedingly resistant to strong mineral acids as well as organic acids. Orlon can be dyed in a wide range of colours and hues.

Orlon has a soft, luxurious hand. The addition of orlon staple fibre can make a low-cost garment look and feel expensive. More than any other synthetic fibre, orlon resembles silk, and has its warm, dry feel. Yet is has some of the insulation characteristics of wool. For this reason, orlon has taken over a large part of the sweater market and is being used alone or in blends in many types of knitted goods. The printing of sweater and jersey orlon fabrics has also been successful. Washable fleece are made from orlon because of its bulk warmth and light weight. Orlon is also often used in making simulated fur coats. Permanently pleated, washable skirts of orlon and wool blends have proved to be very popular.

Of the synthetic fibres, orlon is the least affected by sunlight, weather, insects and mildew. It is therefore a popular material for outdoor use as awnings, porch furniture covers, curtains and auto covers.

Care of orlon

Orlon is an easy-care fabric; it does not soil or stain easily. Washing or dry cleaning renews its freshness. However, mild soaps should be used since strong soaps damage orlon. Household bleaches may be safely used. Knitted garments of orlon tend to shrink and discolour in dry cleaning, and are more satisfactorily cared for by washing them with water.

Soft, bulky orlon yarns will pill, but orlon blended with other fibres reduces this tendency. To avoid pilling, garments like sweaters should be washed inside-out, with as little scrubbing as possible. After rinsing through mild suds and then in lukewarm water, squeeze out the water, turn the garment back out, spread it on a towel and gently brush it with a very soft brush while drying. Thorough rinsing after washing is important. Orlon should be ironed with a moderately hot iron when dry.

Orlon fibre blends

Orlon's desirable properties can be usefully blended with other fibres. Some of their blends are described below.

Orlon and Cotton Orlon adds light weight and body, while the cotton contributes strength and absorbency. The fabric is wrinkle-resistent, retains shape well, and provides easy care. A blend of 80 per cent or more of orlon with cotton has the general characteristies of a wash-and-wear fabric, as in sports shirts.

Orlon and Wool One of the outstanding characteristics of orlon is its bulk, so that when the staple is blended with wool, the resulting fabric is light-weight, yet warm. It also has a soft hand, but there may be some pilling. Fabrics of this combination have very good crease retention and wrinkle recovery. These blends are washable, and when there is a good proportion of orlon, the fabrics seldom need pressing. A good blend for a wash-and-wear tailored garment should have 60 per cent or more orlon, though too much orlon makes the fabric too bulky. Such a blend will also be stronger than an all-wool fabric.

Orlon and Silk provide interesting cross-dyed and textured effects. Such blends have outstanding hand and excellent stability. In addition to the good appearance, the combination gives long wear. The orlon contributes easy-care qualities and shape retention while the silk contributes absorbency and strength. The fabric is very resilient and may be warm, depending on its weight.

Orlon and Rayon To the versatility of rayon, orlon adds wrinkle resistance and stability. New and unusual surface and dye effects, including cross-dyes are possible. Orlon provides a dry, warm, soft hand. A wash-and-wear blend should have at least 70 per cent orlon. If instead of regular rayon, a high wet-modulus rayon is used it will result in a stronger fabric with the same general properties. An orlon and modified rayon blend could, therefore, have a lower proportion of orlon.

Orlon and Acetate A combination of orlon and acetate makes a fabric that has soft, luxurious feel, excellent drapability and shape retention, and good resilience. The fabric launders easily with milk soap and warm water, dries rapidly, and is easy to iron. The orlon also provides greater resistance to sunlight. Neither orlon nor acetate, however, is particularly absorbent, which is a disadvantage in warm, humid weather, making these blends warm and clammy.

Orlon and Nylon The strength and abrasion resistance of nylon, combined with the luxurious hand and covering power of orlon produce attractive, warm, strong fabrics. The similar qualities of orlon and nylon, such as wrinkle resistance, crease retention and easy care, are increased when these fibres are combined. Again such fabrics will not be very absorbent.

Orlon and Polyester Orlon improves the hand of a fabric when combined with a polyester fibre, giving better body comfort and warmth. The polyester fibre contributes even greater wrinkle resistance, especially under humid conditions. A 50/50 blend will provide good wash-and-wear characteristics. Such a fabric will generally wear well because of the strength of the polyster fibres and the good abrasion resistance of orlon. However, it is likely to pill if care is not exercised.

Basic features common to most thermoplastic fibres

Property	From the user's point of view
Wet strength is comparable to dry strength	No danger of holes due to agitation or abrasion during washing or wear.
Elasticity and elongation like wool	Maintains air space for warmth. Regains shape after stretching. Affects stiffness, drape, resiliency.
Low moisture absorption	*Advantages:* Resists spots, easy to remove, washable, dries quickly. *Disadvantages:* Difficult to dye, builds up static electricity charges.
High tensile strength and abrasion resistance	High durability to pilling and rubbing in wear.
High chemical resistance	Not rapidly destroyed by acids, alkalies, bleaches, detergents. Non-hazardous skin irritant.
Heat sensitive	Melts with hot iron, hot cigarette ashes, contact with any hot object.
Heat-setting	Will keep: crush resistant pile, permanent pleats, original size and shape. Knits do not need pressing after washing. Embossed designs possible.
Resilient	Loses wrinkles easily.
High resistance to moth, mildew, insects, mould, etc.	Simplifies storage problems. Economy from little loss due to these causes.

General Care of Synthetics

The following suggestions should prove helpful in caring for garments or other articles made of fabrics containing nylon, orlon, terene or dacron fibres:

1. Wash whites only with other whites.
2. Wash in warm water (100°F) using a synthetic detergent or soap plus or a water softner.
3. Dainty blouses or any garment with fragile trim is best washed

by hand and drip-dried on a non-staining hanger. Do not wring or crush unnecessarily in washing.

4. When 'touchup' pressing is desired, it can be done quickly and easily, using a steam or dry iron at the rayon or nylon setting.

Home sewing

Cutting Use well sharpened shears. Cut with the middle of the blade, using long clean strokes.

Pins and Needles Needles and pins, both for machine and hand sewing, should be fine, with sharp, smooth points. It is best to change the machine needle often, as man-made fibres dull the needle more rapidly than natural fibres.

Thread It is best to use thread that has the same quality as the fabric to be stitched. Thread shoul be cut, not broken, to avoid pulled seams.

Sewing Run sewing machine slowly and evenly. Hold fabric firmly without pulling. Be sure all the linings and tapes are fully shrunk, and of washable construction.

Pressing Each seam should be pressed on the wrong side after stitching. It is important to use low temperature at 250°F, i.e. at the rayon or nylon setting on automatic irons.

Asbetos (Mineral Fibre)

The textile industry makes use of three minerals: asbetos, which is a natural fibre, and glass and metallics which are man-made. These mineral fibres have characteristics in common but behave different from all other fibres. They do not burn, and if they melt, they do so only at very high temperatures, much above those ordinarily encountered by textile fabrics. Glass and asbetos are not attacked by chemicals.

All three fibres have specialised uses and cannot be used interchangeably with most other textile fibres. All three are inorganic and their structure is not typical of the long-chain molecule organic fibres.

The source of asbestos is the mineral rock chrystile serpentine, which occurs as silky fibres of hydrous magnesium silicate. Major deposits of the mineral occur in Canada, former Soviet Union and South Africa. The name asbetos comes from the Greek word for unquenched, because it resists fire. Its use as a textile goes back at least to the Greeks. The lamps in the temples to the vestal virgins of ancient Greece were always kept burning with wicks of Carpathian linen. This Carpathian linen is believed to have been made of asbestos. From the middle ages in Europe, comes the story of Charlemagne's tablecloth made of asbetos. Once, when his empire was threatened by invaders from the east, Charlemagne called a peace conference to hear the demands of his enemies and, during the course of the conference, tossed the tablecloth into the fire and drew it back out unharmed. The ambassadors were convinced that they were dealing with a great magician and the invasion was called off. Commercial production of asbestos began in Canada around 1860.

Properties

Under the microscope, asbestos fibres appears straight, smooth and needle-shaped.

Asbestos dyes easily but the colour is likely to be spotty and have poor fastness. The fibres are coarse and have little strength. Short periods of high temperature (over 600°F) will further decrease its strength. It is absorbent and has wicking ability. Asbestos is acid and alkali resistant.

Uses

Asbestos is an important fibre for production equipment, filters for chemicals and other industrial purposes. It is used for flame-proof clothing for, many kinds for laboratory, industrial and military uses. It is used in all types of protective equipment for fire fighting, fire screens, insulation for steam and hot pipes, brake linings, insulating building materials, tapes and braids for electrical uses and items wherein non-combustibility is essential. Asbestos is also used with glass fibre in making decorative fabrics for curtains and draperies for hospitals, theaters, libraries, schools and other public buildings, and for heat insulation. A major draw back of asbestos is that factory workers, miners or others exposed to asbestos dust, can develop a serious respiratory disorder.

Glass Fibres

Glass fibres are outstanding among textile fibres, both natural and synthetic, as they have very high tensile strength (around 300,000 pounds per square inch compared to 100,000 psi for organic fibres) immunity to micro-organisms causing mildew and deterioration, very high resistance to chemicals, and complete fire-proofness. The drawback of the glass fibres is their lack of resiliency and ability to stretch. They are not soft to the touch, and break if bent too much, and hence are not generally suitable as a clothing commodity.

Coarse fibres were first prepared in 1893 by drawing the heated ends of glass rods. In 1900 a number of patents were issued in Germany and England but it was not till 1936 that the Owens-Corning Corporation succeeded in making glass fibres that were fine and pliable enough to be woven into fabrics.

Manufacture

Glass fibres suited to different purposes are prepared by the proper selection, mixing and melting of raw materials, by varying the ingredients and their proportions, by regulating the temperature, and by controlling the fibre diameter.

The primary ingredients for the various types of glass are silica, sand and limestone. In addition, other minerals are used, according to the end product required. The fibres are manufactured in two main forms: staple of short-length, and continuous.

Glass meant for electrical appliances with good chemical resistance and high durability is a borosilicate glass containing no alkali metal oxides. It is used only in continuous and staple textile fibres. Glass meant for chemical appliances such as filter cloths is produced only in staple fibre form. Borosilicate glass is used for thermal and acoustical insulation. Soda-lime-silicate glass is used in the form of relatively coarse filter fibres.

The ingredients are melted in a furnace, the molten glass coming out in fine jets from the base of the furnace. Jets of high pressure steam or hot air hit the jets of molten glass with terrific force and yank them into thread-like fibres.

Fibres in the form of a fleecy, resilient mass are used for thermal insulation applications. For other purposes it may be treated with a binder, compressed and shaped into rigid or semi-rigid boards.

For the manufacture of textile fibres, the molten glass is transferred to marble-forming machinery, which makes small glass marbles about 5/8 inches in diameter. These are then remelted in electric furnaces.

To make continuous filaments, more than 100 filaments are drawn and gathered into a strand, which is then attached to a high-speed winder, thus reducing the diameter of each filament. From a single marble, singles filament of about 170,000 yards can be drawn. The strands could in fact, be drawn to indefinite lengths, thousands of miles long. These fine filaments are twisted and plied to form yarns by methods similar to those used for making other continuous filament yarns. These yarns are then used to reinforce plastics or are woven into industrial or decorative fabrics, and tyre cords.

To make staple fibres, the molten glass flows in thin streams through small holes in the base of the furnace and is struck by jets of high pressure air or steam which yank the glass into fibres 8 to 15 inches long, longer than the best long-staple cotton. The fibres are driven down, through a spray of fibre lubricant and drying flame,

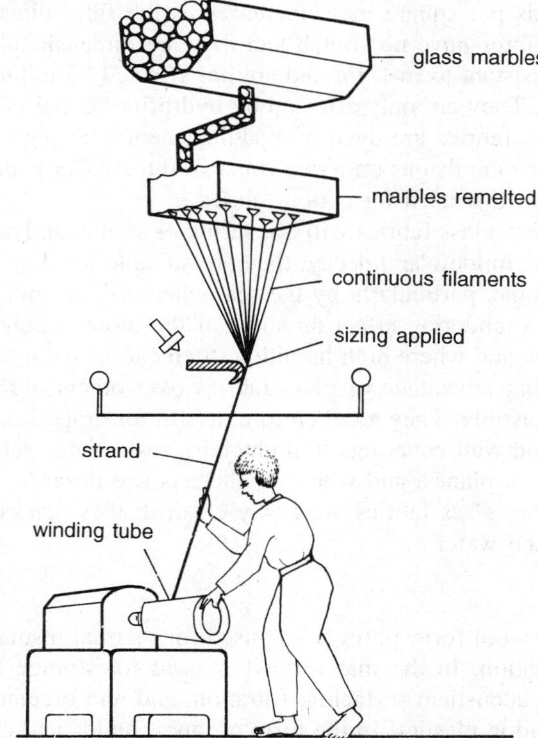

Fig. 3.5 Schematic diagram of the formation of fibreglass filament from marbles

on which they form a veil resembling a cobweb. The web of fibres is then gathered into a sliver which is lightly drafted in the succeeding winding operation, so that the majority of the fibres lie parallel with the length of the strand.

Strands of continuous filaments or staple fibres are twisted and plied into yarns on textile machinery similar to that used for cottons and worsteds. Fabrics woven from continuous filament yarns are thin, smooth and lustrous. Those woven of staple yarns have a slightly fuzzy appearance and are less lustrous. The yarn thus produced is primarily used for tapes and fabrics for industrial purposes where insulation is needed.

Properties

The tensile strength of standard fibreglass textile fibres, about 200, pounds per square inch, increases as the fibre diameter decreases. The fibres have no stretch and they are dimensionally stable. They are resistant to rust, rot and are not affected by mildew and perspiration. They are only affected by hydrofluoric and phosphoric acids.

The fabrics are dyed by padding them with pigmented water-in-oil type emulsions on a two-roller or three-roller padder of the same type as that used for cotton fabrics.

Since glass fabrics will not shrink or stretch and are proof against moths, mildew and decay, they are suitable for drapery materials in the home, particularly by the sea, where salt air and strong sunlight have a tendering effect on some of the more common drapery materials, and where high humidity often causes them to stretch or sag. One big advantage of glass fabrics over others is that they are incombustible. They are therefore, useful for draperies as well as ceiling and wall coverings in nightclubs, restaurants, schools, railroads, ships, airplanes, and wherever there is fire hazard.

Fibre glass fabrics are easily cleaned: they can be sponged with pad and water.

Uses

In its wool form fibreglass is used for thermal insulation and sound absorption. In the mat form it is used for storage battery retainer mats, acoustical surfacing, filtration, and reinforcement of electrical insulation plastics. In the form of tapes, braids and cloths, it is used for electrical insulation, high temperature industrial textiles, reinforcement in laminates, plastics, etc., chemical filtration and dec-

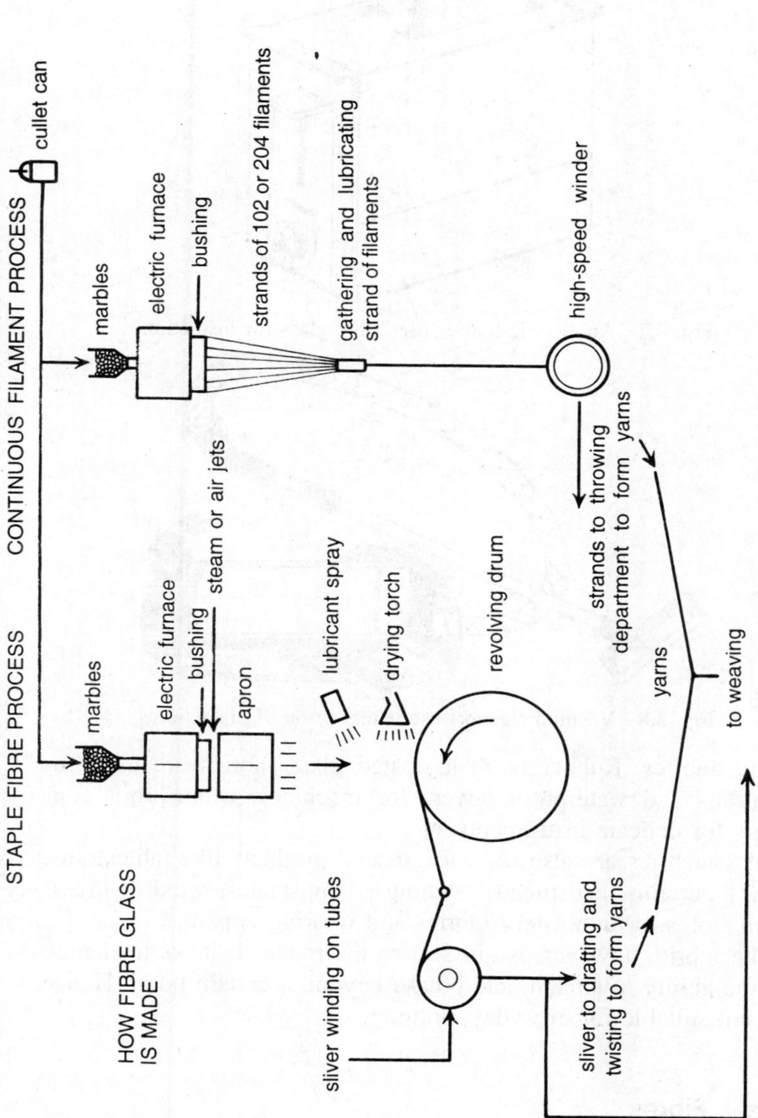

Fig. 3.6 How fibreglass is made

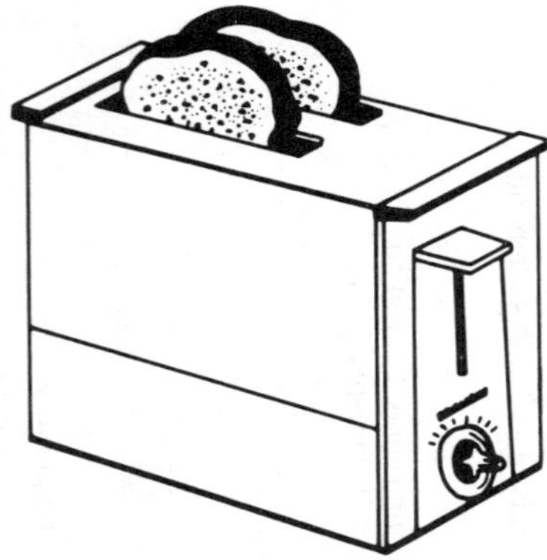

Fig. 3.7 An electric toaster uses fibre glass for insulation

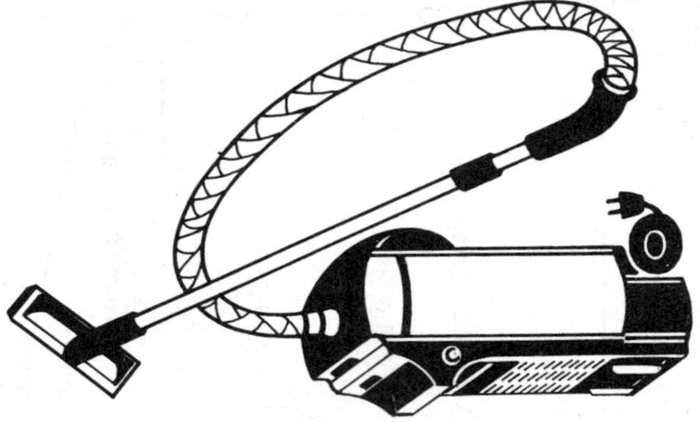

Fig. 3.8 Vacuum cleaners use jetters made of glass fibres

orative fabrics. Rubber or resin-coated glass fabrics are used for tarpaulins and waterproof covers for machines, water-proof containers for delicate instruments, etc.

Glass fabrics are also used for special products like tablecloths, shower curtains, bedspreads, awnings, lampshades, window-dressing in stores, or upholstery fabrics and wearing apparel.

The fabric, however, is not soft to the touch. It lacks resiliency and the ability to stretch, and breaks beyond a certain point. Hence it is not suitable for everyday clothing.

Metalic Fibres

A metallic fibre is a manufactured fibre composed of metal, a plastic coated metal, a metal coated plastic, or a core completely covered by metal.

Threads made of metal, particularly gold and silver, have been used for centuries in hand weaving, sewing and embroidery. In India, the tradition goes far back into the past. Indian metal cloth could also have reached ancient Babylon. Marco Polo writes of India, 'Here are elaborate, diverse cloths in gold and silver of great bravery.' Among well-known Indian metal-weaving centres are Ahmedabad, Murshidabad and Benaras, where gold brocades (*kinkhabs*) are world-famous. Here gold and silver wires are used lavishly to work out delicate patterns, making them the most gorgeous and highly ornamented of Indian textiles. Some of the favourite motifs on brocades are sacred geese and animal patterns in bands. The art of brocade-weaving has survived, and many varieties are still produced, both for the home and foreign markets.

Any of the ductile metals, such as gold, silver, copper or even the cheaper alloys, can be drawn out into fine filaments. Today metal threads are usually made with a core of cotton yarn wrapped within a ribon of metal. Gold thread (*kullabuttoon*) and silver wire is used for richer fabrics. Imitation gold and silver wires are also prevalent, but they get tarnished easily.

Pure and imitation metal threads are used on *jamdanis*. The *jamdanis* or figured muslins of Dacca were much admired by the British. These fabrics may be called loom tapestries. The patterns are inserted by hand as the weaving proceeds; this gives it an embroidered effect. A tiny bobbin with gold coloured or silver thread is passed through and round the warp threads in the manner of tapestries. *Panna-hazara* (thousand jewels), *dorakata* (stripes) toradar (patterns with sprays of flowers), chevrons, and geometrical patterns are some of the favourite designs in *jamdanis*.

Modern metallic yarns, at least those available abroad, are generally made of coloured aluminium ribbons sandwiched between two layers of transparent plastic film. Aluminium, the basic metal used, is softer, lighter and cheaper than the more precious metals and is not so apt to tarnish or cause discolouration. The gold, silver and copper colours of old are also available, as well as a rainbow array of metal-coloured yarns to serve many purposes such as wearing apparel, household furnishings, car upholstery and glamorous packaging materials.

Properties

Metallics are not fibres but light-weight, non-tarnishable and relatively inexpensive yarns. All are bright. The strength varies with the type of film and the width of yarn. Acetate and acetate butyrate laminates are quite weak, do not knot, tie easily and tear readily. So these yarns are usually plied with another textile fibre for weaving, knitting and other types of processing. Polyester films are much stronger than acetate films and can be used unsupported for weaving, knitting and processing even on power looms and knitting machines. They also tie and knot more readily. They have considerable elasticity, resiliency and elongation. All metallics are sensitive to abrasion and the flexing. The heat resistance of acetate film is low, so such yarns must be processed at low temperatures and the fabrics containing them must be washed and ironed at low temperatures. The polyester type of metallic yarns can go through regular processing, including wet and dry-finishing and dyeing without harm. Polyester film-decorated shoes can withstand vulcanizing without harm to the metallic yarn. The yarn can withstand bleaching but dry cleaners are advised to turn articles and garments with metallic yarns inside out when cleaning and processing. Metallics are insect, moth, mildew and rot resistant and completely non-toxic.

Uses

Metallics have been used in carpets and rugs, upholstery and drapery fabrics, slip covers, tablecloths and placements, towels, curtain fabrics, bedspreads, shower curtains and pillow cases. In the apparel field there are few items in which metallic yarns have not appeared. A large amount of metallic yarn goes into automotive upholstery. They also used to appear in radio and television set grills, theatre curtains and eye glass frames. The military uses them for radar scrambling, braids for uniforms, and as tow targets.

A whole new field of 'exotic' materials has arisen to meet the rigorous requirements associated with space exploration and other new developments. Experimental work is going ahead on all fronts. Glass and ceramic fibres, and metallic yarns are among the materials being tried out.

Rubber

Rubber belongs to a class of elastic polymer called elastomers. Yarns can be manufactured from naturally occurring or synthetic rubber. Although not a true thermoplastic, rubber is heat-sensitive and requires much the same care as the thermoplastic fibres.

Latex is a milky fluid obtained from the rubber tree by cutting its bark and collecting the fluid that oozes out. Ammonia and some other type of preservative are added and the latex is packed for sale. The principal sources of the liquid material are Malaysia and Indonesia.

In 1925, scientists at the U.S. Rubber Company discovered that raw rubber liquid could be extruded as a round thread of almost any desired fineness and then cured to maintain this shape. Latex is such a constructed rubber yarn around which are wound filaments of rayon, silk, wool, cotton or synthetics.

Round filaments of latex can be extruded as fine as human hair. The filament is coagulated in an acid bath and then vulcanized (given a permanent set) by means of heat aided by a catalyst. Latex vulcanization extends the life of latex rubber.

Latex yarn can be woven or knitted into fabrics in which elasticity and close conformance to the body is desired.

Latex fabrics have many useful properties, such as ability to stretch in all directions, and conform to the body's contours. The latex core will retain their elasticity throughout the useful life of the garment. The yarn can be even be made fine enough to be woven into such delicate fabrics as laces, nets, voiles and batistes.

The rubber of latex fabrics is not noticeable to the eye, and no odour is discernible. Latex is not affected by washing and can be pressed with a moderately warm iron. However, chlorine bleach turns the yarn yellow.

A thin coating of latex to the backs of rugs and carpets serves to prevent slipping and binds the yarns to the base. Latex is also used to cement garment seams, reinforce the seams of fur coats, close food containers and water-proof paper and fabric. Rubber slippers, raincoats and other water-proof articles are made from latex. Uses for latex also include foundation garments, the elastic hose tops of men's socks, surgical gloves bindings, swim suits and stretchable trimmings.

Alginates

Algin or alginic acid is a linear polymer derived from seaweeds and kelp. The viscous material extracted from these marine plants has many uses outside the textile industry, but around the turn of the century, British chemists managed to process it into filament yarns. Britain was the only country producing or using these yarns. Their use has now become redundant in the advent of the synthetic fibres.

Alginate fibres are produced in the following steps: (1) collecting, drying and milling the seaweed; (2) treating the material with sodium carbonate to produce a thick gelatinous mass of sodium alginate; (3) filtering the mass; (4) bleaching it with sodium hypochlorite; (5) spinning the filament on a viscose spinning system; and (6) coagulating it in a bath containing small amounts of calcium chloride, hydrochloric acid and a cationic agent to prevent filament adhesion.

Calcium alginate fibres have two notable properties: they are fire-resistant and dissolve quickly in very weak solutions of alkalis, even when washing with ordinary soap. It is this negative factor which made alginate fibres useful. They are spun with wool or other fibres or used as core yarns, woven or knitted into fabrics, then dissolved out in the finishing process, leaving shoer fabrics which were difficult to make otherwise. When alginate fibres are used in background fabrics for laces, embroideries, etc., they are washed out after the processes have been completed, leaving the open mesh lace and embroidery structure. Alginate yarns are also used as spacing yarns in open-patterned fabrics and washed out in the finishing process.

Alginate yarns were also used as a carrying yarn in hosiery and fabric mills, and as surgical dressings. Alginate acts as an agent that arrests bleeding, forming an absorbable film over the wound and accelerating the healing. Dentists sometimes use it to fill cavities after extracting teeth. This stops the bleeding, and the fibres left in eventually dissolve into the blood stream.

Paper Yarns

Paper is a cellulose fibre, and it can be cut into strips wet and twisted to make yarn that can then be woven or knitted like the yarns. Paper has also been used in non-woven form to make diapers and other disposable garments, particularly for hospitals. Woven paper yarn fabrics of open construction (webbing or matting), make brightly coloured, strong net bags for transporting fruits and vegetables, cord rugs, automobile seat cushions, hats and handbags.

Paper yarn fabrics take dyes readily and generally have good colour fastness. They are dimensionally stable. Their softness is controlled by the addition of wetting agents. Paper yarns cost less than half as much as cotton yarns of the same size.

Plastics

Saran and Velon are plastic yarns which can be woven like cotton and dyed in many colours. These yarns are very tough, flexible and resistant to wear, water, fire and chemicals. Although fabrics made from these yarns are easily cleaned with soap and water, they shrink excessively at high temperatures, causing the fabric to crumple with permanent wrinkles or folds.

Saran yarns make attractive upholstery and drapery fabrics, and are used for porch furniture. In apparel, they are used for belts, suspenders, handbags and shoes. One outstanding use for these yarns is as plastic window screens which are not affected by rust or extremes of climate.

4

From Fibre to Fabric

The principles of weaving were known very early, perhaps as long ago as 4,000 B.C. Our ancestors knew how to make baskets and mats by interlacing twigs, reeds and grasses. Later they learnt how to twist together short fibres, such as wool and cotton, to form yarn, and to weave the yarn into cloth on a loom. Primitive looms, were built around a convenient horizontal tree-branch, over which the warp threads were tied. The lower ends of the threads were fastened to stones to hold them in position.

Among the discoveries at Mohenjodaro are many needles of bronze and copper. The spinning wheels and other implements for spinning and weaving that have been excavated in the Indus valley are very much like those used today, indicating that finely-spun yarns were being manufactured.

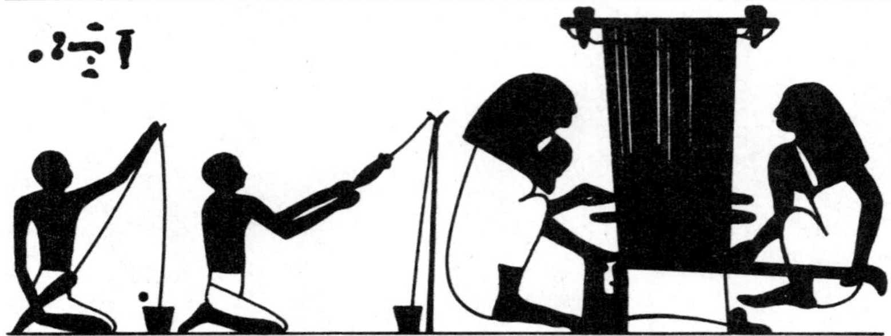

Fig. 4.1 Spinning and weaving in ancient Egypt (The loom appears to be vertical owing to the lack of perspective in the drawing.) (Photo: Science Museum, London)

The mummy cloths unearthed from the Pharoah's tombs in the pyramids bear witness to the fact that Egypt was another region where the art of weaving reached a high standard very early. (see Fig. 4.1)

Making Yarn

Fibre selection

The starting point of the weaving or knitting of fabrics and garments is the selection of a suitable yarn or thread. A yarn is a strand of fibres laid or twisted together by a process called spinning. Yarns may be made from any one or a mixture of the many different natural and man-made textile fibres. Each of these fibres has its own characteristic properties and each is therefore best suited for the particular end use of the woven cloth. Cotton is known for its absorbency, wool for warmth, silk for feel and appearance. In the range of man-made fibres, cellulosic rayon yarns are nearest to the natural fibres, although they cannot fully replace them. They have a silky feel and appearance. Similarly, the synthetic fibres have each their own intrinsic properties such as strength, lustre, crease resistance, handle and drape. Mixtures of these natural and man-made fibres have enabled the spinner to produce a still wider variety of yarns and fabrics for the domestic and industrial uses of today.

When a weaver selects a yarn for a fabric, he looks for such characteristics as thickness, evenness, cleanliness, strength, elasticity, twist, etc. Each of these properties may add to or impair the quality of the fabric required. In short, the first requirement for quality fabrics is the use of quality yarn.

Yarn classification

Yarn is usually made in two forms: long, continuous filaments, or short staple fibres twisted together.

In making staple yarns, loose and entangled fibres of varying lengths and thicknesses are first separated, cleaned and mixed for uniformity. The fibres are then straightened out, made parallel, drawn out into a ropelike form, and then further drawn into a thinner roving (sliver) and still further twisted in order to bind the fibres

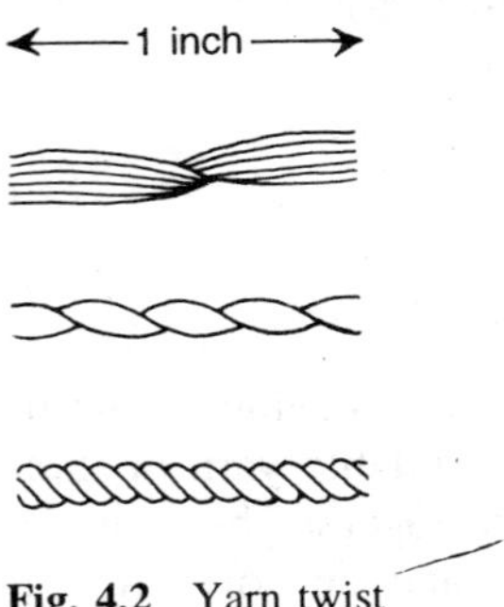

Fig. 4.2 Yarn twist

together and give the yarn strength. Depending on the number of fibres in the cross-section, and the fineness of the fibres, yarns may be spun coarser or finer to suit the qualities of cloth to be woven.

To carry out the various processes mentioned above, a wide range of different types of machines and a great variety of methods are used. Yarn-making could involve some or all of the process known as opening, mixing, carding, combing, drawing and spinning. The important physical properties of the end-product depend on how these processes are carried out. A hand-spun yarn, for instance, cannot be compared with machine-spun yarns, because of the limited number of processes and the crude methods that are used.

Most fabrics are made from yarns with ordinary twist. This is the amount necessary to hold the fibres close enough together to give strength to the yarn and prevent them from slipping apart. The amount of twist is measured by the number of twists per inch (tpi) a low twist is 0-3 tpi; an ordinary twist is 3-7 tpi; and a high twist is 7-12 tpi.

The twist may be made either to the right or to the left. If the yarn is twisted to the right, the fibres form a Z shape, while a left twist forms an S shape (see Fig. 4.3). Regular weaving yarns are usually Z-twist.

Yarns are also differentiated by the terms 'ordinary' and 'fancy.' Ordinary yarns are regular throughout their length in their physical properties. However, one ordinary yarn may differ from another in the material used, in fineness, strength, twist, appearance, etc. They are distinguished by numbers that indicate their fineness or thick-

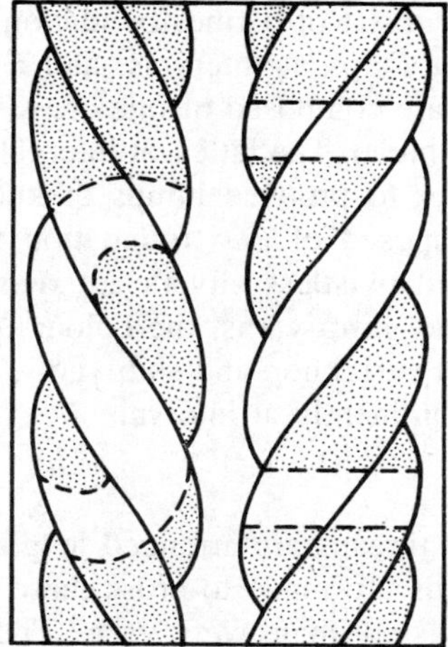

Fig. 4.3 S and Z twists

ness. These numbers are termed *counts* in the case of cotton yarns; *denier* in the case of silk, rayon and synthetics; and *skein* in the case of wool. A coarser yarn is generally stronger than a finer yarn. The strength and extensibility of yarns depend on the physical properties of the fibres, the number of fibres in the cross-section of the yarn and the number of turns or twists inserted in the spinning of the yarn.

A novelty or fancy yarn results

When yarns of different colours and thickness are twisted together without intimate intermingling of the fibres, so that each colour or yarn is seen separately. This breaks the continuity of the resultant yarn and produces effects which are out of the ordinary. Different counts, colours and even different materials are combined in various ways in these fancy yarns.

Many novelty yarns have names, and some of them are described below.

Grandrelle yarns are composed of two or more differently coloured threads twisted together. Spiral yarns have two threads twisted tightly together, and around them a soft spun thread is twisted spirally. Gimp yarns consist of a central hard-twisted thread and a soft-spun thread given in more rapidly than the centre thread. Curl or loop yarns consist of a fine foundation thread, a soft-spun thick thread forming loops at intervals, and a fine binder thread. Knop or knot yarns are composed of one or two foundation threads twisted with a third thread. The latter, at intervals, is wrapped round and round the former to produce lumps or knops. Cloud, slub or flake yarns are composed of two foundation threads with which pieces of short-fibred twistless slivers are twisted at intervals. In grandrelle, spiral, and gimp yarns, the colours of the yarns appear regularly, whereas in curl, knop and slub yarns, a separate colour of yarn can be seen prominently at intervals.

The parts of a loom

In a loom, the *warp* threads are arranged lengthwise, and the *weft, woof* or *filling* threads are made to cross these threads. Warp yarn is usually more twisted than weft yarn. The warp threads are mounted on a *weaving harness*, which is a frame consisting of a number of wires known as heddles (Fig. 4.4). Each heddle contains

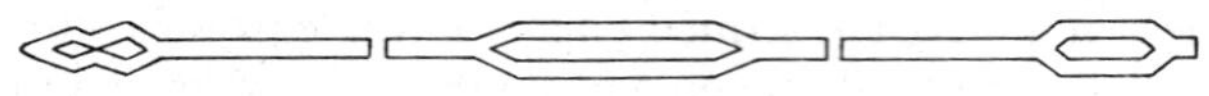

Fig. 4.4 A heddle

an eye through which one or more warp yarns pass. The harness controls the movement of the warp yarn upwards or downwards, and ensures the correct running of the films yarn over or below the warp yarn to produce the desired pattern. The Shuttle holds the filling yarn and is passed back and forth across the loom (Fig. 4.5).

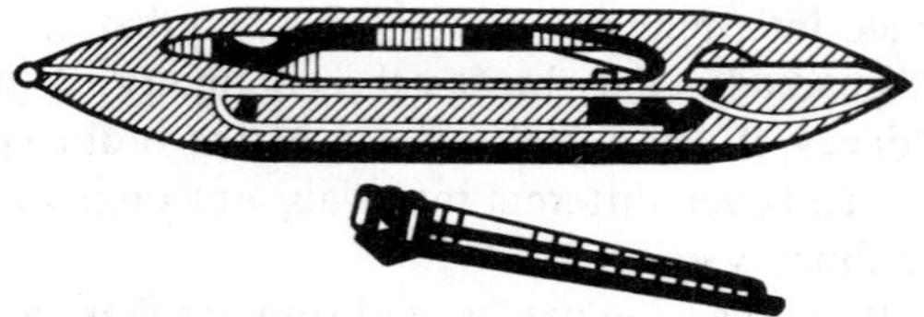

Fig. 4.5 A shuttle

The (Fig. 4.6) reed is a frame which is located directly in front of the harness. This frame pushes forward each time the shuttle

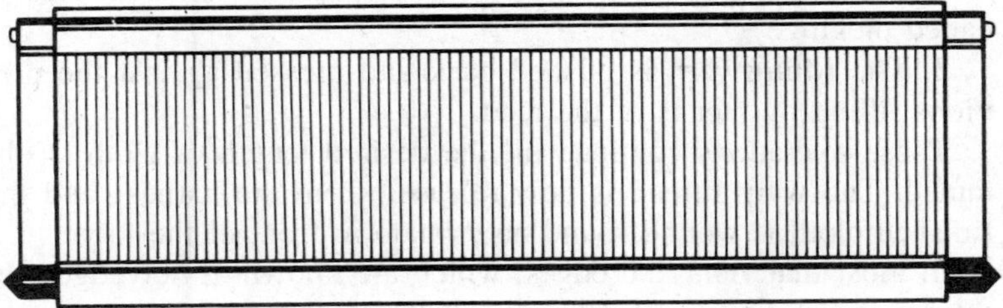

Fig. 4.6 A reed

passes in beteeen the warp yarns, and presses the filling thread back in position.

The sequence of operations carried out on a loom is as follows:

1. One of the harnesses raises a certain number of warp threads and forms a shed or passage for the shuttle to pass through (Fig. 4.7).

2. Passing backwards and forwards through the shed, the shuttle

Fig. 4.7 Throwing the shuttle through the shed

throws the filling yarn between the warp yarns. This process is called picking.

3. The filling yarn is pushed back and pressed against the previous filling by means of the reed.

These operations continue till the desired length of cloth is obtained. The warp thread is now released from the harness and the finished cloth is wound round on a beam in front of the loom.

In most materials, the edges, which are known as selvedges (or selvages) are made with heavier, more closely placed warp yarns, so that they do not unravel easily. The width of the selvedges is generally about one-fourth of an inch, except where it is utilised in a border, e.g., in saris. The warp yarn runs parallel to the selvedges.

Making the fabric

Yarn is turned into fabrics of garments by weaving, knitting or felting.

Weaving

Fabrics are woven in long lengths, from 40 to 100 or more yards, and from about 20 to 60 inches in width. The threads which extend through the length of the fabric are warp threads or *ends*, while those which go across are filling weft or woof threads (also called *picks*).

For a fabric to have strength and compactness combined with a fair degree of elasticity, the warp and filling threads, must be interlaced. This interlacing is called weaving, and it is done on a loom. An interlacing where the filling threads are passed alternately over and under the warp threads is called a plain weave. It is the simplest type of weave.

If the filling threads pass over one and under two or more warp threads, the result is a twill fabric. The surface of such a fabric has a pattern of parallel diagonal ridges. Depending on the weaving process the pattern produced will leave the fabric with a larger proportion of warp threads or a larger proportion of filling threads, showing on its surface. Thus we may make a warp twill or a filling twill fabric. If either the warp or the filling threads are considerably thicker, then a rib-type fabric will be produced.

There are a very large number of variations of the methods for interlacing the warp and filling threads, making it possible to weave a wide variety of fabrics, each of which has its own special properties and uses.

Prior to weaving, the warp threads are brought together side by side just as they would be in the fabric and then wound on to a beam or roller. The length of these threads must, of course, be approximately a multiple of the piece length. The filling thread is wound on tubes to form *cops*. Since the filling thread has to be moved between the warp threads in weaving, it is not possible to make these cops large. So a large number of cops have to be used one after the other in making a long length of fabric.

The beam of warp threads is placed at the back of the loom, and the threads are drawn from it across the loom from back to front to be wound on another roller. For the weaving of plain cloth, the threads are drawn through the eyes of two sets of heddles.

The filling threads pass over and under alternate warp threads, which are lifted and lowered by the corresponding heddles.

The cop with the filling threads in placed in a shuttle, which is moved or 'thrown' from side to side across the loom. Each pass of the shuttle lays one filling thread. The comb-like reed described earlier, beats the filling thread tight against the preceeding fill threads. As the fabric is woven, it is slowly wound on to a roller in front of the loom.

Mechanical loom-attachments called *bobbies* or *jacquards* are used to weave fabrics with complicated designs or lifting-order of the warp threads.

Although the plain weave is the simplest, it can be varied to produce quite a variety of fabrics by the selection of the yarns to be used as warp and filling and by the number of threads per inch or centimetre. The simplest plain cloth (such as long cloth) may be one whose construction is essentially square or balanced, with equal threads and counts of yarns in the warp and filling. A poplin, on the other hand, has more ends than picks in order to produce a ribbed effect. The use of coarser yarns in the filling makes the ribs even more pronounced. A plain fabric may also be varied to give stripes of greater density of warp ends, or by the addition of thicker threads, called cords. A plain weave may also be woven with very fine, medium or coarse yarns as required, each fabric being distinctly different. A voile fabric, for example, is an open, gauze-like fabric made with fine, specially spun and prepared yarns. It has a translucent look and is called a muslin.

There are many weaves of an elementary nature, each with its own distinctive value. Some weaves are bettter suited for fine fabrics, others to coarse fabrics.

It is very difficult to classify the vast number of weaves and their combinations which produce the different woven fabrics of today. The following list includes some of the most common weaves.

1. Plain, including (a) plain and tabby; (b) rib and (c) basket.
2. Floating, which covers the categories (a) twill; (b) satin; (c) huckaback; (d) honeycomb; (e) bird's eye; (f) crepe; (g) corduroy; and (h) velveteen.
3. Fabrics with woven-in pile, including (a) cut; (b) uncut; and (c) looped or terry-pile.
4. Jacquard patterned.
5. Leno.

Plain Weave fabrics are sometimes called cotton, taffeta or tabby weave. The filling yarn is simply passed alternately over and under one warp yarn. Plain weave fabrics have no wrong side. They are cheap and have great utility value. Some popular plain woven fabrics are gingham, voile, calico, muslin and taffeta.

There are two other weaves where the warp yarns are equally divided and are, therefore, regarded as variations of the plain weave. They are the rib and basket weaves; they make plain-weave fabrics more attractive.

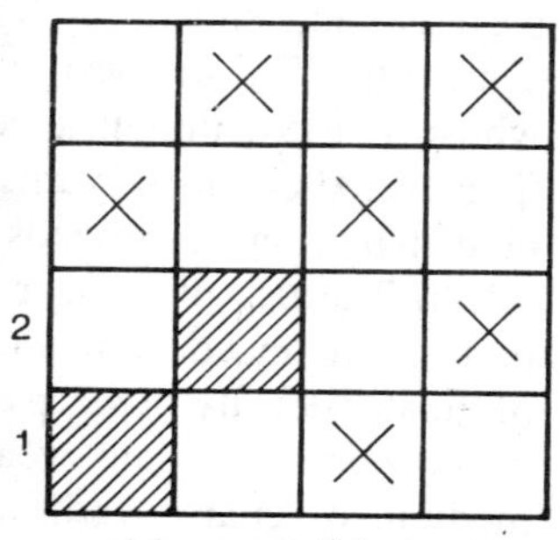

plain weave 2 harness, most widely used weave

Fig. 4.8 Plain weave

Rib-weave fabrics have a ridged surface. The ribs may be woven lengthwise or crosswise. If lengthwise, they lie in the direction of the warp and are formed by the filling yarns passing alternately over and under a group of warp yarns. This is called a filling-rib weave, and an example is rep (or repp). The Crosswise ribs, in the direction of the filling, are formed by the warp yarns passing alternately over and under a group of filling yarns. This is called a warp-rib weave, and poplin is an example.

Basket weave fabrics are made by passing two or more filling yarns over and under two or more warp yarns. The basket weave

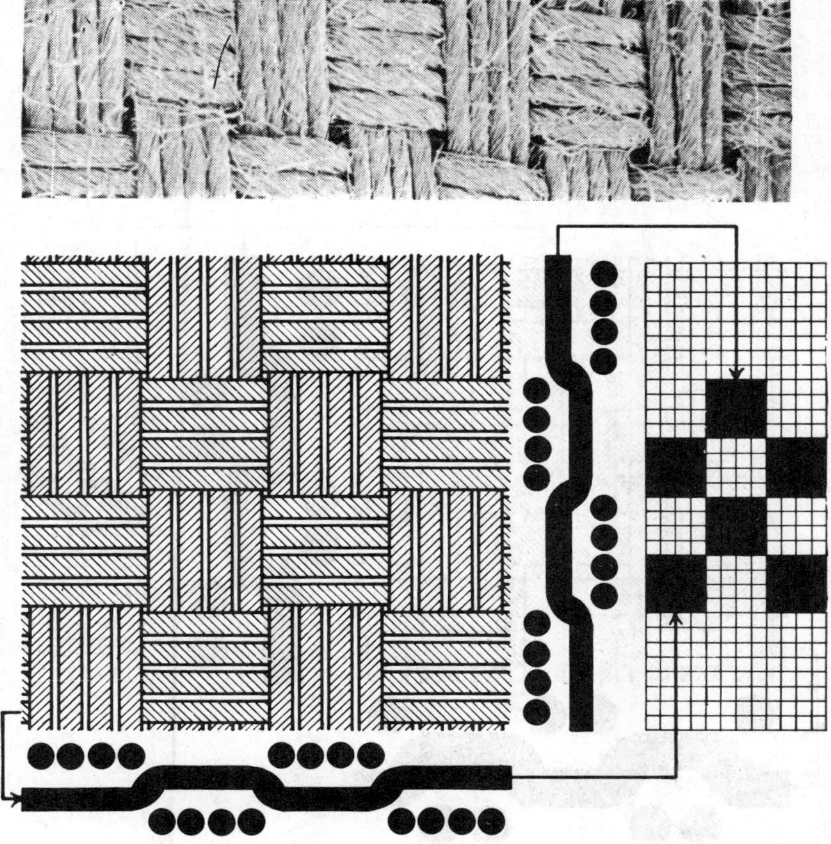

Fig. 4.9 Basket weave

may be three by three, four by four, or any other balanced arrangement (Fig. 4.9). Very attractive fabrics may be woven in plain, basket weave by the use of coloured yarns. This weave produces a rather loose fabric, like monk's cloth, sports coats or suits and dasooti.

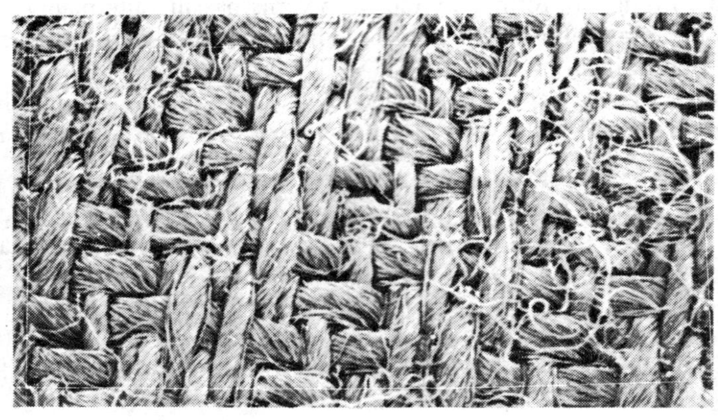

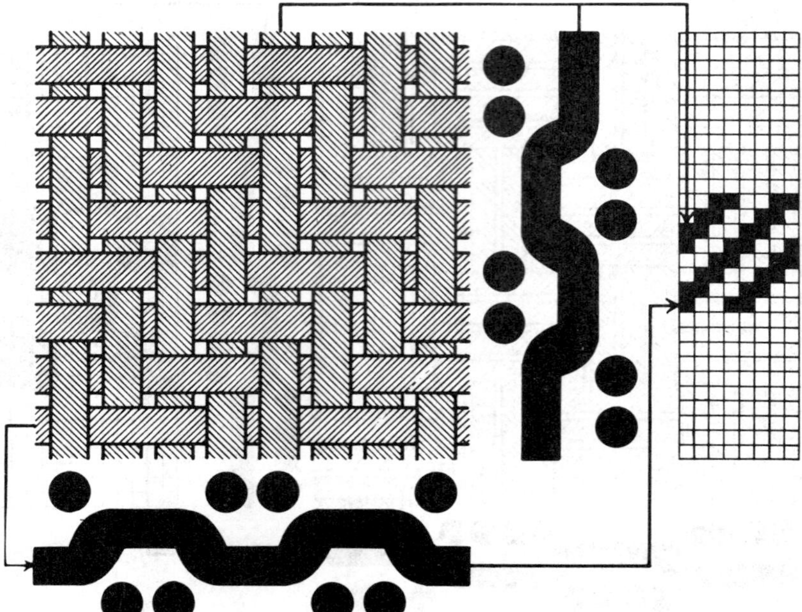

Fig. 4.10 Twill weave

Floating Weaves The wide range covered by this category are the most durable of weaves.

In **twill weave**, the filling yarns float over and under the warp yarns in regular patterns to form diagonal lines. Variations of the twill weave are herring-bone, broken twill and zigzag twill. Twill fabrics include gabardine, denim, drill, khaki and serge in cotton; table linen and towels in linen; cashmere, gabardine, tweed, worsteds and broadcloth in wool; and satin, twill and serge in silk.

Satin Weave produces a solid face on one side of the cloth so as to give it a smooth, lustrous surface. If more warp than weft yarns show on the surface, it is called a warp-face or satin weave. 'Satin' is the name of the weave as well the fabric woven in this weave. Satin originally referred to silk fabrics with the warp predominating on the surface.

Sateen Weave is the reverse of satin weave. That is if more filling yarns show on the surface it is called a filling-face or sateen weave.

Both satin and sateen constructions produce smooth, lustrous, rich-looking fabrics which can withstand a good deal of hard wear. Satin weaves can be done on many fibres. Silks, rayons and wools woven with warp satin-weave produces lustrous fabrics. Wool satin-weave fabrics are often napped. Cotton fabrics are more frequently woven with the sateen weave.

The **huckaback weave** is constructed with warp yarns floating on the face of the fabric. A typical repeat pattern of huckaback weave may have the first and second warp yarns floating over five filling yarns and, in the following five picks, the fifth and sixth warp yarns floating over five filling yarns. The remainder of the fabric is woven with a plain weave. The floating produces short, intermittent, lengthwise ridges.

In the **honeycomb weave**, a cell-like appearance is produced by floating yarns which form ridges. Both the warp and the filling yarns float on both sides of the material, giving a structure suitable for towels. Vertical lines are formed by the floating warp yarns, and horizontal lines by the floating filling yarns.

The **birds-eye weave** is constructed with filling yarns floating on the surface in a pattern of small diamond-shaped designs. The back of the fabric shows the warp yarns over which the filling yarns float.

This kind of woven-in design was originally made only with a dobby attachment.

Crêpe weave (crêpe meaning crinkled in French) gives fabrics a

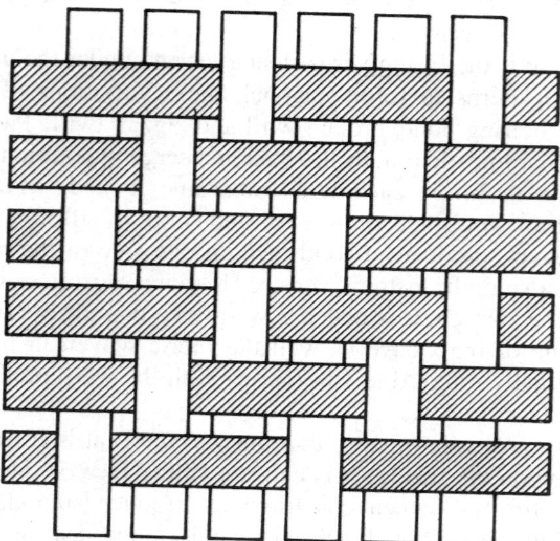

Fig. 4.11 Huckback weave

Fig. 4.12 Bird's eye or dobby-loom weave: diamond-shaped figures with dots in centre

pebbly surface. True crêpe is made by weaving highly twisted yarns alternately with a yarn of right hand twist and yarn that is used in the filling only, in the warp only or in both. They are made in a variety of weights, but mostly present a somewhat open appearance.

Although there are many kinds of crêpe, the principle is to have the floating yarns so placed that the fabric shows no twill, no striped effect and no long floats. The weave may be a variation of the plain or satin weave, but it is frequently a combination of the two. Wool, cotton, silk and synthetic can all be used to make crêpe.

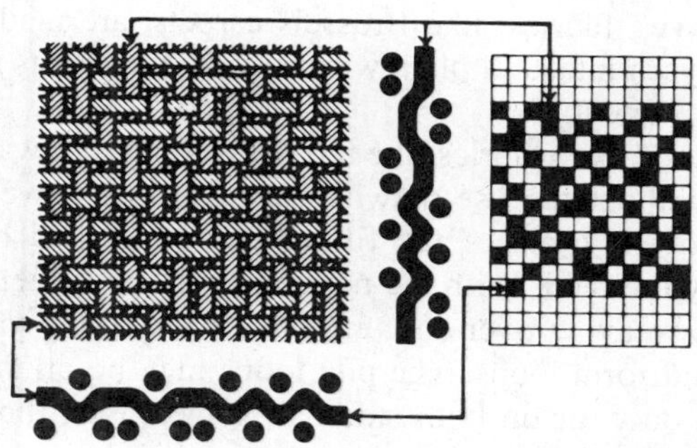

Fig. 4.13 Design and construction of a worsted crêpe weave

Corduroy weave fabrics consist of a ground and pile. The ground fabric is made with filling yarns weaving in a plain weave with the warp yarns. In the pile fabric, the filling yarns interlace with one, two, or three warp yarns, then float over three or more warp yarns, and this pattern is repeated. After the fabric is woven, the floating filling yarns are cut midway between the interlacings. The fabrics are then finished so that the pile forms cords or ridges. Suits, sportswear, drapery, bedspreads, and upholstery are some of the uses of corduroy.

The velveteen weave is similar to corduroy. The ground may be plain, twill or satin. The pile filling does not float uniformly as in corduroy, but are scattered. Velveteen leaves the loom as a flat fabric, which is taken to the cutting machine for the floating yarns to be cut. Since the floats are scattered, a cut pile is formed over the entire surface of the fabric. The length and number of floats determine the depth and closeness of the pile .

Woven-in Pile Weaves All the weaves described so far have either the warp or the filling yarns lying flat, in longitudinal and transverse parallel lines. Fabrics with woven-in pile, have a third set of yarns that stand upright. These include velvet, frieze, plush, turkish towelling, tapestry and carpets. The pile, which is formed with floating warp yarns, may be cut or remain in uncut loops. In all fabrics, the ground cloth is either plain, basket or twill.

In the *cut weave*, the pile is produced by weaving two fabrics simultaneously face to face, with pile warp yarns connecting the two. As the fabric is being woven, a knife cuts the connecting yarns which form the pile on both fabrics. Velvet and velveteen use this technique.

Uncut Weave fabrics, like Brussels carpets, are made by leaving connecting yarn intact. A plain wire is used; when it is removed, the loops remain uncut.

In looped or terry fabrics like terry towelling, the warp pile loops are raised without the use of wires, e.g., turkish towelling. As the fabric is woven, some of the filling yarns are held back and not beaten in by the reed. With the next pick, all are beaten in. The pile warp yarns, weaving over and under the back filling yarns, are also beaten in and form loops. The pile loops may be on the back only, on the face only, or on both sides. In some cases, the tufts of pile yarns are fastened in during the weaving of the warp and filling yarns. Carpets and rugs are woven this way.

Jacquard Patterned Weaves These weaves have elaborate woven-in designs. They are produced on a special type of loom first constructed in 1801 by the Frenchman Joseph Jacquard. The principle involved in these looms is numerical control using a tape or set of cards with holes. Tapes with different patterns of holes produce different weaves.

The Jacquard loom is complicated and expensive. It requires a room with a fairly high ceiling. Several weeks are needed to prepare a loom for a complicated new pattern, and the weaving operation is comparatively slow.

In a Jacquard weave the fabric may be as flat as damask, it may be raised, or it may have a cut or uncut pile. Examples of cloths made in Jacquard weave are damask, tapestry, brocade and terry cloth.

Leno Weave This weave is quite different from those described above. It is produced by means of a loom attachment called a leno (or lino). The weave looks like a figure eight, an effect that can be emphasized by drawing the filling yarns out of the fabric.

Fig. 4.14 Punched-card Jacquard loom

Leno is a strong durable weave. It is sometimes combined with plain or basket weaves to produce lace cloth. Mosquito netting also uses the leno construction.

Cloth counts and cloth balance

In most weaves the warp yarns are more closely spaced than the fillings. How close the warp and weft yarns are to each other may be estimated if the cloth is held up to a light. A more accurate method of ascertaining the closeness of a weave is to count the number of warp and weft yarns in a given area. The number of both warp and filling yarns per inch is known as the count of the cloth.

A *pick glass* is used to measure the count. It is a magnifying instrument that has an opening in its base, 1/4 inch square. In making the count, the warp and filling yarns are unravelled to make a square corner of the material. Pins may be used to indicate the points of measurement. The base of the pick glass is placed along the unravelled yarns that are exposed through the opening. The number of warp yarns exposed multiplied by 4 gives the warp per inch count Likewise, the number of filling yarns counted multiplied by 4 gives the filling count per inch. The more yarns to the inch, the higher the count of the cloth.

The count of a cloth will vary with the kind of fabric. In expressing counts, the number of warp threads is given first. If the count of a cloth is 100 warps and 100 fillings to an inch, the count is expressed as 100 × 100, or 100 square. An average count for surgical gauge is 28 × 24; for cotton sheeting, 74 × 66; for gingham, 96 × 88; and for linen, 121 × 96. Thus as the count of the yarn increases, the fineness also increases (i.e. the diameter of the yarn decreases). Conversely, as the count decreases, the fineness decreases meaning the yarn is coarser (thicker).

The ancient Egyptians wove very fine cloth. The linen cloth wrapped around one mummy was found to contain 549 warp yarns to the inch. The finest cloth woven today has only about 353 warp yarns to the inch.

The proportion of warp yarns to filling yarns is the *balance* of the cloth. If the number of warps and the number of the fillings per inch are nearly the same, a cloth is said to have good balance. A low count in either warp or filling shows a poor balance. For example, a piece of muslin with a thread count of 64 × 60 is considered well balanced, by contrast, a broadcloth with a count of 100 × 60 has poor balance. Materials having high count and balance wear longer and shrink less than those of loose texture and poor balance.

However, the balance alone does not mean that a cloth will wear well. The warp in such a cloth may be loosely twisted and not as coarse or as strong as the weft threads. The tensile strength of both sets of yarns must, therefore, always be taken into consideration when a fabric is being judged. Both yarn count and thread count (number of twists) determine the suitability and value of finished goods. Good balance is very important in fabric like sheets, pillow-slips and shirts that are washed often.

Knitting and knits

Instead of making fabrics by interlacing warp and weft threads on a loom, an alternative method is to make rows of stitches, each row hanging on the row behind and the row in front of it. This is the principle of simple knitted fabrics made either by hand or by machine.

The modern knitting machine is a complicated mechanism. A single operator attending to several such machines can produce fabric, socks, hose and garments shaped and patterned automatically and at great speed. A wide variety of knitting machines are used to make the different types of knitwear now available in the market.

The knitting machine has a number of evenly spaced hooked needles, the spacing being made proportional to the size of stitch. Needles arranged in a circle are used to knit socks and other kinds of tubular garments. If the needles are arranged in a straight row, then a single width of fabric is called a flat knit.

Knitted fabrics have the defect of easily laddering if even a single stitch breaks. This is very common in rayon and silk materials since their fibres are smooth. However, by knitting the fabric so that a locking thread moves through the different courses (rows), laddering can be prevented. Laddering does not occur with rougher, more hairy cotton and wool yarns because the projecting fibre ends get caught in the stitches and prevent their slipping through each other.

All knitted fabrics distort easily when pulled, but return to their original shape when released. For this reason knitwear is exceptionally suitable as underwear and outer garments that need to accommodate movements of the body. Rib knitting, which is similar to purl knitting by hand, is used to give knitwear even more elasticity. In ordinary knitting the thread is presented to the loops on the knitting needles always on the same side, and the freshly formed stitches are always drawn off the needles in the same direction. In rib knitting these movements change direction with every other stitch or with selected groups of stitches. The fabric which results has a ribbed appearance, and because of the rib is very elastic. The tops of men's socks are almost always ribbed. Ladies' garments, too, often have ribbed portions to make them fit the body more snugly.

Another knitting variation is the plaited knit. Here two threads are run simultaneously into the knitting machine in such a way that one of them predominates in the back of the fabric, while the other is mostly seen on the front. Thus if one thread is cotton and the other wool, the fabric can be made to look like a cotton fabric lined with wool or *vice versa*.

Lace

The lace industry employs quite another method of making fabrics out of yarn. It is more restricted in volume than weaving and knitting. The machines used are ingenious and complicated, but they cannot achieve the high volumes of the knitting and weaving industries.

The basic principle is that of having a large number of warp threads, as in weaving, and running filling threads, not straight across, over and under these warp threads, but twisted round them and moved across the fabric in a diagonal direction. This is how lace curtain fabrics are made.

Ornamental lace of the best quality is made with real silk threads as the ground work, and 'effect threads' of rayon or cotton. Such materials may then be dyed with contrasting colours.

Felt

Felt is not made with yarns at all,. but with loose fibres. When a layer of wool or fur is rubbed while wet or in the presence of steam, the fibres become entangled and interlock. This is called felting. It is the principle behind the method used to make felted fabrics. If the fibres are closed up enough, a compact fabric results in which the fibres are so tightly interlocked that it has sufficient strength to withstand considerable pulling about.

Rough felts are used for many domestic purposes, as in *numdhas*, but the best felts are made into men's felt hats. A modern application is in felt-tipped pens.

Finishes and Finishing Materials

A finish is defined as anything that is done to fibre, yarn or fabric to change its appearance. The finish often determines the fabric care required. Finishing alters the surface of a fabric and therefore its look and feel. Fabric finishing processses include scouring and bleaching, dyeing, printing, singering, tentering, calendering, sanforising, mercerising, schrienerising, moireing, weighing and embossing. These finishes may be applied in conjunction with, before, or after manufacture of the cloth.

As yarn and fabric come from the spinner, weaver or knitter, they are often in rough condition. The material may be harsh to handle and contain impurities, either those added to facilitate the manufacturing process, or impurities which are natural to the fibres. The material may also be soiled and have oil stains. In fact, materials fresh from their manufacture are referred to as being in a grey or brown state, after the colours they have at this stage. The finishing processes are required to make the materials attractive. They also improve their serviceability.

Scouring/purifying and bleaching

These operations remove impurities from the material (yarn or fabric) and leave it pure white. Both are wet processes. The substances and methods used are such that they dissolve or destroy impurities but do minimum damage to the material. Different fibres need different purifying agents and machinery, as do woven and knitted fabrics.

The impurities removed during scouring and bleaching are starches, fatty and oily substances, natural nitrogenous bodies, gums, mineral impurities and any natural colouring matter.

Rayons and synthetics are usually the cleanest, so their purification is relatively easy. Cotton is a fairly pure, clean fibre. But wool is the most impure. It contains a large proportion of wool fat. When this is removed and purified it forms the basis of a skin salve called lanoline. Wool also has perspiration residues from the sheep. Flax contains a large proportion of woody impurities, while raw silk has 20 to 30 per cent silk gum. Further, starch and oil impurities are introduced into all textiles to strengthen and lubricate the yarns as they pass through weaving and knitting machines.

Most of the starchy, nitrogenous and gum products are removed by treating the material with alkaline liquors, or with hot or boiling water. Cellulose fibres are resistant to alkalis and are therefore thoroughly boiled in solutions of sodium carbonate, or even caustic soda. On the other hand, wool and silk are sensitive to alkalis; the weaker alkali ammonia is used for them. Or they are saponified, i.e., converted into water-soluble soap. In both cases the impurities are washed out. Real silk is more resistant to alkalis than wool, so raw silk is boiled in a slightly alkaline soap solution to remove the silk gum sericin. Fats, waxes and oils are dissolved in hot, alkaline soap solutions, where they become emulsified. The natural colouring matters are usually resistant to these treatments and must be destroyed by oxidising substances, especially hydrogen peroxide, sodium hypochlorite or other substances containing active chlorline. Acid liquors help in removing mineral substances such as calcium and magnesium compounds.

Acid purification is likely to tender cellulose fibres even if warm, dilute acids are used. In contrast, wool or silk can be boiled in dilute acid solutions.

Rayons and synthetics are fairly white after manufacture. Scouring and bleaching them is therefore simply to remove the dirt accumulated during weaving or knitting. They are more sensitive to acids and alkalis than vegetable and animal fibres.

So far we have dealt with scouring. In most cases scouring leaves the material whiter than before by removing impurities. But this is not so in all cases. Cotton goods may become browner or yellower after scouring. Bleaching is the final treatment that removes the impurities, and the natural colouring matters left in the material produce a good white colour.

Silk and wool are bleached with hydrogen peroxide. All cellulose fibres and rayons can also be bleached with hydrogen peroxide, but just a good or white colour can be produced more cheaply with a solution of active chlorine. This solution is prepared by acidifying a solution of sodium hypochlorine, or by bubbling chlorine gas into water or lime water.

Dyeing and printing

Dyeing is employed to give solid shades all over the fibre, yarn or fabric. When two different fibres with different dyeing properties are used, two different shades may be obtained in one dyed shade by cross dyeing. Dyed shades are obtained by treating the material with a solution of a dye with affinity for the material. The dye liquor penetrates through the innermost parts of the yarn or fabric.

Modern methods of dyeing use pure standardised dyes made synthetically from coal tar and other products. There are thousands of these synthetic dyes, and they can be used to give shades of varying brightness and fastness. Dyes are classified according to their chemical structure, or acording to their affinities for different textile fibres. Generally there are special methods of application for each of these different classes of dyes.

The art of dyeing involves considerable skill, especially when shades of the highest degree of fastness are required. This problem is even more difficult when the yarn or fabric consists of a mixture of different fibres having different affinities for dyes.

To get more colourful effects than plain dyeing, fabrics are *printed.* Yarns, too, can be printed, but this is less common. Some of the common methods of printing are described below.

Block Printing, is the simplest method of printing a pattern on a fabric. It was known to the Chinese and Indians some two thousand years ago. It consists of carving a thick block of wood with a pattern in relief. This block is smeared with a colour paste and pressed on the fabric to transfer the coloured pattern.

Very fine patterns can be made, and the method is still used when exclusive patterns are required. But it has largely given way to machine printing, which is now used all over the world to produce printed fabrics in quantity.

Roller Printing was developed in 1785, about the time all textile operations were becoming mechanised. Roller printing can turn out colour designed fabrics in vast quantities, at the rate of thousands of yards an hour.

In the roller printing machine the fabric passes around a large central cylinder, which rotates with the moving fabric. Against the fabric and the central cylinder, press a number of colour-printing rollers, one for each colour. Thus if there are five colours in the design, there are five colour-printing rollers. Each of these copper rollers has engraved on it that portion of the pattern which is of one colour. Rotating against each colour-printing roller and importing the dye to it, is another roller, the colour furnishing roller, which dips into a trough containing the printing colour or paste. As the fabric moves past, each roller presses its part of the pattern on to the fabric continuously. After leaving the central cylinder, the fabric goes through drying and steaming chambers that fix the colours.

Roller printing machines can have up to fourteen colour-printing rollers, producing patterns in fourteen colours.

As described above, the machine prints only one side of the fabric. To print both sides, the central cylinder, its accompanying printing and furnishing rollers, etc., is duplicated. The fabric is printed first on one side, and then with the same pattern on the other side.

Roller or block printing can be used to print a multi-coloured pattern on white or slightly tinted fabrics. Other methods are used to print on dark fabrics.

In the **discharge** or **extract printing**, colour is expelled from the fabric to produce an attractive multicoloured pattern on backgrounds other than white. To produce a white pattern on, say, brown, the fabric is first dyed with a brown ground shade. Then it is printed with a paste containing chemicals capable of bleaching the brown colour to white. Such a paste is called a discharge paste. Discharge prints are found on cottons and rayons and in some patterned silk with dark backgrounds. However, the chemicals that discharge the dye tend to weaken the fabric in the area of the design. Discharge-printed fabrics should be avoided if they are intended for long-term wear.

In **resist printing** a white fabric is first printed with a paste containing a substance that will prevent or resist the fixation of the dyes that are to be subsequently applied. It is then dried and padded all over with a colour paste containing one or more of these dyes. On drying and steaming, the padded-on dye is fixed everywhere except where the resist pattern has been printed. After washing off any non-fixed dyes, the result is again a white pattern on a coloured ground.

Screen Printing is the development of a process called stencil printing. The stencils are replaced by silk or stainless, wire-mesh fabric fastened to a wooden frame. The screen is coated with a varnish of hardened gelatin, but left unvarnished (or open) in the parts forming the pattern. A separate screen is required for each colour.

The fabric is laid flat in open width, and an operator places the screen on it, forcing a colour paste through with a brush. The screen is then lifted and placed on the next location along the length where its portion of the pattern occurs. Other operators follow the first with screens for the second, third, or more colours of the pattern, until the fabric is completely covered with the pattern. It is then steamed as in roller printing. Screen printing is good for short fabric runs. The screens are inexpensive to prepare, and up to sixteen colours are possible in one pattern. Also, new patterns can be produced quickly by this method. Many people consider screen printed fabrics more pleasing than roller prints.

Pigment Printing is a recent development. It originated in America, where it known as the Aridye process. This method uses pigment dyes, that are water insoluble and very fast to light, ironing and other adverse influences. The pigments are made into a colour-printing paste using, among other ingradients, a synthetic resin to act as a binder to the fabric. The pastes are printed to the fabric by any of the usual methods, such as roller or screen printing, but here the fabric is heated to bind the pigment.

Finishing

Fabrics or garments generally have to be finished to make the material presentable and attractive. It is often the finish which increases the sale value of textile goods. Finish is usually applied to fabrics. The yarns themselves are not finished before being woven or knitted. However, hand-knitting yarns are twisted into skins or balls before sale for home use. The wet processes of scouring, bleaching, dyeing and printing leave fabrics in a distorted condition. One of the important functions of finishing is to straighten the fabric and bring it to the required dimensions.

Dyeing is sometimes considered part of the finishing process. It can sometimes be carried out at the same time that the fabric is straightened and brought to its desired finish, width and length. For other processes, the fabric must be be dried first and then lightly damped for the final finishing treatment. The most common finishing processes are listed below. The list is not a sequence, nor are all the processes used on all kinds of grey fabrics. Some fabrics go through more than one process, while each fabric is given its own characteristic finish.

Singeing The object of singeing is to remove the short fibres from cloth coming off a loom. The cloth is first passed over one or two steam-heated copper cylinders to remove moisture and to raise a nap. The projecting fibres are then singed (burnt) by passing the cloth over a hot plate or through a gas flame at high speed, leaving the cloth with a smooth surface.

Tentering To bring a fabric to the right width, it is passed through a 20-90ft. long tentering machine. The cloth is carried through the machine by two moving chains of clips or pins, one on each side, which grip the selvedge firmly.

Tentering is an important and necessary operation because the fabric has been pulled in length during bleaching, dyeing and drying, and is therefore generally narrower than the required finished width. During the operation, the clip chains diverge from the entry end for about one quarter or slightly less than the length of the machine. As the cloth is carried forward, gripped on either side, it is gradually widened. In order that this stretching may take place easily, the cloth is slightly dampened or steamed. After stretching, it is passed through a hot-air chamber to dry and set at this width.

Calendering Calendering is essentially an ironing process. Most fabrics (and yarns, too) become stiff, board-like when wetted and dried under tension. Running the fabric through a calender removes the stiffness and makes it quite soft. At the same time, calendering flattens the fabric and makes it more lustrous. The process consists of applying a lot of pressure by passing the cloth through the nips of heavily-weighted bowls of compressed cotton and steel. Rayon fabrics are not calendered as heavily as cotton or linen, but silk fabrics often require fairly heavy calendering. Some calenders use waxy substances to give added lustre in addition to friction treatment by steam-heated pressure bowls.

Calendering flattens and closes the threads of the fabric to give it the required smooth feel and appearance. The finish depends chiefly on pressure, temperature and moisture.

Sanforising After weaving or knitting, the interlaced threads of a fabric are in a state of strain, i.e, they are stretched. Therefore, freshly made fabrics are not stable—they are larger than they would be if the strains were relieved. Calendering and other finishing processes further stretch a cloth. Furnishing fabrics are sometimes deliberately stretched to make them longer or wider.

Modern fabrics and garments must not only be well-finished; they should not shrink on washing, or at least shrink only within reasonable limits. The fabric therefore undergoes a process called sanforising, by which its stretch is closed up without spoiling the finish. It is contracted in length by passing the puckered cloth between a blanket and a large steam-heated metal cylinder. As the fabric passes around the cylinder, pressing against the blanket, it is set and smoothed in its closed-up state.

Mercerising Applying caustic soda under controlled conditions, this process gives cotton fabrics a silky lustre and beautiful sheen.

It also gives the cloth greater affinity for colouring matters, especially deeper, brighter shades with dyestuff.

The cloth is impregnated with an 18 to 20 per cent solution of caustic soda for one-half to two minutes at room temperature. The cloth is stretched while saturated and then washed out while it is still under tension. This treatment produces a permanent change in the structure of the cotton fibre.

Schreinerizing Schreinerizing is an inexpensive method of imparting lustre to low priced cottons. The fabric is pressed between steel rollers engraved with fine lines, giving it between 125 and 600 diagonal ridges per inch. When light reflects off these ridges the fabric looks lustrous, like mercerized fabrics. But the lustre is not permanent, because the imprinted ridges reduces the tendency of the fabrics to cling. If the fabric has also been mercerized, the additional Schreinerizing produces a lustre like that of silk.

Moireing A watery moire effect (from the French *moirer*, watered) is sometimes given to cotton fabrics on a calendering machine. Fine engraved lines on the rollers, and special ways of running the fabric around the rollers, produce the effect. The lustre is caused by the divergent reflections of light on the lines of the design.

Weighting Fabrics are sometimes weighted to give them additional body.

The weight and body of the silk fabric is increased by immersing it in a solution containing metallic salts. The salts permeate the yarns and become a permanent part of the fabric but cannot be detected by handling. However, if excessive metallic salts are used, the fabric is eventually weakened.

Only low-grade wool fabrics are weighted. Magnesium chloride makes a woollen fabric absorb more moisture, increasing its weight.

In India, cotton (especially sheets) is often weighted by being heavily starched e.g., sheeting. Fabrics weighted this way feel very compact, but rubbing the fabric between the hands will cause the dry starch to fall out.

Embossing This process produces raised figures or designs in relief on the surfaces of fabrics by passing the cloth through resin and then pressing in the design with engraved rollers. The designs may be large, floral or geor..etric, and of one or more colours. The colour and resin can be added at the same time. The process can be applied to all types of fabrics except wool. The finish is permanent when applied to fabrics made of thermoplastic fibres. It is not permanent on untreated fabrics made of natural fibres or synthetic, non-thermoplastic fibres, except with certain chemical resins. To preserve the embossed finish of such fabrics, they should be washed in lukewarm water with a mild soap, never bleached, or ironed on the wrong side while damp.

Anti-creasing The anti-crease process is exceptionally useful for viscose rayon. Not only is it made resistant to creasing, but also given fuller handle and better appearance.

The anti-crease process is not suitable for acetate rayon, and is not used for wool or silk. The latter are already sufficiently crease-resistant.

Waterproofing Waterproofing is done by coating fabrics. For rough, heavy-duty fabrics like tarpaulins, the coating compound is made of tar products, which are cheap and can be thickly applied.But with fabrics that are to be worn, such as raincoats, a softer handle is necessary.

One method of waterproofing garments is to coat one side with a layer of rubber or, increasingly, a synthetic resin. This makes the fabric resistant to water but also impervious to air, so that moist air from the body cannot escape. Rubber-treated garments are also adversely affected by grease and oil.

A better method is to deposit an insoluble, somewhat greasy aluminium soap on the fabric. This makes it permeable to air but not to water. In an improved version, an emulsion of the aluminium soap is applied to the fabric and dried into it.

The terms waterproof and water-repellant are often used interchangeably, but they have different meanings technically. A waterproof fabric is one which no water can penetrate. A water-repellant fabric is resistant to wetting, but if the water comes on it with enough force, it will penetrate the fabric. The following table enumerate the differences.

Water proof fabrics	Water-repellant fabrics
Extruded fabrics or low-count fabrics with a finish which coats the fabric, filling the spaces between the yarns.	High-count fabrics with a finish which coats the yarns but does not fill up the interstices of the fabric.
Fabrics are stiff, not pliable.	Fabrics are pliable, and are not different from untreated fabrics.

Cheaper to produce.	Fabrics which can 'breathe' are comfortable for raincoats.
Permanent finish.	Durable or renewable finish.

It is more difficult to select a water-repellant garment than a waterproof one because the finish is not obvious, and one must depend on the label for information. However, some guidelines that may be followed are: (1) The cloth construction is far more important than the finish. The closer the weave, the greater the resistance to water penetration. (2) The kind of finish used is important in selection because it influences maintanance costs. (3) Two layers of fabric give increased protection. Two layers are especially useful across the shoulders, but the inner layer must also have a water-repellant finish, otherwise it will act as a blotter and cause more water to penetrate.

Moth-proofing Wool is far more readily attacked by moths than other fabrics. The wool fibres are not eaten by the moths themselves, but by their larvae which hatch out the eggs laid in the material by the moths. Being a complex protein, wool is excellent food for the larvae. They would starve on cotton or linen fibres. The holes left in the material by these grubs give woollens attacked by them a characteristic, moth-eaten look.

Two of the means of controlling moth damage are cold storage and contact poisons like moth balls. Fluorides and silicofluoride finishes are also used on wool. They are fast to dry cleaning, but not fast to washing. Another method is to chemically change the fibre to make it unpalatable to the larvae. These chemicals are added during the dyeing process, they are fast both to washing and dry-cleaning. The chapter on storage has more details on moth protection in the home.

Mildew-proofing Mildew is a fungus. Clothes are susceptible to it in warm, damp conditions. During finishing, a sticky, gelatinous substance called *size* is sometimes applied to the surface of a fabric to stiffen it. Sizing, however, increases the fabrics susceptibility to mildew.

To prevent mildew, inorganic salts such as magnesium chloride, calcium chloride and zinc chloride are used on the yarns as warp sizing. More recently, turpentine and formaldehyde are being used as preventives.

The following household recipe gives good results. Mix 1½ ounces of cadmium chloride (a poison, so use it carefully) in a gallon of hot water. Wash the article with a neutral soap. Do not rinse out the soap. Apply the solution to the fabric. This finish will withstand several such launderings.

Antiseptics, such as boric acid and carbolic acid, also prevent rapid growth of the mildew fungus.

Flame-proofing Fabrics cannot be made absolutely fireproof, but they can be chemically treated to retard inflammability. Flame-proofing is a practical form of fire protection for fabrics used in awnings, matresses, work clothes or draperies.

Textile fabrics may be made fire-resistant by a simple home method. Immerse them in a solution of 7 ounces of borax and 3 ounces of boric acid in 2 quarts of hot water. Wring and dry. Press with a cool iron, (Heat reduces the effectiveness of the finish). This method does not alter the appearance of the fabric, but the treatment must be repeated after each wash.

Durable fire-retardant finishes use chemicals that either precipitate on to the fibres or react chemically with them to add fire-retardant properties. Most of them tend to stiffen the fabric.

Mixed and Blended Fabrics

The combining of fibres in weaving with warp yarns made of one type of fibre and filling yarns of another is an old practice. The trend to combine two or more fibres in one fabric has increased with the advent of synthetic fibres, and is being done more and more scientifically. Blends and mixtures are successfully used in all types of fabrics to make better undergarments, sweaters, shirts, suits, drapery, blankets, work clothes, rainwear, children's wear, sports wear, etc.

Mixed or mixture fabrics are those made up of two or more different kinds of yarns, each of which is composed of only one kind of fibre. The yarns themselves may be made of filament or staple length fibres.

Blended fabrics are made up of yarns in which two or more different kinds of fibres are spun together. Also, various types of monofilaments or filament yarns may be combined or twisted together to form a combination filament yarn.

A mixed or blended fabric can have a larger number of desirable characteristics than one using a single fibre. It can be given increased absorbency, comfort, fastness to light, greater resistance to abrasion, wrinkle resistance, strength, elasticity, resiliency, dimensional stability, fabric attractiveness, better texture, drape and softness, reduced tendency to pilling, mildew, bacterial growth and static electricity accumulation, wider mixtures of colours and designs, permanent pleating, embossing, printing and other special effects. In short, the fabric improves in appearance, behaviour and utility, and becomes cheaper, easier to care for.

When cellulosic fibres are included in the mixture or blend, we get increased absorbency and comfort, decreased static electricity accumulation and pilling, increased washability and greater affinity for dyestuffs and chemicals in finishing. Thermoplastic fibres are used to improve crease resistance, shape retention, abrasion resistance, strength in elongation, drying time, ease in ironing, pleating, etc. Rayon-cotton helps keep costs low, and increases absorbency and washability. Nylon improves toughness and abrasion resistance; terylene improves wrinkle resistance; acetate improves drape texture and resistance to wrinkles.

Some problems with mixtures and blends

Fibres differ in their specific density, length, diameter, texture and hygroscopy (affinity for water). These differences make blending a tough job for manufacturers. It has also been observed that variations can occur both along the length of the blended yarn and from the inside to the outer edges of the fabric. The longer fibres tend to travel towards the centre of the fabric, while the short fibres more towards the outside edges. This is mostly an undesirable characteristic. Also, some fibres (such as the synthetics) may cut others (such as soft cotton). Blends and mixtures cause problems during dyeing and finishing, too, requiring special equipment and handling.

In the care of blends and mixtures, detailed labelling on the fabrics is a must. In its absence, good knowledge of the properties of the fibres is very useful. There is no general procedure; the care of each blend or mixture depends on the particular fibres and finishes that have been used. A safe, beginning procedure is to apply the care required by the most sensitive of the fibres used in the combination.

5

Indigenous and Synthetic Dyes

Traditional Colours of India

In terms of the fabrics used in the old days, India used to be the colour-box of the world, using the earliest natural dyestuffs known to man. Indigo, the 'king of dyes', for blue; madder, lac, safflower and sandalwood for red, cutch for brown; turmeric and saffron for yellow, and many other dyes were known. After the European discovery of the sea route to India, these colours became more widely known, contributing to the image of Indian women in colourful saris, and Indian men wearing bright turbans and *lungis*.

Colour in the past, and perhaps even today in rural India was considered a spiritual necessity, of equal importance to food. Every colour had its significance, and the design, whether mythological or natural, human or floral, its hidden meaning. Blue was a symbol of vitality, it conveyed a sense of splendour. Red indicated joy, happiness, life, truth, virtue and sincerity, an auspicious colour for brides. Rose was the emblem of divine wisdom, and green denoted immortality to the Muslims.

The seasons too, had their own favourite colours—lime green for early summer, and saffron for spring, when the mustard is in full bloom. Even today, many Indian girls dye their saris and dupattas yellow, for the Basant (spring) festival, yellow being another colour traditionally associated with sunshine.

In Rajasthan, the technique of double-dyeing results in different colours on either side of a fabric. These colourful patterns have names: *agnipat* (used to make flame-coloured saris), *meghdambar* (dark clouds), *mayurpankam* (peacock feathers, and *asman-tara* (starlit sky). *Ikat* and *patola*, fabrics use another traditional skill of the Indian *rangrez* (dyer) and *chipigar* (printer): tie-dyeing the yarn before weaving.

Coloured and printed fabrics from India were exported to Europe up to the nineteenth century. They went under the names chidney, chint, palampore (palangposh), Coromandel, Gujarat, Golconda, Mosulipatam and Agra, the latter being the centres where the fabrics were made. But like most arts in India, the craft of dyeing, too, was hereditary. The secrets of extracting dyes were known only to a few and passed down by word of mouth. As with any industry that is not standardised, the old dyes finally made way for the cheaper coal-tar dyes of the West. Today, although rural printers still follow the old process, as the dyes in use are mostly synthetic. However, a few old secrets are still known to the hill tribes, who make wonderful dyes for their fabrics from herbs, leaves and the roots of plants.

Some of India's traditional dyes are described below, using information complied by the I.W.S. and Lady Irwin College, New Delhi. Some of their dyes can even be tried at home.

Cutch, found in Chota Nagpur, Maharashtra and other places, goes by the local names *khair*, *khair-labul* and *katha*.

Indigo, also called *nila*, is grown in Bihar, Tamil Nadu, U.P. and Assam.

Majeeth (*manjit*) is found in Sikkim and Assam.

Pomegranate rinds are used for dyes in east Punjab, Kashmir and Almora district in U.P. Its local names include *anar*, *dhalum* and *dharim*.

Tessoo is abundant in U.P. and Bihar, where it is also called *dhak plas*, *Tesoka-phul* and *kakria*.

Turmeric (*haldi*) is mainly grown in Tamil Nadu.

Walnut rinds (*akhrot*) are used as dyes in the temperate parts of India—Himachal Pradesh, Kashmir and Almora in U.P.

These dyes are applied to fabrics either directly or after the material has been *mordanted*. A mordant is a substance that fixes the dye to the fabric. Fabrics can also be 'developed' with a mordant after dyeing them directly. The table below lists the colours that can be obtained with the natural Indian dyes.

Another traditional dye is henna, the product of a plant widely grown in India. Although mainly employed as a hair-colouring and

INDIGENOUS DYES OF INDIA

Serial No.	*Dye*	*Textile fibre Suitable for*	*Shades obtained by direct dyeing and on development*	*Shades obtained on mordanted material*	*Fastness remarks*	*Local name*	*Where found*
1	Cutch	Cotton, Silk, Wool	Reddish brown (Cr) Deep brown (Cu-Cr) Deep reddish brown (Al-Cr) Dull pinkish brown (Fe-Cr)		Shades are fast to soaping, perspiration and moderately fast to light	Khair, Khair Labul, Katha	Most places in India; Chota Nagpur, Bombay Province
2	Indigo	Cotton, Wool	Blue, yellowish to blueish green when topped with Turmeric on Pomegranate rind		The blue shades are fast to washing, perspiration and light. The green (Turmeric) are poor in fastness but with rind are of moderatefastness	Nila, Indigo	Bihar, Madras, Oudh, Assam
3	Majeeth	Cotton, Wool	Red (Al)	Pinkish red (Al) Crimson to dull red (Cr) Maroon to reddish brown (Fe) Reddish orange (Sn) Brick brown (oxalic acid 8%)		Manjit, Manjith, Manjeeth	Sikkim, Assam

4	Pomegr-anate Rind	Silk, Wool, Cotton	Golden brown (Cr) Straw yellow (Al) Greyish to deep black (Fe) Dark brown (Fe-Cu-Cr) Khaki (Fe-r)	Old Gold (Cr); Yell-owish Brown (Al-Cr); Chocolate brown 8% Oxalic acid: Dove grey 2% Potassium dichr-omate; Old gold with Tinchloride acidified with sulphuric acid	Fast to soaping Diluted acids, diluted alkalies, perspiration and to light. Black only moderately fast	Anar-ka-per, Dhalum Dharm	E. Punjab, Kashmir, Almora
5	Tessoo	Silk, Wool, Cotton	Yellow Clay brown 2% Pot. dichromate. Light Grey 2% aluminium sulphate	Bright Organge (Al) Terra Cotta (Cr) Bright yellow (Sn)	Shades are not quite fast and are fleeting	Dhak Pas, Teso-ka-phul, Kakria	Most places in India: U.P. & Bihar abundance
6	Turmeric	Cotton Silk, Wool	Yellow, Lemon yellow (Bleaching powder)	Bright Yellow (Al) Bright Orangish Yellow (Sn); Olive (Fe); Green (Topped with Indigo)	Moderate fastness to neutral soaping; poor to alkali	Haldi	Madras Presidency
7	Walnut Rind	Cotton Silk, Wool	Warm brown (Cr) Drk brown (Fe-Cr); Olive brown (Fe); Deep brown (Cu-Cr); Full bright Brown (Al-Cr); Dark olive	Bright reddish Brown (Al) Yellowish Brown (Cr)	Very fast to soaping, only moderately fast to light	Akhrot Akrot	Temperate Himalaysa Kashmir, Almora

Mordanting Key: Al: Alum; Cr: Bichromate of soda; Cu: Copper Sulphate; Fe: Iron sulphate; Cu-Cr: Bichromate of Potash and Copper Sulphate; Sn: Tin Chloride; Fe—Cu: Ferrous Sulphate and Copper Sulphate.—(*Courtesy:* I.W.S. and Lady Irwin College)

in make-up, it has also been used to dye textiles. Henna is inexpensive; colours obtained from it are moderately fast, and able to withstand quite a lot of washing, chlorine bleaching and light. As little as one kilogram of henna leaves can yield a substantial amount of colouring matter. The dyeing solution is obtained by soaking crushed henna leaves in water, sieving it through a piece of cloth, mixing it with a small quantity of dilute acetic acid and heating the mixture so obtained. A large variety of colours can be made this way, ranging from reddish- brown to mildly brownish-yellow.

Artificial dyes

Today coal tar derived dyes are available for every sort of article. They can be made fast to sunlight, artifical light, water, perspiration, friction and washing processes. However, the perfect dye, which is totally fast, has yet to be produced.

The artificial dyes are grouped into six main categories:

(1) direct cotton dyes or salt; (2) basic dyes; (3) acid dyes; (4) sulphur dyes; (5) mordant dyes; and (6) vat dyes.

Direct cotton dyes, acid dyes and **basic dyes** possess the common property of dyeing cotton cellulose rayons, linen, silk and nylon in full shades without the help of mordants. They are dyed from neutral or slightly alkaline baths with the addition of common salt or Glauber's salt (crystalline hydrated sodium sulphate). Direct dyes have a wide colour range, but do not produce the brilliant colours of acid dyes. They are cheap, but generally bleed or run, and in general are not suitable for washable material or fabrics exposed to bright daylight. But they can be used for evening wear, since they give very bright and pleasing colours.

Sulphur dyes are very fast to washing and perspiration, but not satisfactorily fast to light and not fast to chlorine bleach. They are dyed at or near boiling point. They are used on cotton, linen, mercerized cotton and cellulose rayons. A commonly used set of sulphur dyes are the thionol series: blue, yellow, green, violet, khaki, maroon, grey and black.

Mordant dyes are generally very fast to light, washing and acids. They are excellent for animal fibres, but used only occassionally on vegetable fibres. Mordant dyes are treated with solutions of metal salts e.g., these of iron, chromium or aluminium, which fix the dyes in the fabrics. Most fast colours on wool are obtained by mordanting. Other mordants are tannic acid and Turkey red oil.

Vat dyes form a very important class of colours, possessing excellent fastness and durability. These dyes are not soluble in water, and must be chemically treated before they can be applied in solution. A hot alkaline solution of a powerful reducing agent, such as sodium hydrosulphite is used. This converts the dye into a colourless, soluble form which can be taken up by the fabric. Upon exposing the cloth to air or treatment with a suitable chemical, the colourless material is oxidized to the coloured form. Indigo is a well-known example of this type of dye. Vat dyes are used on fabrics which will receive hard wear, sunlight exposure and frequent washings. As a class, they outrank any other dye. The coloured borders of towels, table cloths, table napkins, etc., are generally dyed with vat dyes, as they can withstand bleaching (with oxidizing bleaches). But boiling in a solution of soda may cause the dye to mark on to white portions. It is now possible to apply vat dyes to all types of fibres. (For simple home-dyeing, see Chapter 28).

Technically, dyes are distinguished from pigments. The following table illustrate this.

Differences between dyes and pigments

Dyes	Pigments
Small substances which are soluble.	Opaque, colloidal particles.
Penetrate into the fibre and combine chemically with it.	Attach to the fabric do not combine chemically with the fibres.
Dyes must have an affinity for the fibre. Fibres of like chemical composition will take the same dyes. Fibres which are not absorbent are treated to swell them before dyeing.	Pigments are carried by resins which are set on the fibres by heat.
Different dyes react differently to the destructive influences of light, washing, etc.	Different pigments react differently to the destructive influences of light, perspiration, etc.

The care of coloured fabrics

Since no dye, natural or synthetic, is perfect, the following points must be noted when washing coloured articles.

1. Colours are not always fast.

2. Colours are affected by chemical agents.
3. Different colours in one article may behave in different ways.

Although it is not possible for everyone to be an expert on dyes and dyed fabrics, the following general ideas will help in the care of coloured articles.

It is useful to observe how the fabric has been coloured:

1. Coloured yarn may have been used.
2. The fabric may have been dyed after manufacture.
3. A printing process may have produced the coloured pattern.
4. The coloured pattern may be embroidered on to the fabric.

Generally fabrics woven or knitted with coloured yarn do not run, and are the fastest fabrics while those dyed after manufacture may run.

In dyeing cotton fabrics at home, salt or vinegar is added to the dye bath to exhaust the colour, i.e. to get better dye penetration. But there is no firm evidence for this. If colour is to be permanent to washing, it must be set in a factory dyeing process.

Colours that do not bleed under ordinary laundering conditions may do so when kept wet too long. It is not a good idea to roll wet fabrics in a towel and leave them for long periods, or to wash coloured fabrics on a damp day when they will not dry quickly. Bleeding occurs with rayon and acetate more often than with cotton.

Knit fabrics (such as jerseys) are usually screen printed; they stretch so much in roller printing that the designs get blurred. But screen prints are not usually colour fast, and jerseys should be dry cleaned.

Flax fibres do not absorb or hold colour as well as other cellulose fibres. Consequently, the colour in linen fabrics fades.

The presence of size or other finishes applied before dyeing or improperly removed before dyeing, may result in uneven wear or service from a colour.

Piece-dyed fabrics made of large yarns may develop light streaks resembling wrinkles, because the colour has not penetrated the yarn. When the fabric stretches during body movements, the undyed fibres work their way up to the surface. There is no remedy for this except re-dyeing.

Holes may appear in a printed fabric, or a solid-colour fabric may be 'tendered' by the acid formed from the sulphur in a dye and the moisture in the air, or from a combination of sunlight and the sulphur in a dye. Yellow, orange, black and brown are the colours that most often cause this trouble.

Dyeing at Home

The art of dyeing is an old one and goes back several hundreds of years. Dyeing gives a new look to old fabrics. Dyeing is a simple process and if a few rules are followed, the results should be successful. Garments and furnishings may fade or the owner may tire of the shade. Tinting and dyeing at home can make the articles look new at a far less cost than if they are sent to the 'cleaners'.

The fabric and the dye

The dye must be chosen according to the nature of the fibre. Different fibres may react differently to the dye employed.

Vegetable fibres do not react well to dyes but dyes can be boiled in when dark fast colours are required.

Animal fibres have a great affinity for dyes. It is better not to boild them, as it removes the natural oil from fabrics and may cause shrinkage.

Rayon fibres like cottons have only slight affinity for dyes and often take them very badly. Cellulose acetate does not dye well and special dyes need to be used on them.

Stripping. A fabric to be dyed must be 'stripped' first so that the dyeing is even. Cotton fabrics can be bleached by sodium hypochlorite. Sodium hydrosulphite or sodium bisulphite can be used for animal fibres as well.

Types. A number of dyes produced today are suitable for home use.

Liquid dyes are suitable for different materials. Concentrated cold water dyes are suitable for dyeing fabrics that are not intended to be cleaned by washing, e.g., scarves. Paste dye concentrated colouring is made up in paste form and suitable for recolouring leather. Powdered dyes are usually bought in packets or capsules and dissolve easily in a dye bath. They are suitable for most textiles fibres and can be used in cold or warm solutions to tint or at a correct temperature for each fibre for dyeing. They are available in a variety of colours and are easy to use. To use Powdered dyes, some rules are important. The fabric must be perfectly cleaned, free from stains and evenly wet. A lining may take the same colour as a garment, and if it is not to be dyed it should be removed. Lace trimmings, braid, fur, etc., must be removed and treated separately. Button and metal ornaments may also be damaged by the heat of the dye bath and should be removed. Unpick pleats, hems and double thicknesses of the material which will prevent penetration of the dye.

Keep old enamel bowls, wooden spoons or smooth pieces of wood for the purpose. Protect hands and dress with rubber aprons and gloves. The basin must be big enough to hold the dye and article comfortably, so that the garment can be moved without spilling the dye.

Prepare the dye according to the directions and the colour required. Two or more dyes can be mixed to give unusual colours and shades. Dissolve the dye completely in hot water following the directions given and strain through muslin into an enamel bowl.

There must be sufficient dye in the dye bath to allow the entire article being dye to float easily. The dye bath must have the required quantity of water. Test the colour of the dye with a piece of material similar to that being dyed, or a piece of a similar fibre. It must be remembered that the dye when dry is several shades lighter than it appears when wet.

Method. Shake the article. Lower into dye bath. Begin to move at once with two wooden spoons or pieces of wood and keep it moving the whole time the article is in contact with the dye. Keep in the dye bath till the fabric has developed the required colour at the correct temperature for the fibre. Remove to a sink or tub by using dye spoons. Rinse according to the fabric until the water is dye-free. Keep the dye till the article has dried in case it is needed again. The dyes can be stored in close bottles for future use. Squeeze dry and finish according to the fabric. Care should be taken to protect clothes lines and to see that dyed article does not touch other things lest it should stain them. The fastness of colour is ensured. by adding to the dye bath one tablespoonful of salt per gallon for vegetable fibres and 1 tablespoonful of acetic acid or 2 tablespoonful if vinegar per gallon for animal fibres.

Finishing. Dyed articles must be allowed to dry completely before ironing. When this is done, they should be damped down and treated over muslin according to the fabric. As a safeguard against staining the ironing sheet, an old sheet should be used. This can be stripped after the process. Excessive heat may change the colour of the dyed article, hence it is important that the iron should be only moderately hot.

Best results are secured by ironing articles on the wrong side. The part needing special attention should be touched up over muslin on the right side.

Dyeing with Indigenous Dyes

Indigo

The commonest vats used to dye wool with indigo are the soda vat and the potash vat.

The soda vat gives brighter shades on woollen materials and is principally used for light blues. Caustic soda is used in place of lime. Besides indigo that vat contains bran, madder, treacle, soda-ash or caustic soda. Vatting is done at 65°C and the vat is ready within 24–48 hours.

The potash vat is like the soda vat but made up with indigo, madder, potassium carbonate and lime.

Majeeth (maddea)

The dye is almost entirely present in the cordex of the roots, which also contain about 10–15 per cent sugar. The roots are rasped to a coarse powder and boiled with water for two or three hours when most of the colour is extracted. The colour of the liquor after proper extraction is red. After cooling it should be strained through a coarse piece of calico. For faster and fuller shades wool should be dyed on the two-bath principle.

Mordanting (aluminium salts). Wool is mordanted in a bath containing 5–6% of aluminium sulphate of 8.5% alum. The bath also contains about 4–5% cream of tartar. The material is turned in cold in the bath set as above, and the temperature of the bath is raised slowly to boil within two hours. The material is then allowed to lie there at boil for half an hour and then in the cooling bath. When the bath becomes cold it is taken out and washed thoroughly to remove all superfluous particles. The material is then ready for dyeing.

Mordanting (chromium salts). Wool can also be mordanted with chromium floride using a 2% solution and an equivalent quantity of acetic acid. Mordanting is started in cold and then the temperature is gradually raised to boil, the wool is then mordanted within one hour. The chromium floride bath can be reused after replenishing. The acid concentration should not, however, be allowed to increase. The addition of a little tin-chloride crystals in the mordanting bath brightens the shade. In dyeing wool, the temperature of the bath is best of 80°C than 100°C.

Pomegranate rind (*anar*)

The dye is extracted from the coarse powder of the rind by boiling with water. Generally two extractions are necessary to extract most of the colour. The infusion is strained from a piece of calico and the insoluble residue is thrown away. The infusion is coloured yellowish brown.

Wool is dyed a 20% shade by first boiling the material two hours in the infusion of the rind. The material is then left to cool in the bath for 12 hours, then squeezed and developed in a bath containing 3–4% bichromate of potash or soda and about 1–2% acetic acid. The wool is worked in cold for a few minutes and the temperature of the bath is then raised to boil and the wool worked in it for a period of 20–30 minutes. Finally it is washed and thoroughly soaped. The material is then passed through a bath to which a little tartaric is added and dried without washing.

Blacks can be obtained in combination with iron salts. The material is treated in a bath containing 25% of rind infusion at 60°C for about and hour and left to cool overnight. Then it is squeezed and worked up in a lukewarm bath containing 5% ferrous sulphate for bout 10 minutes and then thoroughly washed. A darker shad is obtained by repeating the process taking only 10% of the extracts again and then developing in 3% solution of iron sulphate.

Tesso

A mellow yellow is obtained from the flowers which are dried and steeped in about twice the amount of water for some time, after which the whole is boiled till the volume is reduced by half. It is then strained and allowed to cool.

Wool is dyed in an acid bath with an aqueous extract of tesso flowers. Previous boiling with mineral acid is not necessary, but if the wool is dyed with the decoction of tesso previously boiled with a mineral acid, better results are obtained.

Turmeric

A 10–15% of the dye will give a fairly deep shade of yellow. About 1 or 2% ascetic acid or alum is necessary. If the bath is alkaline to any degree the fibre is not dyed at all and the colouring matter begins to deteriorate gradually in the dye bath. Turmeric is dissolved in hot water and the dyeings are carried out at a temperature never exceeding 60°C when the dyestuffs quickly go on to the fibres. Turmeric, however: does not stand high temperature, and it is found that in dyeing wool temperatures higher than 60°C are most detrimental, since duller and paler shades result. After dyeing for half an hour the material is taken out, squeezed and washed with water to remove all traces of acid if added to the bath. The following shades are obtained when dyeing with different mordants:

Alum	Bright yellow
Bichromate of potash	Brownish yellow
Tin chloride	Bright orange
Ferrous sulphate	Olive

Wool may be either mordanted first and then dyed or the dyeing and mordanting carried out together. Temperature must not be exceeded.

Walnut rind

The rind is ground to a coarse powder and the colouring matter is extracted by boiling repeatedly in water. It should be boiled two or three times.

Equal amounts of wool and rind are boiled for about half an hour in six times the amount of water. The wool is then allowed to be in a cold bath for 8–12 hours. It is then treated with different metallic salts. Ferrous sulphate gives a deep olive brown, bichromate a good yellowish brown.

In place of after-treatment the material may be previously mordanted and then dyed. Alum by such a process gives a bright brown shade. Fastness is good and can be improved by using copper salts in the developing bath.

Batik

Batik has now become an established and popular art. Creating coloured patterns on the cloth, by a method known as 'batik' is an Indonesian art. It is an exciting craft, which is well within the capabilities of the non-specialist.

'Batik' is a resist technique because no dye can penetrate the parts of the fabric covered with wax. The wax is heated and the hot melted wax is appiled on the fabric in the form of a design by using brush or any other such equipment. The waxed material is then dyed in any cold ice dye. In the dyeing process minute cracks occur in the wax, letting in tinyspecks of dye. This produces fine veins of colour which are characteristic of batik. The wax is then removed at the end of the process.

The best materials for batik are cotton, silk and rayon. Among these, cotton is the best suited. The surface of the material should be as smooth as possible. The choice of fabric depends on what one is going to do with the batik piece. The material should be free of starch and properly ironed.

The selected design is drawn on the fabric. The type of wax selected is according to the particular design. A standard combination contains equal quantities of bees wax and paraffin wax. If the quantity of paraffin wax is increased then more cracks result for the higher the paraffin content the more friable the wax.

The wax mixture is heated. It should be uniformly heated and must not smoke or over-boil. This melted wax is applied on the fabric with the help of a brush or a T-janting. For better effect the material should be waxed twice on each side. Only the portions that are required blank (white) should be waxed.

The dyes for batik are called 'naphthol dyes'. They are also known as cold or ice dyes.

Method. Take one teaspoonful of naphthol in a bowl and mix thoroughly with two teaspoons of turkey-red oil. Then add 50 ml of boiling water. Stir well and add 2–3 pallets of caustic soda. Heat it and stir properly till the solution becomes transparent.

Take two teaspoons of naphthol salt in another bowl and add to it 3–4 teaspoons of common salt. Mix well and add to it 50 ml. of water.

Now take two basins and put enough water in then to to dip the waxed fabric. In the first basin add the solution from bowl A and in second add the solution from the bowl B. Next soak the waxed fabric in water, squeeze out excess water, open the fabric and dip it in a naphthol colour solution (first basin). Work for 10 minutes in the above solution, squeeze out the excess dye, open the fabric and then dip it in naphthol salt solution (second basin). Again work for 10 minutes, remove it, wash it, and soap it. Always start with a lighther colour and then proceed with the darker colour.

The wax can be removed by boiling the fabric in a soap solution containing a little caustic soda. But before that it is better to remove excess wax by rubbing. The wax can also be removed with petrol but it is an expensive process.

Some useful dye mixture for reference

Naphthol colour	Naphthol Salt	Result
AT	Bardeaux GP	Golden yellow
BS	Scarlet R	Scarlet red
ASBS	Blue B Salt	Blue
ASBS	Bardeaux GP	Maroon
ASBS	Scarlet R	
	Blue B Salt	Purple
ASBS	Orange GC	Orange
ATAS	Blue B Salt	Black

6

Judging and Selecting Clothes and Textiles

When buying clothes or fabrics, the Indian consumer should be an intelligent shopper. Although required by law, not all fabrics or garments carry the I.S.I. (Indian Standard Institute) mark or the Woolmark, nor are they necessarily labelled adequately regarding content and care. Further, only a few textile merchants sell or advertise their products honestly.

While there are now an increasing number of consumer associations where one can seek redressal in the event of a fraudulent sale, it is more efficient and inexpensive to be cautious before making the purchase. The consumer should plan his or her wardrobe and other fabric needs, and do a lot of comparative shopping.

A general acquaintance with fabrics and fibres will help greatly. During the purchase itself, the buyer should use his senses of sight, touch and even smell in judging the fabric.

Experience and a little background study will teach the buyer about the softness of a Banaras or Kanjeevaram silk sari, the feel of velvet, the warmth of pure wool and the coolness of cotton or linen. He will learn to appreciate the traditional hand-woven fabrics of India—their colour and their feel. The wise shopper will look for flaws in weaving, poor-quality materials or workmanship, poor colour-fastness, uneven colour and other characteristics.

In assessing fabric quality the following general guidelines can be used with regard to the material, its weave and its finish.

The material should have good hand (or handle), i.e. it should be pleasing to the touch. Its durability will depend on the kind and quality of the fibre, the tensile strength of the yarn, the amount of twist in the yarn, and compactness of construction. The latter is one of the most significant factors for durability. A closely-woven fabric has more yarn than a loosely woven one, and is therefore more serviceable. All-wool fabrics should show high resistance to creasing and crushing, with individual threads being strong and regular in outline.

In judging weaves, long 'floats' of individual threads, as sometimes used in fancy weaves, should be avoided. Unless well-secured on both sides, they tend to wear out rapidly. Test the strength of the cloth by applying tension between the two thumbs. The threads should not slip away from each other if the weave is sound. Double clothes should be securely joined so that they will not separate when wet. But the stitches should not be apparent.

With respect to finishes, the cloth should smell clean, and should not feel oily. Look for marks or weak spots due to uneven milling, raising, or cropping. The nap or pile of raised fabrics should be dense and fine. In raising it, the fabric's strength, particularly weft-ways, should not have suffered.

Clothes count for most of us. Right clothes are necessary for health, poise and self-respect. An individual who lives within a planned budget is usually happier, more contented, than one who spends his money as he earns it. It is true, our desires or wants are unlimited. Our needs are comparatively few. While adjustment for needs are essential and important in family life, catering to mere wants is undesirable for the development of personality. There is a difference between what we want and what we need. A good clothing plan may include both.

Some of the following practical tips may prove useful in choosing your fabrics.

Making a Clothing Plan

One of the first steps before shopping is to find out what one's needs are and to make a plan for spending on clothes. This should be in relation to the family budget. Study each member's list of clothing needs, and decide how to spread the purchases through the year. Give essentials priority, and defer less necessary items to later.

Next, consider the purpose for which fabric is to be used. For instance, whether for everyday wear or for a special occasion. Buy only the item you set out to buy. Do not be lured by a pretty pair of chappals when you have to buy a sari. Avoid buying on impulse. Choose the right quality for your purpose. Compare prices and values at different stores.

As far as possible buy good quality; cheap things are rarely an economy. Consider the merits of the fabric and what care it will require. If economy becomes very important, discover ways and means of renovating old garments. If possible, learn to sew simple streamlined kamizes, cholis, dresses and other garments at home.

While keeping up with trends, remember that what one wears shouldn't blindly follow the 'latest fashion'. Good taste is the ability to discern what looks appropriate on you.

Women's Clothes

In buying saris or dress materials, bear in mind the suitability of the fabric to the occasion, the age, and personality of the wearer and the season. Both quality and look are essential features to look for.

If the fabric is to be subjected to hard wear, choose a sturdy material with a firm weave with the yarns packed tightly together. This gives some insurance against holes due to friction, pulling and fraying at the seams, and sagging at the elbows and knees. Handloom cottons are practical for use throughout the year in India. They are durable, easily laundered, and permit circulation of air. If the garment is to be worn frequently over a long period of time, it is wiser to select quality fabrics of plain colour or an inconspicuously patterned material.

For special occasions a more delicate fabric such as a chanderi, may be selected for its effect. But consider also the upkeep. Sheer chanderis or jamdanis need frequent costly dry cleaning, and withdraw the sari from wear for long periods. Handloom silk saris (such as shahpuri, Kanjeevaram or Kollegal) bespeak quality. They are also practical as well as elegant, as they can be washed at home, are durable and do not lose their freshness.

In choosing colours, the following points should be noted.

1. Ensure that the colour suits you, and that the design is effective and pleasing. Colours, like people, have personalities. A well-chosen pattern or colour will be a fashion statement.

2. Decide what colours go together. They must be harmonious and nature provides excellent examples to help in choosing colour combinations.

3. The natural light and colours around us change from season to season and even within one season. A a rule, cool, light colours, such as white, cream and soft blues and pinks are good for summer wear. Darker, subdued colours, such as brown are pleasing for winter wear. Red looks warm and is suggestive of winter.

4. Most Indian women have black hair and therefore are fortunate in being able to use fairly vivid colours, with which dark hair makes a striking contrast.

5. Skin colour should not be forgotten. Coloured fabrics should be held against a clear patch of skin to see if it is suitable. Good contrast is needed especially near the face. For example, a cream or white upper garment contrasts well with a dark complexion.

6. Bright colours can seem to make the wearer appear larger, while dull colours have the opposite effect. It might be necessary to balance such colours.

7. Older women should avoid harsh, bright colours like sharp blue, orange or vivid purple, since they tend to harden the face. Avoiding these colours or using them sparingly would be more flattering.

In selecting designs on saris or other apparel these empirical facts should be kept in mind. If you are stout and wish to appear less so, select a small all-over print where the design does not stand out conspicuously from the background. Avoid large-figured designs, wide borders or broad stripes. If you are short, it is better to choose saris with narrow borders, as broad-bordered saris make one look even shorter. Saris and cholis of the same fabric also help a short person appear to advantage.

The texture of a fabric is important, too. It can make a colour either becoming or otherwise. For example, a lustred, crêpe silk or wool may be flattering because of the softness of the fabric, but the same blue may be harsh in a lustrous satin. There is also a difference in the effect of transparent and non-transparent materials of the same hue. A lavender may be unsuitable in linen, but could look better in a sheer fabric like voile or chiffon, because skin and underwear can show through it attractively.

It is alright to keep in vogue, but extremes in fashion should be avoided, since they are costly. Also both the person wearing the dress and others can tire of it quickly.

In India, most women either sew their own garments or give them to a tailor. Generally you are yourself the designer. To be a successful designer, you have to acquire an instinctive ability to recognise a happy relationship between fabric, style and personality. Whether sewing yourself or getting it tailored, it is wise to purchase the other essentials like thread, buttons and binding at the same time. This way you will not run into delays after starting to sew, or be at the mercy of the tailor's tastes.

When sewing or tailoring, remember that every fabric has a character of its own, and you should learn to recognise the inherent traits of a fabric. When you make your own choli or kamiz for your salwar, you will soon discover that the easiest and most successful sewing occurs when the natural qualities of the fabric are respected. An experienced seamstress studies herself until she finds the colours, lines, and fabrics that match her accessories to enhance the total outfit. She insists on a correct fit before they are finally stitched or completed, she also makes sure that her foundation garments fit well and are comfortable; they should be able to absorb perspiration, and their material should be durable and easy to launder.

Children's Clothes

Children outgrow and outwear their clothes rapidly. The material chosen should depend on where one lives and the season of the year. Children's clothing should be: (1) patterned for growth, ease and freedom, yet not too large; (2) strong enough to withstand hard wear and yet be comfortable; (3) simple but attractive in line and colour; and (4) of closely-woven material that will remain fresh even after several washes.

When having children's clothes tailored, insist on: (1) good workmanship and durable flat seams; (2) fasteners sewn firmly to withstand tugging and pulling; (3) buttonholes closely worked; (4) roomy neck openings; (5) strong reinforcements at all points of strain, such as placket-openings, pocket corners, knees, elbows, armholes and under-buttons.

Shoes

A good pair of shoes has more meaning than just foot protection. It can also be a measure of status, and a personal statement. An adult foot has twenty-six bones, and one hundred and thirty-seven joints, the general structure of the foot being pretty well determined by the age of twelve. On the other hand, an infant's foot has only one bone—the heel bone, and the rest is composed of twenty-five segments of cartlege, easily pushed about. Buying shoes for children should therefore be taken more seriously; comfort and good fit are of primary importance, while style is secondary. Children outgrow their shoes every three months, and they must be changed accordingly. Parents should exercise constant vigilance to ensure perfect foot development.

Some of the points to be remembered in buying a pair of shoes for children are listed below.

1. The shoes should be comfortable and support the feet. Have the child try on both shoes and walk around the shop. Listen carefully to his complaints about pinching or looseness.
2. Correct fit is particularly important in children's shoes. A shoe must neither be too short, nor too long. Correct width is essential too, to let the metatarsals expand. The widest part of the ball-point of the feet should conform to the widest part of the shoe.
3. Buy shoes therefore, half-an-inch or three-fourths of an inch longer than the end of the toes in closed-toe models. Open-toe shoes can be smaller.
4. Shoes should fit snugly around the heel, under the arch and over the instep, without pinching or chafing. A snug fit ensures that the feet are well-supported.
5. The heels should be comfortable, usually no more than one and a quarter inch high.
6. Shoes should be well made and of durable material. The best shoe lining is leather with cloth over the toes.
7. Don't hesitate to throw away outgrown or poorly fitting shoes lest the feet become malformed or foot ailments develop.
8. Resoling children's shoes tends to shorten them.

A sandal is primarily a sole with straps securing it to the foot. They are ideal for the warn Indian climate. In general, the simpler sandal and shoe designs are the best. Sandals, too, must have the right fit, and be attractive, reasonably hard-wearing and comfortable. Avoid loose sandals with only one grip.

Clean, well-polished shoes enhance one's appearance. Taking good care ofshoes also makes them last longer. Allow shoes to rest and dry out between wearings. Attend to repairs promptly. Watch the heels and soles before they have lost shape. Use polish and a brush to keep shoes supple and shining.

Men's Clothes

Shirts

Cotton, including 'old-fashioned' white-cotton broad cloth, is still king in this category of clothing. None of the new synthetics or blends can yet match cotton's pleasant feel and lasting good looks. In fact, almost all shirts at the upper end of the price range are made of high-quality cotton, not synthetics.

However, synthetics do have advantages, particularly their wash-and-wear character. A synthetic shirt can be washed in the basin of a hotel room, hung up to dry, and worn the next day without ironing—a tremendous benefit to travelers. Among the synthetics, dacron and terylene shirts are whiter, less stiff, and have better wash-and-wear than orlon shirts. When blended with cotton—a common blend is 65% dacron staple with 35% cotton—synthetic shirts also feel cool in warm weather and less clammy in cold.

When buying a shirt, note that although a higher count is associated with smoother-looking, more expensive shirts, count alone is not an index of durability. Yarn twist, the number of strands in the yarn, and mercerizing are also important. Mother-of-pearl buttons are sometimes used on expensive shirts, but good-quality plastic buttons last longer, as they do not chip or yellow during laundering. Fused collars are generally superior to soft collars or shirts of the same model, but some teased collars have poor resistance to abrasion.

Some other features to look for in shirts are listed below.

1. Sleeves should extend to the bend of the wrist i.e. covering the wrist bone extending at least one-half inch beyond the sleeves of a coat.

2. The neck line should fit closely, neither too snug nor too loose.

3. A curved yoke seam (with gathers set in over the shoulder blades, not the centre back alone) is recommended.

4. Shirt tails should be rounded and full-cut, both at the front and the back, with a set-in gusset at the side seams.

5. Sleeves should preferably be cut in one piece. However, a shirt with a two-piece sleeve can wear as long.

6. Button holes should be reinforced.

Suits

A good suit should provide comfort, good fit, good outer fabric, good tailoring, and high-quality trimmings, including all linings and hidden materials that help give a suit its shape. Style, pattern and colour are of course, matters of individual preference.

For winter wear, men's suits are almost entirely of wool, either worsteds or woollens. As a rule, worsteds are smoother, firmer fabrics and will hold a crease longer than woollens, which are usually rough-surfaced and loosely woven. Worsteds also keep their good looks longer. Closely-woven worsteds, preferably with two-ply yarn in both warp and weft, are recommended as they wear better.

Whether a summer suit keeps the wearer cool depends on a lot of fabric qualities and other subjective factors. As a rule, a fabric with a porous, open weave is cooler than one with tightly-woven yarns, such as gabardine or flannel. Light weight also helps. Nearly all summer suits have light weight, open-weave construction. Cotton, raw silk, nylon, rayon, dacron or terylene are common fabrics for summer suits. Dacron-worsted (50% dacron, 50% worsted) and dacron-rayon (40%) dacron, 60% rayon) blends are popular.

Even an expert could only properly evaluate a suit by taking it apart, as most of the differences between top-of-the-line and low-priced suits of the same outer fabric lie in the inner, hidden details. However, any buyer should check that the fabric is smooth, with no puckering along the seams, rippling at the labels or elsewhere. If the fabric is patterned, it should be matched at the pockets, sleeves, collar, etc. Shoulder pads should be smooth, light and flexible, and buttonholes should be sewn on both sides of the cloth.

The lining in both body and sleeves should be a firm, closely-woven rayon twill. It should fit the outer layers snugly not bunch up.

All pockets should be lined with a firm, closely-woven cotton. Reinforced corners increase durability, and.seams should be finished in hand-felling or silk piping.

Adjusting the waistband, crotch, sleeve and trouser length, or raising the shoulder are reasonable alternatives to a ready-made suit. But if more work is needed, it is better to try another suit.

When trying out a suit, wear both jacket and trousers, and check the following points of workmanship.

1. The coat should hang straight down from the shoulder, both back and front, with no wrinkles or bulges.

2. The collar should fit snugly at the back and sides of the neck.

3. The lapels should lie closely and smoothly against the chest.

4. The coat should be long enough to cover the seat of the trousers, and should fall close to the body at front and back.

5. The shoulders should form a firm, unbroken line, with no wrinkling across the back. If one of the shoulders is lower than the other, the lining may be opened and a small pad inserted under the shoulder of the coat. But alterations involving the opening of the outside seams of the shoulder or collar are not recommended.

6. Armholes should be comfortably large; the coat should not lift noticeably when you raise your arms. Do not shorten or lengthn sleeves more than one inch. The fabric in front of the coat should not pull when it is buttoned.

7. Trousers should be snug at the waist, hang naturally and straight, and be full enough around the seat and crotch so that they do not feel tight when you walk, bend or sit. They should have substantial seam allowances to make alterations possible.

Household Textiles

These include Turkish towels, huckaback and face towels, dish towels, and dish cloths, table covers and napkins, bed sheets and pillow cases; and yarn goods, i.e., sheeting (*dosuti*).

Turkish towels have a looped-pile surface, which increases their absorbency. The more loops there are, the more absorbent the towel. Choose towels in which the loops are reasonably close together, soft and not too tightly twisted. Striped or checked towels with the stripe or check in plain weave sacrifice some absorbency for appearance. Examine the underweave, by holding the towel up to the light. If wide swathes of light come through the interstices or pores between the weave, the towel is poorly made. Only pinpoints of light will show through a well-made towel. Also check that the selvedges are firm and even.

Huckaback towels are usually made wholly of cotton. The weave is also called honeycomb or diamond weave. For durability the weave must be close and the count must be balanced. That is, the yarns must have the same bulk and diameter in both warp and filling. Absorbency is not as important as looks in huckaback towels, as they are used mainly for the face.

Good dish towels must have just the right twist to the yarn and firmness of weave, so that the moisture is absorbed and the fabric remains lintless. Dish towels made from handloom cloth are very good. For example, *thorth mundu* or *baias,* commonly available in Kerala, serve the purpose well. They can even be used to strain liquids.

Dinner table cloths and napkins often come in sets and include damask. They are available today in beautiful, handloom material, both white and coloured. The weaves may be jacquard, satin, plain, twill or other. Damask tablecloths are usully made of pure linen, pure cotton or mixtures of these fibres. Sometimes rayon is included to make the design more prominent and lustrous. Damasks are made in jacquard weave with a certain warp design over a filling sateen ground. A twill weave is also used for the design, with a satin weave for the ground. Damasks have the advantage of being usable on either side.

Ginghams, twill, *khaddar* and other handloom materials also make good tablecloths. Qualities to look for are appearance, suitability, serviceability, durability, washability and size.

7

Laundry Materials and Equipment

Water

Water can be hard or soft. The former does not lather readily with soap, so in laundry work, it is soft water that is the most important agent. Among the properties of water that make it so useful for washing is the ability of water to adhere to the fabric, so that it can penetrate into the fibre and wet it.

The movement of the water molecules helps to remove nongreasy dirt, so a fabric is partially cleaned by steeping and friction. The salts and alkalis in hard water hinder the movement of particles. Dust particles aggregate and the large ones resettle in the fabric.

Water is an excellent solvent, so most soluble dirt and stains are removed during the steeping process. Cold water is the best solvent for albuminous (food protein) matter. Hot water helps to melt and soften grease, but other cleaning agents are necessary to emulsify and remove greasy matter. In general, the solvent power of a liquid increases when its temperature is raised.

Naturally occurring water is not absolutely pure; its purity depends on the nature of the soil over or through which it has passed before being collected. Rain water is the most pure, but even this contains substances absorbed from the atmosphere, one of which, carbon dioxide, is always present. When free from impurities, rain water is ideal for laundry work for it is soft. Soft water washes whiter, brighter, saves soap and makes fabrics last longer.

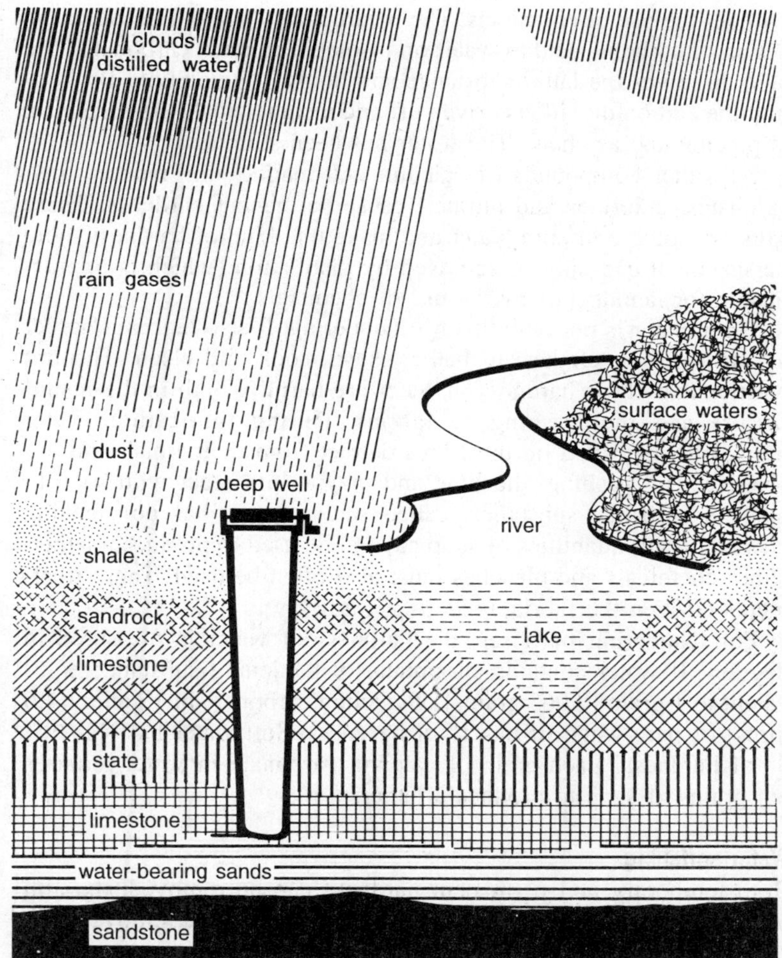

Fig. 7.1 Passage of water through the ground

Water hardness

Most water, especially from chalky districts, contains calcium and magnesium salts in solution, usually as sulphates of bicarbonates. These cause hardness.

If the salt present in water is calcium or magnesium bicarbonate the water has is temporary hardness which can be removed by heat without the use of chemicals. The bicarbonates occur because of the action of carbonic acid in water on insoluble calcium carbonate. The acid dissolves the latter substance and holds it in solution. By boiling, the carbon dioxide is driven off and insoluble calcium carbonate is precipitated as chalk. The water has been softened.

All other compounds of calcium and magnesium, namely their sulphates, chlorides and nitrates, cause permanent hardness. These salts are soluble in pure water and make this kind of hardness more persistent. It can only be removed by distillation (which is impracticable for laundry) or by the use of chemicals.

Hard water is not only bad for laundering, it also makes it harder to wash dishes, clothes, to bathe, shave, cook and clean. The impurities that cause hardness in water are harmful both in the manufacture and the washing of fabrics. During fabrication, water impurities deposited on the fibres detract from their finish and appearance. In washing, the lime and magnesium react with soap to make a curd-like substance, called scum, which has no cleaning power. Larger quantities of soap have to be used to produce a lather. Other chemicals and bleaches must also often be used. These treatments coarsen the fabric, tendering it quickly.

For laundering purposes, the hardness of water is measured in degrees. If water contains an amount of hardening substance equivalent to 1 grain (0.065 grams) of calcium carbonate in 1 gallon (4.6 litres) of pure water, it has 1° of hardness. Soft water has less that 3° of hardness. Each grain of calcium carbonate in water requires ten grains of soap to produce a lather.

Water softening

Both temporary and permanent hardness can be removed, the aim being to soften water without making it alkaline. Soda removes both kinds of hardness and can be used at home. For large scale softening, a combination of lime and soda, or a water-softening plant attached to the household supply can be used. The most common softening plant is a zeolite, which also removes permanent hardness.

Soda is inexpensive and easy to use, making it ideal for softening water in the home. Chalk is precipitated and only harmless salts remain in the water. About 2 grains of soda are needed per degree of hardness to soften 1 gallon of water. However, it is a chemical, and it acts by producing a chemical change in the water. Two facts must be borne in mind: (1) The action is not immediate. The speed at which water is softened by soda depends upon the temperature of the water. Boiling water softens in a few seconds, while cold water may take as long as an hour. (2) No more soda than is required should be used. Any excess, besides being uneconomical, will hinder the cleaning properties of soap, and may also damage certain fabrics.

Some other softening agents are soap, caustic soda, ammonia and borax. Soap combines with the water-hardening substances. However, this happens before a satisfactory lather can be formed. Also, soap is an expensive softening agent compared with soda.

Caustic soda is not used in the home on account of its strength. It removes temporary hardness but reduces permanent hardness slightly.

Solutions of ammonia are used when fabrics may be harmed by soda. However, excess, ammonia may destroy the lustre of rayons, discolour and injure animal fabrics and loosen the dyes of coloured articles. As it is not possible to be certain of the quantity to be used, ammonia is not a very practical softner.

Borax does not harm fabrics if left in the water. It is useful for water containing over 20° of hardness. In practice, borax is usually used to reduce the alkalinity of a soap solution rather than to soften the water, for instance when washing babies' clothes.

Zeolite Water Softeners A zeolite plant attached to the household water supply is a popular means of water softening. It can remove both temporary and permanent hardness. Zeolite plants work on the chemical principle of base or ion exchange, discovered at the turn of the century by Robert Gans. Zeolites are minerals consisting of hydrated aluminium silicates of sodium, potassium, calcium and barium. A zeolite has the property of being able to exchange its sodium or other base for another. When hard water passes through a zeolite, the hardening compounds of calcium and magnesium are caught up by it and become compounds of sodium. Since sodium salts do not precipitate out on heating or form soap curds, the water is called soft. As the water gets softened, the zeolite becomes depleted, having given up all its sodium. However, a zeolite can exchange its base again, and take back sodium in place of calcium and magnesium, in a process called regeneration. It is effected by passing a strong solution of sodium chloride (common salt) through the zeolite. The frequency of regeneration depends on the amount of water which passes through the water softener. A domestic appliance can operate for several days without the need for regeneration. When the zeolite finally deteriorates, it has to be replaced with fresh zeolite.

Zeolite water softeners for domestic use are either connected to the main water supply or fixed to a water tap. In the latter case the appliance is a portable type which can be moved from one tap to another. When installing on the main water-supply, separate plumbing may be provided to flushes and taps where softened water is not needed. A mains water softener does have some disadvantages, though (1) It tends to make drinking water somewhat unpalatable, although better for health. (2) It makes water softer than is good for treating loose-dyed fabrics. (3) It necessitates a larger softener than is really necessary unless separate plumbing has been installed.

Laundry Soaps

Soap is the most widely-used fabric cleaner. It is made by reacting natural oils or animal fats with sodium hydroxide or other strong alkali. The ancients might have stumbled on soap when melted animal fat or tallow got mixed with potash. This naturally occurring alkali is formed, for instance, in wood ash from fires. The Romans used soap, as evidenced by written records and also a soap factory found in the ruins of Pompeii. There was a flourishing soap industry in Italy, Spain and France in the middle ages. Modern soap manufacture based on chemical processes can be traced to the nineteenth century.

Manufacture of soap

During manufacture soap is first made in molten form and them shaped into different sorts of finished products: hard soaps, toilet soaps, powders, flakes, etc.

Most soap today is made by the full-boiled process. In the first step called emulsification and saponification the natural fats are melted, the impurities allowed to settle, and the clear fats pumped into kettles and heated with an open steam coil. A 10 to 15 per cent solution of caustic soda is added. The mixture is further heated by steam until the saponification is about 90-95 per cent complete. This may continue for two or three days. The reaction mass now contains soap, glycerine, excess alkali, water and organic impurities.

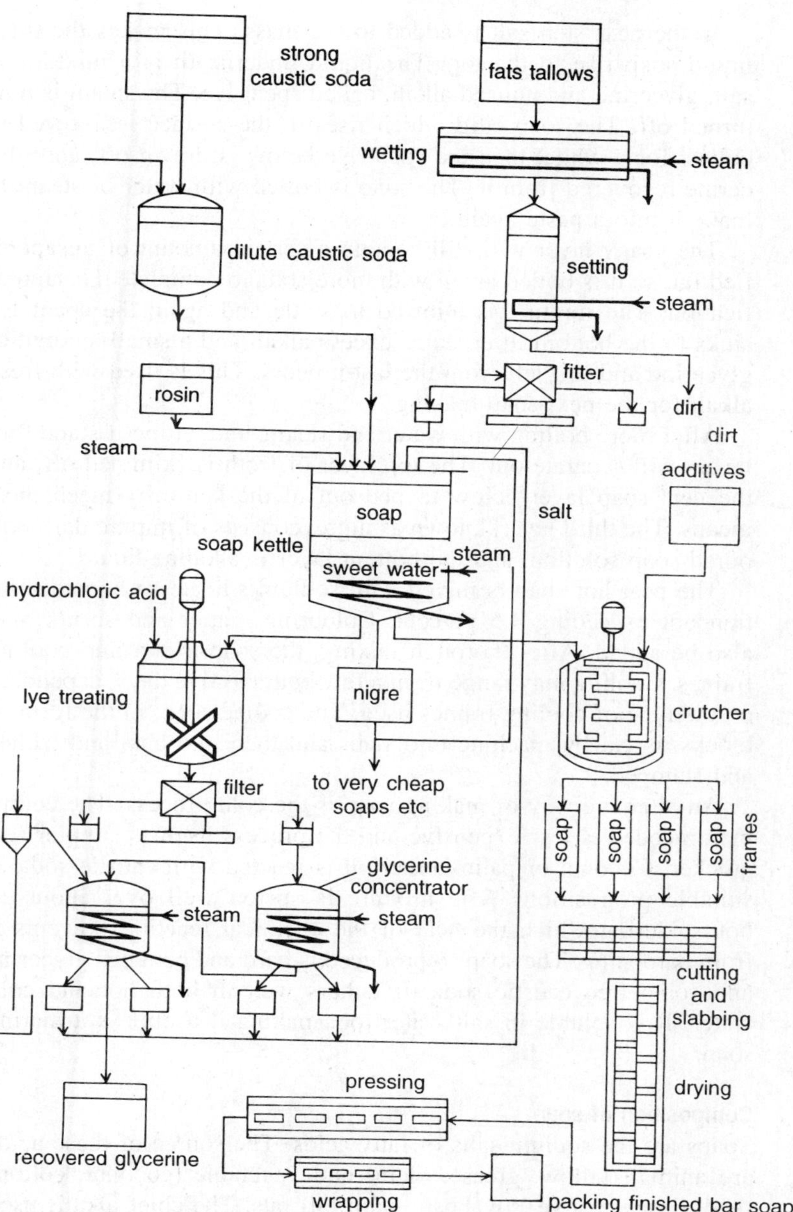

Fig. 7.2 Manufacture of soap (full-boiled process)

In the next step salt is added to the mass. This makes the thick liquid soap rise to the top. The liquid underneath is a mixture of salt, glycerine and unused alkali, called spent lye. The steam is now turned off. The soap curd which rises to the surface is allowed to collect for a while, then the spent lye below is drawn off, and glycerine recovered from it. The soap is boiled with water or steam to make it into a paste again.

The soapy layer will still contain a certain amount of unsaponified fat, so it is boiled again with more soda to complete the saponification. The mixture is allowed to settle and again the spent lye sinks to the bottom. It contains excess alkali and a small amount of glycerine and salt left from the last process. This is used with fresh alkali for the next soap-making.

After more boiling with water and steam, and letting if stand four layers will separate out. The top layer of froth is skimmed off, and the neat soap layer below tapped out of the kettle by mechanical means. The third layer, known as nigre, consists of impure dark-coloured soap solution, and the bottom layer is alkaline liquid.

The neat hot soap is mixed with sodium silicate carbonate solution not exceeding 4.5 percent. Colouring matter and scents may also be added. After thorough mixing, the soap is run into cooling frames. Cooling may range from a few hours to five days, depending on the type of cooling frames used. The cooled soap, in the form of blocks, is cut by machine into slabs and then into bars and tablets and stamped.

An alternate way of making soap is the cold process. The equipment needed is less expensive and the process itself is simpler and quicker. Coconut or palm-kernel oil is reacted with caustic soda in suitable propositions. The mixture is stirred well over about 24 hours, during which the heat of the chemical reaction prevents it from hardening. The soap so produced is hard and contains glycerins and some free caustic soda. It lathers well in both hot and cold water. It is soluble in salt water too, making it useful as a marine soap.

Composition of soap

Soaps are the sodium salts of fatty acids. The source of these acids are animal (tallow, grease, olein) and vegetable (coconut, cottonseed, linseed, olive, soyabean, palm oil) fats. The chief alkalis used are caustic soda and caustic potash.

All soaps contain water, but not more than 30 per cent in good soaps. Additives are also added to give the soap specific properties.

Naptha and a little mineral oil, such as paraffin oil, may be added to help in its cleansing properties and in the removal of grease. Resin and naphthenic acids (obtained from petroleum) may also be added to improve the effectiveness of soap. Their presence makes the soap yellow and translucent, and since they are cheap, the soap can be sold at less unit cost. However, resin has less cleaning power than soap and can also discolour white articles, especially when combined with calcium from hard water.

Other additives include disinfectants, such as carbolic, solvents, and substances used for filling, such as sodium silicate and sodium carbonate (washing soda) and phosphates. Filling also includes certain collodial clays, collodial organic material and other cleaning powders. They act both as detergents and as mechanical aids in cleaning. Together with certain mineral oils, waxes and starches, these additives are often added for the express purpose of cheapening the soap.

In selecting a laundry soap, care should be used, as many kinds of soap can be quite harmful to clothes. For example, soap used to clean wool or silk should be free from alkali; even one per cent alkali is disastrous on coloured silks. The following criteria may be used.

1. The soap should be of a clear plate colour as dark-coloured soap may contain impurities.

2. The soap should feel firm when pressed. If it feels soft, it may contain excess water, and will be wasteful in use.

3. Many hard soaps, especially cheap makes, on the other hand, contain fillers like sodium silicate, to disguise the low percentage of soap.

4. Good laundry soap dries with a firm unspeckled surface. Soaps that develop white crystals should not be used, as this shows the presence of harmful excess alkali.

5. A rough and ready test of good oil soap is to break a bar across the knee, examine the fracture, and then taste it. The fracture should be granular, not striated, and it should taste mild, not sharp to the tongue.

Commonly available types of laundry soap

Laundry soaps are often classified by their strength. Mild soaps have fat and alkali in equal balance. Lux soap flakes is an example. Strong, 'all purpose' soaps, such as Rinso by Hindustan lever and Deep by Godrej have a higher proportion of excess or free alkali. The various types of commonly available soap are listed below.

Yellow bar soaps contain a minimum of 52 per cent resin, a maximum of 36 per cent moisture, and a small amount of free alkali.

Bar soaps are generally used when hard soap is required. They can also be used to make soap solutions. They are economical, and can be bought in large quantities, cut into squares and stored in a cool dry place. The soap hardens, resulting is less waste when washing.

To make soap solution from bar soap, use 4 oz, of soap to 1 pint of water. Grate the soap and stew it in the water for a few minutes until a clear liquid is obtained. Avoid over-boiling. Scraps can be saved and converted into jelly. The solution can be used for non-laundry cleaning too. Neutral soaps are fairly high-priced white soaps of good quality, containing no free alkali.

To make soap flakes (such as Lux), a film of molten soap is spread over the surface of a rotating, water-cooled, steel drum. It comes off the drum as a number of ribbons. These ribbons are then moved backwards and forwards on conveyors inside a drying chamber through which hot air is circulated. To avoid loss, perfume is added to the ribbons after they have been dried. The perfumed ribbons of soap are then passed over five rotating steel rolls until they form a skin as thin as cigarette paper. The soap, stamped out as diamond-shaped flakes by sharp, rotating knives, is skimmed from the top roller and weighed into cartons. Soap flakes are convenient to use and are suitable for washing coloured fabrics which might run in warm water. Modern soap flakes are also soluble in cold water.

In washing with flakes, the correct amount of flakes is measured out and dissolved in a little boiling water. The solution is poured into the wash water, which is then whipped up to form a good lather. If any flakes remain undissolved, particles of soap may find their way into the fabric (particularly woollens) resulting in greasy marks on the garment. Whites should be rinsed well in clear, cold water.

Soap powder is made by pumping molten soap blended with silicates, phosphates and other ingredients to the top of a tower, where it is sprayed through high-pressure nozzles into a current of air. The soap solidifies and falls as granules onto a conveyor belt. The air is extracted by fans; any particles of soap in it are trapped in a dust collection system and recovered. A large variety of soap powders are available today, with a soap content ranging from 5 to 30 per cent. In the cheaper varieties, sodium bicarbonate, sodium silicate and French chalk may be included. They also contain a bleach which acts through the release of oxygen. The directions on the package must be followed carefully in using soap powder. Although no apparent harm may be done in a single wash, the continued use of an inferior washing powder may gradually shorten the life of an article. If the powder contains sodium silicate, lime and iron salts may be deposited on the fabric.

Soap nuts, also called *reetha* nuts in India, make a good alternative to soap. They are the fleshy berries of a moderate-sized tree, *Sapindus mukorossi*, which grows in northern India, or of *Sapindus laurifolius*, found in central and southern India and Sri Lanka. The berries are dried, then cracked open and broken up and dissolved in boiling water in the proportion: 8 oz of soap-nut to two pints of water. The resultant solution is slightly acid, unlike soap, which is alkaline. This is an advantage when washing coloured woollens or silks, which withstand traces of acid better than alkali. Their colours, which often bleed even with good soaps, do not do no with soap-nut. However, it is not as effective on white woollens and silks. Soap-nut is less affected by water hardness than soap, and produces better lather; in fact the pulp is used by the soap industry. Soap-nut can also be used to wash gold and silver, and as a shampoo. The active cleaning agent in soap-nut is a class of chemical called a saponin.

Shikakai is similar to the soap-nut. It comes from the pod of *Acacia concina*, a prickly bush of south India. The choclate-brown pod is dried in the sun and powdered fine. A tablespoon of powder is added to a pint of of water and boiled to a thick paste. Shikakai is excellent for removing grease and washing coloured cottons and silks whose lustre is retained. A mixture of powdered *reetha* nut and *shikakai*, soaked in warm water, makes an excellent shampoo.

Soapless Detergents

Research in Germany in the 30s and 40s into soap substitutes derived from petrochemicals, resulted in the first soapless detergents. This work was spurred by the scarcity during World War II of the fats and oils needed for soap. Detergents had properties similar to soap, such as foaming, wetting and cleaning, but they are able to make soluble salts out of the calcium, magnesium and other metals that make water hard and render ordinary soap insoluble.

Both soaps and detergents act by lowering the surface tension of water. In fact, soap is technically a detergent, while Surf and other products are synthetic or soapless detergents. The lowering of surface tension helps the detergent solution penetrate grease and dirt deposits on fibres. This characteristic property of detergents, because of which they are called *surfactants*, can be demonstrated by a simple experiment.

A dry, clean needle is placed gently on the surface of a glass of water. If care is taken it can be made to float for a very long time. The needle is buoyed up by the skin of outer molecules on the water surface. If a tiny trace of soap or detergent is now added to the water, the needle will immediately sink. This occurs because the soap dissolves in the water and changes the nature of its skin of outer molecules. Techncially, the surface tension of the water has been lowered.

Chemical action of detergents

To see how soaps and detergents do their cleaning, we can depict the long organic chains of their molecules as a 'tail,' depicted R, attached to a 'head.' In soaps, which are fatty acids, the hydrogen atom at the head of the molecule has been replaced by a carboxyl group, COONa or COOK, depending on whether caustic soda (NaOH) or caustic potash (KOH) has been used. In one large class of detergents, on the other hand, the COO-metal head of the soap molecule is replaced by a head consisting of the group O-SO_3-metal or SO_3-metal. If a small amount of detergent is dissolved in a droplet of water, the molecules of the soap or detergent on the surface of the droplet arrange themselves so that the heads of the molecules point towards the centre, while the tails all stick outwards like hairs (see Fig. 7.3). More technically, the tail of the soap molecule is *hydrophobic* i.e.(water-repelling) and head is *hydrophilic* (water attracted). The 'free' tails so created are capable of hanging on to dirt, which can then be rinsed away along with the detergent.

The chemical differences between soaps and detergents give the latter new properties. They can be made to give much more foam than soap. They wet fabrics more readily than soap; they emulsify

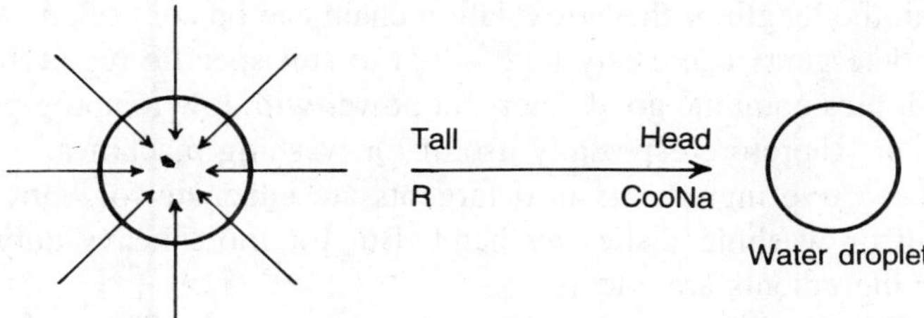

Fig. 7.3 Behaviour of heads and tails of detergent molecules

oils with water as well as soap in certain cases, and they have cleaning properties almost equal to soap.

Detergent manufacture

Soapless detergents are made in both powdered and liquid form. There are three main active ingredients (surfactants):

1. sulphonated alkylbenzene;
2. sulphated fatty alcohols; and
3. non-ionic compounds.

The first two are called anionics. Sulphonated alkylbenzene is the most commonly used surfactant in India. To make it, the petroleum-derived hydrocarbon, alkylbenzene, is reacted with oleum, which is fuming sulphuric acid, produced by dissolving sulphur trioxide in concentrated sulphuric acid. After the reaction, the moisture is diluted with water, when the sulphuric acid separates and is removed to a spent-acid tank. Caustic soda (sodium hydroxide) is now added to neutralize the sulphonated alkylbenzene and make a paste.

Sulphation differs from sulphonation. In the former reaction, the sulphur atom is attached directly to a carbon atom, while in the latter, it is linked via an oxygen atom. During sulphation sulphuric acid is added slowly to a fatty alcohol in a reactor. The reaction temperature is regulated by cooling water and the speed at which the sulphuric acid is added. The sulphated fatty alcohol is again neutralized with caustic soda.

The final group of surfactants, the non-ionics, have become more important lately. A common non-ionic is produced by adding ethylene oxide to alkylphenol, a long-chain alcohol, a process called ethoxylation. The reaction is carried out at a temperature of 180°C using an alkaline catalyst. By altering the quantity of ethylene oxide added, the length of the ethoxylation chain can be controlled, so that such detergents can easily be tailored to suit specific requirements. Non-ionics combine good detergent power with low foaming power. They. are therefore especially useful for washing machines.

The active ingredients in detergents are adequate for light laundering or washing dishes by hand. But for more heavy-duty use, other ingredients are added:

1. Builders of two types, inorganic and organic. The main inorganic builders are phosphates. They do not produce suds but increase detergent action by forming soluble, complex ions that give a repulsive charge to the fibres and help to loosen dirt particles from their surface. Organic builders stabilize the foam or suds of the surfactant. Builders also soften the water, so that the dirt that is removed from the fibre remains in suspension instead of settling back down.

2. Antideposition agents, such as sodium carboxyl methyl cellulose, help to suspend dirt in water after it has been removed from the fabric.

3. Sodium sulphate and sodium silicate ensure that traces of detergent flows out with the rinse water. It also protects aluminium parts of washing machines from pitting.

4. Sodium perborate or other brighteners or optical bleaches to remove stains and whiten fabrics.

5. Perfume, fluorescent substances to counter the natural discoloration of fabrics, foam stabilizers and colouring matter.

To make detergent powder, all ingredients, except the perfume and sodium perborate, are added to the sulphonate, sulphate or non-ionic surfactant, and the mixture, called a slurry, is pumped through nozzles at the top of a long tower. Hot air rising up the tower dries the moisture in the droplets of slurry, which fall as hollow granules of powder to the bottom of the tower. The powder is cooled on a pneumatic conveyor which lifts it to a settling vessel. Perfume and sodium perborate, which would not withstand the heat of the drying tower, are now added. Any fine powder which is carried over from the drying tower or settling vessel is trapped and used again. The final product is then packed into cartons in a high-speed packing unit. Spray-drying produces a uniform dust-free product, easily dissolved in water.

Advantages of modern detergents

1. Greater cleaning efficiency than soap, as they do not combine with the calcium, magnesium and other salts present in varying degrees in water, and thus are not wasted. All the detergent is available for washing. By the same token only one quarter to a half as much detergent is needed compared to soap.

2. While soap may leave soap deposits so that clothes come out stiff and grey, a soapless detergent will remove all deposits. As a result, clothes feel soft and fluffy.

3. More effective than soap against acids, particularly body acids. They also wash effectively in an acid medium, which is an advantage with girdles and slips, for instance, that generally become impregnated with acid dirt.

4. Detergents are soluble in cold water. So they are preferable to soap when cold wash is indicated as for girdles, rubberized garments and fine fabrics.

5. More than one deep, clear water rinse is unnecessary. When it is expedient to omit rinsing, the tiny amount of detergent left after efficient wringing, will not weaken or discolour the garment during ironing or storage.

6. The small amount of foam formed on rinse water by the detergent does no harm. Most detergents foam readily, even at very low concentrations and are easy to rinse out.

7. Detergents penetrate right into the fibres of a garment and effectively remove soil, because the detergent solution has a lower surface tension.

8. Rapid removal of grease is a very desirable characteristic because much of the dirt on clothes is of a greasy nature. Detergents, being highly efficient wetting agents, disperse the oil so that it does not form globules on top of the wash solution.

9. Modern detergents leave the wash clean and pleasant smelling with no heavy, chemical odour.

10. Detergents dissolve instantly in all degrees of hardness. So there is no formation of insoluble compounds that cause greying, stiffening and speckling of clothes, and also clog pipes and drains.

11. Modern detergents are 'one-package' products containing not

only detergent but also builders, optical bleach and water-softeners all built-in.

In order to get the most out of detergents:

- Follow the instructions on the detergent pack.
- Use hot water for white cottons.
- Soak clothes in the detergent solution for half-an-hour or longer.
- Knead the fabric inside the detergent solution.
- Rinse well.
- Check colours for fastness before washing.
- Do not pack in too many clothes; they should be able to move freely in the water.
- Do not beat the clothes.
- Do not use soap together with soapless detergents.

Starch

Clothes sometimes need to be stiffened before wear. Starch is the most frequently used stiffening agent. A good laundry starch must penetrate the fabric well but at the same time leave it pliable, and give it a smooth, glossy finish that will resist dirt, making it look smarter. Starching also makes subsequent washings easier, as soil clings to starch rather than the fabric. Good starch should be safe to all dyestuffs and fabrics, colourless, free from odour and easy to apply.

Starch is a polysaccharide similar to sugar in composition. It is manufactured by green plants during photosynthesis, and stored by them in roots, seeds and tubes. Starch from plants shows up as easily identifiable grains under the microscope.

The grains of rice starch are very small and are suitable for cold-water starching, as they penetrate the fabric thoroughly.However, starch produced from rice is not much used in the textile industry, as it finds most demand in the preparation of foodstuffs.

Wheat and maize starch grains are of intermediate size. They give a strong viscous solution, leaving the fabric very stiff. Maize starch is also called corn starch;

Tapioca starch is made from the roots of the cassava plant. The roots are dried, sliced and crushed to a pulp with water. The mash is washed with several changes of water and then evaporated to dryness. Tapioca starch is in the form of irregularly shaped lumps produced by breaking the solid white mass left after evaporation. Some starches are tinted to give shades of cream, fawn and blue. However, they are not widely used, as the colours may disguise an inferior quality starch. Along the Malabar cost of India, polished tapioca powder and tamarind-seed powder are blended with some commercial starches.

All the starches described are, when processed by modern methods, free from all impurities and in the form of opaque granules of varying sizes. When starch is 'cooked' in water these granules swell and become almost clear. The degree of cohesiveness depends upon the kind of raw starch used. Most starches remain perfectly fluid after cooking, and are said to be stable.

Clothing can be starched in boiling or cold water, and there are some differences in the preparation and use of starch in the two cases.

Boiling-water starch

The following ingredients are used to make a starch jelly:

- 1 tablespoon starch.
- 1/4 teaspoon of borax (optional—helps to make the starch more resistant to atmospheric conditions)
- Shredded wax or a small amount of soap to help the iron to glide more easily over the fabric.
- 2 tablespoons cold water
- 1 pint boiling water

Mix the starch to a smooth paste with two tablespoons of cold water using a wooden spoon. Pour in the boiling water quickly, stirring all the time until the appearance of the liquid changes to a transparent grey. This shows that the starch grains have burst. The starch thus prepared is called starch jelly and must be diluted at once by adding an equal quantity of hot water. If the jelly were not diluted before cooling, the addition of water to make solutions of correct strength would produce lumpy starch. Finally, a little formalin can be added to prevent the starch from becoming sour, and a pinch of wax prevents it from sticking, while ironing. Now, cover the starch at once to prevent a thick skin forming on top.

The starching process is simple. The articles, mostly cottons and linens, are dipped up and down in the starch till they are thoroughly saturated, then wrung out and hung up to dry. Fringes, tassels, and crochets are not starched. When the articles are dry, the fabric is damped evenly before ironing. The amount of starch required depends on the thickness of the fabric, the stiffness required in the fabric, and personal taste. Generally, heavier materials need less starch than light-weight fabrics. White starch shows prominently when used on dark fabrics. It may be tinted with tea of coffee for browns and with blues for white fabrics. The following table indicates the strength needed for various fabrics.

Starch-cold water dilution	Articles
1 to 1	Stiff caps, sun hats, chintz
1 to 2	Stiff cuffs, thin fabrics, cotton dupattas, centre of cake doilies
1 to 3	Stiff aprons
1 to 4	Aprons, overalls, shirts, blouses, table linen, dupattas
1 to 6	Curtains, linen, table napkins, linen table-cloths, salwars, tea cloths
1 to 8	Fine cotton blouses, kameezes
1 to 10	Very fine handkerchiefs

Cold-water starch

The following ingredients make enough starch for six collars or their equivalent. Add 4 drops of turpentine if twice this quantity is to be prepared.

- 1 tablespoon rice starch
- 1/2 teaspoon of borax (to give additional and more permanent stiffness)
- 3 drops of turpentine (instead of wax which would not melt in a cold solution)
- 1/2 pint cold water
- 1 tablespoon boiling water

Dissolve the borax in the boiling water. Add cold water to the dissolved borax and pour this onto the starch. Add turpentine. Mix to a smooth paste. Strain through muslin, cover and leave for half-an-hour before use. This softens the starch grains. Stir thoroughly before use.

Cold starch is used when greater stiffness is required, such as for stiff collars and cuffs and Gandhi caps. The material must be dry for this type of starching. Starch the fabric till the mixture is absorbed into its mesh. Then squeeze out and rub off surface starch grains with a muslin wrung out tightly in cold water. Iron with quick movements, using a clean iron. Great stiffness results.

Other Stiffening Agents

Borax can be used above for slight stiffening. 1 to 4 teaspoonfuls are added to 1/2 pint of water. Borax is useful for stiffening laces.

Dilute solutions of gelatin or gum arabic are often used on delicate fabrics like voiles, organdies and silks to restore their crisp new appearance. Avoid using too much however, as they will leave the fabric feeling sticky.

First a stock solution is made by adding 1 pint cold water to 1 ounce gelatin or gum arabic, and heating to dissolve. The stock solution can be stored with a little borax to help preserve it. Before use, the stock solution is diluted with hot water: 8-15 times for gelatin, and 5-10 times for gum arabic. The actual dilution depends on the kind of material and stiffness required.

Laundry Blues

White fabrics often lose their original, sparkling whiteness and develop a yellow tint. This tint may be due to one of the following causes:

1. Incomplete washing.
2. The deposition of lime or iron particles from soap on fabrics.
3. The reappearance of the natural colouring of the original fibres after repeated washes in which no bleach has been used, or the effect of coarse alkaline soap upon fabrics damaged by cover bleaching.

Contrary to belief, bleaching does not whiten clothes; it merely corrects the yellow tinge that clothes may develop owing to one of the above-mentioned reasons.

Blues are chemicals used during the wash cycle, either at home or by large laundries to correct the yellowing of white fabrics. Ultramarine is a commonly used household blue. It is insoluble in water. Most laundries use soluble blues.

Ultramarine is a safe blue to use. It is not affected by alkaline soaps. It is sometimes used together with soap in boiling water so that the blue is 'boiled in.' Blueing with ultramarine may, however, cause trouble by large particles forming specks on the fabric. This may be avoided by applying the blue before the last rinse. The care required with ultramarine has caused the abandonment of its use by many laundries in favour of the soluble blues and fluorescent washing powders, which are simpler to use.

The soluble blues are actually aniline dyes and are marketed in a great variety. They are easy to prepare, control and apply, producing an even colour and leaving no sediment. They are widely employed in large-scale power laundries. These can be obtained as concentrated solutions or as powders. Purplish-blue is the most popular shade, as it gives a whitish appearance. The aniline dyes have a strong affinity for materials and must be used with care. However, owing to their high solubility, they are easily removed by thorough rinsing, so that correction of over-blueing is no trouble.

Blueing should only be done when the fabric is free from soap. The process, therefore, follows the last or second last rinse. The blue is tied in a piece of muslin and squeezed in cold water until the required depth of colour is obtained. Ultramarine, being insoluble, is held in suspension; so the water must be stirred each time before use.

The article is dipped up and down in the solution once or twice. Any water retained in pockets or other bagshaped parts is shaken out. The articles should be moved constantly, and not allowed to rest in the bath. Blueing and starching may be combined if necessary.

Yellow articles should not be blued, since they turn greenish. Over blueing can be removed by treatment with acetic acid. It should be noted that blueing is not really necessary in India, where there is strong sunlight for nine months of the year. Sunlight is the best natural bleach for properly washed articles.

Additional Laundry Reagents

Other additives are used along with soap or detergents to help in removing grease spots, fruit stains, etc. They can be grouped as alkaline agents, acidic agents, organic solvents and absorbants.

Alkaline agents

Washing Soda (Sodium Carbonate $Na_2CO_3.10H_2O$) is the most commonly used additive. It is usually purchased in the form of soda crystals which readily dissolve in boiling water. It is used along with soap to improve its cleaning power particularly in the boil.

The use of washing soda:

1. Softens the water.

2. Emulsifies grease stains. Heavily soiled articles are steeped overnight in a vessel containing two teaspoons of soda in about one gallon of water).

3. Removes vegetable stains and light scorch marks. (The fabric is treated for 15 minutes in a hot solution of 1 to 4 teaspoons of soda in 1 pint of water.

4. Neutralises the effect of acids, removing acid stains on bleached cottons and linen fabrics. (Saturate in a solution of 1 to 4 teaspoons of soda in 1 pint of water.)

However, washing soda should be used with care. If used in excess, the wash solution becomes alkaline, injuring fabrics. Washing soda tends to make white clothes yellowish, and fades prints. It is also hard on the skin.

Borax Sodium Tetraborate $Na_2B_4O_7.10H_2O$ occurs naturally and is sold as a white powder. It is a mildly alkaline substance, readily soluble in cold-water, and can be used safely on any fibre. The alkalinity is useful in removing acid stains. The addition of borax to starch prevents its scorching or browning at the high temperature used in finishing collars. However, too much borax will make the collars stiff and cause then to crack. The proportion of borax to starch must not be more than 1 : 16. Borax also has a bleaching action. Cotton and linen fabrics yellowed by age are whitened by boiling in a solution of borax. The decomposition product of the cellulose responsible for the yellow colour is dissolved by the borax solution. No other coloured substances are formed at the same time as happens with sodium carbonate, or when a strong alkali is used.

Ammonia (Ammonium hydroxide NH_4OH) is sometimes purchased as a concentrated solution. This must be used with care as its pungent vapours may cause coughing and choking. It is better to use household ammonia, but the strength may vary from make to make.

Ammonia is a strong alkali, capable of yellowing silk and wool, and bleeding colours and, in time, tendering the fabric. A 10 per cent solution may be used safely on coloured fabrics. Ammonia is used to treat grease and mild scorch stains on animal fabrics, the solution being about 1-4 teaspoons to a pint of warm water. Again, it can be used against acid stains.

It is also used to remove the smell left after using Javelle water (sodium or potassium hydrochlorite) used as a bleach or disinfectant.

Acid agents

Oxalic Acid $(COOH)_2$ is a poison and should be kept in a jar labelled as such. It is sold in the form of white crystals. Its uses include

1. The removal of iron mould and obstinate fruit stains.
2. Bleaching the brown stains left after the use of potassium permanganate.
3. Removing the tannin base of ink stains, together with hydrogen peroxide.
4. As a cleanser for white straw hats.

The article is soaked for above ten minutes in a hot solution of 1-4 teaspoons to 1 pint of water and is then thoroughly washed and, if possible, boiled. Oxalic acid has a strong action, and it should be neutralised after use by borax or ammonia to prevent damage to fabrics. Oxalic acid should never be used on wool or silk since it causes brown stains which cannot be removed. Care must be taken not to treat the material at temperatures over 140°F or with too strong a solution, nor must the substance be allowed to dry into the material, since any of these conditions may result in a weakening of the material. Wooden spoons must be used if possible.

Salt of Lemon (COOH COOK) is a compound of potassium oxalate and oxalic acid. It is also called salt of sorrel. It is used in the same way and in the same proportions as oxalic acid. It, too is a poison, and should be used with a wooden spoon.

Acetic Acid (CH_3COOH) is one of the most important acids in use in the laundry. The household form of acetic acid is vinegar which has about 6 per cent acetic acid. Acetic acid is sold in several strengths, glacial acetic acid being the strongest and purest. The acid should not be stored in metal vessels, only in glass, enamel or earthenware vessels.

Acetic acid is used in the following cases.

1. A weak solution of vinegar (about 1 teaspoon to 1 pint of water) is used as a steeping bath to remove overblueing and as a neutralizing agent.

2. Treatment with a weak acetic acid solution during the final rinse will not only fix colours, but also, in many cases, give added brightness to the colours.

3. During manufacture, special finishing processes are applied to silks and rayon to give them their scroop or characteristic rustle. This finish or scroop is removed during laundering, but it may be restored by rinsing the garment in a weak solution of acetic acid.

4. To the dyer of silks, acetic acid is very important as a substitute for the stronger sulphuric acid.

5. Acetic acid is a great aid in the correction of finishing faults on cellulose acetate. If this fibre is finished at too high a temperature, shiny, glazed marks, often mistaken for grease spots are produced on the fabric. To correct this the article is immersed in cold 20% acetic acid solution for about an hour, after which it is wrapped without rinsing in a cloth and hydro-extracted lightly. Drying is carried out at about 140°F. Among the precautions in using acetic acid, too much of it may injure wool or silk. These fabrics have an affinity for acids, and should be rinsed thoroughly. If residual acid is present, it will split a soap solution; the fabric will then be greasy from the free fatty acid and smell abominably.

Oleic Acid ($CH_3(CH_2)_7CH = (CH(CH_2)_7COOH)$) is a straight-chain unsaturated fatty acid. While glyceride, olein, occurs in most natural fats. It produces soap when mixed with an alkali. It is used for the spotting of machine grease and oil stains. The acid is applied to the stain and allowed to remain on it for 15 minutes to dissolve the grease. The part being treated is then twisted and dipped in a weak solution of ammonia, which produces soap. The stain is now rubbed or brushed until it is removed by the lather. Oleic acid is used to treat cotton and linen, but it readily felts wool, tends to discolour silk and is unsuitable for coloured fabrics. It must in all cases be well rinsed from garments, or a rancid odour will remain.

Organic solvents

Appropriate solvents are applied to the most delicate fabrics either to remove stains or to dry clean them. They do not injure the fibres or the colours of the fabrics. There are few solvents suitable for use in the home, as they are not very economical. Some commonly used solvents are described below. The section on drycleaning in the next chapter has more details on their use as spotting agents.

Cleaning Benzene (C_6H_6) or Petrol is obtained from the distillation of shale oil or petroleum. It is highly inflammable and should not be kept or used indoors in any large quantity, and must never be used, even in small quantities, near open fires. It is of great value in removing stains containing grease.

Carbon Tetrachloride (CCL_4) is more expensive than cleaning benzene, but similar in action and has the great advantage of being non-flammable. It is very toxic however, and should be used near an open window or in well-ventilated rooms. It is extremely volatile and evaporates quickly. It is a good solvent for paint, and can be used on all fabrics.

Acetone (CH_3COCH_3) is a useful solvent for many stains. However, it cannot be used on cellulose acetate as it rapidly dissolves the fibre. On fibres other than cellulose acetate and vinyon, acetone is an effective spotting agent for stains caused by cosmetics, nail polish, lipstick, paint, varnish and shoe polish. Acetone, too, is highly inflammable.

Methylated Spirit is ordinary or ethyl alcohol (C_2H_3OH) mixed with methyl alcohol (CH_3OH), which makes it poisonous to drink. It is sold coloured with a violet dye to draw attention to this fact. Although not a very good solvent, it can be used to remove sealing wax, silver nitrate and other silver stains. It can also be employed usefully with soap. It dissolves acetate but can be used safely on all other fabrics.

Paraffin is a mixture of hydrocarbons (C_9H_{20} to C_7H_{36}). It is a white, waxy solid obtained as a residue from the distillation of petroleum and shale. It is used for removing grease and paint stains on the rubber fittings in laundry appliances. The section on the laundering of cottons and linens in the next chapter has details on the paraffin wash technique.

Turpentine ($C_{10}H_{16}$) is more expensive than paraffin. It has a distinctive smell, is inflammable and volatile. It is a solvent for grease, varnish, paint and printer's ink. It is also useful for cleaning rubber rollers. Its one disadvantage is its odour, which is best removed by dry cleaning again. The great advantage of turpentine is that it is safe on acetate.

Absorbents

These substances are suitable for removing grease spots from all fabrics and for general treatment of light-coloured fabrics that are evenly soiled. Some examples of substances that are used as absorbents are common salt, bran, fullers earth, powdered magnesia, French chalk and bread crumbs. The section on dry cleaning in the next chapter has more details.

Bleaches

Bleaches are used to render coloured or discoloured fabrics white. They are used in laundering to remove stains that do not respond to normal washing. Bleaches should not be used as cleansers; it is not possible to 'bleach' dirty laundry.

Bleaching agents are grouped into two classes: oxidizing and reducing. Oxidizing bleaches supply oxygen that combines with stains to form a colourless compound. Normal as well as stained fibres can be oxidized, so the bleach must be in contact with the fabric only till the stain is removed, else the fabric will be weakened. Reducing bleaches work by removing oxygen from the colouring matter of the stain.

Open Air and Sunlight is the world's oldest and cheapest method of bleaching. Hanging clothes out in the sun to dry keeps white clothes sparkling. In many parts of India, clothes are still spread out on grass, sprinkled with water and left exposed to sun, rain and dew until they are bleached. Sunlight bleaching can also be used for stain removal from bleached cotton and linen fabrics. When an article is laid on grass or spread over a bush, additional bleaching may be due to the chlorophyll in the leaves, as it plays its part in making starch for the plant.

Sodium Hypochlorite (Javelle Water) is made using the following ingredients;

- 1 pound washing soda
- 1/4 pound chloride of lime
- 1 quart boiling water
- 2 quarts cold water

Dissolve the washing soda in the boiling water. Mix the chloride of lime with the cold water, allow to settle, and strain off the clear liquid without stirring. Mix this filtrate with the washing soda solution. Allow the precipitate of calcium carbonate that is formed to settle. Again strain off the clear liquid and store the residue in dark-coloured bottles as it is unstable to light. This compound readily gives off nascent oxygen, a powerful bleaching agent. It should only be used to bleach white cottons and linens, never on any other fabrics. Dilute the Javelle water with an equal amount of hot water and dip the stain in the bleach till it is removed. Do not allow the article to soak for more than twenty minutes. To speed up the action, a few drops of vinegar may be added. Rinse very thoroughly, never allowing the bleach to dry into the fabric. A small amount of ammonia in the rinse water will help remove the smell of bleach from the fabric. Sodium hypochlorite should not be used on silk or wool as these fabrics are dissolved in it. The dyes of many coloured fabrics are not fast to sodium hypochlorite or other chlorine bleaches. Also, fabrics should not be boiled in the solution, as this may weaken the material.

Hydrogen Peroxide is an effective bleach, not harmful to most fabrics. It can be used in various concentrations, depending upon the amount of bleaching required. One pint to a gallon of water is an average quantity. A teaspoon of concentrated ammonia solution or of sodium perborate can be added to each gallon of the solution to make the action stronger. After bleaching, the garments should be rinsed thoroughly.

Sodium Perborate is made from borax, caustic soda and hydrogen peroxide. It is used in many 'oxygen' washing powders. It dissolves in water to make an alkaline bleaching solution that contains hydrogen peroxide. To prepare the bleach, dissolve one ounce of sodium perborate in one gallon of water. If animal fabrics are to be treated, the solution is first neutralized with acetic acid, and then made slightly alkaline with a little ammonia. Sodium perborate is especially effective when the action is started from low temperature and the heat gradually increased. Like hydrogen peroxide, its bleaching action is due to oxidation and can consequently tender cotton and linen.

Potassium Permanganate has a high content of oxygen. This enables it to combine with and remove obstinate stains like perspiration and mildew. It can be used on animal as well as vegetable fibres. For the former, half-an-ounce of potassium permanganate is dissolved in one gallon of water at body (warm blood) temperature. For cotton and linen fabrics, one ounce of the bleach is used to one gallon of hot water. The articles are steeped in the solution for a few minutes, then rinsed out. Due to the formation of manganese dioxide, the article will be stained a characteristic brown. This is now removed by dipping in one of the following solutions: (1) Sodium hyprochorite (see above); (2) oxalic acid prepared in the ratio 1 ounce to 1 gallon of water; or (3) two volumes of hydrogen peroxide acidified with a teaspoon of vinegar (acetic acid) to one volume of bleach. The brown stain will disappear almost at once. Finally, the article is thoroughly rinsed.

Reducing bleaches

Sodium Hydrosulphite is a valuable agent for bleaching all fibres, particularly wool and silks, which cannot be treated with sodium hypochlorite.

It acts by taking oxygen out of the stain, especially when dissolved in hot water, and becoming sodium metabisulphite. When the latter is exposed to air, it is split up into sodium sulphate and sulphur dioxide, which is itself a reducing agent. Sodium hydrosulphite should be stored air-tight and moisture free and away from heat, as it can decompose by absorbing oxygen, and sulphur dioxide gas is given off, so windows should be left open. It can be used in concentrated form to remove spots caused by grass, dung, leather, polish, mildew, ink, potassium permanganate and dye stains. Used as a solution, the solution hydrosulphite is dissolved in the ratio 1-4 teaspoons to 1 pint of water. The water may be cold, hot or boiling, depending on the nature of the fibre and the stain to be removed. The article is steeped in the solution for a few minutes, then rinsed well in very soapy water. If the bleach has inadvertantly run into a coloured part of the fabric, the bleached colour can be restored by dipping immediately in an alkaline solution, scrubbing with soap, or sponging with vinegar. When using sodium hydrosulphite bleach, only vessels of wood or earthenware should be used, as contact with metal will leave a black stain on all fabrics.

Sodium Bisulphite is a mild reducing agent produced by the partial neutralisation of sulphurous acid by caustic soda. Like sodium hydrosulphite, its bleaching action is due to the formation of sulphur dioxide, which takes oxygen out of the stain. It is used in the proportion of 2 tablespoons to 1 pint of water. Neutralization or thorough rinsing must follow, otherwise sulphuric acid will appear in the fabric through the action of oxygen.

Sodium Thiosulphate (Hypo) is a bleach for cottons. It is made by mixing 1/4 ounce sodium thiosulphate, 1/8 ounce of 36 per cent acetic acid and 2 quarts of water.

Overbleaching

The overbleaching of cotton and linen goods during laundering is one of the main causes of general weakness of the fabrics. The fibres become brittle and harsh, and give a distinct 'crackle' when rubbed together. To guard against it, use a bleach of known strength, never exceeding 5 grains per gallon. Keep the temperature below 140°F, and add measured quantities of dilute bleach gradually. Chlorine bleach especially, should not be used at temperatures above 160°F. Although most overbleaching is due to chlorine bleaches, oxidising agents have the same effect on cotton and linen. Hydrogen peroxide, for instance is no safer.

Optical brighteners

Optical bleaches or colourless dyes are used on white fabrics. They are fluorescent white compounds; they act by whitening the fabric, and are not true bleaches. Samples are Ranipal (for cotton) and Ranipal-S (for synthetics and blends), made by Ciba Geigy. These compounds are absorbed into the fibre and emit a bluish light that covers up yellow tinges. They do so by converting invisible ultraviolet rays to visible light. The kind of light source under which fabrics so whitened are seen affects their appearance: dazzling white in sunlight but quite different in any other light.

Laundry Equipment

Although most laundry work in India is done by hand with few mechanical or electrical appliances, this situation is changing as incomes rise. Many middle-class households can now afford washing machines, many more models of which are available today than just a few years ago. However, large sections of people in rural India and in small towns use more traditional mechanical wash aids. This section therefore covers a selection of both modern and older appliances.

Storage

Woven or cane clothes baskets can be used during washing, drying, and for storage of soiled linen. They should be lined with oil cloth or heavy paper to keep the dust out. Oil cloth is best if the basket is likely to rest on damp ground. A small cupboard or closet for laundry stores is also useful. Stone jars or wide-mouthed bottles are suitable for storing laundry materials. Poisonous reagents must be labelled as such.

Steeping and washing

Deep copper or brass vessels (*degchis)* and portable galvanised iron tubs are good for hand washing, but perhaps used most in large homes. Since iron is galvanised by coating with a thin film of zinc, hard water and washing soda react with the zinc and discolour it. Whiting paste or a weak acid solution will remove this discolouration, but should be rinsed off after use.

Bath tubs and other purpose built stationary tubs can also be used, if space is available. They should be of a durable, strong material that is easily cleaned. Soapstone, or Mangalore baked-clay tubs with a glazed surface are very satisfactory, better than cement.

Aluminium is unsuitable for laundry vessels because it is corroded by hot solutions of soap or soda. Smaller aluminium utensils can be used to measure cold solutions of soda or alkali so long as they are not allowed to remain unwashed for a long period after use.

Buckets, basins and kitchen sinks can be used to soak handkerchiefs and small quantities of clothes, or for preparing starch. Sinks used for laundry must be about 14-20 inches wide 20 inches long and 12 inches deep, and should be installed 36 inches from the ground to suit the average height. A double sink with draining boards on either side is preferable. The draining plug should be at one end, not in the middle, with a slight slope to the plug.

A wash board or rubbing board (Fig. 7.4) is a useful aid in clean-

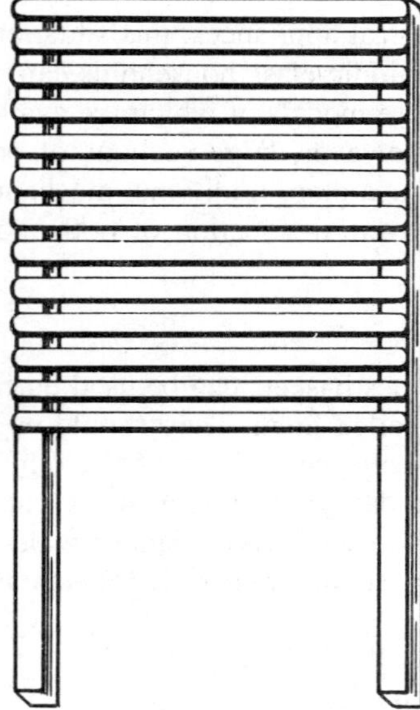

Fig. 7.4 A wash board

ing dirty articles. The board must be rust-proof and should have no rough edges to catch clothing or fingers. Wash boards are less harmful to the fabric than hard scrubbing brushes. Wash boards are made with a variety of materials:

1. Wood, either in the form of a board with a corrugated surface, or as a series of rollers in a frame. Wooden boards are cheap and can be made to order.

2. Zinc in the form of a corrugated sheet held in a frame. This is very satisfactory, but must be kept scrupulously clean, otherwise greasy zinc soap will be formed.

3. Stainless steel rubbing boards with corrugated surfaces are also available, but are more expensive.

4. Glass with a corrugated surface enclosed in a frame is easy to clean and will not stain clothes.

A stiff brush can be used on dirty clothes or soiled patches, but will wear clothing out more easily.

Mechanical washing aids

They may look old-fashioned, but are useful in places with uncertain electric supply. The ones most commonly used in India are the *suction washer* (Fig. 7.5) and *clothes wringer*.

The suction washer consists of a hollow cup of non-rusting material such as copper or chromium with a wooden handle. It usually comes in two sizes: small for fine articles, and a larger one for general household articles. Its use is described in the next chapter. Clothes wringers come in many designs. Some are hand-operated, while others may be electrically driven. They can be placed to swing into position over a sink, or even attached to the tub of a washing machine. Wringers are useful during the monsoons, and in locations with inadequate sunshine.

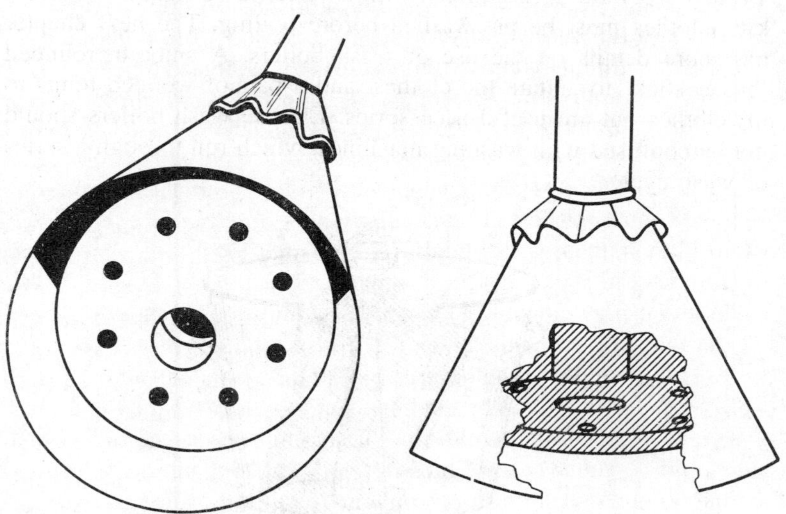

Fig. 7.5 Suction washer

The wringer consists of a number of rubber rollers between which wet garments are forced to squeeze out the water. The spaces and tension between the rollers can be adjusted by a hand screw, and there is a safety release. Some models have a top roller of soft rubber so buttoned garments can be wrung without damage. Wringers can be used for all woollen garments, heavy blankets, most synthetic fabrics, all types of rayon, fine silks and Dacca saris. However, thick garments should not be forced through; the tension between rollers should be adjusted first. In maintaining a wringer, the rubber rollers can be washed with warm, soapy water and dried well, as wet rubber deteriorates. Soiled rollers can also be cleaned with a little paraffin or turpentine, but they should then be washed immediately, as both liquids are rubber solvents.

Wash boilers

For articles that must be washed in boiling water, such as bedsheets, a wash boiler is a useful piece of equipment. Wash boilers used to be made of zinc or galvanized iron and contain electric heating elements, which are covered so they do not contact the clothes. Some models are fitted with agitators to move the clothes around. Typical sizes are 5-10 gallons, with an electric consumption of 2-4 kw. Clothes must be pre-washed before boiling. The next chapter has more details on the use of wash boilers. A smooth, rounded 'boiler stick' to agitate the clothes, and a pair of wooden tongs to lift clothes out are useful accessories. Electric wash boilers should not be confused with washing machines, which run through a series of wash cycles.

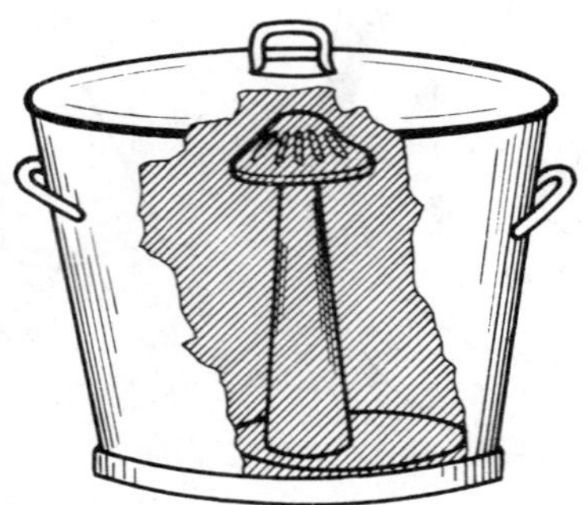

Fig. 7.6 Wash boiler for use on a gas ring

Washing machines

If electric and water supply are steadily available, no appliance can beat the modern washing machine as a labour saver. All washing machines work on the same principle—cleaning clothes by the combined action of water, soap or rather, a specially formulated detergent, and mechanical movement of the clothes through the water. The movement is effected in a cylinder (giving a 'tumble wash') or a vertical tub fitted with an agitator.

Tumble wash machines contain a perforated metal cylinder into which the clothes are loaded (Fig. 7.7). The cylinder has partitions along its inner surface—either short ones in domestic machines, or the whole cylinder is divided into separate compartments in commercial machines. After it has half-filled with soapy water through the preparations, the cylinder rotates a given amount alternately clockwise and anticlockwise. During each of these motions, the clothes are carried around a given distance, then dropped back into the water. The machine must therefore not be packed too tightly with laundry, as this would interfere with the drop, which is an important part of the cleaning action.

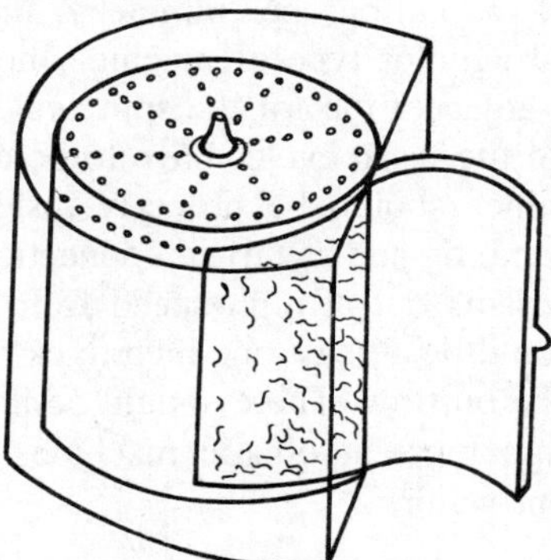

Fig. 7.7 Wash cylinder

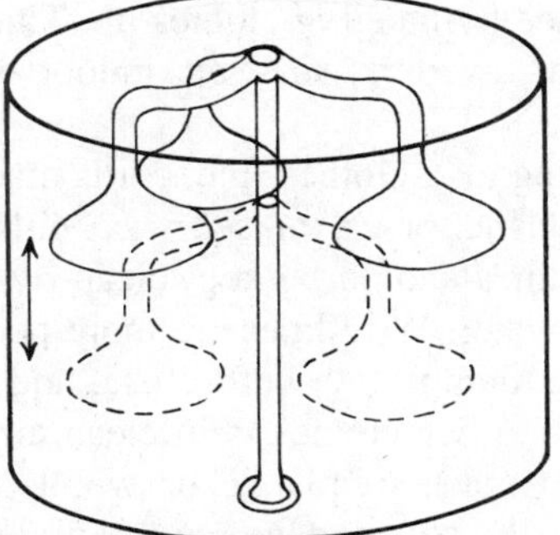

Fig. 7.8 The agitator

In the agitator type of washing machine, the clothes are loaded into a vertical tub. The agitator is located at the bottom of the tub.

It consists of hard plastic or aluminium blades or vanes attached to a rotating shaft that reverses direction periodically (Fig. 7.8). The agitator blades are quite blunt to reduce wear on the clothes. Agitator type machines are less expensive than tumble wash machines, and therefore more commonly purchased in India.

Modern washing machines are fully automatic. The user sets a few wash controls and the water temperature, loads the clothes, turns the machine on and returns in about an hour to take out the washed and wrung clothes to dry. Meanwhile, the machine has put the clothes through a pre-wash, up to three wash and three rinse cycles and a final, fast spin-dry cycle. In the last, the tub, now free of water, spins at over 500 revolutions per minute to thoroughly wring out the clothes. In the agitator type of machine the clothes have to be placed in another adjacent tub for the spin cycle. In semi-automatic machines, some of the wash cycles have to be controlled manually.

Washing machines should be properly installed by a qualified technician. All plumbing and electrical connections should be secure and safe. Water drains out at high speed from these machines, so the outlet pipe should be at least one inch thick and lead into a drain than can handle the outflow. There should be adequate water in the inlet pipe, although most automatic machines will not operate if there is insufficient water.

Drying equipment

Since automatic clothes dryers are not yet freely available in India, all drying takes place by hanging clothes up. This can be a problem for urban apartment dwellers, so some indoor drying methods are described below.

For outdoor drying on a clothes-line, cords made of cotton, hemp, coconut fibres or plastic, or galvanised wire, either solid or twisted, may be used. The lines should be kept clean by washing occasionally with soap and water. Wire lines are more permanent; they must be wiped off with a damp cloth before use, and must be free from rust. The best place to dry clothes is in clean air and sunshine.

Clothes pegs are made of plastic or wood. Unless well made, plastic pegs snap easily, so wooden pegs are preferable. They should be stored in a bag or basket in a dry place. To prevent stooping for them, they can be hooked to the line and moved along it as the clothes are hung up.

For indoor drying, necessary during the monsoons or in cramped

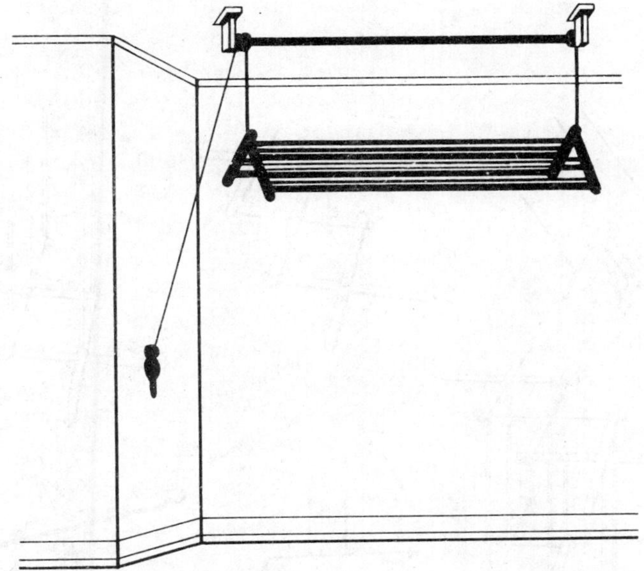

Fig. 7.9 Ceiling drying rack (Courtesy: Lady Irwin College, Delhi)

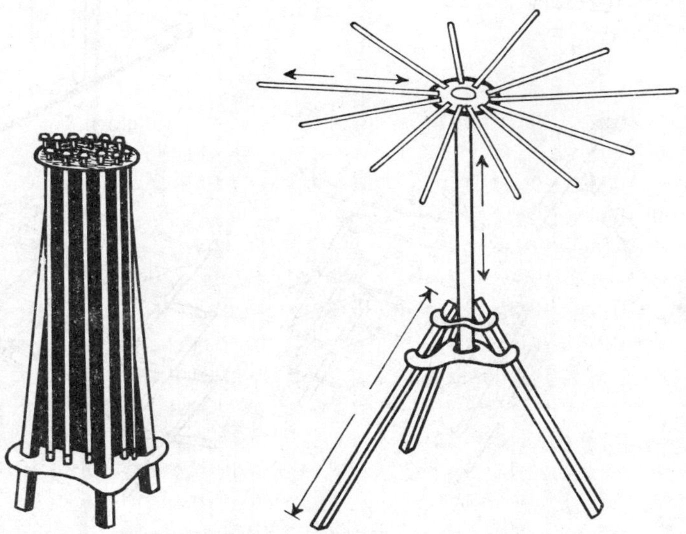

Fig. 7.10 Indoor dryers

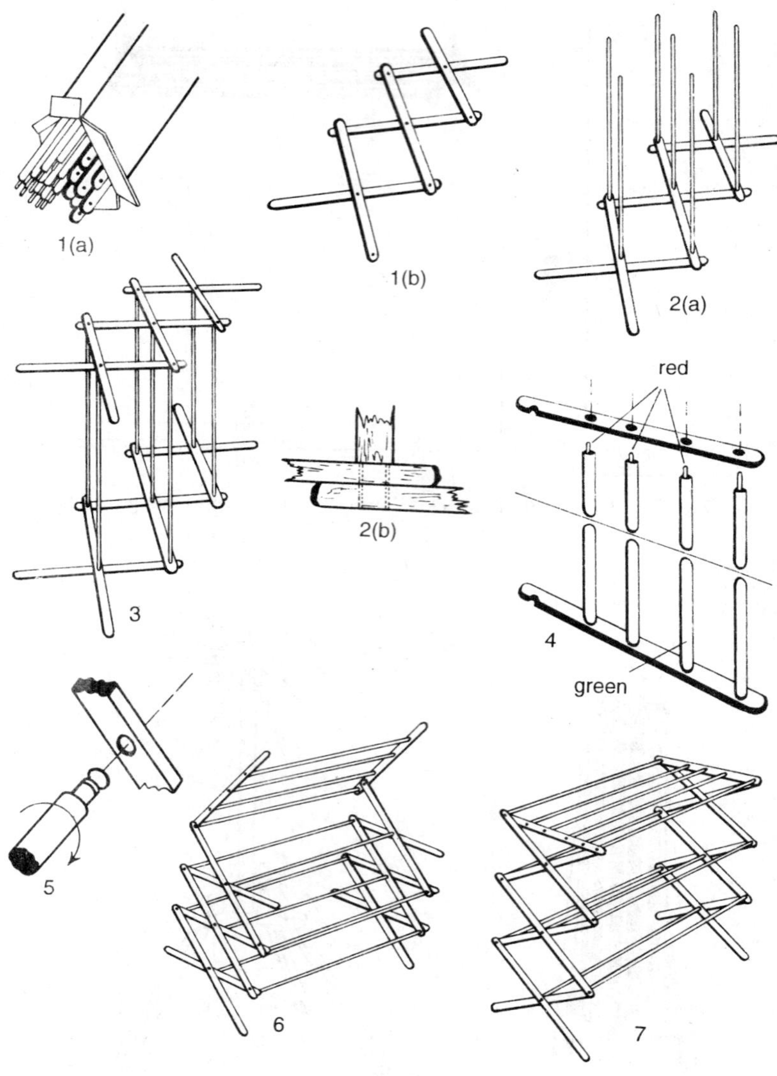

Fig. 7.11 Construction of a collapsible indoor dryer

apartments, several kinds of racks can be used. Those living in older homes with high ceilings can have the rack shown in Fig. 7.9 constructed of wood and bamboo. It uses ropes and pulleys and hoists up to the ceiling, out of the way. Other indoor dryers are shown in Fig. 7.10, while Fig. 7.11 shows the do-it yourself enthusiast how to construct a collapsible drying rack.

Irons and Ironing Boards

Irons in use in India fall into two categories: older models using an external heat source and electric irons. The former can be used in places with unreliable electric supply. They are the irons used by the ubiquitous *presswalas* of urban India who iron clothes on street corners on pushcarts. They use heavy charcoal, flat or box irons (Figs. 7.12).

In a charcoal iron, the top lid opens out and the inside is packed with heated charcoal. There is a draught door in the back to let air in. Coconut shells can be used instead of charcoal. While this type of iron is fairly clean, it is heavy and difficult to manipulate. It has to be replenished periodically with fresh live charcoal, tiny pieces of which may escape and singe clothes.

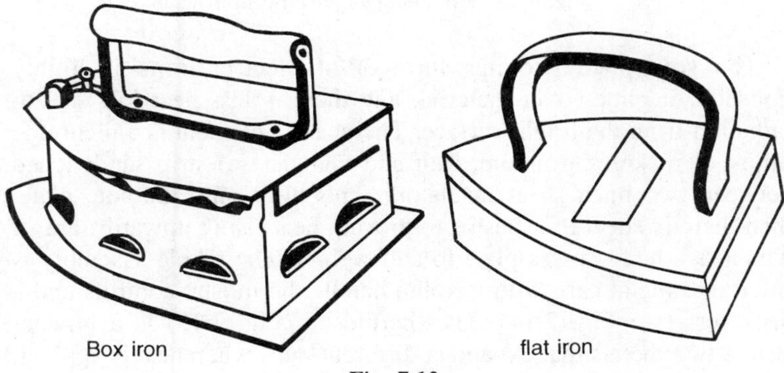

Fig. 7.12

The flat iron is made of heavy, cast iron, faced with polished steel. They weigh from four to five pounds, and are heated over a stove. The ironing surface is cleaned by rubbing on a hard surface sprinkled with powdered Bath brick or other metal cleaning compounds. Box irons are similar. Their cavities are filled with a heated bolt. A small, externally heated polishing iron with a convex box is also sometimes used to press collars, shirts and chintz. An iron holder or iron stand is necessary when these older irons are used. These can be thick, cotton-covered pads, or a slab made of stone or asbestos.

Electric irons (Fig. 7.13) are much lighter and easier to use than traditional irons. Heat, not weight, does the work in automatic, thermostatically-controlled irons. The thermostat makes it possible to reduce the weight of the iron by as much as three pounds. It allows the selection of different temperature settings for various fabrics, and maintains the iron at these temperatures. Thus electric iron can be used at hotter temperatures than traditional irons.

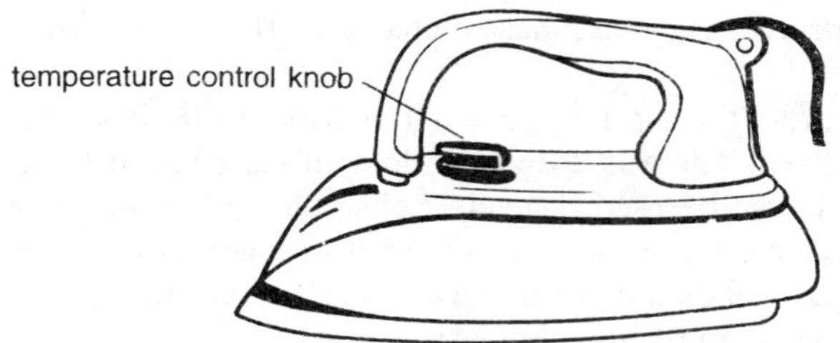

Fig. 7.13 An automatic electric iron

The sole plate (ironing surface) of electric irons is highly polished. It glides over material, and there is less heat loss due to radiation from the bright surface. The heating element is a nichrome (alloy of nickel, chromium, iron and manganese) strip sandwiched between two mica sheet insulators. This goes onto the sole plate, then there is sheet of asbestos to prevent heat rising upwards, above which is a heavy press plate to add weight. The whole assembly is fitted in a metal case with bakelite handle thermostat controls and a back rest (see Fig. 7.14). The thermostat (Fig. 7.15) is a bimetal strip—two metals that expand at different rates when heat is applied. This strip opens and closes a contact to maintain a steady temperature. An indicator lamp glows to show when the current is being switched on and off by the thermostat.

There are some very compact models of electric iron that can be packed into a suitcase by frequent travellers. Other models are cordless. They are plugged into a base unit which heats them up very

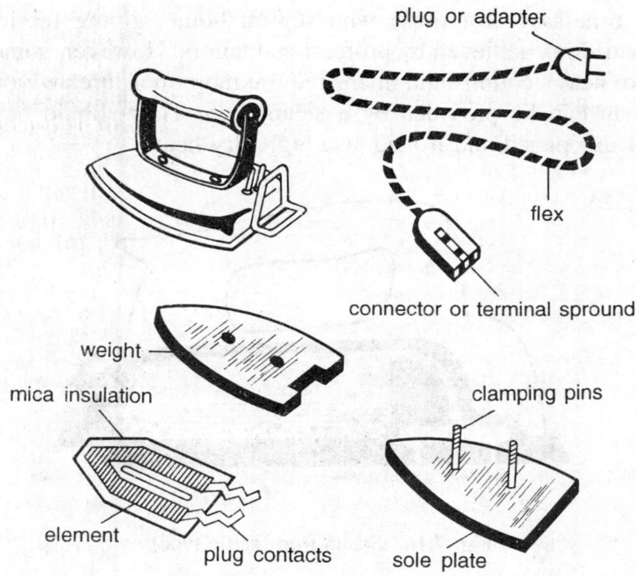

Fig. 7.14 An electric iron

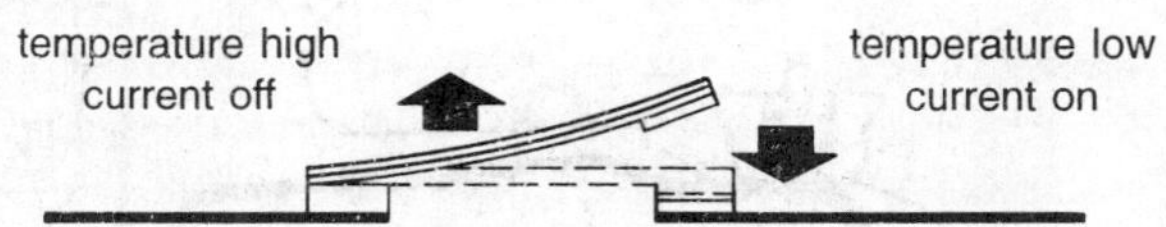

Fig. 7.15 How the thermostat works

quickly. Some other modern features of electric irons are chromium-plated surfaces, bevelled edges with special grooves for ironing under buttons, thumb-rests, and handles that open at one end to facilitate ironing in difficult places like sleeves.

Steam irons eliminate the need to moisten clothes or use a damp cloth while ironing. Water filled into a compartment or reservoir in kettle-type steam irons (Fig. 7.16) is brought to the boil. At the press of a button on the handle, a shot of steam emerges from perforations and grooves in the sole plate. Flash-boiler type steam irons (Fig. 7.17) make instantaneous steam when individual drops of water come in contact with a heated chamber. Steam ironing is a considerable time-saver for those who sew at home, giving fabrics the 'finished' look achieved by professional tailors. However, some fabrics like heavy cottons and linens require more moisture and a hotter iron than can be provided by a steam iron. They should be thoroughly dampened and ironed at a high, dry heat.

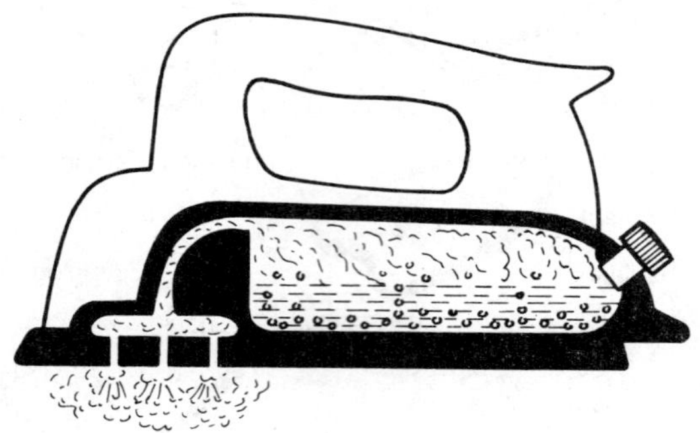

Fig. 7.16 Steam iron (kettle type)

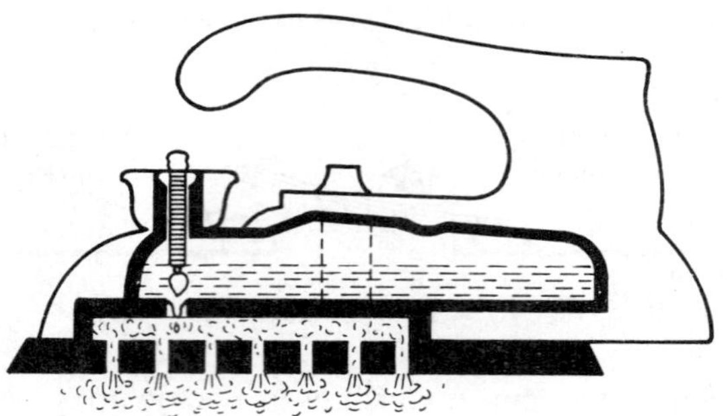

Fig. 7.17 Steam iron (flash-boiler type)

Electric irons draw around 1,000 watts of electricity, though portable models use less. The higher wattage irons make pressing clothes easier, with less physical effort. Irons should be used carefully to prolong their life. The sole plate, especially, should not be damaged by overheating, resting on abrasive surfaces, or ironing over zippers. The use of an ironing board with iron rest is recommended. Some models are shown in Figs. 7.18, 7.19 and 7.20. A

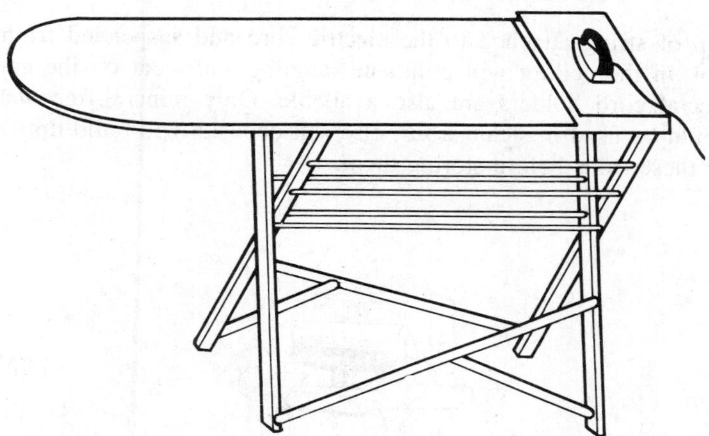

Fig. 7.18 Skirt-board or ironing board (Courtesy: Lady Irwin College)

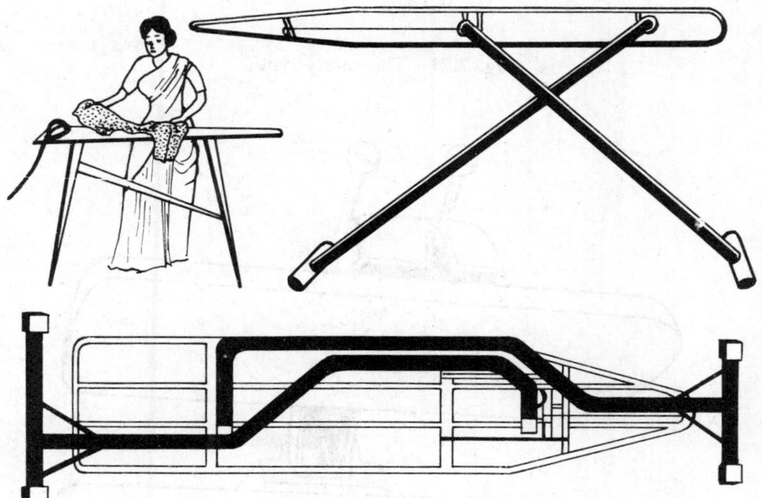

Fig. 7.19 Adjustable ironing board (Courtesy: Lady Irwin College)

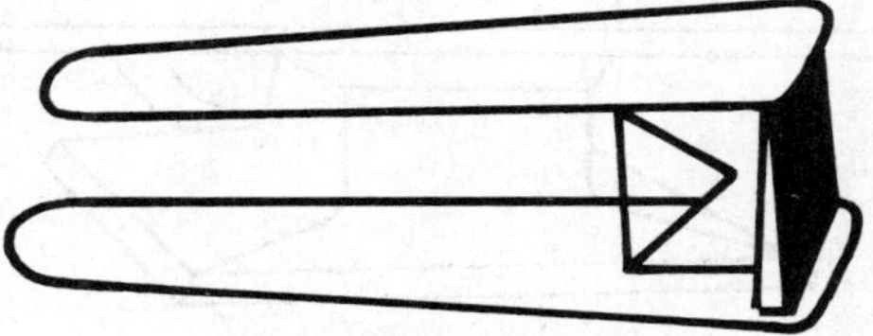

Fig. 7.20 Sleeve board

loop of string attached to the electric cord and suspended from a hook in the ceiling will eliminate tangling and wear on the cord. Special cord holders are also available. Only mineral-free water should be used in steam irons, else salt deposits will build up. Dry out these irons before storing them.

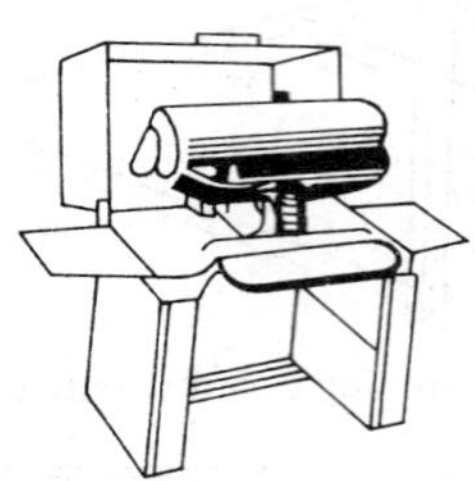

Fig. 7.21 The rotary type

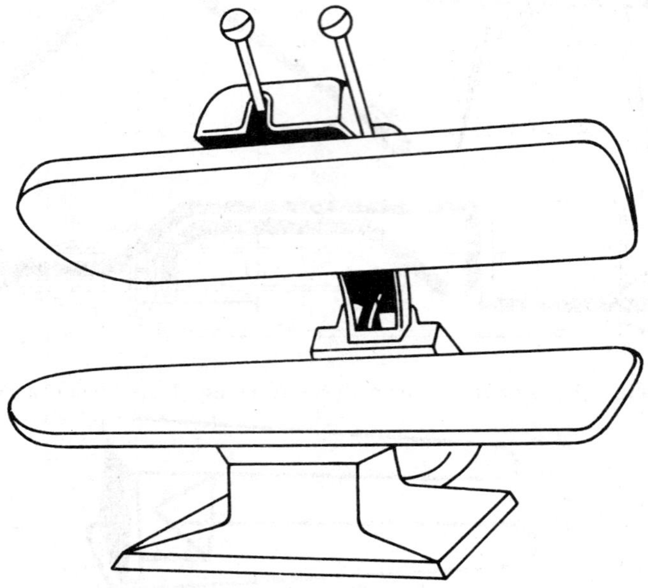

Fig. 7.22 Pressure type of ironing machine

Laundromats, hotels and other establishments use large presses or ironers to iron large volume of clothes quickly. These presses can be in a variety of shape and designs, among them the rotary press (Fig. 7.21) and the flat press (Fig. 7.22).

In a rotary press, the material is passed between a padded roller and a concave metal 'shoe' heated by one or more electrical elements with separate thermostatic controls. The rollers are from 18 inches to 30 inches wide, are well padded and rigidly supported to maintain pressure. The roll covers are removable for cleaning. The heating elements in the shoe can be individually turned off when ironing small articles, so that unused portions of the roller are not scorched. Rotary irons also have a pressing action, in which the roller is stopped momentarily. Damp portions of the article can then be held in longer contact with the heated shoe.

The flat press has two equal-sized metal boards. The upper board or shoe has one or more thermostatically controlled heating elements. The article to be ironed is placed on the lower padded board or buck, and the shoe is brought on to it with pressure. Flat presses are built on a steel and aluminium base, but portable models can be used on a table top. The lower board is of cast aluminium, covered with a thick padding and a removable muslin cover, and flexibly mounted to allow adjustments for garments of varying thickness. The temperature of the elements varies from 200°F to 500°F. There are two hinged arms attaching the shoe to the base, one to raise and lower the shoe, and the other to apply pressure.

8

Laundering, Ironing and Storage

Principles of Washing and Their Application

Home laundering is a process that requires patience and practice and a knowledge of the right techniques. No one method can solve every washing problem.

The dirt in fabrics can be classified as loose dirt resting on the fibres, or fixed dirt which is held fast by grease.

Loose dirt is removed by soaking, or brushing and shaking. Fixed dirt is removed by means of absorption, washing and dry cleaning. Soaps play an important part in removing dirt.

The dhobi first boils and steams the dirty garments in *bhutti*, and then washes the clothes by beating them with a wooden beater or on a stone. This kind of laundering is incorrect.

The former damages the garment by making the dirt get into the fabric and tenderizing it. The latter only weakens the article by causing uneven friction, stretches the fabric in parts and causes them to wear out quickly.

Clothes must be washed as soon as possible after wear. Otherwise the dirt becomes 'fixed' and harder to remove. Soak the garment for about three to four hours. Coloured clothes should be soaked only if the colours are fast. Make sure the detergent powder is completely dissolved in water because it works quicker that way. Do not pack too tightly. It is better to wet the clothes in plain water before soaking them in the detergent. Wetting clothes before soaking saves detergent powder.

Friction washing

By hand. 1. Wring the article out of the water in which it is soaked. 2. Apply soap to the most soiled parts and rub one part against the other until the dirt is loosened. 3. Work over the whole article in this way on both sides until it is fully cleansed. 4. Rinse out the soap with warm water.

This method is useful for cleaning very soiled small articles made of cotton or linen. It is economical in the use of soap.

With a plastic scrubbing brush. You will need hot water, good soap and a plastic brush.

1. Wring the article out of the water. 2. Soak well with the hot washing water and wring out. 3. Spread on a flat surface and rub over with a cake of soap. 4. Rub in the soap, causing a lather in the fabric as it is scrubbed, and work over the whole of the fabric in this way. 5. Rinse in warm washing water.

This method is used for very soiled household articles of any coarse strong fibre e.g. kitchen towels.

Using the rubbing board. You will need hot water in a washing tub, good soap, and a rubbing board.The washing can be conveniently carried out in a deep sink or tub.

1. Saturate the article with hot washing water. 2. Place a part of it on the rubbing board and soap well. 3. Rub one part of the soaped material on another part over the corrugations of the board. This causes a permanent lather in the part of the material being rubbed. 4. Work over the whole article in this way. 5. Rinse well in warm water. It is now ready for the boiler.

This method is used for articles of any size that are very soiled. Rubbing and squeezing on a board is less harmful to the fabric than using a hard scrubbing brush.

Suction washing

With a suction washer. A suction washer is made of some non-rusting material. It may be of a small size for use in a bowl or large for use in a tub.

1. Heat the washing water to the required temperature. 2. Make a permanent lather in the water with soap solution or soap flakes. 3. Place the soiled articles in the softened soapy water and repeatedly press the suction washer down on the immersed article, so that the soap solution circulates through the clothes. Do not pack in the clothes too tightly. When the hollow cup of the suction washer

is pressed down on the clothes, air is forced, from inside the cup, out through the holes at the side. This causes the soapy water to be drawn through the clothes. The repeated suction of the soapy water through the clothes cleans the fabric. This method is sufficient to cleanse normally soiled articles, but very dirty parts need special attention. 4. Use as many waters as required to cleanse. 5. Rinse out the soapy water. The fabric is now ready for the boiler.

This is a quick and practical method to clean large quantities of dirty articles, e.g., sheets, sarees. The fabrics are squeezed and lifted up by the suction of the cup. It can be used on garments of any fabric and colour.

The suction washer must be kept clean and dry when not in use, otherwise it will corrode and become discoloured.

Washing by kneading and squeezing

1. Heat water to the correct temperature for the fabric being treated, i.e., usual temperature 100–110°F. 2. Prepare one or two washing waters with a permanent lather according to the number of articles to be washed. 3. Prepare rinsing water of the correct temperature; the first rinse after washing must always be warm. 4. Knead and squeeze the soiled fabric in the warm soapy water without lifting it out of the water more than is necessary. Very soiled parts should be placed on the palm of the left hand and have additional lather patted through them until the dirt is loosened. Use as many soapy waters as required to cleanse. 5. Rinse thoroughly to remove all traces of soap.

This method is suitable for delicate fabrics to which hand friction cannot be applied such as wool, silk, rayon and coloured fabrics.

Washing by machine

Before using a washing machine, it is important to study the instruction manual. Here are a few general hints.

1. Fill the machine to the water line with warm water. The water must be softened if necessary before adding soap. Add detergent or flakes.
2. Work up a good lather.
3. See that heavily soiled garments have some soap rubbed in before being placed in the machine.
4. Sort clothes into white, coloured and delicate fabrics, e.g., silk, rayon, woollens, etc. For the main wash of white cottons and linens,

use really hot water 120–140°F—rather hotter than the hand can bear. For all delicate fabrics, e.g. rayon, nylon, wool and silk, use only luke-warm water about 90°F.

5. Set the agitator in motion and put in the clothes, one at a time and well opened out. (The cleansing takes place by the movement of soiled fabric through the soapy water so that the soiled matter in moved into the water.)

6. A typical household machine takes a load of 6 to 7 lbs. See that the machine is never overloaded.

7. It is better not to wash more than one sheet at a time and to make up the loads with small things. Babies' clothes or exceptionally delicate garments may be tied in a pillow slip before putting them in the machine.

8. When washing a load of mixed fabrics, always treat according to the most delicate fabric. Collars and cuffs may need gentle rubbing by hand to completely remove the already loosened dirt. Rinse thoroughly, at least twice. Switch off.

9. Swing in position the electrically driven wringer and pass the clothes through the rollers. All articles should be roughly folded lengthwise to avoid straining them.

10. Before putting away, clean the inside of the machine with hot water and wipe dry. The rollers should be wiped carefully and if very soiled, cleaned with a rag soaked in turpentine.

There are several fully automatic washing machines available these days. Just follow the instruction manual carefully. They are efficient and easy to use.

Laundering Cottons and Linens

The safest way to clean soiled clothes and preserve their strength and freshness is to launder them at home.

Bleached cotton and linen fabrics, if carefully handled, can withstand heat, friction and the action of most stain-removing agents and so are fairly easy to wash.

Sorting

Sort the clothes according to their colour, texture, and use.

Fine cottons such as mulmuls, chanderi saris, delicate cottons must be separated and sorted colour-wise: white and light fast colours; dark fast colours and non-fast colours.

Empty pockets and turn set-in pockets inside-out for thorough washing. Clothes are also sorted according to their use: table linen, bed linen, personal garments, handkerchiefs, kitchen towels and or dusters.

Mend garments and remove stains (see section on Removing Stains). Remove all shoulder pads, buttons, belt buckles and trimmings (not washable) and close side-fastners.

Soak all white clothes overnight in cold water. A short soak is better than no soak. *Do not soak for more than 24 hours in the same water,* as bacterial action makes the water sour and the clothes may be damaged. Place dirty linen at the bottom of the tub, and build up to the cleanest. Badly soiled articles must be separated from lightly soiled ones. Rub soap on the very soiled part before soaking. Shirt collars and cuffs should be scrubbed with hot, soapy water and a soft brush. This helps to loosen the dirt and insoluble matter. The articles should be opened out and immersed thoroughly. Washing soda helps to emulsify the grease and loosen dirt—1 oz. washing soda to 1 gallon water. Handkerchiefs must be soaked separately with salt in water—1 tablespoonful to 1 quart of water. When there is danger of infection as in colds, it is desirable to also add a disinfectant—one tablespoonful of lysol or carbolic acid to one quart of water.

Washing

Remove clothes from the tub and wring. The most practical method of washing will depend on the type of fabric and the amount of dirt.

All methods of washing are suitable for bleached cottons and linens. Warm softened water and good soap must be used. Temperatures recommended for washing cottons are:

White cotton and linens	...	160 to 180°F.
Coloured shirtings	...	140 to 180°F.

Wash the whole garment, paying particular attention to specially soiled areas such as the collar and cuffs of a shirt, front and inside of pockets, and the centre of pillow cases.

Rinse out of the first washing water, and repeat a second time, turning double articles on to wrong side. In the second washing less soap is required, as there is already some soap left in the article and it is cleaner. Rinse and boil if necessary.

Boiling

Boiling whitens clothes, dissolves protein deposits, helps to remove stains and partially disinfects.

While clothes are still soaking prepare the boiler as follows:

Fill a boiler half-full with cold water. If the water is hard, it should be softened with soda to avoid washing soap. When there is grease to be emulsified during the process, the quantity of soap must be increased—the average amount of soda required for the two purposes being from half to one teaspoonful to each gallon of water. The softening action of soda is effective only when the water is very hot, therefore, the soda is put into the boiler shortly before the boiling point is reached and then, a few minutes later when the water is softened, the shredded soap is added, about 2 to 3 tablespoonfuls to each gallon of water. A rough estimate is one handful of shredded soap or soap-powder to each gallon of water.

Put the clothes in the boiler before the water reaches boiling point and leave them in the boiling water for 10 to 15 minutes. More soap must be added, if there is less lather otherwise a scum will form which discolours the fabric and damages the threads. Push the clothes down with the boiler-stick into the water.

Fine and small things may be placed in a 'boiler-bag' or an old pillow-case with its corners cut off and hemmed round to allow water to pass through it. This keeps them together and helps to take them out of the boiler. Lift out clothes, using a boiler stick and put them in a tub of cold water.

- In India where there is plenty of sunshine, clothes need to be boiled only every third or fourth wash.
- If white clothes have become yellow or discoloured, put them into cool soapy water, stew or slowly bring to the boil and keep below boiling point for about an hour, adding soap whenever necessary to preserve the lather. If yellowness still persists, give three or four small 'boils' until the whiteness comes back. A void one long 'boil' as it may weaken the fabric.
- Never boil acetate-rayon and nylon fabrics, as this will crease the material and nothing can remove the creases.
- Do not leave clothes lying in soapy water, they will bleed and transfer colour to other clothes.

Rinsing

Rinse clothes well in warm water to remove all traces of soap. Adequate rinsing is important. Three rinses are desirable, two are necessary. For the first rinse use plenty of hot, clear soft or softened water. Hard water curdles soap and cold water hardens it, making it difficult to remove. Detergents may weaken or yellow the fabrics, is they are not thoroughly rinsed out.

Merely putting clothes in the water and then wringing them out does not remove all the soap. A good method is to push each article up and down two or three times before wringing it.

Starching and bleaching

Cotton and linen can be bleached and starched in one operation.

The starched solution is made up to the required strength and the blue is squeezed carefully into it. The moisture from the fabric is wrung out and it is hung up to dry.

Caps, men's dress-shirts and collars need extra stiffness, and may be stiffened with cold water starch.

The following articles are not starched:

Cellular cotton, flannelette, organdie, velveteen, georgette, turkish and huckaback towelling, cotton hosiery, babies' clothes, bed-linen and underwear.

Drying

Outdoor drying is best as this helps to retain whiteness and gives a certain freshness to clothes.

For longer wear, easier folding, sprinkling and ironing, hang clothes on the line in the following manner.

Hang sheets over the line with hems together, or fold with hems together, then turn hem 8 to 12 inches over the line. Shake straight. Running the fingers down the selvage edges helps to smooth out the sheet.

Small straight pieces may be hung together—handkerchiefs, napkins, small towles, washcloths, and doilies.

Avoid hanging any article by its corners. Let if drape six inches over the line and secure with a peg.

Hang socks and stockings by their toes.

Hang clothing by its strongest part: men's shirts and women's dresses by the hems, shorts by the waistband, men's cotton knitted shirts by the shoulders.

Coloured articles should be dried in the shade—hang them up inside out. Two ropes-twisted together make a good clothes-line. The clothes can be inserted between the twists of the ropes.

Washing defects

Yellowness is caused due to use, wear and tear, too much alkali on fabric from cheap bazar soaps, and failure to attain boiling temperature in the boil.

Greyness is caused by calcium soaps penetrating the fabric or by extra blue in the garment. Another cause may be due to the dirt re-settling on the fabric after having been removed at a previous stage of the washing process. It may also be due to insufficient cleaning or overloading of the washing machine.

This can be corrected by ensuring that the ratio of alkali to soap in the boil is at least 3 : 1 and that the full boiling temperature of over 200°F is reached and maintained for ten full minutes. When yellowing has been allowed to develop for a fairly long period, it may be necessary to boil for 20 minutes during several washes before whiteness is regained. In order to obtain white colour, the soiling matter should not only be removed from the fabric, but also kept in suspension. It is easily done by using soft water, on which no scum is formed. Thorough rinsings after boiling, the correct use of blue, and open air drying are other factors which prevent greyness in fabrics.

Washing of special fabrics

Knitted fabrics are soft and pliable. They are comfortable to wear, specially in summer, and absorb perspiration well. These fabrics last for a long time, if properly handled during washing. They are generally cream in colour or dyed in pale shades. e.g. jersey material. They require no boiling, no starching and very little finishing.

When top garments are almost dry and when undergarments are quite dry, they should be placed flat and pressed with a moderately hot iron. White knitted vests and underwear may be boiled.

Velveteen is a cotton pile fabric, and is treated like coloured cotton as regards temperature of water and method of washing. Velveteen may lose colour during washing, so it must be kept apart from other clothes and washed quickly. Between washing and rinsing waters, hold up the garment and allow to drip. Do not squeeze.

Give a final acid rinse to revive colour, hang up, and allow to drip from the last rinsing water.

Dry in a warm place. If the velveteen hangs straight while drying it will require little ironing.

All that is necessary will be slight steam pressing on the back of the material using a damp muslin to provide steam, and holding a moderately hot iron above it without allowing the weight of the iron to rest on the fabric and flatten the pile.

Organdie is a fabric—stiff, transparent fine longstaple cotton is used for its yarn, which is spun with many twists. Organdie can be washed like coloured cotton and generally does not require any stiffening as it becomes stiff when ironed damp. If any stiffening is necessary, dilute boiling water starch is used. Organdie dries quickly and should be ironed after squeezing from the last rinse.

Flannelette is washed like knitted cotton. Wring thoroughly as it holds moisture. Finish when almost dry with a moderately hot iron.

Fire-proofing material may be done as follows:

Dissolve 2 oz. of boric acid and 4 oz. of borax in a quart of warm water. Immerse the material in it for 15 minutes to 1 hour according to the ease with which it penetrates the fabric. Wring and dry the garment. The mixture forms a non-crystalline almost invisible layer on the surface of the fabric which melts on heating to form a glassy covering which does not catch fire.

Washing removes fire-proofing. Hence the treatment has to be repeated after every wash.

Unbleached cotton and linen Wash as for cotton. Use thin starch, but no blue.

Finishing cotton and linen

The look of a garment depends on the finish it gets. Washed fabrics that require finishing fall under the following three broad classes.

Fabrics finished when evenly damp. This is the most suitable condition for finishing all woven fabrics and clothes that have not been starched. They are taken out when half-dry and rolled up tightly for a short time until they can be finished by 'pressing'.

Fabrics finished when dry. This is suitable for knitted garments, some kinds of rayon, nylon, crepes, and crease-resistant fabrics. They give a good finish when dry. They are stretched into shape while still damp and allowed to dry straight. It helps to make the finishing easier. A moderately hot iron is used for finishing.

Fabrics dried and re-damped for finishing. Starched cottons and linens give an excellent finish when they are allowed to dry completely. They are then damped evenly and rolled up tightly for half an hour before being finished. This prevents the starch from sticking to the article and causing problems in ironing.

Use warm water for sprinkling; it penetrates fabrics better.

A bottle fitted with a perforated top or a small vegetable brush or whisk-broom is easy to handle and scatters the water evenly.

Shake out flat pieces of about the same size and place in a pile. Sprinkle about every third piece and roll together, smoothening fabric as you go; roll tightly. Sprinkle large articles one at a time, smoothing wrinkles as you go. This makes ironing easier. Heavily starched articles take more sprinkling than medium, and medium take more than those with light starch. Place all sprinkled, rolled, or folded articles in a basket, arranging them so that those which are to be ironed first are on top. Wrap or cover with waterproof material such as plastic cloth or oil cloth.

Watch for mildew in humid weather. Do not leave any dampened articles longer than 24 hours in hot, wet weather.

Pressing

Ironing is a quick method of finishing many present-day fabrics, flat articles of daily use like towels, dusters, kitchen cloths and bed linen.

The articles should be evenly damped, stretched into shape and folded right side out and pressed with a hot iron over the folds. A bottle with a perforated top may be used for sprinkling. Warm water dampens the clothes more quickly and evenly than cold water.

The iron is pressed, lifted and replaced, but not moved on the surface of the material as in ironing. This is done to economize time and labour. It also prevents the shine on woollen clothes.

Ironing

Use a suitable table. Cover it with an uncoloured blanket or thick sheet, and keep it smooth by tying the corners with tapes. You can also use a well-padded ironing board with a suitable cover, firmly tied in position. The ironing board should be high enough to eliminate bending.

Place a bowl of water and a damping muslin at the top left-hand corner of the table and a suitable iron stand (of stone or asbestos) at the right hand. Turn all articles on to the right side and dampen them. A bottle with an improvised perforated lid (as sprinkler top) may be used (see Fig. 8.1). The first essential thing in all ironing is

Fig. 8.1 Warm water sprinkler

to see that the articles are of the correct degree of dampness. If they are too dry, a good finish is not achieved; if they are too wet, it is only a waste of time and fuel. Have a small damp turkish towel handy and also a pressing cloth convenient for use.

Heat the iron. A trained hand easily finds out the difference in heat that is required. A practical test for a beginner is to hold the iron on tissue paper. A moderately hot iron will not make a mark on the paper on counting six, a hot iron on counting four. White and light-coloured linens and cottons should be ironed on the right side. Iron dark-coloured linens and cottons wrong side out to eliminate shine. Iron small parts such as tapes, lace, trimmings first, then do the hems and seams on the wrong-side. Use the left hand to smooth and arrange work while ironing, but never to stretch material. With the top of the article on the left-hand side, iron the main portion by the selvedge way of threads, ironing part furthest away first.

Iron a single layer of material where possible, moving the iron from right to left and in straight lines (see Fig. 8.2). Develop the habit of using long, slow strokes. Iron embroidery and lace over a piece of flannel or a towel from the wrong side. This will make the pattern stand out. Iron material until quite dry or the dampness will spread over the ironed parts and give a rough dried appearance if this is not done. Remember it is the moisture and heat that does the job, not extra pressure. Iron small articles at the centre keeping the thread of the material straight and the iron outward. Air all articles thoroughly to prevent mildew and moths and in case of personal articles to prevent chill. Avoid ironing the elastic parts of garments.

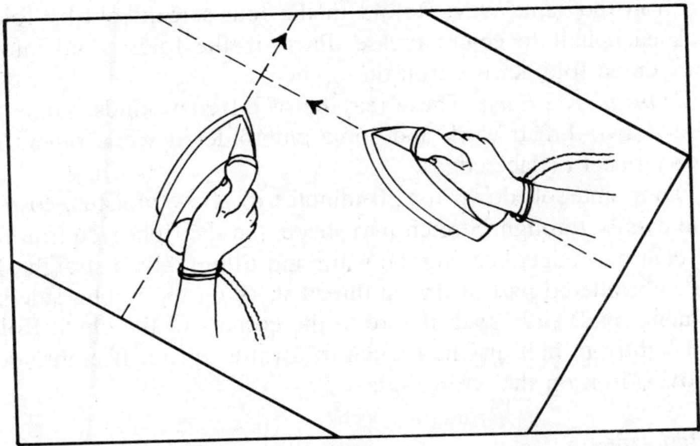

Fig. 8.2 The iron should travel in straight lines

Table linen

Tray-cloths and table-mats. These are usually made of good hand-spun and hand-woven material or of ramie linen—no starch is required.

Fringes may be damped and straightened to shape either with a metal comb or a stiff nail brush. Leave tray-cloth flat or roll from end to end.

Round mats. Lay on table, iron on the right side from the centre outwards to the edge. Keep the threads of the material straight.

Tea cosy cover. Iron on the wrong side. If heavily embroidered, press on the wrong side over a flannel pad by pressing from inside. On the right side, iron the centre and work outwards. Touch up and store after airing.

Table napkins. Damp, stretch and fold table-napkins into a three-screen fold with hems in each hand, rightside uppermost. Roll down for half an hour. First iron the top third (right side), open out and iron the rest together. Refold. Iron lightly at first and then more heavily to finish. Fold in a three-screen fold across and press again on top for gloss.

Table cloths. Damp, stretch to shape and fold in a screen-fold of four. Press in the centre fold on the wrong side. Iron half of the cloth, working with the warp threads. Spread out the second half and iron the same way. Refold in the four-screen fold by folding back each half to centre crease. Press in the folds. Fold into the four-screen fold across. Iron on top across.

Embroidered linen. These may be of different kinds. Some may have drawn-thread work and some embroidered while others may have crochet or lace edges.

Damp and roll down for 30 minutes to allow moisture to penetrate evenly through. Stretch into shape. On the right side iron from the centre to edge, keeping the warp and filling thread straight. Iron the embroidered part or drawn thread work on the wrong side over a flannel pad. Give special care to the corners of the cloth. Roll or fold lightly in half and half again to form a square. If embroidered all over, iron on the wrong side.

Cotton saris

Damp the starched sari, particularly the borders. Fold into two lengthwise, stretch to shape, and fold border to border. The article can be held between two persons or placed on a table. To obtain a better finish, knock the folded parts on the edge of the table to remove creases. Fold again twice over. Iron with pressure, so as to smooth all the 4 layers together. Avoid making a crease at the fold. Re-fold, thus making eight folds. Press on the opposite side. Arrange the borders in place where necessary. Ensure that every part is well pressed. Fold and press—thus making sixteen layers. Fold the sari breadthwise to make it rectangular in shape. Press lightly on top to give it the finishing touch. The sari should have no creases. It should be one long stretch of ironed material. Fine quality saris may be damped, stretched to shape and ironed on single thickness.

Sari petticoat

Method 1. These are not starched, and must be ironed when the garment is evenly damp. Iron double parts and seams on the wrong side. Place petticoat flat on the table, seam to seam with the hem of the garment to the right and the waist band to the left. Use the left hand to smooth and stretch where necessary. Work from hem to waist making the iron travel in straight lines. Iron each panel on both sides.

Method 2. Use a skirt board if available, as this creases and give a better finish to the garment. Iron double parts and seams on the wrong side. Slip the petticoat on the skirt board—with the hem to the right and the waist band on the left. Iron. Roll the petticoat over until every part is ironed.

To fold, place it flat on the table with the placket opening on the right-hand side. Fold the sides towards the centre so that the petticoat forms a rectangle. Fold over in two.

An alternate way is to fold it in the centre, bringing the two side seams together. Turn over the lower ends of the panels at the hem, forming a rectangle. Fold the width into two.

Blouse

Iron double parts and seams on the wrong side. Use the left hand to stretch the darts and hold them in position for the iron. continue ironing until quite dry. Slip the sleeve on the sleeve board and iron from shoulder downwards. Arrange the blouse on the board so that the neck lies to the left hand. Iron the right side passing the work away from you as you do it. Iron neck line working from the front towards the shoulder line. Touch up and air thoroughly on a hanger before folding neatly. Front bands should be stretched and ironed lengthwise, along the selvedge threads. If sleeve boards are not available, the edge of the skirt board or a thick pad may be used as a substitute.

Blouses can be ironed better on a skirt board. They can be ironed flat on the table, but without making a crease down the centre back. They retain better shape when stored away on hangers.

To fold fasten blouse. Fold into two, lightly down the centre back, holding the two shoulder ends together. Lay on the table and arrange the two side seams together. Turn back the sleeves at shoulder-point towards the centre. Unfasten buttons, and store.

You can also fasten the blouse and lay face down on table. Fold the sides towards the centre back about half an inch from the shoulder point. Lay sleeves on top of side pieces. Fold over into two, so as to form a light neat square.

Salwar

Damp salwar—specially the bottom hem and roll tightly to enable the dampness to penetrate evenly through. Iron one leg at a time beginning with the bottom hem and the waist band on the wrong side. Turn over to the right. Arrange together the two centre seams and press together. Iron along with the seam of the leg and work outwards. Form a straight crease in the centre. Remember this crease is as important as the crease of a flannel trouser. Iron the other half in the same way.

To fold, place one leg over the other—folding at the centre of the forkline. Fold the salwar into 3 equal parts lengthwise, one fold being at the end of the hem, or lower end of the 'poncha'. Fold 'kundas' into two, lengthwise. In other words turn back panel one, over panel two and panel two over panel three to form one long rectangle. Press to give a good finish but do not form a crease. Fold the length into two and over, to form two weft folds, thus forming a neat square.

Kameez

Turn the kameez and sleeves to the wrong side. Iron all double parts and pockets. Open up the seams and iron them flat. Press embroidery, if any, with a pad placed under the embroidery in order to raise the pattern, work with the toe of the iron in and out to dry the fabric around the embroidery. Any rough dry place should be damped with muslin and touched up. Iron shoulder pads, if any—otherwise the damp pads will mark the sleeves and spoil the appearance of the kameez.

Place the lower end of the sleeve on a sleeve board and iron until quite dry. With long sleeves, cuffs and gathers need special care. Press the toe of the iron well into the gathers. Finish sleeve. Iron shoulder and as far down into the front and back of the yoke as possible. The pointed end of the skirt board or a padded corner of the table or a stiff pad makes a good substitute for a sleeve board. Iron the collar, if any, first on the wrong side and then on the right Press until a good finish is obtained. Iron the top of the kameez. Do the back first and then the front. Finish the lower half of the kameez working from the hem to waist, taking care to see that the iron travels the selvedge way always. Take the kameez off the board, touch up the pleats, button holes and hem. Glaze marks may be removed by lightly pressing over a damp muslin. Hang on a clothes hanger to air.

To fold, fasten placket opening in front. Lay front down on table, fold sides towards the centre back, lay the sleeves on the top of the side piece. Fold in half across. See that the placket opening is in the centre.

Dresses

Dresses are best ironed on a skirt and sleeve board. If the shoulder pads are not removable, begin by ironing these till quite dry. Otherwise, the damp pad will mark the sleeves, and spoil the look of the finished garment. Next dry off all seams, pockets and double parts on the wrong side.

Turn the garment on to the right side. Iron the sleeves. Finish the crown of the sleeve; iron the shoulder and as far down into the front and back of the yoke as possible. Iron the bodice first. Slip top over end of board, spread out skirt and iron from hem to waist. Gathers, pleats and tucks need special care. Spread out the gathers, press the toe of the iron weli up into the gather and allow them to drape of their own accord. Do not press on the gathers. For pleats and tucks, run the iron on single material along the seam under the lip or the fold of each pleat. Then arrange the pleats damp and press keeping them down with the weight of the iron. Ironing over damp muslin may be necessary to give a smart finish. Avoid 'tram lines'.

Shorts

Turn on to the wrong side. Iron seams and all double parts and pockets. Turn garment to the right side. Iron till dry. Fold one leg placing it seam to seam. Iron on the inner side moving outwards. Crease at the centre both in front as well as the back of the leg. Iron the other leg in the same way.

Fold legs together placing fronts inside. Fold back fullness over legs. Then, fold across.

Kurtas

If it is made of fine material such as 'mulmul' it is sufficient to iron it on the right side over the two thicknesses.

Dampen the kurta. Iron the sleeves to dryness. Place kurta flat on the table, front uppermost, neck to the left hand side and hem on the right hand side. Iron along the seam and proceed inwards. Iron from hem to neck across the whole front. Turn and iron back on front.

To fold place kurta flat on table, back of kurta uppermost. Fold sides towards centre back, about one inch from the point of the shoulder. These folds are sometimes done twice over. Fold sleeves down sideways. Fold in half to form a neat square.

Pyjamas

Pull the pyjamas into shape, turn to the wrong side and iron the hem, seams and double parts practically dry.

Lay the pyjama leg on the table and continue ironing up the whole length of the pyjama, guiding the iron up the seam and working across to the fold. Make the centre crease from the hem to the waist band. Turn the pyjama over, 'deal with the back in the same ways.

Men's Shirt

Iron first on the wrong side. Iron seams and double parts placing the yoke flat on the table for ironing.

On the right side, iron yoke until dry. Iron the collar and then the cuffs and sleeves. Fold back in half; side seams together, and iron the back with fold down the centre. Ironing half the back, then turn and iron the other half on the ironed part. With the front uppermost, fold and press in the back pleat, working from inside. Fasten shirt front on back and fold and press in the front pleat, so that the front lies evenly on the back.

To fold, place the shirt on the table with the back uppermost. Fold sides towards centre about an inch from the point of the shoulder. Fold the sleeves down straight and then fold cuffs. Fold over the tail, fold in half.

Shirt collars. Most collars and cuffs today are permanently stiffened during manufacture. This is achieved by placing between the layers of the fabric a cellulose acetate material specially treated to melt and stiffen when heat is applied. This heat brings the materials together in such a way that the stiffness is unaffected by subsequent washing and ironing. Such materials must be ironed when very damp to get good results. The entire process can be seen in Figs. 8.3 to 8.9.

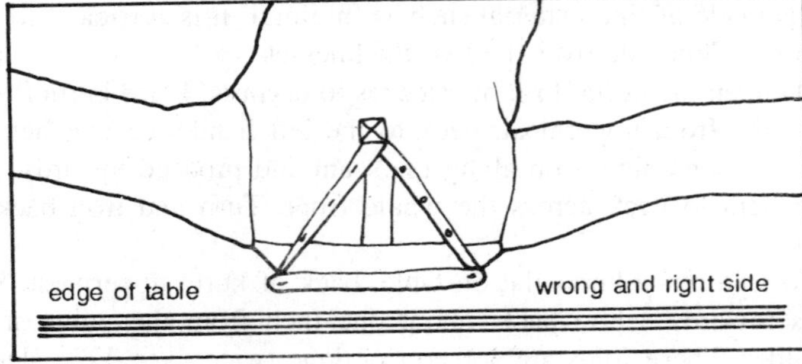

Fig. 8.3 Ironing the collar band

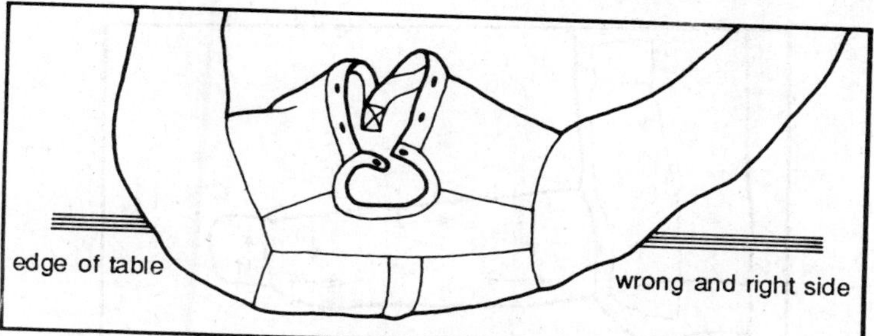

Fig. 8.4 Ironing the yoke

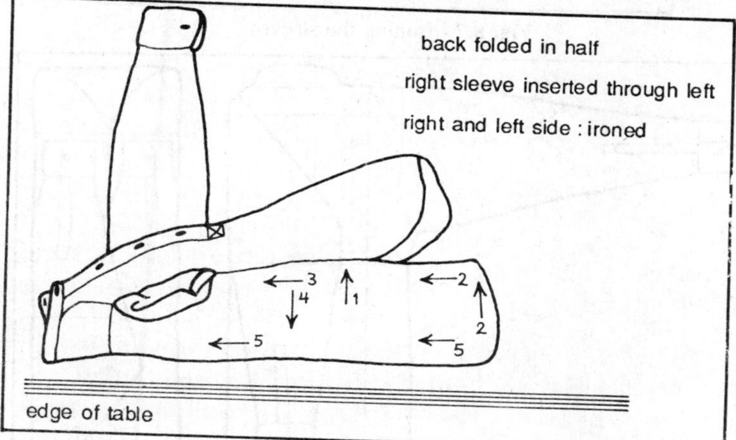

Fig. 8.5 Ironing the back

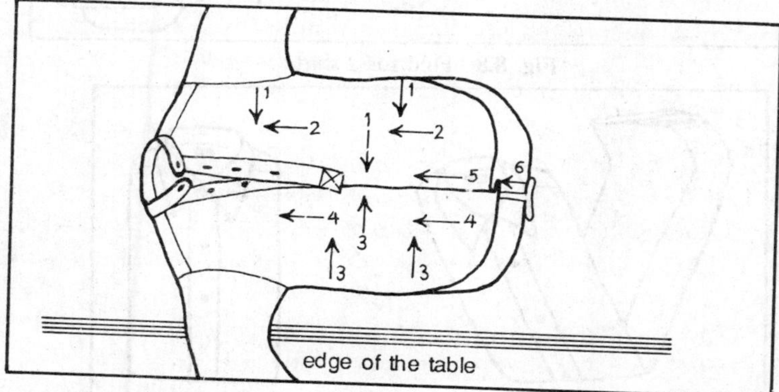

Fig. 8.6 Ironing the front-also putting in back and front pleats

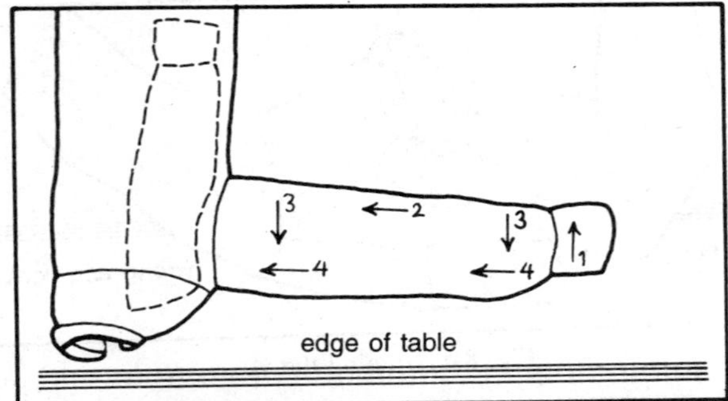

Fig. 8.7 Ironing the sleeves

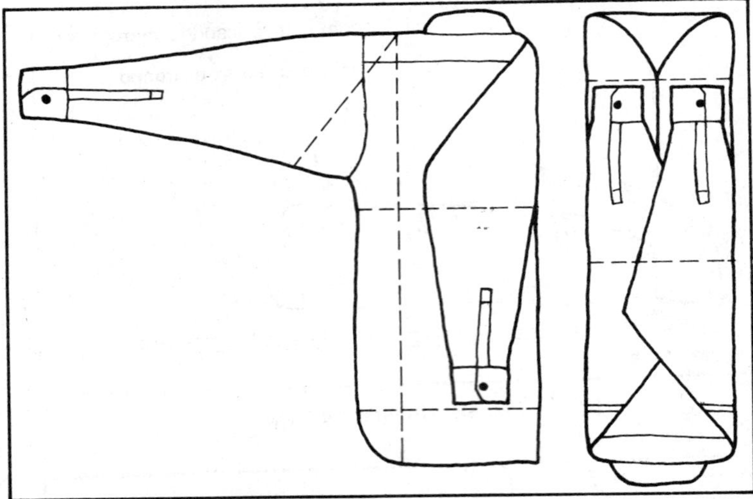

Fig. 8.8 Fold for a shirt

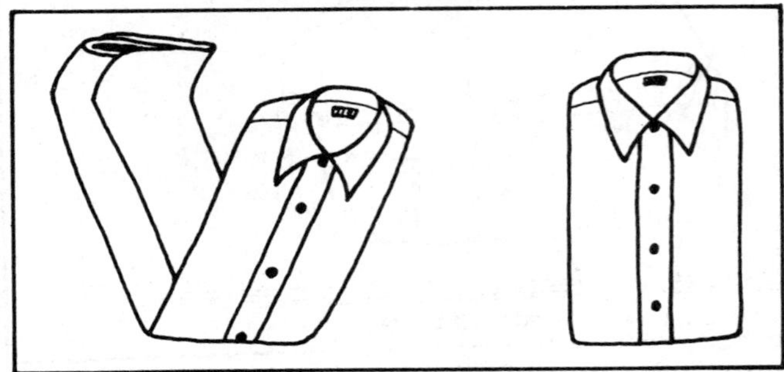

Fig. 8.9 Fold for a shirt

Half-sleeved shirt

Iron the collar, the yoke, the back and the sleeves in turn in the same way as a full-sleeved shirt. White ironing sleeves see that the link holes are carefully closed before setting takes place. Iron front, first lightly to shrink and then heavily to set—iron up and down the front to smoothen all creases. Fold as for the other shirt.

Some helpful hints

Sleeves. Slip the sleeve over the small end of the board. Rotate until completely ironed.

Pleats. Work pleats into place with fingers, a few at a time. Pin

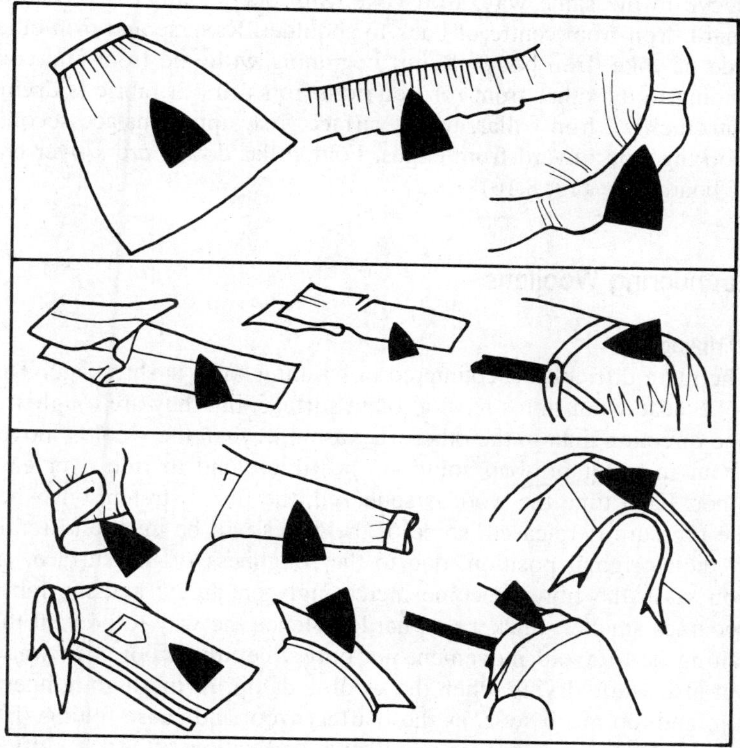

Fig. 8.10 Methods of ironing

or even baste at hem if difficult to keep in place. Iron hem first and work upward, pulling garment slightly against the iron. Work on the wrong side of fabric, if possible.

Gathers and ruffles. Manipulate garment or iron so that the point of the iron works into the fullness. Use in-and-out strokes. Don't iron gathers over the surface.

Creased slacks and shorts. Lay one leg flat on board, underleg side up, with the other leg folded back over top. Fold so that creases appear in the centre front and centre back of the leg. Iron. Turn over and iron outer leg upto point where crotch begins. Repeat with the other leg. Finish the top over the end of the board.

Shirt. Iron cuffs first, inner surface first and then the outer surface. Iron body of sleeve, cuff opening side first. Iron the other sleeve in the same way. Iron yoke. Slip one shoulder over end of board. Iron from centre of back to shoulder. Reverse and iron other side of yoke. Iron body of shirt beginning with one front and continuing to the other front (or iron both fronts first if fabric is drying out quickly). Iron collar, under surface first, upper surface second, working iron inward from edges. Fold collar down, press over end of board (see Fig. 8.10).

Laundering Woollens

Shrinkage

The main difficulty encountered in washing wool is shrinkage. This is because wool fibres have a rough surface, but they are rougher in one direction than in the other. In washing, when the wool is moved about in water or soap solution, the fibres tend to ride over each other. Each time the wool is squeezed, the fibres stretch, but when the pressure is released, some of the fibres will be unable to return to their original position, due to the roughness of the surface. As you wash the fibres become increasingly entangled and the fabric becomes smaller, thicker and harder. Hence the way to prevent this felting is: to avoid movement not only when the wool is in water, but also while drying when the wool is damp. Avoid high temperature and too much soda, as these affect wool and cause felting. Too much alkali in soap makes wool harsh and yellow after it has dried. Many of the dyes used on wool are very sensitive to alkalis and the colours may bleed. Hence use pure soap or soap-flakes for white or light-coloured woollens. For coloured woollens use a solution of *reetha* or a specially formulated washing liquid like Genteel or Ezee. For white woollens, never use a domestic bleach liquor sold in bottles. If some sort of bleaching treatment is necessary, a very weak solution of hydrogen peroxide made faintly alkaline with ammonia or borax may be used. Add a trace of blue to the final rinsing water. It is wiser to wash before the woolen garment gets very dirty since it may be impossible to wash it completely clean without doing some damage to the wool.

Washing

Mend all holes to prevent them getting larger. Fine woolens and knitwear are liable to stretch out of shape. It is best for all beginners to mark the outline on a sheet of plain paper before wetting the garment. The garment after being washed can be placed on this outline and dried flat on the paper over a table. This way the shape of the garment will be retained. Examine the garment for stains and remove them before washing. Soaking weakens the fibres. Hence do not soak longer than it takes to become saturated with the suds.

Put sufficient soap into the water to produce a satisfactory lather. The water must be soft. The temperature of the water should be lukewarm around 90° to 100°F. It is best to use at least three rinsing waters. Only soft water must be used for rinsing and the temperature of the water should be lukewarm between 90° and 100°F. Have a soft nail brush and a turkish towel ready at hand.

Shake the garment free of dust. Immerse it in water. Cleanse by kneading and squeezing, keeping the garment under water as far as possible. Soiled parts may be placed on the palm of the left hand and extra soap solution may be patted gently over them until the dirt is loosened. A soft nail brush can be used to remove persistent dirt. Do not rub. Lift the article out of the washing water, support it with the hands, squeezing out the soapy water. Rinse to remove all soap. Squeeze all water by hand, lay it on a clean turkish towel lightly, pull it into shape. Wrap it in the towel and press out excess moisture. This will remove a great deal of the water without any vigorous handling.

A wringer is good to squeeze out water from heavier articles. Set the wringer on loose tension so that the fabric does not mat (see Fig. 8.11).

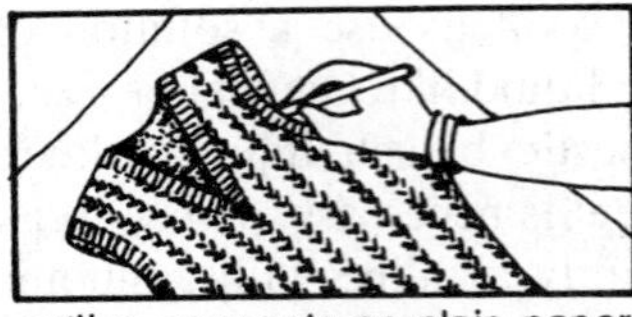
outline garments on plain paper

prepare washing water and work up a lather

lifft extra dirty parts and pat suds over these until dirt is removed

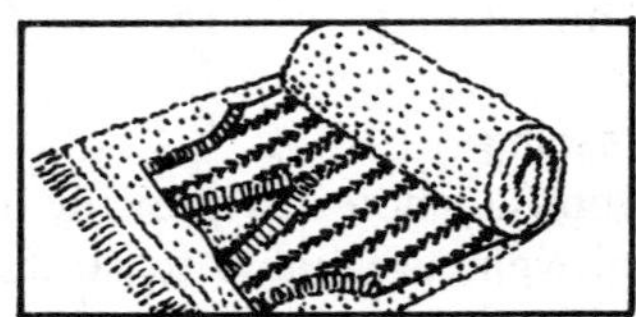
roll the garment in a towel to remove extra moisture

Fig. 8.11 Washing woollens

Drying

Shake, stretch into shape and hang up to dry on a hanger in dry moving air where the moisture will evaporate quickly. Fine delicate articles that are liable to stretch out of shape can be dried flat on a on the back of a chair or a table to enable free circulation of air. Always dry woollens in the shade. Lift, shape and turn occasionally.

1. Never boil or twist.
2. Never hang wool garments near heated radiators or in the hot sun, because heat dries up the wool fibre causing it to become brittle and break.
3. Do not use washing soda.

Ironing knitted woollens

Knitted woollens need little or no finishing. Outer knitted garments, like pullovers, jumpers and cardigans, should be dried completely and ironed on the right or wrong side, according to colour and surface finish required. Woollens that require a fluffy finish can be brushed with a stiff dry brush. Crepe woollen garments should be measured before washing, stretched during drying, and steam pressed to correct shape and size in finishing. They should be pressed on the wrong side when almost dry.

Woven woollens

A well washed garment should be nearly ironed. Essential equipment for pressing consists of a smooth well padded ironing board, a heavy nap woollen pressing cloth, and cotton cloths, or muslin. Cotton cloth or thin wrapping paper can be used to cover the damp clothing to prevent the iron from sticking to the fabric. A padded roll makes the pressing of seams and sleeves much easier. This can be made by wrapping a folded magazine with a heavy towel. A sleeve form, which is made of muslin cut into a plain sleeve pattern and stuffed firmly, is an excellent aid in sleeve pressing. Always use steam for pressing wool. As far as possible press on the wrong side. Use an old piece of fine cloth. Dampen and wring it out thoroughly. Press lightly with a hot iron.

Woven woollens may be 'steam pressed', that is, pressed with a fairly hot iron over a damp cloth. This should be done on the wrong side, except when surface pressing is needed for finishing. Use the iron lightly. Lift and press with your iron, do not glide it. Press lightly at first until the moisture forms steam, then use more pressure. Where the press cloth has been lifted, there should be a small amount of steam rising from the garment. Then take a flat backed brush and knock it down hard on the part you have just pressed. Hold it there for a second or two; lift and hit smartly again. Continue till no steam is visible. This is known as 'knocking the steam in'. Garments such as trousers, coats and jackets can be pressed only in this way. If a steam iron is used, no pressing cloth is needed if the garment can be pressed on the wrong side but a cloth should be used when pressing on the right side in order to prevent shine. Always follow the warp or weft threads of the material. Be careful not to hold the iron in one place until the material dries. Pressing dry makes the fabric shine. While pressing the leg of a pair of trousers, place a piece of thin cardboard or heavy wrapping paper underneath. Follow the same process for seams, darts, pleats or pocket flaps—this will prevent the press mark of a pleat on the right side of the garment. Iron one leg at a time.

Suits

Begin at the top of the garment and work down first pressing the sleeves and other parts that fall off the board. Start on the wrong side to case into the correct position and repeat this process on the right side. Press the sleeve, with crease about 1/4 inch in front of the forward seam. Press the underside of the sleeve first, then the other.

In pressing the shoulders of the coat, curve them round the edge of the table or ironing board, or better still lay a tailor's pad underneath and press. If you do not have a pressing pad, roll up a turkish towel and slip it under the arm-hole. Place a strip of heavy paper,

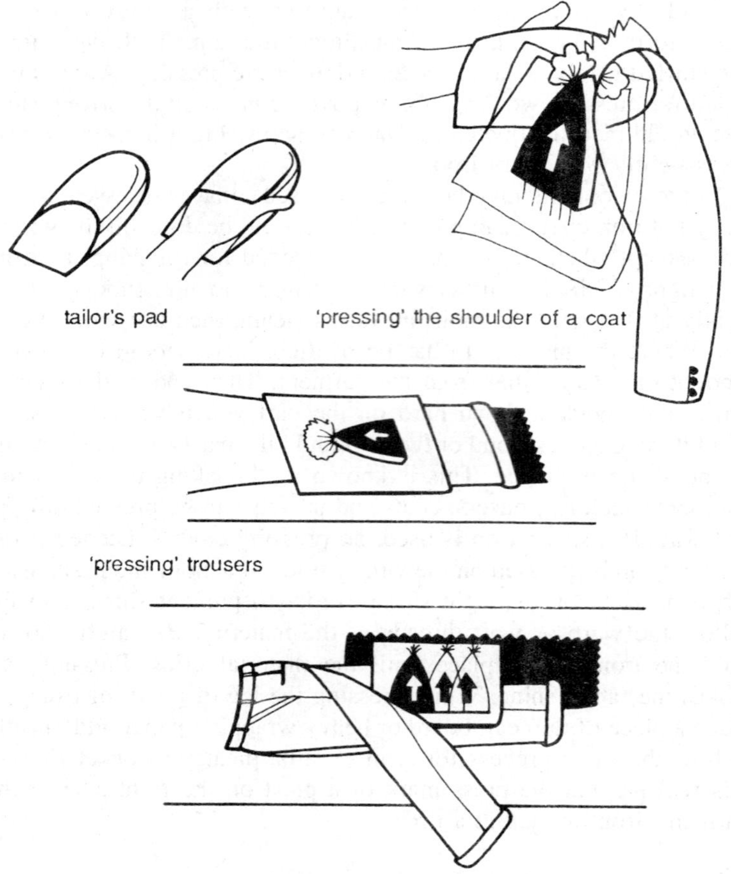

Fig. 8.12 Ironing a suit

cardboard or a piece of garment material, under the seams, pockets, flaps, hems or between the folds of pleats. This helps to equalise the thickness and prevents edge marks or lines from showing on the right side of the garment after pressing (see Fig. 8.12).

In pressing trousers, the chief necessity is to avoid double creasing. Nothing looks worse than 'tram lines'. Bagginess in the knees and shine on the seams, elbows, wrists, collar, pockets, back and seat are things to be corrected in pressing a suit. They are all remedied, to a limited extent, by light pressing or steaming through a moist cloth which leaves the material still damp. The reason why wool fabrics often become shiny after continued use is that the nap is worn off or flattened with wear. If the nap is merely flattened the shine can be removed, at least temporarily. Place the garment right side up on the ironing board. Cover with a woollen cloth and then with the dampened and dry cloths. Press lightly, then brush with a stiff bristled brush, steam and press again. The brushing and steaming may have to be repeated.

Socks and stockings

Shake well to free loose dust and sand. If they have become muddy through wear dry them, and then rub or brush off the mud. Wash by kneading and squeezing in lukewarm soapy water, paying particular attention to the soles and ankle parts. Rinse as for other woollens. A dark-blue in the water improves the colour of navy-blue or black stockings. Wring as explained above on a towel. Then fold evenly by seam at the back of the leg and dry flat as for knitted woollens.

Hand-knitted socks can be folded or rolled up when dry. Machine-made stockings can be pressed on the right side with a moderately hot iron. If this glazes black stockings, put a piece of thin muslin over the stockings. Iron over the muslin.

Kashmir shawls

These fine delicate fabrics must be washed with great care.

Use a solution of reetanut and make a heavy lather. Wash by kneading or squeezing. Rinse at least thrice in soft lukewarm water. A little lemon juice or khatta juice, about a desertspoon to one gallon of water, may be added to the rinse.

In Kashmir, an indigenous product called *krith* is used to clean shawls.

Fold the shawl lightly (do not lift as far as possible). Lay it on a large towel and press to remove moisture.

The following synthetic detergents may also be used:

— Lissapol N: 3 tablespoons to one gallon of lukewarm water.
— Teepol: 3 tablespoons to one gallon of lukewarm water.
— Astol A: This is a solvent emulsion containing trichloroethylene. It washes greasy woollens and shawls. It is marketed as a yellowish brown liquid. Use half a teaspoon of Astol A to one gallon of water.

To remove stains Astol A should be used undiluted being worked into the soiled portion of the fabric and then rinsed out.

The most satisfactory method of drying a shawl is to lay it on an old sheet on the floor and spread it into shape. Change its position from time to time and stretch occasionally in both directions if it has a raised pattern.

Knitted shawls may be pinned by each corner to an old sheet and dried. If small, the shawl may be pinned onto the ironing table.

Blankets and heavy woolens

Blankets and heavy woollens can be washed well in a large tub and with a long-handled suction washer or a washing machine. If you do not possess either you will have to knead and squeeze by hand. Blankets must be washed quickly, else they will shrink. A continuous supply of softened lukewarm water (temperature 100°F is needed. The article must be immersed in plenty of soapy water. The working of the suction washer on the woollens must be light. If the woollen garment is put in the machine, it must be made to work at a slow rate and kept in the machine for only two minutes. The rinsing must be thorough and only soft water must be used. The water may be squeezed out with the help of a rubber wringer from the machine and then hung up to dry. Never rub or twist blankets. Hang the blankets over two parallel lines so that air can circulate all around them.

The glue method. This is a fairly useful method for washing blankets. Only glue is used. Thus there is no risk of soap being left in the blanket and making it hard.

Use carpenter's glue. Dissolve one oz. in a pint of water for every blanket. Shake blankets thoroughly. Prepare a tub of hot water and add the glue solution. If the blanket is very dirty, one tablespoonful of ammonia may be used. Soak the blankets in this mixture for half an hour, covering the tub to retain heat. While soaking, turn the blanket once or twice in the solution. Pass the blanket through a wringer. Rinse in several warm waters to remove all dirty water and all traces of glue.

Glue forms a colloidal solution and so has some cleaning properties. This method is also suitable for washing tweeds, serge, gaberdine and dark colours which are inclined to look white and streaky if soap is used. The whiteness is caused by deposits obtained by an incorrect use of soap. These do not show up on light coloured articles, but colours reveal the defects in washing. Washing with glue is less effective than washing with soap and water or soapless soaps.

To finish treat lightly with a teazle brush. Press binding carefully with moderately hot iron over damp muslin, then dry.

Shirts, gym tunics and trousers

These garments can be washed with suitable synthetic detergents. They may also be cleaned with a sal-ammoniac wash (ammonium chloride).

To make a sal-ammoniac solution, dissolve one tablespoonful of sal-ammoniac with boiling water. Pour into a bath. Add hot or cold water to make up a gallon of warm solution.

Place the garment in the bath. Stir occasionally; knead and squeeze in the water. Rinse well in warm water. Do not squeeze out water, but allow to drip dry. The slight acidity of the solution protects the colours of dark-coloured woollens and also helps remove the dressing in the fabric. This releases dirt and other water-soluble stains.

Wool mixtures

Examine garments of different materials where wool is mixed with other fibres. The mixture may be cotton, silk or rayon or casein fibre. The mixing of another fibre with wool reduces the tendency of wool to felt owing to the separation of the wool fibres from one another. These fabrics combine the properties of both kinds of fibres. They usually launder very well. An example of mixed fabrics is Viyella.

The one general rule is to treat then as woollen fabrics, because wool is a fibre that needs most care.

Baby's woollens

A baby's clothes must receive special attention, because of the great delicacy of a baby's skin. They should not be washed with the family wash. When a baby is young, it is best to wash the clothes every day. Never use soda. Only good quality soap must be used. Thorough rising necessary as a baby's skin chafes so easily and the least trace of soap may cause irritation. Do not use blue, as it has a slightly irritant effect. Never starch parts of clothes that come into contact with a baby's skin. Dry the clothes out in the open.

If possible, use soapless washing powers. These are very useful for washing woollens, because they do not form a scum with hard water, and the woollens are easily rinsed clear of lather.

Woollen toys

Shampoo with utmost speed, not allowing water to soak into stuffing. Wrap in dry towel and pat. Hang up to dry. Treat lightly with teazle brush.

Ribbons can be washed and dyed and trimmed.

Laundering Coloured Fabrics

There is a wide range of coloured fabrics in all materials available today. Coloured fabrics are of two kinds: one made of thread in which the dye is produced within the fibre itself. These materials are colour fast to washing, bleaching, and light, e.g. shirtings, ginghams, zephyrs, household materials like casement, and printed materials on which patterns are stamped by machinery. These cannot be washed by ordinary methods as the colours are likely to run.

Testing colour-fastness

All coloured and printed fabrics can be tested. Wet a small piece of the fabric in lukewarm water. Place this between two layers of white cloth. Press with a hot iron. An unstable dye, if any will be marked off on the white cloth.

Washing

Mend where required. Look out for stains. Tack or run round the stain with ordinary thread, as it is impossible to see the stains when the fabric is wet. Treat stain with required reagent.

First test it for colour fastness. If washing is necessary, it should be carried out quickly in cool soapy water followed by thorough rinsing and immediate finishing.

The most important point to remember is speed in order to minimise the risk of colours running. If several articles are to be washed at the same time, they should be graded as far as possible, the lighter colours being treated before the darker ones. When the dye appears over-saturated and liable to bleed during washing, a treatment with acetic acid will fix the colours. A good synthetic detergent will not harm coloured clothes but colours may run because of poor dyes. Always check first by soaking a part of the cloth that does not show.

Wash using a suction washer or kneading and squeezing in a soapy lather. The temperature of the water should never exceed 110°F. Lower the temperature if the colour runs. Gentle friction can be applied on soiled parts. Rinse in warm water to remove the soapy washing water, then in soft cold water. Give a final acid rinse. An additional solution of weak acetic acid (1 tablespoon to 1 gallon of vinegar (2 tablespoonfuls to 1 gallon) will give an added brightness to the colours and neutralise any alkalinity caused by the soap. Salt (1 teaspoonful to 1 gallon) may also be added to the last rinse, as it decreases the imperceptible movement of the water, and so prevents any loosening of the day caused by the rinsing waters. Vinegar is necessary when soap is used.

To prevent transference of the dye from the dark to the light parts, lay the article on a piece of thick clean cloth, cover with another piece and wring without folding. Wring out as much moisture as possible before hanging up to dry in a shady place. Remove garments when they have reached the correct dryness for ironing, and iron at once. Avoid redamping. If starching is required, as in the case of cretonne or chintz, the article is treated in a cold boiling-water starch. Bran water is often used to stiffen dark-coloured fabrics when moderate stiffness is required, because it prevents the white shiny marks caused by starch.

Laundering Silks

Washing

The first lesson in silk washing is 'never soak or boil it'. It should always be washed by hand in tepid water in tepid soap solids.

Prepare warm soapy water, using a soap solution or soap flakes to make a lather. For coloured silks, use a reetanut solution. Reetanut not only cleanses but also prevents the colour from bleeding.

Use sufficient soapy water and clean by kneading and squeezing by hand for small garments, or suction washing for large garments. Pat extra soap solution through the very soiled parts. Rinse in warm water to remove soapy water This is most important, for if the water is not warm enough to dissolve the soap, a fine white powder is formed on the surface of the silk.

Rinse finally in cold water to which a little lime juice is added; this clears the colour, restores the sheen and stiffens the silk.

Silk articles can also be washed with soapless detergents like Genteel or Teepol which have a rapid cleansing action and do not call for any harsh washing processes that wear away the garments.

Move the silk gently in this solution for 15 to 30 minutes. Knead and squeeze. Finally take out, wash well with water. Wring in a turkish towel. For heavily soiled silk goods, add half an ounce of ammonia solution.

Silk seldom needs to be stiffened, as it usually becomes stiff when ironed damp. If thin silk needs to be stiffened use a little gum solution in the rinse; 1 teaspoonful to 1/2 pint of cold water.

Squeeze out by hand. Large articles of strong silk can be put through a rubber wringer. Thin silks can be wrapped in a cloth and rolled up for half an hour before being ironed.

Dry in a shady place, as sunlight acts on silk and causes white silk to become yellow. The fading of colours by sunlight takes place at a greater rate while the fabric is wet. For this reason coloured materials should never be dried in direct sunlight. Thin silks do not need to be dried. Wrap them up in a towel for 10–15 minutes to be ready for ironing. Thick silks need to be half dry.

Ironing

Most silks are ironed when evenly damp; they must not be dry in one part and damp in another. Silk will not dampen by sprinkling with water like cotton, as there are no small hairs to carry the moisture along the fibres; when parts become too dry they must be damped by putting into water again. Therefore, do not sprinkle water, as it leaves water marks. Sarees are best wrapped in damp towels and unrolled gradually for ironing. White silks are generally ironed on the right side. They have a natural sheen which is heightened by ironing. Tussar and shanting silks are ironed dry (on the wrong side) because the natural gum is left in the fibre, and this allows it to straighten under the heat and pressure of the iron. If the fabric is wet when ironed, it becomes lustrous and greasy-looking. Dark-coloured and corded silks are ironed on the wrong side. iron heavily over stitchings to dry the thread before airing. All silks must be ironed until they are dry, or creases will reappear on the portions left damp. Use a moderately hot iron, as silk scorches easily.

To test whether the iron is the correct heat, hold it onto a white paper and count to six; no mark should be left on the paper. An iron that is too cool will drag and crease the surface of the silk, and may cause a brown cold-iron mark. Scorches and cold-iron marks may be difficult to remove, so it is very necessary to have the iron on the right heat for silk.

If 'greasy' patches occur because of faulty ironing, they can be removed by dabbing the affected area with ten-volume hydrogen peroxide and a trace of ammonia; and soaking it for four to six hours until the marks have disappeared.

Air after ironing. Fold silk garments lightly by hand.

Coloured silks

Most silk sarees—whether Kollegal, Arni or Bangalore—are likely to run colour in the first wash. Do not be alarmed at this as it is only the superfluous dye that comes off in the water. In Kornad sarees where the borders are of a different colour from the 'body', one has to be particularly careful while washing them for the first time; for if the colours run into one another, they can never be removed later. Wash or rinse them in plain water even when they are new. This makes the sarees loss their crispness and rustle, and gives them a better 'fall' when worn after the wash.

Kornad silk sarees with wide borders of different colours may be washed as follows: Tie the border and pallu tightly. Wash the light part first. Wring out the moisture. Then treat the part with the darker colour. Remove as much moisture as possible. Wrap in a turkish towel; and dry flat on the grass in the shade.

Kornad sarees can also be washed in reetanut solution or with synthetic detergents. There are many advantages in using these soapless detergents—the use of cooler or cold water and a non-alkaline solution, the possibility of adding vinegar and salt, and in most cases the application of pure detergents direct to any particularly soiled parts. Even if traces of the detergent are left behind in the fabric it does not harm the fibre.

Avoid over-soaking, heat, strong alkalis and acids or washing powders containing too much soda and friction. All these affect colours easily.

Kollegal or Bangalore sarees must be taken down when just damp, pleated breadthwise, wrapped in a slightly damp turkish towel and ironed along the selvedge threads. This method helps to maintain the dampness of the saree, and thus gives a good finish. Sarees pressed after being completely dried give a poor finish.

Velvet

This is a silk pile fabric. Most velvets are spoilt by washing, and it is best to dry clean them. Examine velvets well before touching with water; the surface can be spoilt very easily, as the soft pile does not recover from wetting. Do not attempt any stain removal with water solutions; grease solvents can be tried.

Steaming is the only way to renovate the fabric and remove creases. Hang or hold the velvet so that a continual flow of steam from a kettle strikes the crease; or stand a moderately hot iron on its heel, place a damp cloth over it and draw the velvet across the steam that this causes. Hang the velvet up till dry before folding, as it will crease again if folded damp. If you are working on a large piece of velvet, it should be held firmly between two persons, while a third places a wet rag over the wrong side and irons it.

Crepe-de-chine and georgette

These are silk crepe materials and their colour and pattern must decide the treatment. White and all light colours will wash and finish well when ironed damp. If the garment shrinks while washing, stretch on a wooden roller and iron both sides of the material so that it is stretched to its original size. It should be measured before wetting.

Crepe materials may shrink while washing; they need to be stretched during drying to their original size and finished by ironing on the wrong side when almost or quite dry. This will help to preserve the crepe surface.

Weighted silks

Weighted silks are likely to split when friction is applied. Hence they must be washed with great care. Silks which contain a minimum percentage of weighting wash more satisfactorily than other weighted silks, though the inevitable loss of weighting may spoil the finish.

In the case of South Indian Silks, which are hand-woven and hand-spun, it is better to give them a rinse in cold soft water before wearing for the first time. This helps to remove the weighting thus making the silks last longer. Do not store away sarees with weighting for more than two years, as the weighting weakens the fabric.

Laundering Rayon and Nylon

Washing

Rayons can be laundered much in the same may as real silk, although there are a few important differences.

Greater care in handling is necessary because rayons lose their strength when wet, and occasionally a fabric is encountered which combined with it loses most of its strength. With acetate the loss is about 35%, and with viscose rayon about 55%. Rayons need no bleaches. A white rayon blouse remains white to the end.

Gentle squeezing in warm soapy water is usually sufficient to clean rayons, and when the fabric is to be lifted out of the liquid, support it with the hand and do not pull it out by the corners. The rinsing must be thorough.

As in the case of silk, twisting and wringing must be avoided. If further removal of water is necessary, place the article between two dry turkish towels and press the water out. In case of a printed fabric, a piece of muslin inserted between the folds will prevent the marking off of the colours when they tend to bleed.

Knitted garments like stockings should be gently eased and smoothed to shape and allowed to dry flat. They can ladder and lengthen if hung up wet.

Drying

Hang up to dry as soon as possible after ensuring that the weight of the garment is evenly distributed. It is a good tip to suspend a kameez or dress by throwing it over the line at the waist. Garments that may stretch out of shape can be dried flat.

Ironing and finishing

Each type of fabric has to be dealt with differently. Garments often have a label attached giving directions for finishing. This is a useful guide. When ironing fine fabrics, it may not be possible to follow the usual method in finishing a garment.

As a general rule, rayon must be slightly and evenly moistened and in some cases ironed dry like crepe and suede. Taffetas and satins should be ironed almost wet, after the excess moisture has been pressed out into a towel. Use a cool iron. A hot iron first puts glaze marks on the fabric, which also develops a series of ripples and a hornlike texture. It then sticks to the iron and finally melts. All this may occur within seconds. Finish shiny fabrics like satins on the right side. Dark rayons and crepe fabrics must be ironed on the wrong side, using a moderately hot iron. Heavy-spun rayon fabrics are best pressed under a damp cloth. To ensure a uniform result, the single material may have to be ironed first. It is unwise to iron over buttons and press fasteners, or many thicknesses of these fabrics, for example, seams over single fabrics, as pressure on the thick part may cause it to split. Keep the iron moving and do not press heavily. If creases are not easily removed, it may be because the material is too dry. This should be remedied by rewetting or placing between two damp towels and *not* by sprinkling with water because this is liable to produce unevenness of lustre or water marks particularly on dull finish fabrics like crepes.

Fold lightly without pressing in the folds and air. Glazed parts can often be corrected by wetting the whole article and exposing the glazed parts to the steam of a kettle. If the material is white and the glazing so bad that the garment is unwearable, acetate in a soap solution is a last resort.

A steam electric iron is very useful for finishing rayons particularly crepe fabrics.

Dry cleaning

Some garments by their very nature are difficult to wash, e.g., elaborate *gararas*, suits, etc., so in these instances it is advisable to dryclean the garment. It is helpful to the cleaners if such garments are marked 'rayon'.

Note that non-inflammable cleaning solvents such as carbon tetrachloride are not advisable, as they sometimes extract the colour from acetate.

Special Types of Laundering

However efficient the normal dry-cleaning process may be stains still remain in garments which are not soluble in spirit. Such stains have to be water-brushed, and the garments wet-cleaned. Fabrics such as raincoats and tennis-flannels require special care. Each of these need to be treated individually and are described below.

Water-brushing is different from wet-cleaning in that no soap is used and the water, is used cold. Water-brushing removes a larger amount of water-soluble soiling with as little disturbance or distortion of paddings and inner linings as possible. It is a specialised job that requires an abundance of soft water, a large tub and some stiff brushes.

The article to be water-brushed should be treated one at a tune. Each piece is plunged in and out of a large bowl or tub. It is then thrown on a slab or table and scrubbed with quick light movements with a wet brush. When the whole surface is done, it is rinsed at once in a tub of fresh water If the colours are loose, a little half per cent solution of acetic acid is added. The garment is then drained off of all its water, well shaken to remove creases and dried quickly in an airy place.

All types of fabrics are suitable for water-brushing except modern silver and gold brocades.

Water-proofed coats

These must be divided into groups for treatment:

Rubber-proofed garments. They may be 'single' where the rubber is the direct backing of the facing fabric and usually cotton or they may be 'double' where the rubber is placed between two layers of fabric, as for example, a khaki cotton surface with checklining welded to it by the rubber.

Examine the proofing. If the fabric is of the 'single' variety, and if it is sticky or hardened and cracking, it is best not to take the risk of cleaning it. If it is rain-proofed, it can usually be dry-cleaned with any grease solvent or the surface of the coat may be sponged with soap solution and rinsed in warm waters. The best way to do this is to rinse in a sink so that plenty of water passes over the material and all the soap is removed. It should then be hung out in the open so as to dry quickly. Do not press.

Mackintoshes or rubber-proofed coats. Spread french chalk or magnesium carbonate thickly over the surface to remove grease marks. Do not use any grease solvent, as it will dissolve the rubber. Make a warm concentrated solution of good cleaning detergent. Lightly scrub the whole article with a solution with a soft bristled brush making long sweeps. Pay special attention to those parts that are heavily soiled such as the collar, sleeves and pockets. Use no chemicals for stain removal, as such substances cannot be cleaned from these articles without causing damage. Machine-cleaning or wringing must be forbidden; the proofing will not stand it. Rinse thoroughly in warm water by plunging articles in a big tub. Traces of soap left on the garment will appear as white streaks when the coat has dried.

Lift the coat on to a wooden hanger, allow it to drip into the sink or in some convenient place and hang in a draught to dry. Keep the coat as uncreased as possible and straighten during drying, as it cannot be pressed in any way. Pieces of the same material should be stuffed in the pockets, which should be emptied of water. Peg or pin sleeves in such a way that the do not rest against the body. This will ensure even drying and prevent 'sweals' on the body along with sleeves.The drying must be away from direct sunlight. Rubber deteriorates by exposure to sunlight.

Tennis flannels

It is safe to measure flannel before laundering. The recording of measurements avoids the risk of likely over-shrinkage during steam-pressing.

Method I. Turn out pockets. Remove badges (unless the colours are fast) and dry-clean. Remove stains. Wash as for woollens in a fairly thick lukewarm soap solution in a tub. Add a little ammonia. Work on it for 2 or 3 minutes paying special attention to the knees, turn-ups and pockets. Rinse thoroughly in warm water of about 100°F. The last but one rinse should be soured with sulphuric acid (about 1/2 oz. to 10 gallons of water). This makes the water just sharp to the taste. It helps to decolorise all brown stains and also counter-acts yellowing or the bialkalinity of the soap bath, making other bleaching unnecessary. Throw a teaspoonful of salt into this acid bath. This protects the stitchings and pockets even if too much acid has been used.

Method II. Wash with a detergent. A safer bleach to use with this detergent is sodium perborate. Add 3 to 4 oz. (say, a handful or two) to the wash so as to cover the garment easily. Put the trousers in this and pour in a little formic acid moving the garment as we do so. The oxygen in the perborate is liberated. This gives a powerful yet safe bleaching effect to the fabric. Rinse well, dry and finish as for woollen trousers.

Men's Silk Ties

If there is an inner lining, tack it into place. Wash as for silk using a detergent. Add 1 teaspoonful of gum for each half pint of last rinsing water, in order to stiffen. Place flat on a towel. Squeeze out the water. Pull into shape, and iron both the wrong and right sides over muslin until dry. When almost dry, gently remove the tacking thread. Air thoroughly.

Gloves and leather goods

Chamois. Dissolve one teaspoonful of washing soda in boiling water and add it to a basin of lukewarm water. Shake the leather, put it in and cover with a plate to prevent the water becoming cold and the leather hard. Never soak gloves for a long time, as they may shrink. Squeeze out, then wash by squeezing and drying through the 'wooden hands' in two, or, if necessary, more lukewarm waters with ammonia and soap jelly added. A soap containing a grease solvent is very effective. Very soiled finger tips can be lightly brushed with a soft bristled or rubber brush. Rinse well in clean lukewarm water. Remove from the water. Wrap it in a towel and lightly beat out all surplus water. It is often better to wipe off without rinsing. Stretch into shape, then rub and stretch frequently while drying to keep the leather soft. If a glove frame is not available for drying, blow into the fingers to open them up. Hang the gloves out to dry slowly in a cool airy place.

Suede. Wash as for chamois leather gloves. These gloves do not soften after treatment until fitted on the hand. Suedes sponged with 15% solution of formic acid get a brighter and fresher appearance. When nearly dry, press into shape with a moderately hot iron. If the gloves are white, dip the leather into french chalk occasionally as it is used. This rubbing must be firm, for it is to the glove what pressing is to other garments.

Leather goods such as coats and hand-bags are treated the same way as gloves.

Wet a piece of flannel in warm soap solution (good cleansing soap is required) Sponge the surface evenly working with another flannel wrung from clean warm water. Treat the whole coat and dry in a draught. When dry, treat with a good polishing cream.

A seven per cent solution of oxalic or formic acid may be rubbed with a stiff brush. The coat is allowed to dry in the cold and the surface set by brushing in the way of the 'pile' with a soft wire brush. This method gives good results.

For stains do not use dry-cleansing solvents, as these leave behind 'sweal' marks. Clean with a powder suitable for the colour of the coat, for example, natural fuller's earth, rub this into the stain, leave for a short time and then brush up. Touch the surface of the leather lightly with a piece of emery paper to remove shiny marks. This must be done by rubbing lightly in one direction only. Rubber-cleaners are specially useful for suede leather. Natural fuller's earth or suitable powders may be used for cleaning the leather.

Faded or much-used coats can be dyed with leather dyes; and when dry, polished with a suitable cream.

Furs

If the lining is very soiled, it is best to remove it for separate cleaning, dry or wet, as may be required.

For dark furs, apply hot bran and shake out. A slight sheen may be secured by rubbing with a cloth dipped in methylated spirit.

For white furs sprinkle with magnesia or french chalk, wrap up and leave to dry before shaking out. If very dirty, treat with a paste made by mixing french chalk or fuller's earth and a dry-cleaning solvent. When dry, brush the powder. Brush in the direction of the fur, but never against it. Dry in the open air.

Moth-proofing agents can also be added to give a very high degree of immunity from moths.

Steam is required only when the fur is severely crushed. A special cloth or paper is put over the fur to protect it, and the iron is allowed to skim over the surface. This calls for expertise, and should not be attempted by beginners.

Plastics

Plastic fabrics must be treated with great care, as they tear very easily. Lay flat on a table and sponge with warm soapy water, then with clean warm water. Hang straight in a cool place to dry.

Plastic handbags can be polished with a small amount of machine oil. If dirty, they can be first treated with warm soapy water.

Lace

As real lace is very valuable and also very delicate, great care is required in dressing it. If the lace is white, the dirt can be drawn out using a little powdered borax added to the cold water. If it is very dry, a little soap jelly may also be added. Soak for about an hour, then squeeze out very gently.

Real lace may be washed gently by squeezing in two lukewarm soapy waters or by taking the lace on to a piece of flannel and squeezing the flannel carefully in the soapy water.

Cover a bottle with flannel, then wind the lace over the flannel and tack the ends. Make a good soap solution in a basin, place the bottle well down into the water, press the lace well with the soapy water, turning the bottle round and round. You can also take a wide-necked bottle, put into it some soapy water, slip in the lace, then close the bottle. Shake the bottle well, tip out the lace and repeat the process till the lace is really clean. If the lace is still not clean, it may be boiled. It is not a good idea to do this often, as high temperature weakens the delicate threads of the lace. One of the following methods may be adopted.

Wrap the lace in an old handkerchief and put it into a small pan with cold water, shredded curd soap, and dissolve powdered borax (1 tablespoonful to 1 quart water), and a little milk. Simmer gently for 10 minutes. You can also fill half a jar with boiling water, some powdered borax and a little soapy jelly. Put the lace into this, and then put the jar into a pan with sufficient water to come half way up the jar and allow to steam from 10 to 15 minutes.

If white lace is still not white, bleach in the open air and to prevent the lace being blown away or picked up by birds, tack it on to a towel or old sheet, keep it wet by sprinkling with dissolved borax. Rinse well in lukewarm water to remove soap and in cold water to clear the colour.

To make lace keep clean longer and to give a slight firmness as when new, stiffen slightly by one of the following methods:

- Use two teaspoonfuls of borax dissolved in half a pint of water.
- Dissolve two lumps of sugar in half a pint of water.
- Use equal parts of milk and water.

- Add one tablespoonful cooked hot water starch to half a pint of water.
- Add one and a half tablespoonfuls gum water to half a pint of water.
- The water in which rice has been boiled is a good stiffening agent, but, if used for lace, should be diluted in strength.

A little blue may be added to the stiffening waters for white lace; and few drops of tea, coffee, or cream starch, for cream lace, if a deeper shade is desired.

Thick Irish or crochet laces require no stiffening agents.

Fold lace evenly and pass through wringer, or, if it is very fragile, beat well in a towel.

Lace may be ironed when half dry, or it may be pinned out on a board covered with flannel, or if large, on a table with ironing blanket pinned tightly on it. Use good quality pins and put them through the holes in the pattern to avoid tearing the lace. Pin out straight edges first and then the pointed. Pin tightly enough to stretch the lace well without straining it and to make the net ground-work mesh open (see Fig. 8.13).

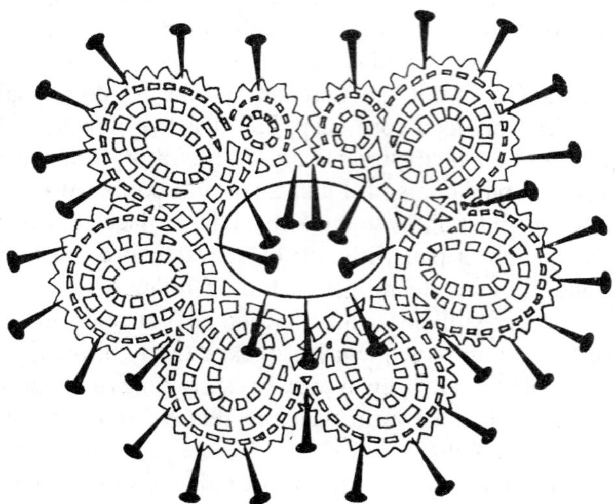

Fig. 8.13 Method of pinning lace to a board covered with a felt

Leave the lace till dry, then unpin it and stretch it gently into

shape. Iron it with a moderately cool iron on the wrong side over flannel.

Iron lightly, then more heavily to press the thicker parts of the pattern on the right side. Iron well into the loops of the lace, with the point of iron.

If real lace is to be stored away for a long time it should be washed, dried and folded in sheets of blue paper to prevent it becoming discoloured.

To wash black laces add a little ammonia in washing water. After rinsing pass through deep blue water or strong tea respectively depending on the dye coming out blue or brown. Add gum arabic, about one tablespoon to one pint of tea. Squeeze well in towel or cloth.

To iron lace. Place a piece of flannel on the table and cover it with a piece of tissue paper. Place the lace on this, right side down, cover with paper again, putting the glazed side next to the lace. Iron till dry, but never with the bare iron next to the lace. Fold lightly.

Machine-made lace can be washed like hand-made lace. Stiffen with very weak boiling water starch, gum, borax or sugar. Tint with dye, weak tea or weak coffee, placed in stiffening solution. Squeeze and press on the wrong side.

Lace curtains should be soaked in warm soapy water overnight. Wash as above. Rinse in warm water. If white, rinse in cold blue water also. Be very careful.

If you wish to have the curtain in a deeper shade, add a little tea, coffee or cream starch to the ordinary hot water starch. To test the shade, dip a corner of the curtain in the starch, then squeeze out lightly to judge the shade. Remember that material when it is wet is always a deeper shade than when it is dry. Sqeeze.

Stretch curtain gently into shape, then hang up very evenly on the lines or on the pulley to dry.

Lace curtains are ironed on the wrong side when almost dry. Fold selvedge to selvedge. Iron lengthways, keeping straight by the edge of the table.

Metallic lace can be cleaned by squeezing in any dry-cleaning solvent. Follow up by rubbing on to the threads (before the solvent dries up) a fine powder such as French chalk or fuller's earth. Leave this for a short time, then shake off and brush.

Gold and silver lace also called *mukaish and salma tilla* or gold embroidered work can be cleaned in reetanut or an S.F.A. solution.

Make a good lather. Place the lace on the palm of your hand and work the lather gently on the laces. If necessary, gently rub the surface with a soft nail brush. Sponge in clan water. Wrap it in a turkish towel or another soft cloth to remove extra moisture. Press on the wrong side when slightly damp.

Note:—Lace with a border of real gold and silver threads can be cleaned wet. Imitation metal threads get easily tarnished and no water should be applied on them. They can be cleaned with a grease solvent or a paste made of french chalk, powdered magnesia and a grease solvent. When dry, brush it off and lightly polish with a soft cloth.

Dry Cleaning

Although cleaning using water is by far the cheapest method of laundering clothes, many a rich and fine fabric has to be laundered by dry cleaning. Dry cleaning was formerly known as 'French cleaning' or 'chemical cleaning'.

Dry cleaning is based on the fact that most of the dirt or 'soiling matter' is held by grease. When this grease is removed, the dirt is removed along with it.

It must be remembered that dirt in ordinary washing is removed by the emulsification and saponification of grease, whereas dry cleaning indicates the removal of grease by the solvent action of certain liquids and by dry powder which act as grease absorbents.

The word 'dry' is somewhat misleading, as it suggests teatment with only a dry agent, but really the word is used in contrast to 'wet', as the solvents used for cleansing do not penetrate the fabric as water does in ordinary washing. As a rule, the liquids have no effect on the colour of the fabric, as the material does not shrink, loose shape or finish as is frequently the case in 'wet cleaning'.

Dry-cleaning at home may be done by the use of (a) absorbents and (b) grease solvents.

Using absorbents

This method is suitable for removing grease spots from all kinds of material, for cleaning light-coloured fabrics that are evenly soiled, and for articles such as furs and dark-coloured gloves that cannot be cleaned by solvents alone.

The common absorbents are starch, magnesium carbonate (powdered magnesia), french chalk, fuller's earth, bran, moong powder, bread crumbs and other commercial dry-cleaning powders sold in perforated-top tins.

The above absorbents are useful for cleaning grease marks on light-coloured fabrics, white lace, white furs, white shawls, and white felt hats.

Shake or brush off loose dirt from the garment. Spread a thick layer of the absorbent powder over it and rub it lightly with a circular motion. Leave for half an hour to allow the powder to absorb the grease. Evenly soiled fabrics can be wrapped up with the powder and left longer. White fur and felt are better cleaned if a paste is made of any of the white powders and a dry cleaning solvent. This is spread lightly over the surface of the fur, left to dry, and then brushed or shaken off. Shake off the powder and brush the whole garment in the direction of the pile. White kid gloves that have been cleaned with a dry cleaning solvent get a better finish if french chalk is rubbed on it.

Bran moong powder (green gram powder) and bread crumbs are used warm. They are useful for cleaning dark coloured felt, dark furs, camel hair cloth and teddy- bear coats and also grease soiled saris.

Heat the bran powder till dry to improve its absorbing power. Rub well into the articles being cleaned. Leave for 30 minutes. Shake and brush out until all the absorbent is removed. Absorbents have this advantage over grease solvents: they absorb and clean grease marks and leave no 'sweal' or ring on the fabric. Hence they are suitable for spotting. They are, however, not so effective for cleaning heavily soiled articles with greasy dirt.

Using grease solvents

Grease solvents in dry cleaning include inflammable solvents like aviation petrol, benzine, and non-inflammable like carbon tetrachloride, benzene and trichlorethylene and tetrachlorethane, and other commercial preparations.

These are good grease solvents and are completely non-inflammable. The principle underlying the use is the same in both cases.

Commercial preparations, like dry cleaning soaps, are available. The use of this soap increases the cleansing power of dry-cleaning solvents. A very small amount should be spread over the grease spots and solid parts, before the garment is immersed for cleansing. Mineral turpentine is a good solvent for grease particularly for paint stains.

The work must be done out of doors or in some place where there is good cross-ventilation. All petroleum products are highly inflammable and give off vapours, which are capable of being ignited by flames many feet away and for this reason must never be used in a room containing a flame.

Brush the garment well to remove all dust. Have sufficient petrol in bowls to clean the garment by hand squeezing, or using a suction washer and cleaning petrol to rinse. Immerse the article in an ordinary bath, as it is cleaned by means of a suction washer. After cleaning, squeeze out as much petrol as possible, wrap in a dry towel or cloth and beat.

Hang outside to dry for one day to remove the odour left behind by the solvent, after which any creases and other parts needing attention are pressed. Press when thoroughly dry.

Leave the used petrol in a covered bowl to allow the dirt to settle. After settling, the petrol should be carefully poured off the top, and the sediment thrown over open ground. Never throw it down the drain or over grass. Petrol can also be reclaimed by straining through chamois leather. This petrol can be used as the first petrol for the next cleaning.

Dry cleaning is necessary for fabrics which cannot be washed such as fur, felt, dark-skin gloves. Crepe fabrics can be dry cleaned. This causes no shrinkage as water does. Velvet and other pile fabrics can be easily dry cleaned. The pile is flattened by washing, but not flattened by dry cleaning. Fabrics finished by moir's marking, lacquered fabrics and imitation fur may be dry cleaned. The surface marking may be affected by this treatment, but it does less damage than washing. Dry cleaning is the best method of cleaning garments with pleats; it does not remove the pleats, as it does not wet the fabric.

Removing Stains

Stain removal and 'spotting' are skills which call for long experience and demand special attention. Two factors must be borne in mind. They are the composition and colour of the fabric, and the nature and age of the stain.

All stains are easily removed when fresh. If the nature of the stain is unknown it should be treated by the least harmful method passing from one process to the next until an effective agent is reached before it is passed from one solution to another.

1. Soak in cold water.
2. Soak in warm water.
3. Bleach in the open air, if time permits.
4. Treat with an alkaline solution.
5. Treat with an acid solution.
6. Treat with an oxidizing bleach, if the above fail.
7. Treat with a reducing bleach.
8. In the event of stain still persisting, which is unlikely, repeat processes (4) and (7).

Known stains should be treated with their specific reagents. Bleaching treatments should only be tried as a last resort, and these should take the form of several applications of weak solution rather than one application of strong solution. Reagents may be spread on to white cotton and linen fabrics and boiling water may be poured through the fabric. They must be made into a solution when used on coloured linen, wool, silk, rayon. The fabric should stay in the reagent only until the stain is removed, and then be taken out at once. If the reagent is allowed to dry into the fabric it may damage it. An acid stain removal agent should be neutralised by an alkaline rinse.

The spotting table should be near a window so that the vapour from any other solvents used may be carried away from the worker.

Stain-removal has no short cuts. If the water and chemicals used fade or change colours, one will have to choose between a stain and a faded spot. Some chemicals make colour change. In such cases the original colour may sometimes be restored by the application of a weak solution of ammonia or by holding the material over an open ammonia bottle. A detailed table for removing particular stains is given on page 260.

Cleaning Carpets

Routine cleaning

In caring for a carpet, the most important consideration is correct

AN ALPHABET FOR THE TREATMENT OF PARTICULAR STAINS

Treatment for all fabrics unless otherwise stated

Stain	*Reagent required*	*Method of application*
Animal stains	Acetic acid Ammonia	In all cases of animal staining on coloured articles (e.g. carpets), the treatment consists of alternate application with a moderately strong solution of acetic acid (up to 20%) and 5% solution of household ammonia. The stained area is thoroughly soaked with the acid for about 2 hours after rising the acid with water. The ammonia is applied to ensure complete neutralisation.
Ball point stains	Methylated spirit	Rub lightly with methylated spirit.
Boot polish	Solvents Methylated spirit	(Boot polish is made by dissolving certain colours in wax). The wax is removed by means of solvents. This will also remove the colour. If the colour still remains, treatment with methylated spirit will completely remove the stain.
Dye stains	Warm soap solution Ammonia Suitable bleach	Treatment of dye stuffs is a difficult operation or series of operations according to the nature of the fabric, its colour, and nature of the stain. The greatest success is obtained on white materials. *White wool* 1. Treat with warm soap solution containing S.F.A. for half an hour. Repeat if improvement is seen. 2. Treat with 1% of .88 ammonia containing a trace of S.F.A. Use at almost boiling point. 3. Treat stains with hot sodium hydrosulphite solution (1 oz. per gallon). 4. Bleach with hydrogen peroxide solution. Leave it in contact with material for half to one hour.

Dye stains	Warm soapy solution Alkali or acid Suitable bleach	*White silk* 1. Treat with hot soap solution with a little S.F.A. The time of application must be only 5–10 minutes. 2. Bleach as for wool. Try hydrosulphite solution first and then hydrogen peroxide. *White cotton and linen* Soap either in dilute alkali or dilute acid. Some dye stains respond to one, and some to the other. Stronger alkaline liquors and higher temperatures are permissible on these fabrics. Immerse the article in hot (nearly boiling) sodium hydrosulphite solution (4 oz per gallon) for 5–10 minutes.
Food stains	Javelle water	*On cotton and linen* 1. Treatment with laundry bleach (sodium hypochlorite solutions or javelle water). 2. A weak solution of the above for a long time is the safest method. The progress of the treatment should be noted every 15 minutes.
Glue and gum stains	Hot water and Glycerine or Acetic acid or Methylated spirit	Treat with hot water to soften and dissolve the stain. The addition of a few drops of glycerine will assist in the dissolving of stains in some cases while a few drops of acetic acid will help in others. Spirit gum must be dissolved by methylated spirit.
Hard-court stains	Hydrosulphite of soda	*On white flannels* 1. Remove with soap and water and brush 'turns ups' by hand. 2. Bleach red colour with a solution of hydrosulphite of soda.

(continued)

Stain	*Reagent required*	*Method of application*
Iodine	Ammonia solution Photographer's hypo (Sodium thiosulphate)	1. Ammonia solution. 2. Photographer's hypo. Dissolve 1 tablespoonful hypo in ¾ pint water; apply immediately over the mark.
Lead pencil stains	Oleic acid Ammonia	1. Generally removed by normal washing. 2. Treat with oleic acid. Then dip in a warm solution of ammonia.
Lipstick	Bleach	1. Treat as grease. 2. Bleach.
Medicine	Ethyl alcohol, Surgical spirit	Steep in ethyl alcohol or surgical spirit.
Mercurochrome	Denatured alcohol, Glycerine. Ammonia and soap water	Mercurochrome stains are very hard to remove unless you treat them promptly. First sponge the stain well with a liquid made of equal parts of alcohol and water. On acetate rayon and coloured materials use 1 part alcohol and 2 parts water. Next work glycerine into the cloth to help to loosen the stain, and continue using as long as any colour bleeds from the stain. Then wash well in soap suds, and rinse with water to which a few drops of ammonia water have been added. If a stain remains after the above treatment, apply 10 per cent acetic acid with a medicine dropper; then rinse well in water.
Mildew	Javelle water	This is formed by the growth of fungus on damp fabric.

Mildew	Potassium permanganate, Oxalic acid	1. Bleach by sunlight. 2. Bleach with javelle water. 3. Bleach with potassium permanganate. 4. Bleach with hydrogen peroxide.
	Potassium permanganate	*Cotton and linen.* 1 oz. permanganate crystals to 1 gallon water. *Silk and wool.* 1/2 oz. permanganate crystals to 1 gallon water. *Method.* Steep material for 5 minutes until it becomes dark brown. Than remove brown stains by applying any of the following dilute solutions of sulphuric acid, or oxalic acid or acidified hydrogen peroxide. Rinse thoroughly in three waters. Wash according to material. *Mildew proofing* The following household recipe is helpful to give a protective finish against mildew; 1 1/2 oz. of cadmium chloride (poison), 1 gallon of hot water } ... mix 1. Wash fabric in a neutral soap. Do not rinse out the soap. 2. Apply the above solution

(continued)

Stain	*Reagent required*	*Method of application*
Mineral	Oxalic acid Bleach	(a) *Iron rust*
	Lime juice Salts of lemon Sour milk Oxalic acid	1. Spread mild acid, e.g., milk, lemon, vinegar or salts of lemon; pour boiling water through. 2. Use oxalic acid solution for obstinate stains. 3. Use bleach.
		Note:—Iron-rust stains should be removed before the fabric is wetted as dampness spreads the stains. Avoid javelle water, as it fixes iron rust into the fabric.
		(b) *Ink, black; Quink fresh* 1. Wash out as much as possible or soak the stain in lime juice, curds or sour milk overnight. Then wash out. 2. Spread salts of lemon over the stain. Pour boiling water through. Wash and boil. 3. Bleach in a hot solution of potassium permanganate and use oxalic acid solution to remove the brown stain.
		(c) *Red Ink*
	Borax	1. Steep in borax solution (1/4 pint warm water with 1 teaspoonful borax).
	Ammonia	2. Steep in ammonia solution.
	Bleach	3. Bleach according to fabric.

		(d) *Marking Ink:*
	Iodine solution Sodium thiosulphate	1. Steep in iodine solution and follow by steeping in sodium thiosulphate solution. Wash.
		2. Bleach according to fabric.
Nail varnish	Acetone	1. Use acetone. (Do not use on acetate rayon).
	Sodium hydrosulphate	2. Bleach with sodium hydrosulphite.
Nose drops		(Consists of eucalyptus oil and methol)
	Solvent acetic acid	Use a solvent, further treat with water containing a few drops of acetic acid.
Orange Juice		1. Wash with hot soapy water. Rinse. For obstinate stains, apply glycerine to the stained area. Rinse thoroughly.
	Glycerine	2. Apply hydrogen-peroxide. Rinse thoroughly after a little while.
	Hydrogen-peroxide	Scrape and steep in turpentine. Any resulting colour stain should be washed out. Strip if necessary. Varnish and lacquer paint will dissolve in methylated spirit.
Paint	Turpentine Methylated spirit	Paint stains are easily removed when wet.
Perfume	Methylated spirit Acetic acid	Consists of alcohol and essential oils.
		1. Remove oil by dry cleaning, or methylated spirit in water, or weak solution of acetic acid.
		2. If dye is affected—strip and re-dye.
Perspiration		Same as for mildew.

(continued)

Stain	*Reagent required*	*Method of application*		
			For vegetable fibres	*For animal fibres*
Protein	Cold water Bleach	Milk, eggs, blood, etc.	1. Steep in cold water or tepid salt water, wash and boil. *Unwashable fabric* 1. Cover the stain with a paste of starch and cold water. Leave for a short time to absorb the stain. Repeat if necessary. 2. Hydro-sulphite. 3. Hypochlorite bleach.	1. Soak in a tepid salt water wash. 2. Hydrogen peroxide bleach. 3. Hydro-sulphite bleach. *Note:* For human blood avoid hydrogen peroxide.
		Note: For human blood avoid hypochlorite.		
Rouge	Petrol, ammonia	Apply petrol to remove grease. Wash with hot soapy water and a few drops of ammonia. Rinse thoroughly.		
Sealing wax	Methylated spirit	Soften with methylated spirit and dissolve in warm dry cleaning solvent.		
Scorch	(1) Sunlight and soapy water (2) Hydrogen peroxide (3) Potassium permanganate	When the fibres of the material are burnt, bleaching is the only method which is effective. 1. When light, remove by gently brushing the surface and then rewash the article. Sunlight bleach. 2. Bleach with hydrogen peroxide or potassium permanganate or other chemical bleaches according to fabric for severe scorch.		

		Scorch mixture: 2 oz. washing soda…half-pint vinegar 2 oz. fuller's earth…1 onion *Method:* 1. Peal, slice and pound the onion. 2. Mix with other ingredients. 3. Boil for 10 minutes. Strain and bottle. Spread a little on the scorch, let it dry and repeat until mark disappears.	
Tar	Oil Grease-solvent	1. If necessary scrape first. 2. Rub with oil or grease using a clean cloth and working from the edge of the stain. 3. Treat material with grease-solvent.	
Transfer	Methylated spirit, Ethyl alcohol, Hot soapy water	Steep in surgical spirit or ethyl alcohol; wash according to fabric.	
Turmeric and Kumkum	Sun and grass	1. Soak in hot soapy water and dry in the sun on grass.	
	Hydrogen peroxide	2. Apply a few drops of hydrogen peroxide, leave for a few moments, rinse thoroughly and dry in the sun.	
		For vegetable fibres	*For animal fibres*
Vegetable	Tea, coffee, cocoa beer, etc., pan, fruit wine	*Fresh.* Pour boiling water through the stain.	*Fresh.* Steep in warm water, repeat until stain is removed.

(continued)

Stain	Reagent required	Method of application
		Cold. 1. Steep in boiling water containing soda or borax or both or apply glycerine and put into hot soda water. 2. Bleach with javelle water. 3. Bleach with sodium perborate. *Cold.* 1. Apply glycerine and steep in warm borax or weak, ammonia solution. 2. Hydrogen peroxide bleach. 3. Hydrosulphite bleach (also called photographer's hypo).
Varnish	Methylated spirit	Steep in surgical spirit or commercial methylated spirit.
Unknown stains		Bleaching may be carried out when necessary by means of (1) hyprochlorite bleach for vegetable and rayon fibres. hydrogen peroxide—for animal fibres. If this is not effective, use (2) hydrosulphite bleach—for all fibres. Fabrics must be thoroughly rinsed after the process.

cleaning. New carpets sometimes 'fluff'. This need not cause any concern. When the yarn is woven in the loom, it is cut and a number of short over-lapping fibres meet adhering only to the main strand. This is the 'fluff' that gives way when the carpet is cleaned during the early days of wear. Carpets have a natural tendency to 'felt' as they settle down and this should not be disturbed by hard sweeping.

The dirt that accumulates in a carpet is mainly of three kinds: light dirt or dust, litter that clings such as threads, fluff, hairs, and grit which is destructive, dangerous, germ-laden and is carried in from the streets on the shoes; it sinks to the roots of the pile and its razor-like edges are pressed against the pile by the feet so that most of the fibres are broken from the base.

Each kind of dirt needs a special cleaning process. Light dirt can be removed by suction. Sweeping removes fluff and litter. For heavy grit at the base on the pile, the carpet needs beating. A good vacuum-cleaner which has the triple action of suction, beating and sweeping is the best. A vacuum-cleaner is designed to give maximum efficiency with a slow movement. The carpet sweeper may be used regularly for the daily round so that brushes of the agitator rotate the pile of the carpet. It is effective for picking up crumbs, threads and other litter. For daily cleaning, a soft bristle brush is equally good, if it is not applied too vigorously. Always brush in the direction of the pile. If brushed against the pile, dirt and grit are pushed into the carpet, and this tends to damage the wool.

If a vacuum-cleaner is not available, lay the carpet face down wards on a dry lawn and beat it well on the back with a long stick. Brush off as much of this superfluous dust as possible on either side of the carpet. Never beat it over a clothesline because such treatment is harmful to the fabric.

Shampooing

Dissolve two tablespoonfuls of a mild synthetic detergent and half an ounce of acetic acid or vinegar (40%) in one gallon of hot water at 115° to 120°F. A teaspoonful of salt may be added to prevent colours from running. A small amount of methylated spirit may also be added to facilitate drying. (The last is optional.)

Work up a good lather of the detergent. Rub the carpet gently a small area at a time, with the solution using a soft bristle brush or a pad of absorbent undyed cotton material, in a circular motion until cleaned. Use the suds as far as possible. Be careful to wet the surface only. The back of the rug should never feel wet. Follow with a few rubbings with a damp cloth, rinsing the cloth between each treatment. While finishing, leave the pile inclined in the right direction. If carelessly done, it may cause patchiness. Make sure that no one walks on the carpet while it is still damp. Dry in a airy place.

Some do's and dont's

- Over-handling should be avoided, as it felts wool. The same temperature must be maintained right through for washing and rinsing.
- Remember that a detergent is better than any soap or even reeta nut solution, as it does not turn rancid and leave an unpleasant odour in the carpet.

Although the above processes and proportions are based on the successful results of numerous practical trials, they may be subject to alteration to suit individual conditions.

- Under no circumstances should you use soap, powder, soda, or ammonia, as they contain alkalies. Another point to bear in mind is that repeated treatments are not recommended. The solutions leave behind a slight residue, which eventually leads to a more rapid rate of resoiling.
- Do not saturate the carpet; not only does it weaken the backing but also mildew or bacterial action may start during the long time taken in drying.
- With a fresh stain act quickly, mopping up as much of the liquid as possible with blotting paper or absorbent undyed cotton cloth.

Tips on carpet care

- Always line your carpet with underfelt. It is well-worth the little extra expense. Use newspaper underneath the carpets, as this stops the cold air from rising. It also serves to protect the carpet.
- Wherever possible plan so that carpets can be lifted and turned round to spread the wear evenly. Bad spots for wear are obvious—just inside doorways, around the tables, in the dining rooms and so on.
- In the case of fitted carpets, re-arrange the furniture often to redirect traffic and equalise wear over the surface.

- Rugs can be useful in protecting the main carpet at key points, such as outside a door or under a desk.
- Always see that a pile stair carpet is laid with the pile running towards the bottom of the stairs. Always buy a sufficient length so that it can be moved up or down a few inches 3 or 4 times a year. Otherwise if will wear quickly where the carpet bends over the edge of the stair.
- Moth-proofing agents can be purchased which are either spirit or water soluble. Add the right amount to the last rinse or sponging water. New patent insectisides containing D.D.T. or Dieldren are now available. All that is required for protection is an occasional spraying with one of these insectiides, particularly, under the edge of the carpet. Remember wool-eating insects like dark corners where they can remain undisturbed.

Disinfecting Clothing

Simple disinfection

Disinfection of clothing is necessary in the home as a precaution against the spreading of infectious diseases by bacteria or other organisms.

Fresh air, sunlight, dryness, and cleanliness are conditions in which bacteria are less likely to be prevalent. Clothing is disinfected by boiling and otherwise.

Disinfection by boiling. This method is suitable for all bleached cottons and linens, and is used to disinfect bed linen and personal garments. The use of paper handkerchiefs or tissues is recommended. Where it is not possible, handkerchiefs should be steeped with disinfectant in the water, washed separately, then boiled with other infected clothing. All bed linen that has been used by an infected person and has to be sent to a public laundry must be steeped in a disinfectant solution like a 3 per cent carbolic solution for 12 hours, machine wrung and dried. The laundry must be notified of the state of this clothing. Infected clothing can also be treated at home.

Clothing should be steeped for 12 hours in one of the following solutions:

Carbolic acid	1	tablespoonful to	1 quart	water
Lysol	1	”	3 quarts	”
Izal	1	”	1 gallon	”
Dettol	1	”	1 quart	”

Wash by mechanical means. Put into the boiler in softened soapy water, allow to come to boiling point and boil for 1 hour. Rinse very thoroughly. Dry out of doors. Clothing treated like this should be free from any infection.

Clothing that cannot be boiled may be treated by spraying with a solution of one tablespoonful of formalin in a pint of warm water or by pouring half a pint of formalin over 5 oz of potassium permanganate in a metal dish and leaving the clothing near it in a closed room for five to six hours.

Storing Clothes

The quantum of damage to garments made of animal fibre, especially wool by clothes moths and other insects is sufficient to make prevention a top priority. Constant care can prevent damage to woollen and other fabrics vulnerable to moths.

- Brush garments thoroughly and often to keep them free from dust. Empty out pockets. Shake well before brushing. Sun and air kill the grubs and keep moths away.
- Garments which have been worn should not be put away until they have been thoroughly aired. Cupboards, boxes, and clothes-closets should be aired frequently.
- Washable garments should be laundered frequently. Woollen coats, suits and shawls should be sponged and ironed. Garments which cannot be laundered should be dry-cleaned. Do not let a suit become dirty before sending it to the dry-cleaner.
- Suits and overcoats should be hung away on clothes hangers. The sleeves of coats will keep their shape much better if they are stuffed with tissue paper. Make sure that the shoulders sit properly on the hanger.
- Light often makes the colour of fabrics fade. Protect them with

covers made for that purpose Keep such garments in dark closets which can be frequently aired.

- Do not put away garments when they are damp. Moisture causes mildew, which penetrates into the fibre, changes its colour and may even cause it to fall to pieces. This can be easily prevented by brushing the garment each time after wearing, and hanging and storing it away in a dry place in a perfectly dry condition.
- Protect fabric from destructive insects. The moth grubs feed upon wool fabrics, carpets, furs, and feathers. The moth is gray in colour. These pests can be prevented by:
  - — Spraying: Wool and its storage places must be sprayed with a fluid or powder insecticide in which D.D.T. is incorporated to give it a measure of permament protection.
  - — Repellants such as tobacco, dried neem leaves, cedar chips, camphor, and moth- balls are of doubtful value and cannot be relied on. These repellents, will not have any effect upon the eggs or larvae in the garment. Moth balls are effective only as long as a sufficient concentration of vapour is maintained. Naphthalene flakes are more efficient than the traditional moth balls. Paradichlorbenzene is best but it is expensive.
  - — Pack away all woollens and furs in newspapers, as moths dislike printer's ink. The box may be lined and covered with tarred paper. Cedar chips, sandal wood dust, dry eucalyptus and neem leaves are good as long as their odour lasts. Delicate textiles that are kept folded for a long time, weaken at the folds and ultimately teal in those portions. The best way is store them on rollers or tubes. The ends of the rollers should project beyond the textiles so that no folds are formed. Several rollers can be fixed one over the other. Textiles with gold work are susceptible to damage by folding for a long time. Careful padding is required for their storage. Handle textiles with care and never with soiled hands.
  - — Fumigation with a poisonous gas, e.g., hydrocyanic acid destroys grubs and moths, but it is dangerous to use and calls for specialist handling.
  - — Add an insecticide to the wool: This entails adding a

substance to the wool which either poisons the larvae or renders the wool indigestible.

To sum up, it may be said that although there is no perfect and completely moth-proofing agent, there are many varieties and a reasonably satisfactory one can be selected for a particular purpose.

Index